MURDER AT THE PIRATE FESTIVAL

BERRYPORT MYSTERIES
BOOK 1

ABIGAIL YARDIMCI

Soft Rebel
PUBLISHING

Published in 2024 by:

Soft Rebel Publishing Ltd

20-22 Wenlock Road, London, N1 7GU

Cover art by Manuel Diaz

Cover design by Abigail Yardımcı

ISBN: 978-1-7385290-0-1

For Baran and Azad...
...because not all treasure is silver and gold

CONTENTS

1

"Will you be alright out there on your own for a few minutes, luvver? I'm just making another batch of doubloons."

More doubloons? Paulie didn't understand how the people of Berryport weren't fed up of her Aunt Meg's 'Doubloon Delight' cookies. They were sickly sweet and dusted in a fine golden powder that somehow always found its way onto the glass display cases in the bakery. Oily, glistening arcs that Paulie had the honour of swooshing off with a damp cloth every half an hour. Ugh.

"Yeah. All cool out here," Paulie called back in the direction of the kitchen. "There's only Fickle Fergus. And I'm just finishing off these cupcakes for the festival." Paulie paused her task for a moment and glanced over her shoulder. Fergus had finally sat down with his signature crossword, a frothy coffee and the jam doughnut it had taken him the standard seventeen minutes to decide on. He patted down the flouncy frills on the front of the shirt that demonstrated his inexplicable commitment to wear one item of pirate paraphernalia every day. Then he smiled at her warmly. He bit into his sweet treat and a healthy dollop of blueberry jam landed with a splat on the ruffled lapels. *Bless him, he'd be embarrassed if he knew he'd done that.* Paulie thought. *Would it be too much if I wiped it off for him?*

Paulie fought down the urge to grab a napkin and tried to turn her attention back to what she was supposed to be doing. Luckily she still had a fondant eye patch grasped between her fingertips so she didn't have to scroll the recent activity in her brain for long before remembering what the task was. *Oh yes. Eye patches. On all the pirate cupcakes.*

The lunchtime rush was over and Meg was busy, so Paulie took the opportunity to pop out her earbuds and let the bakery Bluetooth do its thing. Instantly the synthetic pops and whirs of 'Glitter Freeze' by Gorillaz pounded around, bouncing off the walls and streaming through the open doors onto the sunny harbour. Paulie grinned to herself, imagining the questionable melody chasing the holidaymakers away from the bakery and off to the end of the famous pier perhaps, the impressive Nautical Gardens or the Arching Angel – Berryport's very own replica pirate ship. Paulie didn't care where they went, as long as she could have this little break from the internal ache of customer service and ALL the smiling.

The eye patches were coming on pretty well. As the music drove on, Paulie felt her brain wake up in notches. With every beat, a tightening of attention. Her focus pinched pleasantly as the familiar notes hit not just her ears but her insides. It was a gratifying process she knew all too well. The pirate eye patches were being placed with such precision now, it seemed that the cakes were suddenly vibrant, alive even. Every swoop of her fingers meant that yet another cake was stunning and she could feel it in her very bones that 'Booty Bakes' would be the talk of the town at this year's pirate festival.

Paulie turned the music up louder.

"Erm. Young lady? Did you not hear us the first few hundred times?" Somebody was shrieking. Which meant she had to turn around. Like, now.

"Ah finally. Can we *please* get some cakes?" The man looking at her had his arms folded across his sunburned chest and black eyebrows that pushed together to a furious point. He held tight fists of money and wore an expression of the purest cake-rage Paulie had ever seen. How long had he been waiting?

"Yes, us too please!"

"We've been waiting for ages!"

"All we want is some doughnuts!"

Paulie's fingers found their way to her phone and she lowered the volume of the music at once, feeling that tight focus slip away along with her joy. There was a queue of grumbling, mumbling people reaching almost to the door and even Fickle Fergus looked up from his crossword to see what was going on. Aunt Meg would have a fit if she knew Paulie had let a queue like this build up. She could already hear the lecture in her mind: *'If I've told you once, I've told you a million times, Paulie. The magic words of customer service are: friendly, attentive and QUICK.'*

She suddenly knew how to sort this mess out.

Paulie hit her phone so that Gorillaz whacked out another tune. Louder this time. "Free cakes for everyone!" She picked up the nearest tray of completed pirate cupcakes and scooted round to the other side of the counter.

"Wah?" The money-wielding, cake-raging man gasped.

"That's right! Free pirate cupcakes for our valued customers at Booty Bakes. Congratulations!" Paulie shouted over the music and beamed out a smile she could feel down to her toes.

Before she knew it, hands were grabbing at her from every

which way as she brandished the tray of cupcakes like her life depended on it. The sudden onslaught of bodies pushed Paulie towards the door of the bakery and within seconds she was standing on the pavement outside, whilst people yelled, "This girl's giving out free cakes!" Yet more hungry holidaymakers threw themselves at her, interrupting selfies in the Devon sunshine, souvenir-searching and lager lunches to jump on the free-cake bandwagon. This unashamed demand brought Paulie a brief thrill of popularity and she thought, just for a moment, *I could get used to this.*

Gorillaz continued to blare unapologetically across Berryport Harbour and the merry May sunshine winking on the water clashed insanely with the rhythm. Paulie felt sweat gather in the palms of her hands and she thought she might lose her grip on the tray as people continued to push and shove. The frenzied grin on her face began to slide and any thrill she might have felt was chased away by a startling wave of confusion. *This is actually awful.* She tried to focus on Aunt Meg's magic words of customer service but it seemed they'd been snatched by one of the circling seagulls overhead, never to return.

The music stopped.

"What on earth? Paulie? Oh, not this *again!*" The disappointment in Meg's voice was as solid as a rock hurled into Paulie's chest. Without turning to face her aunt, she already knew the exact lines that would be etched onto her usually kindly face. The exact pose of hands on hips and a tapping foot. The way her mouth would be drawn into a crooked bunch and the softness of her brown eyes would be edged with distress. It was too much to bear.

Paulie dropped the tray with a shocking clatter. People jumped back, scavenging seagulls screeched and the chubby, fondant pirate faces rolled across the road towards the sea with a sickening cheerfulness. That very image tugged at her brain as she sprinted past her aunt, into the bakery and through the back door to the upstairs flat.

Aunt Meg sighed. "Alright, everyone. The free cakes are over."

2

The landing door rattled behind her as Paulie stumbled, breathless, into the cluttered living room. There was nowhere to sit. Neither she nor her aunt were very good at keeping a tidy home. However, a streak of sunshine poured through the skylight, pooling in a spot on the bright orange carpet just big enough for her to stand in. So she did.

Paulie focused on slowing her breathing and her skin woke up to the warmth. Goosebumps brushed the fabric of her clothes and she tilted her face so that the sun would kiss her cheeks, her forehead and her closed eyelids. She stood in that orange spot and twisted the sparkly rope she always wore around her neck so that the tiny fibres prickled and pinched the skin. *That.* Twist. *Was.* Twist. *Horrendous.* Twist. *But.* Twist. *I'm.* Twist. *Okay.* Twist. *Now.*

Yes, Aunt Meg would have something to say about the whole free cake thing as soon as she got the opportunity. She had dealt with Paulie's spontaneous giveaways before and it always triggered an outpour of worries. Eventually though, the outpour would slow to a trickle and she'd kiss Paulie's cheek, or draw her in enough that Paulie could breathe in the buttery scent of coconut oil embedded in her springy curls. *"It's alright, luvver,"* she'd say. *"I know you mean well."* That's the feeling Paulie was focusing on right now, rather than the adrenalin still clinging to her organs, the shame whispering to her heart.

Paulie pulled her phone from her pocket and checked for messages. Nothing from Wren. So today's drama class must be going ahead as normal. Ah, there it was. That familiar push and pull of emotions. Pleased to have finally found a class that she enjoyed. Dreading having to go and actually be with people. She twisted the necklace again.

She was about to step out of the sunny, orange spot, to force herself to get ready, when her phone chirped. It was the BeYu app. Although Paulie had other social media apps on her phone, this was the only one she actually used because, quite honestly? Social media was totally draining. Having said that, if Paulie had a gun to her head and was forced to choose one platform for the rest of her life, she would definitely choose BeYu. It didn't take anywhere near as much emotional energy as the others and if there was one thing Paulie needed to conserve, it was emotional energy. Twist.

All it took was snapping a double-photo (front and back of the camera simultaneously) once a day at a random time determined by the app. Everybody with BeYu got the notification at the same time and you only had two minutes to take your pictures, so you didn't have time to mess about with stupid filters. Then the photos were shared across your network and it disappeared into thin air after twenty four hours.

Simple. Authentic. Real.

Paulie liked those things.

She lifted the phone and focused on the window behind the battered old sofa. She gazed at the jumble of items stacked up along the windowsill. There were those candles, that she'd ordered a few months ago, setting in their moulds. The salt dough magnets which had been waiting at least three months for their next coat of varnish. And a small mountain of folded paper in faded pink and yellow, supposedly origami swans. All of these things were gathering a glittering crust of silver dust. They were kind of beautiful if you looked at them in a certain way. Even if they did represent yet more abandoned hobbies. Twist.

Paulie arranged her face in a vaguely neutral manner and took the double-photo. Then she added the caption:

`My window crafts are better than your window crafts.`

Done. What now? Oh yeah. Drama class.

Paulie peeled off her work clothes and dropped them to the floordrobe in her bedroom. As she scoured the ground for an outfit that would not only be appropriate for drama activities but also feel okay on her skin, Paulie grabbed a piece of last night's toast off a saucer on the edge of her bed. It was chewy and cold and the butter had congealed into a tasteless gloop. Ugh. Why hadn't she remembered to eat it last night when it was all hot and delicious? She spat it out and vowed to herself she'd eat later.

Sighing, Paulie pulled on a pair of old jeans and a Gorillaz t-shirt. If she'd known anything at all about how to 'style-up' an outfit she'd have no doubt knotted the hem of the t-shirt or done something artful with her hair. As it was, the thought of making such an effort on her appearance filled her with fear and excitement in equal measure. So, for the sake of staying in her comfort zone, she spritzed her sandy locks with a random pick from her plethora of 'root lifts' on the top of her dresser and chucked on her standard swish of lip balm.

As she turned to leave the room, Paulie spotted a jumbo sticky note strategically placed at eye level on the back of her bedroom door.

Drink.

She hated to admit it, but this sticky note system – masterminded by Aunt Meg – seemed to be working. She stepped into the kitchen and hastily chugged back a pint of water, which had the added bonus of helping her swallow down the discomfort of the impromptu cake giveaway. She stepped into her favourite pair of Converse and grabbed a sloppy cardigan which was draped over the pile of recently delivered parcels in the hallway. Underneath the cardi and slapped to the top of one of the parcels was another sticky note in garish green:

What have you ordered this time?

Paulie felt comforted by the fact that her aunt would be more enthusiastic when there were funky, seventies tile stickers in the bathroom, or when they could have fresh juices every morning thanks to the new juicer. This was about lifestyle. And that was important. Romano, her college counsellor said so.

All suited and booted, Paulie's plan was to breeze through the bakery unnoticed, hoping that there would be yet another queue of cake-rage customers keeping Aunt Meg busy. No such luck. As soon as she stepped out of the flat's dingy porch and onto the bakery's linoleum floor (which posed as antique oak, à la pirate ship), it was as if Meg had been voice-activated. "Honestly, luvver. Why did you do that? I told you after the last time we absolutely cannot afford to give out cakes randomly. Especially the very cakes we've been saving for the pirate festival. I'll be up all night making a fresh batch now. I just don't understand what got into you!"

"I am nothing if not an enigma." Paulie treated her aunt to a smile she hoped would soften the blow then kissed her flour-covered cheek. "I'm off to drama. See you later."

"You got your bus pass? Your keys? Some money?" Meg punctuated each question with a straightening, a tug or an adjustment of Paulie's appearance. Paulie didn't mind. This was a ritual she was used to. "And, most of all, are you *okay*?"

"Yes. Yes. A bit. And, what was the last one?"

"Are you *okay*?"

"Oh. Right. I think so. Who knows? It's the nature of an enigma."

Meg laughed as if against her will and gave Paulie one last squeeze. "God, you're weird. Off you go then. Have fun. We'll deal with the cake fiasco later. Oh, and here's a flapjack to keep you going."

"Sweet." Paulie nodded, took the paper bag and turned to leave. She knew the bus would be leaving Berryport depot around now and did not want to be late yet again. She picked up her pace but slammed headfirst into Fickle Fergus, who was on his way back from the gents.

"A state of mass approval or evidenced admiration."

"What?"

"Four down. Seven letters. First three letters – P.O.P."

"Oh, I see. Erm, not a clue, Fergus. I'm late for a bus. Can't help you with your crossword today."

"But you should know this one, Little Paulie." His lips twitched with a glimpse of mischief. "Last letter, 'R'? No? Okay, well here's another clue . . . you don't got to give away them fancy cakes to keep folk happy. We all love you just as you are."

He flickered the cuffs of his piratey shirt as if to punctuate his point and stepped out of her way.

"Yeah, yeah. Okay, Fergus. Gotta go now. Thanks for the inspo!" And she whirled out of the door, onto the harbour, slipping past the Arching Angel pirate ship. She had a bus to catch and that, like many other things, was not her forte.

3

"I can't believe you caught the right bus for the third time in a row! Dude, that's a record." Wren grabbed the paper bag off Paulie before even saying hello, and took a huge bite of the flapjack inside. Even Paulie knew that was rude.

"Do you always have to pinch my snacks? You're worse than the seagulls." Paulie fell into step with Wren and they paced down the tarmac path that led away from the bus stop, across a stretch of green, daisy-dotted wasteland and onto the college campus. Wren was meticulous about her timing and was always there to greet Paulie. Even though she'd never been asked to.

"Not really. Seagulls are scavengers, predators and kleptoparasites. I'm merely relieving you of a delicious baked product that you will – let's face it – forget to eat and leave in the drama studio. Mmm, Meg's bakes are so good."

Paulie's guts somersaulted at the recent memory of pirate cupcakes rolling away from her across the ground. She twisted her necklace until her skin burned, then dropped it and took a deep breath. "Yeah. You're right. Anyway. What are we doing in drama today?"

Wren stopped walking abruptly and turned towards Paulie

with military precision. She lifted her rounded sunglasses onto her forehead and squinted right at her with an unnecessary amount of incredulity. "Dude, how can you even ask that?"

"Oh yeah. Right. Skirmish. I forgot."

"You forgot? We've been working on it for seventeen and a half weeks. Swanny would have a fit if he heard you talking like that." Wren puffed out her chest and belly, started a series of wild hand gesticulations and crafted a tone of voice so effeminate, it would have put any drag queen to shame. "My darlings! This pirate skirmish is going to be the best that Berryport has seen for decades. This, my beautiful belles of the thespian world, will be the skirmish to end all skirmishes and one day – you mark my words – Hollywood will come knocking!"

"That is scarily accurate." Paulie meant it. Wren, despite her notoriously neutral appearance, was insanely good at 'becoming' a different person. That was a mighty good impression of their drama teacher, Josiah Swan.

Wren shrugged, plopped her sunglasses back onto her nose and started up the bonkers-fast walking again. "It's not hard. You just study the precise details of a person's stock characteristics looking for patterns within the finite limitations of their persona. It's logic. Like a jigsaw."

"You and your bloody jigsaws. Okay. Well not for me. I'll stick to backstage stuff, thanks."

"Whatever floats your pirate ship, dude. Now let's hurry up and get there. It's our last rehearsal in the studio today." Paulie followed Wren into the college building and tried, without much success, to keep up with her. Watching her stride on ahead, Paulie reflected on how on earth she'd managed to attract Wren into her life. They had virtually nothing in common. She wasn't even sure they could call themselves 'friends'.

Paulie ached to be popular, to know seamlessly how to make

friends, keep friends and enjoy friends, but hadn't really meant to find somebody like Wren.

Wren was an outsider. She wore nothing but browns and beiges. She cut her own hair (really short), was often mistaken for a boy and didn't even seem to care. She spouted facts and statistics at the most random times. She obsessed over jigsaws and packed them into her army-style rucksack to do over lunch breaks. She even had one of those cringey roll-up mats and a plastic tube to keep them in. The current one was one thousand five hundred pieces and because of their current drama studies, depicted some famous pirate battle from 1722 or something. This hobby, along with Wren's other characteristics, were not – according to Paulie's understanding of the world – conducive to becoming *popular*.

Despite all of that, Wren wasn't a bad person to hang around with. At least for now. The transition from school had been tough and Wren perhaps smoothed it a bit. Having left school with a virtually non-existent haul of GCSEs, Paulie had to re-sit her maths and science straight away. But focusing, for her, was just as impossible at college as it had been at school. Anything where she was expected to sit down at a desk and make sense of words or numbers was a joke. A horrible, terrifying joke.

At primary school, a lot of 'accidents' happened to Paulie's books. They were dropped in puddles. Drinks were spilled on them. They ended up in the washing machine at home. She could still picture them drying on the big old iron radiators at school. Damp clusters of pages, torn and curling at the edges. Yet another teacher tutting and shaking their head as black ink smeared across margins, creating blurry shapes and drowning any chance of legibility, sparking an agonising combination of hope and shame in Paulie's soul.

Now, just turned seventeen years old, she couldn't keep that kind of thing up. Instead she was familiar with a huge, black cloud of confusion that swallowed her up whenever 'traditional' concentration was required. She managed to disguise it for quite a while at secondary school, with smart remarks, jokes and stories that made the whole class laugh – usually the teachers too. These efforts sapped her energy down to zero and she'd go home flooded with fatigue, still not really feeling like her efforts had won her any friends. People laughed with her in the classroom, yes, but in the corridors they shifted away, avoided her eyes. Paulie often felt utterly unlikeable.

Two key things had happened since she started at college . . .

Number One: It had been a long day and the tiny lines, words and numbers captured behind the plastic sign on the bus stop outside college were so stubbornly refusing to permeate her brain, it had actually made her freeze. This wasn't unusual for Paulie. Whether it was exhaustion, stress or good old historical trauma (the latter, according to Aunt Meg), Paulie would sometimes enter a state of inertia. It felt unbearably and emotionally chaotic on the inside, but on the outside probably looked pretty uneventful because, quite often, nobody even noticed. On this particular day, Wren had spotted it instantly and helped Paulie without judgement. Since then, Wren had stuck to her like a whelk. And as grateful as Paulie was for the help at the bus stop, she often wondered if having this weirdo cling to her was actually stopping new friendships from forming.

Number Two: Berryport High hadn't been the most pupil-centred environment in the world but once Paulie enrolled at college, it wasn't long before her struggles with concentration were noticed. Some boring meetings with Aunt Meg and college heads, a laborious succession of appointments with specialists, and Paulie was diagnosed with ADHD. She wasn't sure how she felt about this, but had to admit that many of the symptoms did fit. And if it meant the college would let her drop maths and science for now and take up a full-time course in drama, then she was happy.

Drama was scary, of course. Lording it up in front of other people was definitely not Paulie's thing. In fact, that kind of attention filled her with a cold fear matched only by the thought of never having it at all. Drama class, to her, was the most beautiful and terrifying paradox. She was lured by the intoxicating promise of confidence, popularity, adoration . . . but equally repelled by ever standing up and having to do anything in front of anyone. That's why she stuck to backstage stuff.

"You got a session with Peg Leg Romano today?" Wren's voice snapped Paulie out of her thoughts. They were passing the pastoral block, where the college counsellors were based. Paulie had been assigned Romano Smith since her diagnosis, and had to report to him at least once a fortnight. He was a laid back kind of person, with a tendency to craft conversations above and beyond the usual platitudes she shared with everyone else. This small but courageous personality trait was one of the reasons she kind of liked him.

"Woah, Wren, you can't call him 'Peg Leg'. Do you want to be kicked out for hate speech?"

"That's what he calls himself! Can't wait to see his get-up at the weekend. He'll be the only genuinely one-legged pirate there!"

"Oh yeah." That made Paulie giggle. "Anyway, no. I can't even remember when I'm supposed to be seeing him. But he always texts me a reminder. It'll be fine."

"I love how you ADHD your way out of keeping a diary. Dude, it would drive me crazy not to have it all in my phone!"

"I don't ADHD my way out of anything. Did you swallow a bigot pill today or something?"

"Relax! Anyway, we're here. Ready?" Wren leaned her ruck-sacked back up against the heavy double doors to the drama studio. She looked at Paulie, wide-eyed with concern, knowing that even turning up to class at all was often enough to knock her flat.

Paulie flicked her gaze downwards and noticed the golden studio lights leaking out from the gap under the door. She felt the usual surge in her tummy and twisted the rope of her necklace into her skin just one last time. "Yep. I'm ready. Let's go in."

4

The drama studio doors swooped open with familiar ease. Paulie followed Wren inside and despite her apprehension about being there, was suddenly soothed by the amber wash of stage lights, which she knew so well.

"Delectable darlings! Nice of you to join us. Come on in – the skirmish is afoot!" Josiah Swan practically sang at them, signalling he was far less bothered about their slightly late arrival than he was about the action going on in front of him. He turned towards the group of students currently frozen in battle-like poses and drummed his fingers against his ample belly. "Now those skirmish poses are glorious, but remember that on Saturday, the blasting of the cannons will be ear-crushingly loud. And you lot – the conquering pirates – will have to get into alignment just moments before the first blast to shoot your guns into the air at precisely the right time. Remember, you're trying to intimidate the rest of us with your fancy pistols. This is going to be beyond epic, my show-stopping sugar cubes!"

The students broke their poses and started chatting excitedly about the performance. As she dumped her bag and got settled, Paulie could sense the current of anticipation amongst the group. She kind of shared it, she really did. But she was glad that she had her Saturday shift at the bakery as an excuse to not actually perform aboard the Arching Angel with the rest of them. This way, she got to stay involved with costume, but wouldn't have to endure the chaos, noise and unpredictability of the festival.

Before she could even make her way over to the costume store, Wren pushed her phone in Paulie's face. "Dude. Have you seen what Tantastic Tanya Withers posted on BeYu? She's crapped all over your 'window crafts'."

"W-what?" Paulie looked across the studio and saw that 'tantastic' Tanya was currently perfecting her dagger-brandishing skills, closely monitored by her equally 'tantastic' boyfriend, Sage Bretton, who was casually juggling at least four replica pistols. These two were the absolute golden couple of Berryport, and not just in skin tone either. Tanya was a stunningly good performer, landing the leading role in pretty much everything (word had it that Swanny had already lined up an agent for her in London), whilst Sage was the only son of the owners of Bretton Inc – the property company that owned just about every commercial property in town. Paulie had been trying for months to find a reason to spend time with them outside of drama class. It was obvious that her ticket to gaining popularity was to get them onside. After that, the rest would be easy and social efforts could run at an absolute minimum.

Paulie tried to focus on Wren's phone. There, in the main picture of Tanya's BeYu post, was a cheerfully vivid photo of a window bedecked in hundreds of stained glass sun-catchers. Pink, jewelled hearts; icy blue stars; fiery orange suns; flowers in every colour imaginable. They hung at different angles and heights, the same afternoon sun Paulie had enjoyed through the skylight in her cluttered living room, streaking through them with breath-taking beauty. The caption read:

Nice try, @paulie_trinket but whose window
crafts do YOU prefer?

And the selfie photo was a close-up of Tanya's more-than-perfect face arranged in an adorable pout.

Paulie hated herself for it but her first thought was: *at least she knows who I am.*

Wren huffed, putting her phone away and shook off her rucksack. Then she stood up tall, flicked a non-existent mane of hair off her face and pushed her chest right out. "Look at me, I've got the richest, most handsome boy in town, more dramatic talent in my little finger than everybody here combined AND a face to launch a thousand ships." The impression was astoundingly good. "I ALSO know how to wield BeYu like a weapon of mass destruction."

Paulie laughed but then shrugged. "It's okay. She's just vibing with me."

"Vibing? Dude, you need to wake up."

Before Paulie could assemble an answer, Swanny was stamping across the studio, keeping everybody on task. "Pirates? Work on your agonising deaths please. Wenches? I want pouting, bosoms and cackles galore. Sage, enough with juggling the pistols – I've told you umpteen times we'll never get that past health and safety. Juggle some doubloons or something instead." Swanny paused by a bottle of anti-bac gel sitting on one of the studio chairs. Many of the college staff were still obsessed over handwashing since the pandemic, and Swanny was certainly no exception. The acrid stench of it torpedoed into Paulie's nose as he slapped a massive dollop of it into his hands and rubbed hard. Maybe he clocked her not-very-well-hidden grimace because he swung his wide, brown eyes right over to where she was standing. "Paulie, Paulie, angel of my heart! If you absolutely insist that you're not taking part, I need you on costume duty. Get over there and do a check through of every single sash, medallion and eye patch. I need to know my artistes are adequately bedecked! Oh, and be careful of your fingers if you come across my skull and cutlass belt buckle - it's an antique and rather a pointy one at that."

"On it, Swanny."

Whilst everyone else was rehearsing, Paulie sorted through a jumbled haul of costumes and accessories. She found Swanny's frighteningly jagged belt buckle first and placed it out of the way, then put everything else into name-labelled piles ready for the big dress rehearsal.The irony of how brilliant she was at this was not lost on her. It was standard Paulie that she could carry this kind of task through to completion for the wider good of the drama department, yet couldn't graduate from her floordrobe to her wardrobe back at home.

Just as Paulie's stomach began to scream in protest that she hadn't eaten Meg's slab of flapjack before Wren had, she sensed a distinct change of energy in the room. She lifted her head from the now precisely categorised costume and saw everyone gathered in a circle in the centre of the sprung dance floor, heads bowed inwards, arms slung around each other's shoulders. They were doing a kind of chant. It was one of Swanny's theatrical techniques to bring them together as a group, to harness a collective energy that would fan the fires of the dress rehearsal they were about to undertake. That there, as far as Paulie was concerned, was the visual epitome of why she loved drama class. Yet here she was, on the outside of it.

The chanting grew to a crescendo, the articulation of the words building with an arrogance you could only ever get away with in these four walls: "A pirate's private property plagues Polly Parrot properly, a pirate's private property plagues Polly Parrot PROPERLY . . ." And just as Paulie was stretching her own tongue around those words, considering shimmying her way into the circle, Swanny exploded away with an extravagant spin and shrieked, "Costumes ahoy!"

The students rushed over to Paulie's costume store with frenzied cries of "Shiver me timbers!" and "All hands on deck!" As each of them found their labelled pile of clothes, Paulie shrank back into the heavy fabric of the curtains lining the room. She was glad her work meant everybody could get on with their costume change quickly and easily, but the chaos of the moment was all a bit much.

"What the hell is this?! A random bit of rope?" Tanya Withers was halfway dressed in voluminous purple skirts, a purple bandana and a crop top when she yelled the question out. Everybody turned and stared, Swanny included, as she held her arm aloft, something swinging from her fingertips. Whatever it was glinted rhythmically under the studio lights as it dangled from her beautifully manicured nails. "Surely this isn't supposed to be part of my costume? It's a bit . . . juvenile."

"Give me that," Sage strode in, juggling various pirate trinkets as he moved. He snatched the thing away from Tanya mid-juggle and kept the whirl of items going, an arc of satisfaction on his lips. "Aw. I recognise this. The costume girl, isn't it? I think it belongs to her."

Paulie's fingers flew to her throat where she felt nothing but bare skin. Her necklace was gone. And now it was in Sage Bretton's hands.

"Ah, s-sorry. Must have fallen off when I was sorting everything out." She shuffled forwards, out of the shadows, holding out her hand and aching to have the necklace placed in it straight away.

"Wait a minute, let me see it again." Tanya, who seemed to be in a fantastically bad mood, grabbed the necklace back as it flew through the air between Sage's hands and held it up to the light once more. "A battered compass and a random glittery eye.

They look like those bits of tat you get in the two pence machines at the amusements." Laughter rippled through the room. "Is that where you got them, Pauline?"

"No. A-actually, my mum gave them to me." Paulie's cheeks burned almost as ferociously as the huge chasm in her heart. She never usually spoke about her mum.

"Whatever." Tanya sighed as if that was enough now, and threw the necklace across the room. "Here you go, Pauline."

"It's Paulie." But the words trailed off into the chaos of costume-fitting, line-learning and stage-blocking and it was only Wren who was looking straight at her, eyes broad with concern. Paulie turned away, picking the necklace up off the floor, checking the two pendants were still in one piece and securing it back around her neck. Only this time, she made sure to tie an extra secure double-knot.

5

Friday morning didn't get a look-in.

Luckily, Paulie wasn't on shift at the bakery and there was no college so the fact that she woke up gone midday didn't trigger the usual nagging feeling that she was letting somebody down. Instead, she managed a miniscule stretching of fingers and toes, before allowing the mattress to reclaim her body and the duvet to settle with a stuffy warmth back over her limbs.

Aunt Meg must have opened all of the windows in the flat because the hustle and bustle of Berryport Harbour was audible even with a pillow over your head. Beyond the cawing of seagulls, the hum of slow-moving traffic and the sloshing of harbour waters, Paulie thought she could hear a bell clanging. *Where on earth is that coming from?* The Arching Angel had a bell, but it usually only rang during school children's visits and at the festival itself, and then it would be rhythmical, deliberate. This ringing was almost frenzied with a chaotic insistence to be heard.

Gratefully, Paulie was distracted by the seductively sweet scent of baked goods at various stages of preparation. Down in the bakery Meg had enlisted the help of her entire team, including their cleaning lady, Rita, to get everything ready for the bank holiday weekend and the festival. She was yet to ask Paulie, which was hardly surprising.

The blended aroma of cookies, muffins, traybakes and pastries was enough to remind Paulie's stomach that it hadn't been fed in ages. In fact, before the yucky toast incident yesterday, she couldn't remember the last time she had eaten. The efforts of getting the bus, dealing with Wren, sorting all the costumes and then the temporary yet humiliating loss of her necklace had sapped so much of Paulie's energy, she'd fallen straight into bed when she got home. She trailed her fingers from where they rested on the pillow over her head, to her neckline. Good. It was still there. The tiny golden compass and sparkling blue eye nestled in the soft dip where her neck met her chest. No need to twist the necklace right now. Her skin would thank her for that.

Her tummy, however, told her with a mighty roar that it was time to eat.

As she made her way to the kitchen, Paulie tripped over at least four things, each of them demanding her attention in an excruciating way. Potted lily – nearly dead, needed chucking away or some kind of sophisticated, green-fingered resuscitation. Yoga mat – filthy, needed a wipe-down after a failed attempt at beach yoga three weeks ago. Bumper pack of A4 folders – empty, needed filling with drama notes from last term. Plastic bag full of pebbles from the beach – dusty, needed rinsing before they could be painted and used as paperweights.

Paulie had just opened the door to her aunt's crafts cupboard to look for paints for the paperweight project, when her tummy, yet again, reminded her there was more important business to attend to. *Oh yeah. Food.*

Good old Aunt Meg. Inside the fridge was a huge platter of

savoury pastries and salad veg, wrapped in cling film and a
signature sticky note plastered on top.

Here. I know you won't eat otherwise.

Paulie took the plate out and turned to the kitchen counter
where she saw, lined up in a row: a can of orange Fanta, a bottle
filled with iced water, and her favourite ceramic mug with a tea
bag and two sugars already in it. The kettle was partially filled,
ready to be flicked on. That aunt of hers knew her better than
she knew herself.

Paulie was halfway through the platter, joyfully alternating
bites of food with gulps of sweet, fizzy orange, refreshing water
and comforting tea, when her phone chirped. It was a message
via WhatsApp, from Romano Smith, who Wren had the
audacity to call 'Peg Leg' yesterday.

> Paulie. We have a session booked on
> Tuesday at 2pm. Pastoral block. Still okay
> for you?

It was still okay. She didn't mind going to see Romano, even
if she wasn't quite clear on how the 'sessions' were of benefit.
She liked that he kept the pressure off. Take this message, for
example. They had an agreement that she only needed to reply
to him if she wasn't able to make it. WhatsApp let him see that
she'd read the message and he knew she'd only be in touch if
there was a problem. It was a breath of fresh air dealing with this
man, who was doing his best to keep her from being kicked out
of college.

Paulie smiled to herself and kept on eating.

Some time later, Meg burst into the kitchen, flapping her
doughy apron and clapping her hands together. "Paulie, luvver.
We're finally all closed up. I had a right job getting rid of Fergus.

He was squawking on about some superstitious rubbish. Yet again."

"What was it this time? Did a fisherman catch a left boot? Was there a dead seagull? A shark doing laps in the harbour?"

"Oh, I don't know. Something about the bell on the Arching Angel ringing for no reason and the foretelling of imminent death. He was in a right state. I had to give him a whole bag of pasties just to get him out the door. Anyway, the shop's empty now so I don't suppose you could pop downstairs and . . . flippin' 'eck did you eat all of that?" Meg gestured at the cleared platter from the fridge, several empty crisp packets and a family pot of banana yogurt that was down to the last dregs. Paulie dropped the spoon and licked her lips, as if being snapped out of a trance.

"Oh, um. Yeah. I guess I did. Didn't eat nothing yesterday though, really."

"Okay, fine. I'm just glad you're eating something now. What do you say, luvver? Can you come down and help me and the girls? I made those extra pirate cupcakes last night so you can finally do those eye patches. That's if you can resist parading them out on the street for all to devour?" Eugh. Paulie did not want to be reminded of *that*. "Rita's going to scrub the place from top to bottom so we can do the décor. We've got the bunting to put up, the pirate skeletons to go in the window, the Doubloon Delights need arranging in that treasure chest thingie. Then we have to sort our costumes. Oh, Paulie, there's so much to *do*!"

"Can I play my music?" Paulie asked, knowing Gorillaz hadn't gone down all that well last time she'd pulled a night shift with Meg and 'the girls'.

"I've already briefed them," Meg answered. "You can go as loud as you like, luvver. I know your music helps you work. I don't care as long as we get everything done before midnight. We're going to need at least a bit of beauty sleep before we open those doors in the morning. What do you say? I'll ply you with sweet, baked goods?"

"What, like you have been since I landed on your doorstep eleven years ago?"

Meg slipped behind Paulie's chair at the kitchen table and wrapped her arms around her shoulders, nuzzling her neck like she always used to when she was doing her hair as a child. "You betcha, maid. There's nobody I'd rather bake for than you."

"Alright, alright. You've won me over. Fire up the Bluetooth. I'm coming down."

6

It was May bank holiday weekend and Berryport Pirate Festival was in full swing.

Or at least, Paulie assumed it was from her safety spot behind the counter of Booty Bakes.

It was definitely the busiest day the bakery had seen this year, and that much chaos would usually have had Paulie running for the hills. However, she far preferred doling out baked goods to venturing onto the streets of Berryport where there were seemingly millions of humans auditioning for Pirates of the Caribbean. If she lifted her head for a second and looked out of the doors towards the harbour, she'd get flashes of rippling pirate flags, glittering mermaid tails, glinting swords and enough stripey t-shirts to make your eyes go funny. Every now and then, when the wind got fickle, clashing smells skittered through the bakery: candy floss, fish and chips, spilled rum and, of course, the unmistakeable sulphur scent of harbour dregs.

The noise, on top of everything else, was almost unbearable. Paulie tried to focus on the voices of the people in front of her, the polite and not-so-polite requests for bags of Doubloon Delights or Polly Parrot Pasties. However, it was impossible to block out the auditory evidence of the festivities outside: music pounding from the live stage, street vendors hollering on about their over-priced souvenirs, impromptu bursts of sea shanties from acapella choirs and let's not forget the seagulls squawking like it was their last day on earth.

To anybody else, Paulie would have seemed like a vaguely capable sales assistant. She was being 'friendly, attentive and quick' as per Aunt Meg's magic words. Deep inside though, she wanted it all to be over. She ached for her bed so much and felt her body might erupt in convulsions if she thought too hard about it. Instead, she swallowed down an immense lump in her throat by swigging Fanta whenever she got a moment, and twisting her necklace tightly against the skin at the side of her neck.

The college gang had already been in. Fully adorned in their costumes, they'd chosen the biggest booth at the back of the bakery and slurped coffee whilst Swanny briefed them diligently. If Paulie's hunch was right – he was immensely nervous. He flapped his chubby hands about, and fiddled precariously with his giant, skull and cutlass belt buckle to the point where Paulie wondered how he hadn't sliced off his actual fingertips. It was no secret that he hankered after fame and had been in talks with big important movie-type people about filming a pirate-themed epic in Berryport. Maybe they were coming along today or maybe he just wanted to send them a decent showreel. Whatever the reason, even Aunt Meg noticed Swanny's edginess. "Luvver, take that man a jumbo doughnut and shove it in his mouth, would you? If he mentions pistols and cannon blasts one more time I might fire one at him myself."

In the end, Paulie served jumbo doughnuts to everybody because Sage had snapped his fingers and declared something about landlord perks. Bretton Inc leased Booty Bakes and the upstairs flat to Aunt Meg, and Paulie had watched her stress out for weeks over the fact that the contract was up for renewal within the year. Best keep him sweet for now.

Wren had a stab at getting Paulie to abandon her spot behind the counter. It was hard to take her seriously, what with the fake beard flopping around on her every word. "Come on, dude," she'd said. "You'd already give Keira Knightley a run for her money in that get-up. Just tell Meg you'll be ten minutes. There's tension among the troops, especially Sage and Tanya. We can swashbuckle our way out of it together."

Paulie looked over at the golden couple and saw immediately what Wren meant. Whether it was her ADHD or just a plain old god-given gift, Paulie could always see it when other people were upset. No, not see it. *Feel* it. Sage was juggling some left over doughnuts, his handsome brow wrinkled with effort, but the stiff curve of Tanya's usually smiling lips hit Paulie like an arrow on target. They weren't actually speaking to each other but they were saying *so much.*

"Soz, Wren but there's no way I'm going out there today. I'm sure you'll manage the swashbuckling yourself."

Before Wren could voice her disappointment, Swanny was striding towards the doors in thigh-high boots that jangled with every step and waving a skull and crossbones flag on a pole twice his height. "Avast! See here, me beauties – the Arching Angel lies in wait. The time has come for a skiiirrrrrmish!"

And just like that, they were gone.

Shortly afterwards, Romano Smith popped in for a spiced vegetable filo tart. Paulie nearly dropped a whole tray of them when he rocked up to the counter. He was dressed from head to toe in black, apart from a blood red sash tied around his waist, layered with a leather band and scabbard which was peace-tied at his hip. He had a knee-high black leather boot on his one good leg and his usual shiny prosthetic was replaced with an actual wooden stump. There were strings of shells dripping from his neck and his normally tidy ginger beard was twisted into little dreads and dotted with pearly beads. "Ahoy there, Paulie," he cried, not doing anything at all to limit the cringe factor. "Me name's Cap'n Corvus and I've come ashore to ravage the fine rum stores of Berryport. And pastries too – though I'll not plunder them from you, me sweet girl. You needn' worry."

"Erm. Not worried." Paulie wrapped up his pastry for him, hoping he'd stop with the pirate drawl. "Oh my god. I've just noticed your hat. What have you got in there? Gross."

"This old thing?" Romano went back to his normal voice, smiled and patted his tricorne with both hands. "Well 'corvus' means 'crow' in Latin so these are crow's feathers."

"Yuck."

"And if you look closely you'll see an actual crow's skull with eyes that glow red. What do you think, Paulie? Good enough for your drama department?"

"Yuck again."

"Ah well, I just wanted to be a bit different from all the Johnny Depps out there. Aren't you joining the drama crew on the boat? It's nearly time for the skirmish you know."

Paulie did her best not to roll her eyes at having to explain, yet again, that no, she wasn't having anything to do with the skirmish. "Work. Gotta work."

"Ah, I see." Then he did that thing where he looked at her, nodding, wearing an expression of understanding that went far deeper than she was comfortable with. "Maybe next year. Oh, by the way, is Tanya Withers on the Angel with your lot? I think she wants to speak to me about something."

"Yeah. She was in here with them all earlier. She's probably on the ship now, getting ready. You'll have to find her afterwards."

"Yes. I will. Right, I'm off to watch the skirmish then. Enjoy the festivities!" Romano swept out of the bakery in a whoosh of black and red, taking his disgusting crow hat with him. It was a good job Paulie had prior evidence that he was a decent guy, otherwise he might just have given her the fright of her life.

"Luvver. Bin bags. Out. Now please." Aunt Meg had a tendency to speak in ultra-short sentences when she was busy, tired or stressed. Far from taking it personally, Paulie sometimes preferred it when she spoke like this. It was refreshing to have clear and simple instructions and she loved that she had such a deep connection to her aunt that manners didn't matter. If anyone else had spoken to her like that, of course, she'd have cried for days.

Paulie grabbed the knotted bin bags and pushed her way through the door at the back of the kitchen, which led out onto a narrow alleyway.

Alleyways. They were not fun for Paulie. They brought back some bad memories. Or one particular bad memory, to be precise. However, she knew this alleyway well so once she'd jumped down off the concrete step, she tuned in to the fact that it was cool and calm out here. That the tall, grey stone walls did quite a lot to muffle the sounds that moments ago had been so acute. She walked over to the trade waste wheelie bins, lifted the orange lid and dropped the bin bags inside. There. That wasn't so hard.

Just as she was turning back to the side door, Paulie heard the clopping of booted feet at the opposite end, where the alleyway curled round to the back of the buildings. Something in the heavy urgency of the step told her it wasn't just a shop owner getting on with outside chores. Then there was a voice.

"What's wrong with you? Do you have to follow me everywhere?"

Paulie knew the voice instantly, but the person had already appeared. Swishing layers of purple skirts and hands on belted hips, Tanya Withers stood at the end of the alleyway, addressing somebody just feet away from her but out of sight to Paulie. Her cheeks were flushed and her usually dazzling green, feline eyes were bulging with exertion. Then she shouted, "It's like you've got a death wish or something. Just leave me alone!"

Next thing Paulie knew, Tanya was sprinting down to her end of the alleyway, a flurry of skirts, ruffles, buckles and honest-to-god tears. She was running so hard, so full of fury, that she swayed as she ran, knocking into the walls on either side.

In a distant part of her brain, Paulie knew that if she didn't shift backwards, Tanya might knock her over but the alarming concoction of panic and urgency in the moment – as well as enduring echoes of her own trauma – meant that paralysis was beginning its familiar onslaught.

Tanya rammed into Paulie's shoulder – bam. She let out a thundering cry and threw Paulie a look brimming with – what was it? Hope? Desperation? She kept on running for the harbour, leaving Paulie pounded to the ground. Shocked and shivering, Paulie lifted her cheek from the tarmac and looked backwards to the other end of the alleyway, hunting for the person Tanya had been shouting at. But no matter how keen and searching her eyes may have been, they landed on nothing but a blank wall.

And that's when she froze . . .

"Luvver? You've got to be done putting the bins out by now?" Meg's voice was the first sound to rouse Paulie. She scraped her hands along the ground and pushed herself up into a sitting position.

Then there was an ear-cracking BOOM that shook not only the ground she was sitting on and the wheelie bins she was collapsed against, but also – seemingly – the whole of Berryport.

Then there was another one.

BOOM.

Paulie's hands dashed to her neck and she twisted the necklace hard. *It's okay. It's just the cannon shots down on the harbour. It just means the skirmish is underway.*

Meg appeared in the doorway to the kitchen and heaved a sigh of relief when she spotted Paulie. "Oh, thank god. I thought you'd got lost in one of them there bins. What are you doing on the ground? Let's go back in. There'll be another rush after the skirmish."

Paulie was just regaining her balance, trying to deal with the thunder of the cannons and following her aunt back into the bakery, when both women were stopped in their tracks by another, completely different sound barrelling down the alleyway towards them, straight from the direction of the Arching Angel.

It was a scream.

Followed by another.

And then, the screams just didn't stop.

7

After all of the screaming, it seemed nobody was capable of anything but a murmur.

The police had got to the scene like lightning. They must have been nearby anyway, considering that Berryport Pirate Festival was one of the biggest gatherings of its kind in the world. You couldn't stage an event like that without the close involvement of the authorities.

The Arching Angel had been completely evacuated, which left hundreds of people on the harbour-side, murmuring so that an eerie hum drenched the air. The mid afternoon sun beat down on worried brows, whispering lips. Parents gripped the hands of toddlers, buckled babies into pushchairs, led them silently away. The only people left were those without children. A mass of pirates, wenches, mermaids and ship mates suddenly stripped of their merriment. Trapped by a forced sobriety, in a collective trauma that was yet to be revealed.

Police officers wove in and out of the crowd, telling some people to move back, others to stay put. They scribbled furiously in jotters, presumably taking contact details and asking for clues about what people had seen and heard. They'd already been into the bakery, asking Aunt Meg to keep everybody there for the time being – querying who had been where when, and what had happened since the screams tore through the harbour. Paulie had shrunk back behind the counter, the very proximity of the officers causing her breath to stop, and let Aunt Meg lead the way through whatever this actually was.

Right now though, Paulie was stuck to the frame of the bakery door. Her aunt was following police instructions to the letter and hadn't allowed anybody in or out of Booty Bakes. Paulie had been stationed there to man the exit though she wasn't actually taking much notice. All she knew was that something very wrong had happened aboard the Arching Angel.

She spotted the college crew, gathered in a small cluster next to the railings surrounding the pirate ship. Every single one of them had a gaze glued to the deck, where police officers were securing the site with tape, blocking off the view with speedily assembled screens. They stood so tightly packed together, Paulie assumed they'd been told to stand there and not move.

Wren stood at the edge of the group and even from this distance, Paulie could see her shirt was drenched in sweat. Usually, sweat was Wren's absolute nemesis but she wasn't even attempting to peel the shirt from her back. She was deathly still. Other members of the class huddled and clung to each other, a small mass of colliding bodies. Swanny stood at the front of the cluster, hanging onto the metal railings with both hands. His small, rounded body angled forwards, as if it might tip right over into the sea and Paulie got a sense that although he was staring hard at the ship, that he wasn't actually seeing anything.

Romano was there too. He stood with one hand clamped over his mouth and the other clutching his crow-feathered hat tightly to his chest. The shock of ginger hair on his head was somewhat cheery but his face was in staunch opposition. Sage stood next to him, his mouth slack and his arms folded against his stomach. He was no less handsome in this strange and chilling moment, but his good looks were frayed so that he was hardly recognisable.

"Do we know what happened yet?" Meg appeared next to Paulie and gathered her niece into her arms. "It looks pretty, serious, doesn't it? I can't believe how quickly they've locked down the festival."

It was true. Aside from the attire of the people brave enough to stick around on the streets, the festival had died a horrible death. The music had stopped. Nobody was selling anything anymore. The smells of food and drink were abruptly vacant. Even the seagulls had slowed their overhead streaks through the sky.

"You okay, luvver? Whatever's going on out here, there was something up with you first. Why were you up close and personal with the wheelie bins? Did the alleyway freak you out again?"

Paulie opened her mouth to coax the words out. The collision with Tanya. The mystery person she'd been arguing with. The inability to see who it was and the cold, blank, stone wall dominating her view. Paulie remembered with startling clarity the grain of the stone, the glittering rough of the wall, the tarmac beneath her palms. And then the agonising reality that she couldn't add up all of the elements from the scene. The paralysis had hit her hard. She wanted to tell Aunt Meg all of this but something in Paulie remained frozen. The words locked away.

"It's okay, luvver. I get it. Alleyways are hard." Meg's words did something to thaw Paulie's limbs and she felt the full wrap of her aunt's arms like a luxuriously warm wash of love. Whatever the hell was going on, at least she had that.

"Oh god. Things are moving up there." Meg tightened her hold as they both looked up towards the Sika. A new vehicle had parked up as close as it could get to the entrance to the ship and three figures in white overalls climbed out, their heads angled low. "Tell me, luvver. My eyesight's not what it used to be. What does it say on the side of that van?"

The words barely creaked out of Paulie. "Forensic Services."

The figures made their way up to the gangplank to the tented area on the main deck. One of them held back the flap of canvas for the other and there was a period of about three seconds where, from their vantage point on the dock, a very particular combination of visual factors gave the college kids all the information they needed. Paulie couldn't be sure, but she thought she captured it too. Blood. Blonde hair. Purple skirts.

It was Tanya.

8

Billowbreak Beach was eerily quiet. A quick glance around the stony shore showed some evidence of festivities – candy floss sticks, empty beer cans, even the odd pirate hat or eye patch caught in the rock pools, soaking into heavy, black smudges along with the dark green seaweed. Seagulls perched on empty gazebo frames and scavenged for half-eaten pasties, discarded bags of chips. They squawked occasionally, protesting into the sea air with an ardour perhaps less fervent than usual. Maybe they weren't the beasts everybody assumed they were and by some fluke of nature they sensed that a great loss was present and blooming. That loss billowed now, across the waves, the rocks, and into the hearts of the students currently walking across the beach.

They moved slowly. A huddle of bodies that took comfort in moving as one. As Paulie picked her steps across the pebbly beach by tracing those of the person in front of her, she whispered to Wren by her side, "Tell me again why we're here?"

"Dude, I'm just following the crowd. I mean, all of us apart from you were on that ship and didn't even notice what happened to her. I think we just need to be together, yeah?"

"Okay," Paulie whispered. "What did the police say though? Did you get a grilling?"

"A bit. They need to speak to us all individually again tomorrow. They took in all of the pistols as evidence but, I mean, they were checked and safe, weren't they? The college brought in the best theatrical firearms company in the country. And they were blanks anyway, right? I don't even see how an accident could have happened."

"I don't know. It's all so surreal."

Paulie felt the pace slow down and looked ahead. They were coming to a stop at a corner of Billowbreak where the rockpools rose up and transformed into cliffs so it wasn't possible to go much further unless you wanted to climb. Even though it was only late afternoon, the sun's rays had softened and poured over the rocks in generous, golden lashings, as if they were hurrying towards the end of the day. Paulie wished they would.

Sage was at the head of the group and the first to reach the rockpools. He stopped and turned to face everyone. His usually broad shoulders were slumped and he was running his hands over his face repeatedly, as if trying to rub something away. It was such a strange sight. He – along with everyone else – had removed his pirate hat, but the oversize shirt, tatty scarves, knuckleduster rings and even smudged eyeliner remained. It was a devastatingly bizarre sight to see such raw emotions encased in what now seemed like ridiculously inappropriate regalia.

"I-I don't know why we came here. But . . . well . . . Tanya likes . . . *liked* it here." A couple of the girls from class leapt to Sage's side, patting his arms and making soothing sounds. Swanny, who'd walked along with the students, locked into an abnormally stiff silence, stared at Sage, offering nothing but a slight nod of the head. Romano Smith was nowhere to be seen. Sage sniffed a bit and carried on. "Shall we all just sit down? I-I don't really know . . . I just c-can't believe . . . Let's just sit."

So they did. They all sat on the pebbly shore and looked out to sea, as that seemed the appropriate thing to do. Not that any of them knew what was appropriate. A girl had just died. In close proximity to all of them. A girl who was the beating heart of their drama class – so bright, talented and vivacious just hours ago, now reduced to a lifeless wreck.

Paulie sat next to Wren and looked back towards Berryport Harbour. She could just about make out the curve of the harbour bowl, the line of shops, cafes and restaurants and there, anchored in the centre of it all, was the Arching Angel. The temporary screens so hurriedly assembled that afternoon, were gone. That meant Tanya was too. In a couple of hours the fairy lights strung across the rigging of the ship would flicker to life like they always did, illuminating the very place nobody wanted to see. She wondered if anybody would have the foresight to knock off the timer and save everyone from the distress.

Even though the students were still huddled together in shock, there were little micro-cliques forming, whispering questions and mumbling theories. It created an oddly reassuring hum that helped the moments tick by. At one point, the owners of Billowbreak Bistro trudged down to the shore with trays of hot chocolates, which was incredibly thoughtful, considering they'd had to shut up shop like the rest of town.

Once Paulie had the warm paper cup in hand, she realised the shadows were getting longer and smoother across the beach. Soon the light would be completely gone. Would that mean they'd all go home, left alone with their minds replaying the afternoon's events? Even though Paulie hadn't been on the ship, she couldn't get the encounter in the alleyway out of her head.

"It's like you've got a death wish or something."

Who had Tanya been speaking to and what did that mean? Why had she looked at Paulie with such a deep streak of vulnerability and hope? As if Paulie could somehow save her? She rubbed her shoulder where Tanya had hit it. There would be a bruise, she was sure of it. How strange to have a mark left on her by somebody who was no longer breathing.

Ever so gradually, Paulie was waking up to the cold, hard facts. As real as she could feel the waistband of her pirate skirts digging into her tummy and the stick of the fake leather boots suckered against her shins, she also felt the deep imprint of the alleyway. Should she tell someone? Would it make a difference?

The students started to shift slightly as the sun dipped down and Paulie watched as Sage and Swanny rose to their feet. They traipsed up to the Bistro and followed the owner to the hatch where drinks were usually served. They appeared to gather some objects up from the counter. Objects which chinked and clinked as they walked back down with them towards the gathering.

"What are they doing?" Wren mused, the first words she'd uttered for a while. Then she turned to look at Paulie and saw something that immediately plastered her face in worry lines. "Dude, you okay? Your neck looks so sore from your necklace."

Paulie dropped the charms and knotted her knuckles together. "I think so. It's just, well, you know. All this."

"Yeah. But you're also white. Properly white. When did you last eat something? Here. Finish my hot chocolate." She shoved the cup into Paulie's hands and gave her an expectant look. "Well? Is it low blood sugar or something else?"

"It's probs nothing. I just . . . well, I saw Tanya today."

"I know. We were all there, remember? You brought us doughnuts and Sage juggled them like a dick."

"No, no. I mean after that. After you all left."

"But I thought you were stuck at work?"

"I was, I mean, I went out for a bit. Into the alleyway to put the bins out. And that's when I saw her." Paulie explained the scene in as much detail as she could knowing that Wren, for all her faults, wouldn't repeat the matter to anybody else.

"Woah. But who was she talking to? You must have seen them? Didn't you go have a look around the corner?"

Paulie gulped her age-old trauma into her gullet and ploughed on. "I didn't. I couldn't. I kind of froze."

"Again?"

"Yeah. So they disappeared before I could get a look. But Wren, she was proper upset with them. Whoever it was. And she looked at me as if I should know what to do. As if I should have *done* something."

"You're going to have to tell the police." She locked eyes with Paulie, her grey-blue stare wide and strong. "I'll go with you."

Paulie set the hot chocolate cup down into a crevice in the pebbles and pretended to consider Wren's suggestion. "I doubt that's necessary. I mean, it might even complicate matters."

"Let them worry about that. You need to tell them. It could be important." Paulie was spared from replying because now Swanny and Sage were standing up in front of everybody, clearing their throats.

"Sage would like to say a few words, my sweetlings."

Sage gave Swanny a slow, shaky nod and then turned to the group. He lifted his chin but his gaze went out over and above the tops of everybody's heads. He looked truly awful. "You know, it means a lot to me that you're all here and we're getting through this day together. We're going to light some candles now and invite you all . . ." he paused, a sob ripping at his throat but Swanny gave him a little nudge and he got back on track.

"Each one of you can come up here and add a stone to the pile for Tanya. Oh, and we've lit some candles. Thanks to the Bistro people."

Swanny and Sage stepped back to reveal a circle of tealights in little glass holders placed on the rocks behind them. The glass holders were a combination of different colours – reds, yellows, ambers, pinks and greens – and they instantly brought to mind Tanya's BeYu photo from a couple of days ago. The assortment of sun-catchers that literally outshone Paulie's crafts gathering dust on her windowsill.

Sage looked down at his feet and picked up a few smooth, silvery rocks. For one bizarre moment, Paulie thought he might juggle them, like the Sage from this morning might have done. Instead, he selected one, leaned into the candlelit circle and placed it down, giving it a pat before turning back to address everyone. He took a huge breath that Paulie would have thought impossible given the depths of his despair and said in a slightly louder voice, "I loved you, Tanya."

In turn, members of the group shuffled over to the glowing circle and placed their rocks inside. As Paulie put down her rock, she reflected that what had started out as a confusing, magnetic pull to the beach for a stunned group of youngsters, had fast become an impromptu memorial for a girl whose body was probably still warm. Once everybody had added their rock, and they towered dramatically against an emerging night sky, there was a sudden wave of buzzes, chirps and beeps emitting from pockets and bags. It was the BeYu app, signalling that it was time to take the photo of the day.

Without even speaking to each other, the whole group of students took out their phones and positioned them for a simultaneous selfie and portrait of the rock pile. There was a momentary, dazzling ring of shining screens and flash-lit faces before the precious moment that was meant for Tanya got zapped, thirty times over, into the digital world. Paulie felt her phone buzz with the clash of notifications and all she could think as she unlocked her screen, saw different versions of the same photo cascade across her feed and an abundance of hashtags nudge their way into existence was: *This feels staged.*

9

"Woah, luvver, It feels a bit like a ghost town, doesn't it?"

Aunt Meg drove her dodgy old van into the college car park and pulled to a stop in a space overlooking what the students called the 'Meadow'. Paulie had always thought it was more like a wasteland but the wide patches of stubborn daisies that embellished the shabby grass prettied it up some way to earning the name. It was where students usually gathered to eat lunch. Where staff members sometimes held outdoor meetings. In fine weather the Meadow accommodated choir practice, cricket matches, science experiments, art classes, meditation sessions and more. But today it was desolate. As if the only thing to have touched it was the still-stunned gaze of Paulie and Aunt Meg.

Today was Tuesday and college was closed. Everybody had received texts from the principal to say that as a mark of respect to Tanya and her family, all timetables were called off and main buildings would be closed. The only part of the college that remained open was the pastoral block, so that anybody with pre-arranged counselling sessions could make use of them and anybody who needed impromptu support could come in and ask for it. Apparently, things were to go back to normal next week.

Whatever that meant.

"Yeah. It is a bit ghost-like," agreed Paulie. "Thanks for the lift."

"Couldn't have you stressing over buses with everything that's going on now, could I?" Meg smiled and reached over to squeeze Paulie's hand. "It's important you get your counselling now more than ever. Anyway, what with the bakery being closed, I've got the time." She released her grip on Paulie's hands and drummed her fingers across the arch of the steering wheel.

"Are you going to open tomorrow?" Paulie wondered if the town would ever wake up properly after what happened to Tanya. The pirate festival had disappeared amazingly promptly and not one shop had opened its shutters since Saturday afternoon.

"Not sure. I'll chat to the other business owners around the harbour and see what's what. I don't want to be insensitive but we have got to earn a living. And, let's be honest, some of my cakes might be just the thing right now."

"Maybe." Paulie took a deep breath and twisted her necklace tight. "I don't think they know what they need."

"Luvver, your neck looks so sore. Doesn't it hurt? Let me see." Meg leaned over to the passenger side and tried to brush Paulie's hair away to examine the small, red welts smattering her skin. Paulie knew they looked bad right now. She'd spent the bank holiday weekend agonising over what to do about Tanya's words in the alleyway, her neck bearing the brunt of her worries. But she had her hair arranged around her shoulders for that very reason and wasn't about to undergo a physical examination right there in the van.

"It's fine, I'm fine." She opened the van door and jumped out, blowing Meg a dismissive kiss. "I'll see you back here in an hour or so?" Then she purposefully turned her back, feeling the pendants on her necklace sway beneath her top as she jogged over the Meadow, towards the pastoral block. She heard the engine of the van sputter to life, then the crush of gravel as her aunt drove away.

Paulie dipped her head towards her lap as Romano waited for an answer to his question. She was distracted by a text from Wren.

> So, are you going to tell the police or what?

She felt an immediate tightness across her chest and gulped for the early summer air streaming through the open window, shimmering across the leaves of Romano's houseplant collection. If only she could utilise the oxygen as easily as they could.

"Paulie, can you remember what we agreed about phones during our sessions? Mine is switched off."

"What? Oh yeah. Okay." Paulie turned off her phone and zipped it away in her rucksack on the chair next to her. "Sorry, what was the question?"

"I was asking you about the marks on your neck. You've told me that you twist your necklace when you're stressed. I'm guessing what happened to Tanya is hitting you quite hard." Romano was maintaining the friendly eye contact he was oh so good at, but Paulie felt his sorrow like a wave rolling slowly over her. There was no way he could hide it.

"Yeah. It's hard for everyone."

"And twisting the necklace helps?"

"'Helps' might not be the right word. But it brings me back. Wakes me up, if you know what I mean."

"I think I do." Romano picked up a spray bottle from a shelf behind him and sprayed some miniature potted plants. "Maybe it's a bit like me with my plants. They keep me in the moment, tending to their needs. But I guess I'm lucky I've got something that doesn't, you know, harm me. Your neck looks like it must hurt?"

"Not really. I'm used to it."

"And tell me again about how you got your necklace."

"Again?"

"Again."

Paulie sighed and squirmed in her seat. She didn't know why Romano was so bloody interested in her necklace. Okay, so twisting it into her skin perhaps wasn't the best of ideas, but there were far worse things she could be doing. And if it was the only thing that made her feel closer to her mum, then surely that was a good thing?

"My mum bought the necklace for me when I was six years old. I wanted the compass pendant because we'd been learning about them at school and I thought they were like magic, always pointing North."

"And this was when you lived up in the Midlands with your parents? Birmingham I think it was?"

"Yep. I was out shopping with my mum on New Street. It was always so busy there because it's, like, the main place for shoppers. But it was okay because my mum knew how to calm me down. Distract me. So it was nice. Really nice."

"It sounds it. What about the eye pendant?" Romano sprayed another plant, wiping around the pot with a tissue he took out of a box on the coffee table between them. "Are you okay to tell me about that?"

"S'pose. My mum bought me the eye too because she caught me looking at it. I liked glittery things. I remember thinking I couldn't possibly ask for both charms because we never had any money but she said they were special treats and I deserved it."

"That's lovely."

"It was." Paulie's voice cracked slightly and she fought the urge to twist the necklace as she was speaking about it. She had a feeling it might have loosened the thickness in her throat. "Then she spotted the rope necklaces hanging up on a stand at the till and got me one of those too, to hang the pendants on. I remember the lady in the shop said I was a very lucky little girl."

"Did you feel lucky?"

"I did . . ." Paulie remembered the grip and swing of her mum's hand as they walked along the street. The excited chatter about the pendants and her mum explaining that the compass was for guidance and protection – that she'd never be alone as long as she wore it. That the eye was a reminder to trust her intuition, which had seemed like a very big word at the time, but her mum explained, *"It's like a spark of truth deep inside you. A bright, powerful spark that leads to wonderful things."* It had felt like a very grown-up conversation and Paulie devoured the memory of it, the sweet scent of her mum's perfume, the flutter and flap of her orange dress as she walked.

She recalled with precision the pleading notes her own voice had hit as she asked to put the necklace on before they got home. The amused sigh her mum gave and the swift dip into a nearby alleyway where they could put down their shopping bags without getting in the way of the high street crowds. Those last, divine moments of contact: her mum's fingers brushing the nape of her neck, a soft kiss applied to her forehead, the warm, solid hug she'd given Paulie before stepping back and admiring the charms with a smile that just glowed. These memories were so precious, so full of light, it was a sick joke that they sat next to shadows of such horror.

"Paulie? You okay?" Romano was leaning forwards, elbows on knees, the creak of his prosthetic rousing her back to reality. His eyebrows arched and his brow wrinkled as if waiting to be smoothed out by her next words.

"What? Yes. I'm okay. It's just hard, remembering what happened to her."

"Of course. And you were so young. Do you want to talk about what happened next? I don't want to push you. It's totally up to you." He remained leaning forwards, his brow slightly less wrinkled but his expression still open and engaged.

"You probably have it all on file. I doubt you need to hear it from me."

"It's not about what I need, Paulie. These sessions are for you."

Paulie took a deep breath whose sickening origin seemed to reside in her actual toes and hoped the next words to come out of her mouth would make sense. "Some bloke appeared out of nowhere, grabbed Mum's handbag off her shoulder and tried to run off with it. She wouldn't let it go and they kind of fought for a few seconds." Was it a few seconds? Paulie had no idea. It could have gone on for ages for all she knew because, stupidly, she'd frozen stiff against the alleyway wall, fear cheating her into submission. "All I remember after that is the sound of Mum's head hitting against something hard and the man's footsteps sprinting away. I - I just kept staring at the ground. I couldn't look up." The breath she'd brought up from her toes got stuck in her chest as her heart roared in pain. Romano held his own heart with an open palm, not even attempting to speak. They sat in silence for several moments.

"Paulie, I'm so sorry. Did they ever catch the mugger?"

Paulie shook her head and her pendants chinked together. "Nope. Even though I was the only one to see it, I couldn't help the police. I couldn't answer any of their questions. I didn't see anything useful like his face or distinctive clothing or even hear his voice because I'd gone into that stupid frozen state. I remember her going down and her head hitting something with a horrible crack. Apparently it was a pile of bricks stacked up behind her, so her skull never had a chance. And I was pretty much useless."

"A six year old can't be useless, Paulie."

"Well, like, whatever. All I know is that some idiot was desperate for a few pathetic pounds so my mum died. Whether he actually intended that or not." Paulie sat back in defeat, spread her palms out and found Romano's eyes as a way to anchor herself back to now.

"I'm so sorry this happened to you, Paulie."

"It didn't happen to me. It happened to my mum."

"I understand. So, now, for seventeen year-old Paulie, is it a good thing to always wear the necklace, to always have the pendants on . . ?"

"Yes." Paulie said it so that it cut over the end of his question. "Yes. Wearing the necklace helps." And as if to prove it, she grabbed it with both hands and twisted it right into the front and centre of her neck, causing an intense burning sensation as well as a torrent of tears as hot and spirited as the memories she'd just described.

Romano handed her some tissues. She spent the rest of the session crying and apologising. So much apologising. Like many sessions before it, Romano provided just the right amount of warmth and safety throughout. Paulie knew by now that it was no use holding the tears back, so reluctantly she let them fall. It wasn't like she had much choice in the matter.

And with the same kind of intuition symbolised by the glittering eye hanging around her neck, Paulie knew that the memories of her mum in the alleyway were now inexorably fused with the chaotic images of purple skirts and booted feet, flushed cheeks and terrified eyes. *"It's like you've got a death wish or something."* That begging look Tanya had given her after she'd rammed into her shoulder scorched her mind with an impending responsibility. And it wasn't something the tears could wash away.

Eventually time ran out so Paulie picked up her bag and mumbled her thanks. She knew the general direction of the door and headed for it, attempting to blink back the dream-like blur. She mapped out the familiar objects with this strange new vision: the atlas lampshade on a stand in the corner, the packed bookshelves lining the walls, the sprawling spider plant hanging inside a metal tub. And the filing cabinet, just next to the door on her way out, with a messy pile of papers sitting on top of it. Paulie blinked when she saw shapes scrawled across the cover sheet on top – shapes that, with a few more blinks, became letters with a tugging sense of familiarity. One more blink and Paulie was certain. The name was unmistakeable.

Tanya Jane Withers.

10

Aunt Meg turned the volume down on Paulie's music for what seemed like the fiftieth time that morning. She turned to Paulie, sighing but arranging her face into a smile. "I'm sorry, luvver. It just doesn't feel right, playing music that loud right now."

"But I chose those Gorillaz songs specifically. To fit the . . . I don't know, the mood?"

"I get that, maid, I do. But look around you. Nobody wants to hear about 'dead butterflies' or 'demon days'. It's all so morose." Meg switched the bakery Bluetooth to link with her own phone and scrolled until she found the Booty Bakes sea shanty playlist. The rejection of Paulie's music hurt an inexplicable amount, but she couldn't find the words to question it. Best just swallow that hurt down.

Booty Bakes had only been open a few hours and already nearly all the freshly baked produce was gone. Aunt Meg had anticipated a high need for comforting bakes like warm, fluffy white loaves, soft and chewy caramel cookies and full to brimming butter pecan pies. She'd been right, and the steady stream of customers who'd been through the doors since they opened, meant the goods were in high demand.

As Paulie wiped the counter tops she looked up and saw grief in abundance. Shaking heads bowed inwards over drinks, hands clasped next to platters of half-eaten cookies. Everybody's eyes, as they'd approached the counter, were torn with grief. Paulie didn't know which way to look and felt physically immersed in the sadness.

Fickle Fergus was a wreck. Paulie didn't understand his connection to Tanya, but when he'd rocked up to the counter with a mere golden hoop in his ear and ordering a doorstep ham sandwich and a tea in less than thirty seconds flat, it was obvious he was in a state. "You be careful, Little Paulie," he'd said. "Something's afoot."

Paulie was just hacking into some fresh white loaves to make sandwiches, when she felt a hush settle like a lead blanket over the bakery. Not that it had been very noisy to begin with, but suddenly the tear-loaded sniffs and whispers were deathly absent. Then her aunt gasped, "Wendy, luvver. What on earth are you doing here?"

There, in the anchor-adorned doorway of Booty Bakes, stood Wendy Withers. Tanya's mum.

Well, she was less standing, more leaning, on a wire rack of crisps and snacks. Meg rushed out from behind the counter and caught Wendy as she took a shaky step forwards. She held her in her arms, embracing her small, sobbing body which was clothed in fleece pyjamas and a heavy winter coat. Paulie remembered reading somewhere that shock could make you feel cold.

Every single customer sitting in the bakery watched as Meg led Wendy over to the nearest table. She was recognisable to so many not just because her face had been splashed all over the press recently, but because she really was Berryport's finest manicurist. She ran a salon on Middle Street called, 'Infinity Nails' which had obviously been shut since the pirate festival and now the locals were bereft of perfect nails as well as happiness. Right now, Wendy's face was hidden by lashings of wavy blonde hair and it was spooky how easily she could have been mistaken for Tanya. Except Tanya would never have let her hair go unwashed like that. Paulie knew that for certain.

Meg flashed Paulie a look which she'd seen hundreds of times before. A look that if it could speak, would say, "Hot, sweet tea. Now." It wasn't the first time somebody had sought comfort at the bakery. And it certainly wasn't the first time Aunt Meg had given it. But in the after-effects of murder? Now that was a first.

Paulie brought them a pot of tea heavily laced with sugar and cinnamon. She knew that's how Aunt Meg would have made it herself. She wondered if she should say something as she added two empty cups and a jug of warm milk, because Wendy's shaking shoulders were surely an indication that some words of sympathy were in order. However, they got stuck in her throat as if tiny claws were holding them back and that was that.

Wandering back to her spot behind the counter, and picking up a cloth without really knowing what to do with it, Paulie pondered on the file she'd seen at Romano's office yesterday, with Tanya's name on it. In the broad scheme of things, it wasn't a surprise that Romano had been seeing Tanya. He counselled loads of students so why shouldn't she be one of them? But that, paired with his quest to find her at the pirate festival only minutes before her death, left Paulie a bit queasy. Peg Leg Romano had all the trappings of a good guy but was that just what they were? Trappings?

There was every chance that the person at the other end of the alleyway could have been him. Certainly, he wouldn't have been able to run quickly after Tanya with that wooden leg he'd worn as part of his costume. What if he'd gone and found Tanya before the skirmish and put her into some kind of emotional tail-spin that somehow caused her death? Or what if he followed her after the argument, passing Paulie in her weird, frozen state, and found a vantage point where he could get a good aim with his gun? Paulie recalled his pirate costume with the gross crow-feathered hat. Was a gun part of the get-up? She just couldn't remember.

"Paulie, what are you *doing*?" It was Aunt Meg, leaning over the counter, half-whispering, half-seething at her. Paulie looked down at her hands, where the cloth still was, and realised she had spent the last few moments wiping clean the blackboard sign that usually hung behind the counter. Aunt Meg had spent ages on it that morning, writing a message of sympathy for the town. "Good lord, I spent the best part of the day composing that. How will I ever remember what I wrote? I'll have to start all over again." Meg's curls bounced around her face in outrage. Lines dragged her pretty eyes downwards and she flashed a look back at Wendy who was still and quiet now, but staring blankly into her teacup.

"I-I'm so sorry. I was just thinking about . . . well, about everything that's happened. Sorry, Aunt Meg." Paulie really meant it. And felt that familiar drag on her gut that she never knew what to do with.

"Fine. Whatever. Another pot of tea please. And then go back upstairs. I can't have you down here when you're like this. I'll call one of the girls to step in, okay?"

Being sent home from work wasn't new to Paulie, but today it felt worse because she knew how much her aunt needed her. But Meg was probably right, she was no use to anyone right now. Just before she left, she cleared Fergus's table (actually used the cloth for what it was meant for) and realised he'd been observing everything over his ham sandwich.

"Little Paulie. Don't fret, will you? Meg's got a lot on what with looking after Tanya's mum. That poor woman. Lost her husband and her daughter now. Why do some people get so much tragedy in their lives, eh?"

"Her husband? You mean, Tanya's dad?" Paulie knew Tanya only lived with her mum but had just assumed the dad had upped sticks and left, just like hers had. In fact, she'd been thinking of using the whole 'our dads are crap' line as a way of getting in with Tanya. Too late for that now.

"Aye. Arthur his name was. Such a nice chap, if troubled at times. He just disappeared one day. Way back when Tanya was knee high to a grasshopper. Of course, Berryport folk think she had him, you know . . ." Fergus took his index finger and dragged it across his stubbly throat.

Paulie gasped. "But why? Why on earth would she do that?"

"I don't believe it myself, but you know what folk are like. She's got a liking for the finer things in life and he always had money troubles. He liked the booze. Or it liked him."

"Oh," Paulie murmured. Then she felt eyes on her and looked up. It was Aunt Meg, giving Wendy yet another hug and over the trembling shoulder flicking her eyes upwards as if to indicate that Paulie could go. Or *should* go.

Once Paulie was upstairs and lying flat out on her bed, she tried to settle her mind. It was no use. Her attention jerked around in different directions like a million elastic bands twanging and snapping. Was it Wendy at the other end of the alleyway? Had her and Tanya had a fall-out that day? If she really had offed her husband, is it possible she could do the same to her daughter? Was Paulie a truly horrible person for even entertaining the idea?

Her thoughts catapulted to what the police must be doing right now. Gathering statements, evidence, ideas, theories. It must be like finding needles in haystacks. What if the one piece of information they needed was the one Paulie was sitting on?

What if whatever went on in that alleyway just moments before Tanya's death was the key to understanding why she was no longer in this world? Paulie remembered Sage's voice ragged with shock at Billowbreak Beach and the keening, clustered bodies of the students trying to support each other. Maybe, just maybe, if she talked to the police about what she witnessed, everybody would realise that she was actually a normal, decent person. That all she wanted was to be friends.

Paulie felt her phone buzz somewhere beneath the layers of clothing plastered to her bed. She dug it out and saw there was a voice note from Wren.

"Dude, have you been to see the police yet? You can't keep this stuff to yourself. It could be important. Just get on with it. I can come with you if you like, okay? Over and out."

Bloody Wren. How did she have timing like that? Paulie took a deep breath – probably the biggest breath she'd taken all day – and tried not to let the thought of a police station, uniformed officers, tapping pencils on notebooks and red buttons on Dictaphones flood her brain. She reached round and twisted her necklace right at the back of her neck where she knew there was a fresh, undamaged patch of skin. A surge of relief washed over her. Maybe she *could* do this.

But for now . . . sleep.

11

Feeling like her chest might actually be on fire, Paulie took the final steps to the top of the hill where Berryport Police Station sat. As much as she loved living right on the harbour, it did mean that walking pretty much anywhere else in the town involved hills. A lot of hills.

Carrying a huge box of doughnuts didn't help. Okay, so assuming police officers would enjoy doughnuts was a tad cliché but sometimes the obvious choice is the right one. She'd been up most of the night, music blaring and attention sharpening, baking and decorating them just as Aunt Meg had shown her before. Meg had been surprised to see her so industrious in the kitchen out of hours, but seemed to accept it when Paulie said she was 'just practicing'. Nipping out unnoticed with the doughnuts this morning had been tricky but she'd taken her chance just as a coach load of tourists had streamed through the doors.

Paulie stopped and took a breath. It was slightly cooler today, which was a blessing right now. She took great gulps of air and waited for her lungs to relax. Wren was always telling her she needed to exercise more and perhaps she was right, because that hill had just about finished her off.

Steadying her heart was slightly trickier than calming her lungs. Paulie could feel the full, unforgiving beat of it as sure as the ground beneath her feet. She didn't quite know how she'd got here, standing alone right in front of the police station. Somehow the childhood memories of police interviews were too complex to even begin to explain to somebody else who might have been able to come with her. No. She needed to do this by herself. And show everyone that she was committed to helping Tanya get some kind of justice.

"Hi. I'm here about the Tanya Withers case," Paulie said, placing the box on the smooth blue counter at reception. She funnelled her efforts into ignoring the shaking of her knees.

A lady sitting on the other side of the counter, with a ginger perm straight out of an eighties brat pack movie, didn't even look up from playing Candy Crush on her phone. She slid a contact form over to Paulie which crumpled as soon as it collided with the box. Finally, she lifted her head and looked straight at the box. "Are those Meg's classic doughnuts? From Booty Bakes?"

"Yeah. But about the case. I have some inf-"

"Raymond!" The lady interrupted, squawking backwards over her shoulder. "There are doughnuts here."

"Erm, I need to see somebody. An officer, or someone."

"Well, here's a pen. You'll need to put your contact details down first." Perm Lady dropped her phone with a clatter and reached for the box. Paulie pushed it along the counter, out of her reach. They locked eyes and in that second totally understood each other.

"I told you. I have information. About the case."

"Raymond! This young lady has information. About the case." Perm Lady kept up eye contact with Paulie whilst they both waited for Raymond to materialise. As soon as he did, Paulie pushed the box back and Perm Lady jumped out of her seat, whipped the lid off, and began making whimpering noises about syn allowances and calories.

"Ooh, are those from Booty Bakes?" Raymond, a police officer in full uniform and, weirdly, a spiral of glittery red paper hanging off his ear lobe, eagerly asked, "For the party? Meg's classics?"

"The very same," Perm Lady said, through thick and doughy mouthfuls.

Paulie cleared her throat and Raymond looked up, perhaps noticing her for the first time. "I have some information that might be useful in the Tanya Withers case. Can I speak to you about it?" She tried her best not let her voice crack. Or her resolve.

"What, now?" Raymond bit into a doughnut covered in multi-coloured sugar pearls. His eyelids fluttered in momentary bliss but when he opened them again his face became flatter, more serious. Perhaps it was dawning on him that Paulie was more than just a delivery girl.

"Yes, now."

He made a failed attempt at concealing a sigh, dropped his doughnut back into the box and said, "Come on then, Miss."

Paulie scooped up the contact form and pen and followed Raymond into a room around the corner from reception. She sat down on a scratchy couch with big, plump cushions printed with famous scenes from Berryport. The Arching Angel. Billowbreak Beach. The Nautical Gardens. Raymond gestured that she should first fill in the form so she leaned on a small coffee table to scribble down her name and contact number.

"Okay, I'll have that now, if I may Miss . . ." He scanned the form and cleared his throat. "Trinket. Paulie Trinket. If you could just tell me roughly what this is about, then I can figure out what to do next." The glittery spiral was still swinging from his ear. The unexplained jollity of it was terribly distracting but Paulie tried her best to stick to her cause.

"I saw Tanya. On the day she was murdered."

"Well, we're still ascertaining what actually happened," Raymond said. "Murder has not been confirmed."

A hammering in her heart increased but Paulie drowned it out with her voice. "Okay. Yes, but I work at Booty Bakes and I was round the back putting the bins out. I saw her have an argument with someone in the alleyway and then she ran away from them. She said something about a 'death wish', and I got the sense the person was like, an enemy or something."

Raymond crouched down at the table and scribbled something onto the form, but not with the urgency Paulie had expected. "I take it you didn't see the person she was arguing with?"

"Well, no. Sometimes I kind of freeze and, well, don't experience things like other people do. I know that's not ideal but I thought you'd want to know about the argument. I mean, it was right before she was hurt and she distinctly said the words, 'death wish'. That's got to be significant. Right?"

"Well, it might be but I can tell you this actually isn't new information to us." He stood back up, his knees clicking on the way. "I tell you what, I'll file this as corroborating evidence and we'll be in touch if we need to know more. For now, you're free to go."

"Hang on a minute. No, it can't be that simple." Paulie felt an icy cold prickle across the surface of her skin. "So, you know who it was? In the alleyway?"

"I can't divulge that right now, Miss. But I can tell you that we have this scenario you've described covered. Are you quite alright? You've gone a bit pale."

Paulie tried to stand, but her legs buckled slightly beneath her. The printed images on the cushions blurred into each other and she squeezed her eyes shut, hoping that everything would be straight again when she opened them. They weren't quite, but they would do enough for her to get out of this place.

Like, now.

12

The doughnut-loving police officer, Raymond, took Paulie's arm and led her back out to reception. "Come on now, Miss. Let's see if we can't get you one of those doughnuts you brought in to get your strength up."

"I-I-I'm okay, really." Paulie's blood rushed back to her extremities and the bright interior of the now empty reception space was slowly coming into focus. There was still a sense of crushing disappointment hovering around her, but she was pretty sure she would be okay.

"Maxine! Bloody Maxine. She'd better not have done off with that whole box." Raymond was livid and left Paulie's side to lean over the counter and inexplicably look for Perm Lady on the floor. "Maxine! What have you done with Meg's classics?!"

Just then, a door to Paulie's left swung open and a tough-looking, middle-aged woman stepped out. "Raymond. What in the great oceans of Neptune are you squealing about? Maxine's in here with the rest of us. She has doughnuts." Through the open door came a gush of tinny pop music as well as the whoops and cheers of adults who were quite possibly on their way to inebriation. Paulie noticed the spin of a disco light and watched it cast its rainbow glare on clumps of spiral streamers on the floor, just like the one Raymond had hanging off his ear. *Oh, so there's some sort of party going on.*

The woman who was now standing in reception, facing Paulie head-on, had a plastic cup of something brown and frothy in one hand and a doughnut in the other. Her entire forearms, hands and fingers were covered in tattoos which jarred alarmingly with her formal trouser suit, not to mention her long, black hair pulled back into a bun so tight it made the grey streaks throughout look like they'd been painted on. With a ruler.

The woman sighed so that her pinched-in cheeks puffed out for a millisecond and she looked Raymond up and down like he was a contestant on one of those scathing talent shows. Then she turned to Paulie. "Is Raymond looking after you?" Those eyes gave Paulie something of a jolt. There wasn't a cruelty about them, as such, but something stern. And Paulie had never seen a green quite like it. If she'd had to compare it to anything, she would have chosen dark, glossy seaweed.

"Yeah. I'm . . . yeah, I was just . . ."

Raymond strode over and eyed up the woman's doughnut. "Yes, yes this young lady just came in because she thought she had something for the Withers case. I've done an initial account and it's nothing new. Now, Detective Bombora, are we getting back in there and celebrating your retirement or what?"

"Raymond. Have some heart." The detective handed over her drink and her doughnut to him. Then she turned to Paulie, with seemingly no heart whatsoever and a monotone voice to rival a smart speaker. "I'm sorry for your loss. Did you know Miss Withers? I'm Detective Coral Bombora. Oh, actually . . . not detective anymore. As of today." All of this was delivered quickly whilst brushing streamers and bits of confetti off her suit, but never really breaking eye contact. "If you're finished here, can we call anyone for you?"

"No, I'm fine thanks. Wow. I really like your tattoos." Paulie wanted to kick herself into a spiky coffin with a self-locking lid for saying that, but this detective woman made her jumpy and anyway, she meant it. The tattoos were incredible. Getting a closer look at them, she saw they all had a nautical theme. Ornate seashells, swirling waves, shipwreck scenes, messages in bottles, gnarled and crumbling anchors, twisted ropes and sea birds in flight. Every one of Coral's fingers had a different coloured gem across the knuckle and they flexed beautifully as she moved.

Paulie wondered if she'd ever have the guts to get a tattoo. Probably not. But she'd heard that people with ADHD often found tattoos to be a calming experience – channelling the pain in a different way to people with neurotypical brains. It was a shame really, as there was no way she was brave enough – or cool enough – to find out. This awesome woman standing in front of her right now was a convenient case in point.

"Years in the making. Did most of them myself."

"Oh here she goes," Raymond spoke up from behind the detective, between mouthfuls of beer and doughnut. "Listen, all you need to know, love, is that this here detective has done her time in a 'proper job' apparently, and now she's leaving us in the lurch to go and draw all over people. Isn't that right, Detective? Do you know 'Sailor Boy Tattoos' on the high street?" Paulie nodded. She kind of knew the place he meant. It was close to the community seascape mural but not as far along as the row of fudge shops. "Well that's Coral's now. She's taking early retirement and doing the place right up. What's the new name again, Detective?"

"Odyssey Ink." That was the first time even a twitch of a smile had touched the detective's mouth.

"Wow. Very cool," Paulie murmured, still staring at the detective's forearms, knowing full well, with some faraway part of her brain there was something else she should be asking, which had nothing to do with tattoos. Whatever it was, pulled at her brain like an impatient child. It was something about why she was here in the first place. Why she'd stayed up all night making doughnuts. Why she had even contemplated stepping foot into a police station after over a decade of vowing she never would.

Then, in a practical lightning bolt, it came to her. "Tanya! What about Tanya? Surely you can't just retire now that there's been a local murder. Shouldn't you be leading the case?"

"Might not be a murder!" Piped up Raymond. "Nobody's confirmed anything about a murder."

"It is awkward timing," Coral admitted. "I have had my own demons to fight on this one. But my retirement's been on the books for a long time and the admin's been an odyssey on its own. There's no going back." Coral glanced downwards and did, to her credit, look quite sorry about it.

"Okay, but there will be somebody else to take over, right? We're going to find out what happened to Tanya?"

Raymond guffawed and a bit of doughnut sprayed out across the carpet, but Coral ignored him. "Naturally. The South West Bay team will take over and the case will be managed from Torquay. No stone will go unturned." Then Raymond muttered something about funding cuts before Coral booted him right on the shin.

"So nobody's replacing you?"

"The kid's quick. Right, Detective?" Raymond polished off his doughnut and wiped his greasy hand on his trousers, specially rubbing the shin Coral had just kicked. "If you need a detective, you'll find her at Odyssey Ink, marking people for life. Not that she hasn't done that already."

Coral looked at Paulie with a sharpened glance. "How old are you? Eighteen?"

"Seventeen . . . just," Paulie whispered, hardly able to believe what she was hearing.

"When you turn eighteen, come see me. If you want a tattoo, of course." Coral turned her gaze and her body towards the exit and Paulie found herself mirroring the action. "Thanks for being a concerned citizen."

Paulie left the station and stepped into the midday sun which struck the grey pavement with alarming precision, just like the streaks in Coral's hair. With the tinny pop music of the retirement party fading slowly behind her, she took one step after another until she was so far away from the station her mind began to clear a little.

The very thought that the information from the alleyway was no good to the police, was nauseating. How could that Raymond have been so flippant? And how would people now know that she'd tried to do a good thing? That she'd been brave enough to share what she'd witnessed? Fatigue would soon hit her like a lorry leaving hell and it had all been for nothing.

On top of that, she'd just learned that there was nobody to solve Tanya's mysterious death. What were the people of Berryport supposed to do without a detective? The South West Bay was huge and there was no way somebody from all the way over in Torquay could understand the nuances, the subtle complexities of the Berryport community. A case like this required a deep local knowledge, and Paulie was gutted that somebody as seemingly well equipped as Coral Bombora – despite her jarring presence – could bow out at a time like this.

None of this was fair. None of this was right. And she really didn't know what to do next.

13

"Well, at least you tried, dude." Wren licked a bright blue trail of bubblegum ice cream off her waffle cone and smiled the best she could. "You couldn't have just sat on that kind of information."

Paulie nodded silently, squinting at the reflection of intricate flower arrangements and cloudless blue skies in Wren's rosy, mirrored sunglasses. They were sitting on a bench in a quiet corner of the Nautical Gardens, in an effort to avoid the tourists who stopped to ooh and aah at every single shrub, bush and flower display. It was half term so the number of tourists – or 'grockles' as they were affectionately known – had increased, despite the harrowing news of Tanya's death. Or maybe because of.

The gardens were situated in an undeniably stunning, elevated spot overlooking Berryport harbour, with the view stretching out across the twinkling waters to Torquay and beyond. A hardy team of OAP volunteers was responsible for the upkeep of the gardens and to be fair to them, they did an incredible job. Even amongst the younger population, there seemed to be an uncharacteristically high level of respect for the preservation of the gardens. It seemed that no matter how bored and disillusioned the teenagers of Berryport got, they never touched the gardens. It was always someone's nana who'd planted that rose bush, or someone's grandpa who'd spread those bark chippings.

"Yeah. At least I tried," Paulie replied, recalling even now the courage it had taken to walk into that police station with the ridiculous box of doughnuts.

"And, were you okay, dude? Like, I can't believe you went there on your own."

"Well, I'm still here, aren't I? I don't think the monsters of my past devoured me entirely." Paulie looked up and down her body, as if inspecting for bite marks.

"Cool. I'm glad. You're proper tough, you know that? Anyway, eat your ice cream." Paulie had almost forgotten she too had an ice cream in hand. Caramel popcorn. Wren had practically forced it onto her. "So, no detective for Berryport then? Shame. Sounds like that Bombora woman would have got the job done."

"Yeah. She was kind of arresting, if you know what I mean?"

"Dude. Apt wording."

Paulie remembered Coral's eyes as those deep pools of green. All the tattoos. The undeniable coolness of the woman. She'd gone home and asked Aunt Meg about her immediately. "Aunt Meg says she knows her. Apparently they hung out a bit at school. You know that one tattoo Aunt Meg has on her wrist? Well, Coral did that when they were teenagers."

"The one of the smoking gun? Woah. That's weirdly appropriate right now."

"Right? That's exactly what I thought. Aunt Meg didn't say much more about it. Just that it was a spur-of-the-moment, teenaged thing." In fact, Meg had busied herself quite quickly with washing baking trays after divulging the info about the tattoo. Paulie could have sworn she'd got a bit dreamy talking about her younger days, but adults could be like that about the past sometimes. If that was the state nostalgia put you in, Paulie wasn't sure she ever wanted it.

Wren continued, "If she's not being replaced, do you think they'll send somebody over to work in residence here? Surely this has got to be one of the biggest cases in the Bay for a while?"

"Well, it must be. I mean, not only was Tanya all 'bright and promising' but there was, you know, all the beauty. Nothing like a stunning, dead teenager to light up the Torbay Gazette socials."

Wren nodded in agreement, her lips now tinged with blue from her ice cream. "Plus it was such a messed-up thing. I mean, to be shot in front of all those people and nobody to even notice at first? A thousand eye witnesses and nobody saw what happened. Even I didn't see what happened and I was literally feet away. Dude, it's so sad."

"Crap, Wren, I haven't even asked you how *you* are." It suddenly dawned on Paulie that Wren must be going through her own stuff right now. She was on the actual ship where it all happened. For all they might not be the closest of friends, Paulie knew she should do the right thing and at least check in with her. And she realised now she probably should have done that ages ago. "Are you okay?"

"Yeah. Most of the time, anyway. I just remember trying to get through my choreography for the skirmish and I was wrestling with those stupid girls who freak out over Sage all the time. The cannons were mad loud, weren't they? My ears were still ringing so when the screaming started, I didn't even notice it at first." Wren popped the end of her waffle cone in her definitely-blue-by-now mouth and munched. "Then, well, the whole atmosphere changed and we all stopped with the choreography. Swanny was the last one to stop performing. It wasn't until we were being virtually pushed off the ship by the police and security people that he finally realised it was game over."

"Do you think one of our lot did it? You know, on purpose?" Paulie couldn't help herself.

"Oh poor you, Wren. Are you okay, Wren? What can I do to help you get through this traumatic experience, Wren?" Paulie flinched to hear her own voice streaming so accurately from Wren's mouth and also noticed she no longer wore her trademark smile.

"Sorry. I-I'm just a bit . . ."

"Obsessed. You're obsessed, Paulie. Just like you were when Tanya was alive. I can't believe you're suspecting somebody from our class. It was probably just an awful accident and we need to let the police get on with things. Tanya Withers is not a key to anything for you anymore. You can let her go now."

Paulie couldn't explain it but tears sprang instantly into her eyes with hot, stinging sincerity. She turned her face away from Wren's to hide them and then noticed that her ice cream had completely melted and was about to dowse her hand in caramel popcorn goo. Wren chucked a couple of paper tissues at her and she cleaned it all up, moving over to a nearby bin to throw the ice cream away. There was no way she could eat it in that state. Her stomach turned at the mere thought.

By the time she got back from the bin, the tears had retreated slightly. Wren sighed. "Shall we walk back into town? I know it's sad as hell but I've got a jigsaw waiting for me at home." She turned and started quickly down the path towards town, the panoramic harbour views on the left and the multi-coloured vibrancy of the gardens to the right.

As Paulie followed, she noticed that every other lamppost had an A4 laminated poster cable-tied to it. Looking closer, she saw it was a photo of Tanya, all pearly-white smiles and long, blonde locks, with a solemn appeal for information and a QR code underneath it. As they kept walking, and the posters kept coming, it all felt like a macabre domino rally.

"Woah. Those posters are getting more attention than the actual gardens," Wren observed. And she was right. Dog walkers, grockles, even whole families were stopped at virtually every poster, looking it over, scanning the QR code, making dramatic gasps and shudders.

"Who's he, though?" Paulie asked in a whisper, as the two of them moved past a boy, maybe a little older than them, who was inspecting one of the posters particularly closely. He stood hauntingly still, holding the edge of the poster in one hand and a stack of what appeared to be sketchbooks in the other, his fingertips smudged with ink. He wore a long black coat which almost reached his skinny-jeaned ankles, had a dramatic flash of blue and black hair streaking in front of his pale face and an expression intent on giving nothing away.

"I think I might recognise him," Wren replied, also in a bit of a whisper. "Maybe he's an art student?"

"Well done, Sherlock."

"He's got that look about him though, right? I'm positive I've seen him somewhere around. I think he's called Brock, or Bruise or something?"

"Bruise? Come on."

"Really. I think that's his name. Anyway, he looks pretty bruised by what happened to Tanya."

As they continued to walk away, Paulie looked back over her shoulder. Something about that boy made her breath stop in her throat even though she didn't think she recognised him like Wren did. Why was he so gripped to the spot by that poster? Surely it wasn't the first he'd heard of Tanya's death? It had been the talk of the actual country, never mind the town. Paulie was frustrated that she couldn't just run over to him, pull back his ridiculous hair and see the full expression on his face. Or better still, just ask him what he was doing. Did he know something about this whole sorry mess? What was his relationship with Tanya? Could he be the mystery person at the end of the alleyway?

Paulie was just about to open her mouth and say those exact words to Wren, when she could have sworn, even it was just for a millisecond, that the boy changed the angle of his head, looked through the shards of his dark hair, locked eyes with her and gave her a tiny, but totally perceptible, nod.

"Wren," Paulie breathed. "Let's keep going."

14

"Sorry about that, Sir. She's a new starter." Meg handed the furious man a full refund before he waltzed out of the bakery with a complimentary bag of custard slices. Then she turned to Paulie, her entire face a brand new shade of red. "You want to bloody well wish you were a new starter. I honestly don't know if I can even look at you right now."

"Look, I'm sorry if I overcharged him but he was humming something unidentifiable, jangling every coin in his pocket, tapping his keys on the counter, shouting at his barking dog outside *and* asking me, like, a bazillion questions about the ingredients of the Polly Parrot Pasties all at the same time. How can anyone think in those conditions, let alone work?"

Meg heaved a huge sigh that was fuelled with anger as much as exhaustion. "I can understand one mistake, luvver, of course I can. But you're on a roll today. What about those poor girls whose bright white trainers you ruined with raspberry bubble tea?"

"They were watching socials on their phones far too loudly. Can I help it if that stupid viral song about Tanya sets my nerves on edge?"

"The Debbie Devon one? Tanya's Tune? But everybody loves Debbie Devon."

"Not me. I think you should take away the wireless password in here. Stop people from going on their socials. It's ridiculous. That song's ridiculous. And, quite honestly, now that I think about it, your customers are RIDICULOUS." Paulie's voice ricocheted off virtually every surface in the bakery at precisely the same time that the current sea shanty ended. Her words fell into the ears of every single customer inside and also those hovering at the entrance wondering whether or not to come in.

Meg took one look at the family of six who backed away from the entrance and into a café across the street and almost spontaneously combusted. Instead, she grabbed Paulie's wrist, dragged her into the kitchen and hollered over her shoulder at a bewildered Fergus who had been at the display case for the last fifteen minutes, "Give me a shout when you've decided," and then under her breath, "you absolute nutter."

"Hey!" Paulie protested, as she had a dishcloth shoved into her hand and an apron flung in her face. "Leave Fergus out of this. He's harmless."

"Unlike you, by the way," Meg fumed. "Look, I know you've been through it these past few weeks. I know what happened to Tanya has hit you – everybody – really hard. But we have to keep running this business and we have to rely on each other for that. When you got your diagnosis you said you wanted to work here rather than anywhere else and I was fine with that. I do my best to learn along with you what ADHD means and how I can support you. But honestly, luvver, I need to know you've got my back on this. I need your support too."

"I'm trying, Aunt Meg. I am."

"Well, we need to do better. The both of us. You know, the lease is up for renewal soon and I just want the bakery to be doing so well that the Brettons will just restart it, no questions asked. You know how people talk in this town and if word gets out that Booty Bakes isn't up to scratch, lord knows they'll probably turn the place into luxury harbour flats or something. Then what have I got to offer you, eh?"

"A luxury harbour flat?" Paulie tried a smile.

"Chance'd be a fine thing." Meg took a huge breath and strung her fingers through the tight coils of her hair. She looked over at the industrial sink which was filled with dishes. "Okay. For now you can get on with those. I'll stay out front for today. Let's both simmer down and chat again later. Maybe you can get off early if I can talk somebody else into coming in. Rita might come in before her cleaning shift."

Paulie managed to fill the sink with hot, soapy water and was about ten minutes into staring at the dirty dishes in defiance when she heard that bloody awful song by Debbie Devon yet again. Meg clearly hadn't taken her advice about the wi-fi password and yet more customers were helping this so called 'influencer' to go viral by filling the bakery with more replays of Tanya's Tune than anyone could possibly deem necessary.

Debbie Devon was a local girl, living a couple of towns away in Nestot, supposedly the hippie capital of the world. She was hardly what you'd call a hippie herself, swanning around in top designer brands, ginger curls tumbling as far down her back as extension glue would allow, jewelled acrylic nails for days and, inexplicably, an army of miniature poodles as white as the driven snow always by her side. It was unnerving.

She got her name by promoting and advocating for local Devon brands in everything from organic soap to dog chews and whilst Paulie liked the idea of supporting small business, she wasn't convinced Debbie ever knew with any accuracy what she was talking about. Her reviews featured outstandingly neutral phrases like 'crowd-pleaser', 'gem of the south west' and 'one to watch', to the extent that it didn't even really matter whether she was talking about organic soap or dog chews, actually. Nevertheless, she was devoured by organisations like the National Trust, the Tourism Board and even Bretton Inc. She was unstoppable.

Paulie picked up a scrubbing brush and tried to create enough noise in her task to block out the absurd lyrics and awkward melody quite clearly composed on some sort of music app for toddlers. If she closed her eyes and thought about Gorillaz hard enough, maybe it would all go away . . .

Stray bullet on a pirate ship,
One girl whose sacred life has slipped
Into a void we just don't get.
Tanya, you were so loved by the internet.

Or maybe not.

Paulie almost heaved into the soap suds but stopped herself just as Meg burst through the door and lowered a stack of empty cupcake trays into the sink. She offered Paulie a small smile which indicated they might even be on proper speaking terms later and Paulie felt her soul settle somewhat.

Just before Meg turned to go back into the bakery where the offensive song played on repeat on an equally offensive number of phones, she flicked her fingers into the sink, shaking off the hot, soapy bubbles. The smoking gun tattoo on her wrist flashed up above the dirty dishes and Paulie – who had traced that very tattoo with her fingertips since she was a little girl – suddenly saw it in a new light.

That new light told her Meg had a connection that could perhaps offer some answers. That new light told her to hold on tight to her instincts. That new light told her to stop what she was doing, put the scrubbing brush down, and follow her gut.

So, that's exactly what she did.

15

As the 'Sailor Boy Tattoos' sign came down, a shower of rotting, black plywood rained down on the high street below. Luckily, there were no shoppers passing at the time, but Coral Bombora ducked out of the way, shielding her head and almost bashing into one of the ladders propped either side of the shop front.

"Bilge rat balls! Come on now, lads. Can we get it down without the whole shop front collapsing?" The men teetering at the top of the ladders, muttered their apologies then tentatively stepped down holding the rotting, garish sign at either end. They propped it against the filthy shop window after Coral gestured – with an extremely harsh glare – that's where it should go. "Enough. Go have a break. Clean up when you get back." The men scuttled off, reminiscent of little crab characters from a Disney movie or something, and Coral strode into the darkened depths of her new business venture. Paulie took a deep breath and followed her.

She stood just inside the door way and gave her eyelids a rub. It took a few seconds to adjust to the lack of light, but when she did, Paulie saw that Coral was totally gutting the place. Whilst there were echoes of a tattoo parlour – ageing benches lining one wall; a gaping chasm where a reception counter would have been; tawny, tattered papers with a million tattoo designs pinned to a wall like ancient treasure maps – it felt like an abandoned movie set. Paulie took another deep breath and the musty scent of dust spurred her on.

"Detective Bombora? Erm, I mean, Coral?" Paulie took a step forwards and could just make out that Coral was leaning over a desk at the back of the shop, sifting through a stack of papers. Her hair was loose and straight, hanging over her face, the streaks of grey providing startling stripes that glowed like road markings at night. She was dressed in dark jeans and a torn, black t-shirt and such casual clothes, together with her hair loose and free, showed Paulie there might be more to Coral Bombora than the uptight detective she'd met at the police station.

"Yes?" Coral looked up and her hair parted with a graceful slice across her face. All at once Paulie felt the relief of being able to see her expression and the scrutiny of those intense green eyes. There was no escaping them, even in the half-light of the empty shop.

"Er, hi. I'm Paulie. We kind of met at the station the other week. It was your leaving party."

Coral dropped the papers, straightened up and took a few steps forwards to see Paulie better. "Oh yes. I remember. Did you have something to do with the doughnuts?"

"Yes. I brought them. Meg, who runs the bakery – Booty Bakes, that is – she's my aunt."

"Oh my. Paulie? Little Paulie?" Coral brought a decorated hand to her mouth, covering up a gasp.

"Yeah. Not little though. Like, at all. I think you know Aunt Meg? You gave her a tattoo once?"

Coral dropped her hand and stared a little before replying. "Yes. I do. I did. Anyway, what can I do for you, Paulie? You know you're too young for a tattoo? And I'm hardly ready for clients yet, as you can see."

Paulie laughed but suddenly didn't know how to find the words she'd come here to say. Because of her swift disappearance, Aunt Meg would be fuming and there'd need to be an explanation when she got back. The conviction she'd had standing back at the kitchen sink had quite clearly waltzed off somewhere and Paulie wasn't sure how to get it back. Was this visit to Coral really all that urgent? The familiar pull of dread crept up her spine, across her nerves and under her very skin so she grabbed the little compass and eye pendants hanging on her necklace and gave them an almighty twist at the front of her neck. Immediately, the pain stabbed hard but it was enough to get her back on track.

"It's about Tanya. I told that officer who liked the doughnuts so much . . ."

"Raymond?"

"Yeah. Raymond. I told him that I heard – well actually, saw – Tanya having a fight with somebody in the alleyway outside the bakery just before the shooting. I didn't see who she was arguing with but they were really scaring her and she said they had a death wish. Don't you think that's relevant? Those precise words?"

"It's not really my place to say."

"Okay, fine. You're retired now. I get that. But all Raymond did was put my account in a tiny little note on a form. I was hoping you might be able to have a word."

"I won't be having any words, Paulie. I've officially left the force now. And, as I think Raymond told you, as it's not new information to us, I mean, to *them*. And it's been filed as corroborating evidence. The South West Bay team will be considering all angles, you can be sure of that."

"Really? Because at the moment it just feels like they've put up a load of posters round town and that's it."

"The public appeal is a major component in the strategy, but there's plenty more going on behind the scenes, I can promise you. Now, if you don't mind, you can see I've got my work cut out for me here. I need to be getting on." Coral stepped towards the door and tried to usher Paulie out in exactly the same way she had at the station only days before. Paulie was having none of it today.

"Well if you won't help me, then I guess I'll have to do some detective work myself."

"I strongly advise against that."

"I'll do it with or without you. I was close to Tanya. She was in my drama class. I reckon something's up and it wasn't just an accident."

Coral – most surprisingly – stood quietly for a moment. The sounds of the busy high street filtered through the open door and seemed all the more potent for Coral's sudden silence: a seagull squawking, a child shouting, a busker singing. The skin on Paulie's neck smarted where she'd twisted the pendants, but she used the sensation to remember why she was here. For Tanya.

"Fine. Are you listening?"

"I am," Paulie breathed.

"Number one, document everything."

"Got it."

"Number two, find a motive. Get into the minds of the people around Tanya."

"Sweet. I mean, I will."

"Number three, treat everything as evidence. Everything."

"Everything."

"Number four, persevere. Never, ever give up."

"I won't."

"Number five, don't underestimate the power of your intuition." Coral finally broke her gaze with Paulie and looked down towards the sparkling eye pendant lying against her neck. Paulie felt her own pulse – suddenly beating so strong – make the pendant rise and fall in tiny judders. Then Coral coughed, cleared her throat and started brushing dust off her jeans. "Right. You didn't get any of this from me." This time Coral moved towards the door with a certainty Paulie didn't dare challenge. Her time was up, and she knew it.

"Okay, thank you so much. Can I come back sometime to . . ."

"Nope." Coral quickly disappeared back into the dark cave of the shop, leaving Paulie standing on the pavement, square in the middle of the rotten woodchips from the old sign, which were yet to be swept away. She closed her eyes for a moment and found that the familiar sounds of everyday commotion took on an almost melodic quality, lulling her into a tiredness that was much more manageable than the fatigue that usually floored her.

"You know why they don't give a crap about your alleyway story, right?"

Paulie jumped as her heart nearly sprang out of its cavity. She spun around and saw a boy, lurking in the shadows beneath the shop front, dressed in a practically floor-length black coat and a disturbingly familiar shock of dark hair smothering his face. Jeez, could this Odyssey Ink place get any more macabre?

He stepped with confidence into the sunlight and Paulie realised there was a blue streak slashing through that shock of black hair. *It's him,* she thought. *It's the boy who was obsessing over Tanya's poster in the Nautical Gardens. Bruise?*

"Wh-what? Were you listening to my conversation with Detective Bombora?"

"Oh, you mean my auntie? Yeah. I was. The end of it, anyway."

"Rude."

"So, do you want to know why? Why they don't think it's a big thing?"

Paulie's mind flitted over the points Coral had just made. *Number One, document everything.* She took out her phone and opened up the notes app. "Okay then. Go."

The boy took a couple of steps closer to Paulie and lowered his voice to barely a whisper. His hair flopped forwards and seemingly invited her into a private space where only they could hear the words about to be spoken. "After Tanya ran out of the alleyway, she bumped right into Raymond, the doughnut guy. He asked her what was wrong. She said she'd just had an argument with her boyfriend but she was okay. Raymond took her to the Arseing Angel . . ."

"I'm sorry, the what?" He was playing with her, not to mention the very heritage of Berryport.

"The ship. It's called the 'Arseing Angel', right? Anyway, Raymond left her with her drama class there and that was that. They questioned the boyfriend about it later – for quite a while, apparently – and he said they made up before the skirmish. So, old news." Bruise, or whatever he was called, flicked his head back and smiled in a way that could barely even be a smile. More like a mischievous arch of the lips. "Did you get all that?"

Paulie attempted to bury her attention in the notes she'd tried to write on her phone but all she'd managed was, 'Arseing Angel'. She adapted an expression she hoped screamed 'unflappable' and tapped her phone screen in a final flourish before pocketing it and looking at the boy. "Yeah. Thanks. Might be helpful."

"Why are you so bothered about Tanya anyway?"

Coral's nephew or not, Paulie had no reason to trust this boy and the fact that his presence made her muscles twitch was a weird, confusing sign. She couldn't tell him that solving what happened to Tanya was the most important thing in the world to her right now. That if she couldn't, as a child, help with her own mother's death, then at least she could help with this one as a grown teenager. That her appetite to make and keep friends was so voracious that she thought solving this murder just might hold the key to collective (at least) acceptance and (at most) admiration. How could this pretentious weirdo understand her motivations, let alone keep them to himself? So instead, she asked, "What about you? What did Tanya mean to you?"

The boy did that weird, curvy smile again and brushed the hair off his face so Paulie could see not only the same severe green eyes of his auntie, but a sense of relish that graced his entire expression. It was agitating. And annoyingly captivating. He stuck out his ink-stained hand and said, "Never mind that. I'm Breeze. Pleased to meet you, Paulie."

16

It was the first day of rain in weeks and, on any other day, that would have been fine. Welcome, even.

Whilst the dried-up summer blooms in the neat and tidy flower beds must have been drinking it greedily from their darkened, searching roots, everywhere Paulie looked, people were trying their best to avoid it. It was kind of ironic how well the grey clouds above matched the murky clothing choices of the people below. You could have even seen it as an opportunity for people and nature to breathe, cry and actually *be* together. Properly together. In sync.

Paulie had always loved the rain. Whether it came in a pattering whisper or a drumming roar, she enjoyed the predictable, rhythmical sounds, the cooler, denser air and the intimation that getting cosy and comfortable was suddenly socially acceptable. But, according to the number of figures darting under blossom-covered arbours and wielding black umbrellas like weapons, the rain was not welcome today. At all.

"Bloody rain," Aunt Meg sighed, as she checked the backs of her legs for mud splatters. "I knew I should have worn trousers. You okay, luvver? Holding up?"

"Yeah. S'pose." Paulie was holding up, as long as she was out here, outside of the actual crematorium. The coroner had finally released Tanya's body for the funeral, and although cause of death had not yet been formally announced, all the headlines hinted that Tanya's death might be ruled as accidental. This was a lot to take in. Ever since that gathering on Billowbreak Beach Paulie had been engulfed by a heavy intuition that something wasn't right. She felt it now, waiting in line to honour Tanya's memory. She was dreading going inside the building, crammed in with all of those people and their brimming emotions that clashed so heavily with hers. It wasn't her first funeral, of course, but she could scarcely remember her mum's all those years ago. Only what happened shortly afterwards.

"Here. I brought you something." Meg fished around in her handbag and produced a bashed-up paper bag. "I'm betting you didn't eat anything this morning, right?"

"Top marks," Paulie said. It wasn't that she was actively avoiding food. She just hadn't remembered that normal people ate breakfast. *Do they though? On the day of a funeral?*

"Pop this in your pocket, maid. It's just a sausage roll. Can't have that tummy of yours rumbling during the service now, can we?" Paulie took the bag but already knew she wouldn't be eating it. She liked sausage rolls ordinarily, sure, but not when they had been allowed to cool in a sweaty paper packet, roll around in someone's handbag and become crushed to within an inch of their life. Ugh.

"Dudes. Is it okay if I, like, sit with you for the service?" Wren appeared by their side, ducking under the crematorium's roofed walkway. In any other circumstances, it would have been seen as queue-jumping, but looking around her, Paulie could see that nobody cared, dowsed as they were in grief.

"Aren't your parents coming?"

"Paulie! That's so rude. Wren, luvver, of course you can sit with us." Meg shot Paulie a look that combined disappointment so potently, she may as well have punched her.

"My parents couldn't get back from Singapore in time. They're saving some on-its-knees hotel, as per. They send thoughts and prayers and all that."

"Of course they do, luvver. Wow. Singapore. So you're staying in that lonesome old cottage all by yourself then? You must be rattling round like a marble in a shoe box."

"It's not too bad. I'm used to it now." Wren, so she'd told Paulie, lived in an ancient cottage on an isolated peninsula just outside of Berryport, which overlooked a famously barren beach called Kingsands. Her parents were mobile hoteliers which basically meant they travelled the world visiting failing luxury hotels, pulling them back from the brink of bankruptcy. It sounded pretty glamorous but what it amounted to for Wren was a lot of time alone in a spooky old house, having to walk over a mile to the nearest bus stop so she could access civilization. She'd invited Paulie there numerous times but the very thought of the combination of buses needed to complete the journey, sent Paulie into a not-so-mild panic.

"Looks like it's time to go in. You okay, you two?" Meg positioned herself between Paulie and Wren, slinging an arm around each of their shoulders and beginning the slow shuffle forwards. "I'm here, okay? We'll do this together." The procession of sniffling, shuddering bodies drove slowly forwards and Paulie felt a spiral of nerves swirl through her tummy that she wished would spring open and catapult her away.

The room where the service would be held was surprisingly small. It didn't seem likely that the hordes of people who'd been waiting outside in the rain would all squeeze inside and as Rihanna's 'Umbrella' played on repeat for maybe the third time, it became apparent that they wouldn't. "Dude, they chose the right song, at least," Wren whispered. "I wonder if they've got any spare umbrellas for everybody still stuck outside."

Paulie tried to turn and look over her shoulder from the tight spot she was sitting in, squidged up against Aunt Meg and Wren. She couldn't see all the way outside but she could see that the double doors were left wide open and that all the people dressed in dark, glistening raincoats were standing, packed so closely together they looked like a shoal of fish. A quiet buzz of whispers played beneath Rihanna's sultry tones and a trembling stillness from the crowd overflowed with sorrow. Paulie found the pendants around her neck and felt the comforting press of them against her fingertips.

"It's good that Wendy's got support," Meg said, gesturing to the front of the room. Paulie craned her neck and saw Tanya's heartbroken mum sitting on a front bench, her shoulders already shaking and her face embedded in a huge cloth handkerchief. Next to her was a man of a similar age, his arm firmly around her and his stare fixed forwards at the coffin, which was partially shrouded by a heavy red curtain. "That's her brother. He must have flown down from Scotland. Oh, luvvers, doesn't the coffin look lovely?"

Wren and Paulie exchanged a glance. 'Lovely' was hardly the word. The whole thing was festooned in gold glitter and the handles were encrusted with diamanté gems. The black and white flowers on top were arranged to look like movie-making clapperboards and Tanya's name, constructed out of white roses, was lit up with the kinds of lightbulbs you get bordering an A-list celebrity's dressing room mirror. "It's like Steven Spielberg threw up on her coffin," Wren muttered and Paulie couldn't help but laugh.

"Girls. Please." Meg looked totally distraught so Paulie swallowed back the hilarity and decided it would be a good idea to stop making eye contact with Wren.

The service itself was fairly uneventful. It was a Humanist ceremony, meaning there was no religious content, and just lots of meaningful words about Tanya and her vivacious character, the joy she brought to her loved ones and the glittering acting career she could have had. The celebrant did a good job of keeping the appropriate balance of compassion and profession- alism and it wasn't until Wendy stepped up to the podium, propped up by her brother, that things kind of fell apart.

Wendy gripped the wooden lectern and her knuckles turned as white as the handkerchief still clutched in one hand. She obviously couldn't bear to look up at the sea of faces in front of her, but she managed to raise her voice just enough to push the words out. "Thank you all for coming today. I haven't got anything to say that hasn't already been said, except . . . Tanya, I love you so much. And I hope you're with your . . . your dad now. This last song is one that my Arthur, used to sing to get Tanya to sleep when she was a baby." The familiar tune of 'My Girl' by the Temptations streamed into the room whilst a rolling slideshow of stunning pictures of Tanya appeared on a screen above the podium. That was when sniffles transformed into sobs, whispers into wails and the people of Berryport dived head first into mourning.

It was a wonder anybody made it outside after that. During the second playing of 'My Girl' the celebrant ushered people gently from their seats and, little by little, everyone moved outside.

"This is a bit weird, right?" Paulie whispered to Aunt Meg and Wren, as they stood in line to speak to Wendy and her brother. "I'm sure they'll just want to go home and be done with the day. I mean, there's nothing anyone can say to make them feel any better."

"Dude, it's about energies. Mutual grief. Respect." Wren shook her head then allowed the movement to flow down through her whole body. It looked like she was doing one of Swanny's warm-up exercises. "That speaks way more than words."

Aunt Meg managed a smile for both of them. "Wren's right. And it's the done thing, luvver. At least it's stopped raining." Meg's gaze flickered over the queue of people in front of them and Paulie followed it. Now that umbrellas had been put away, it was easier to recognise a lot of the faces who had shown up. In fact, just a few feet ahead of them, was Coral Bombora and Breeze, looking as deathly dark and inscrutable as could be. Paulie might have been imagining it, but she was certain the moment Meg clocked them, she gave a tiny gasp. Then she said, "Actually, girls, can you make your own way back? I'll speak to Wendy later. I need to get back to pop the boilers on ready for the wake."

"B-but, that means I'll have to get the bus." Today of all days, Paulie couldn't believe Aunt Meg was going to drive off without her.

"Dude, it's fine. You're with me. We'll go back to the bakery together. I didn't realise there even was a wake, never mind it being at your place." Wren scratched her head and looked at Paulie with some sort of unfathomable expectation.

"What? Yeah. We're doing the wake." There was no use in Paulie calling after Meg now, as she'd already disappeared around the corner. "Let's just say whatever we're supposed to say and get out of here."

"That weird boy with the anime hair keeps staring at you. The one from the lamppost the other day. Did you notice?"

"What? Oh. Him. I forgot to tell you. I found out his auntie is the ex-detective. The one who's starting up the new tattoo place?"

"Is that her with him then? Resemblance much?"

"I know, right? He's called Breeze, not Bruise."

"Missed opportunity."

"He told me some stuff about the alleyway. I know who Tanya was arguing with."

Wren's eyes widened to epic proportions. "Dude. Spill." Paulie nodded down the line towards the spot where Sage was standing, alongside his tycoon parents. They all wore flawless suits that screamed quality and Paulie wondered why they were standing just a few feet from Wendy, almost like they were part of the family line-up. It's not like him and Tanya had been married or anything. "Sage?" Wren gasped. "I guess they had been pretty tense with each other that morning."

"Sssh!" Paulie warned. "I don't think Breeze was supposed to tell me anything." Paulie filled Wren in on what Breeze had told her outside Odyssey Ink, including the fact that the police had already spoken to Sage about it. "Plus, Coral gave me some tips. About detecting."

"What? Okay, now it's getting weird."

"Not really. She's left her job but probably wants to solve what happened as much as I do."

"You reckon?"

"I think so. She could see it meant a lot to me so she gave me her best detecting tips to get me off the starting blocks. The first one was to document everything."

"Dude, the starting blocks are eating your dust right now. Can you even remember all of these tips? I know what your brain's like."

"That's the weird thing. I can *so* remember them. It's like they're imprinted." Paulie tapped the side of her head and recalled the five tips immediately. They weren't going anywhere.

"We need to shelve this, dude. It's our turn." Wren was right. The people in front of them were just about done hugging Wendy, her brother and Sage's crew so Paulie and

Wren shuffled forwards, ready to somehow convey their sympathies.

It wasn't quite as hard as Paulie had expected, to look at somebody, acknowledge the pain in their eyes and say the words, "I'm so sorry." Because she really was sorry. She also wanted to say, *"Don't worry, Mrs Withers. I'm going to find out who did this to your daughter and I'm going to bring them to justice and the whole of Berryport will know about it."* Luckily, Wren had a grip on her arm and pulled her along at a suitable speed so havoc like that couldn't be wreaked. At least, not today.

She had been just about ready to murmur some kind of platitude to Sage and his parents, when she was pushed gently aside by Wendy's brother. It wasn't so that many people would have noticed, but she was close enough to hear the words that were spoken into Sage's ear. The words that caused his face to change from a mournful crease into an outraged sheet of surprise.

"That's enough. Just back off now, will you, Sage? Wendy doesn't want you here."

Before Sage could say or do anything, his parents took each of his elbows and silently led him away. He opened and closed his mouth as if a barrage of swear words was about to shoot out, but a cold, striking look from his dad put a sudden stop to that. To anybody nearby who had blinked, they would have missed the whole exchange. One minute Sage and his parents were there, accepting condolences from a factory line of mourners, and the next minute they weren't. But Paulie and Wren had witnessed it all and as they walked away from that awful bubble of grief, they looked back to see Wendy crumple to her knees.

"Woah. This is getting heavy. I need Meg's pastries to get over all of this." Wren was striding ahead, obviously eager to get to the bus stop. But then she stopped dead in her tracks so that Paulie almost slammed right into her back. "Woah. Look. Is that . . ? Oh crap-on-a-ginger-snap. It is! It's Devon-based social media influencer, renowned digital creator, with four hundred and eighty five thousand followers, sixteen Muddy Stilettoes awards and Consumer Influencer of the Year five years running It is, dude. It bloody is!"

Debbie Devon?

There was absolutely no mistaking her. Almost as soon as Sage had rounded the corner to the car park with his parents, she had appeared out of nowhere, four poodles circling her high-heeled ankles, fiery tresses flicking around like nobody's business and an absolute homage to death in a flowing, cape-like black dress that looked like it had been swiped from the wardrobe department of Game of Thrones. She made some very loud noises that landed somewhere between squealing and cooing and flung her arms around Sage, whilst his parents took on the poodles, grinning from ear to ear.

"What the actual hell is Cersei Lannister doing here?" Paulie tried to nudge Wren out of her stupor. "Come on. It's not like you to be starstruck."

"Not starstruck, exactly, more number-struck. I can't believe her BeYu figures, dude. They're way impressive."

"Forget all that. Why is she hugging Sage? What's the story there? Wren, what if that's what – or who – Tanya and Sage were fighting about on the day of her death?" Paulie looked back over at the weird assemblage of personalities and tried to figure out how Sage was acting towards Debbie Devon. She couldn't see his face because it was buried into Debbie's ample bosom. Was he into that hug? On second thoughts, he was a red-blooded, heterosexual male. How could he not be?

"Looks to me like his parents are enjoying that more than he is." Wren checked her phone for the time and gave a little yelp. "Let's get going, dude. I don't want to miss out on the Doubloon Delights. Meg made plenty, right?"

"What? I don't know. Yeah . . . probably."

"Come on. A bus is due in two minutes and thirty seven seconds. You can make like a proper detective, get your phone out and write notes about all of . . ." Wren gestured towards the bizarre hugathon, ". . . this."

And just because Paulie had not a single clue what else to do, she allowed Wren to pull her away and along the path to the nearest bus stop. Maybe it was time to get on with Coral's number one tip for solving this murder: document everything.

17

The mood in Booty Bakes was practically jubilant.

Sure, there were pockets of people shrinking into corners who still wore the pained expressions of exhausted bereavement, but mostly, there was laughing and smiling. On one level, Paulie found this a bit of a relief after the heaviness of the funeral, but on another it jarred quite strangely in her body.

Aunt Meg had closed the bakery to the general public and brought in a couple of staff members to help out. There was a huge trestle table at the back of the room, which was laden with good old fashioned scones, cream and jam plus soft drinks and cafetières so that everybody could help themselves. It was a simple set-up, but it was working.

Paulie noticed that Tanya's mum and uncle were nowhere to be seen. Aunt Meg mused that the funeral had probably been quite enough for them to cope with, and so she had sent a basket to the Withers' home laden with scones, sandwiches and flasks of hot soup. "It's not much, but it's something," she'd sighed.

Maybe it was selfish, but Paulie was grateful the crowd in the bakery was smaller than the one at the funeral. There was something about big crowds that set her on edge and she'd always had trouble explaining it out loud. Romano had asked her about it once in a counselling session and although he'd focused on the sensory challenges of it, Paulie knew somehow that it was more than that. It was something about feeling like a number rather than a person. An anonymous figure amongst more anonymous figures with no real opportunity for intimacy or connection. It was ironic really, considering intimacy and connection were things she found difficult to attain with most people. But when the sheer possibility of that was absent, it seemed that she was too.

Right now, Paulie was attempting to embed herself amongst the college crew. There were lots of familiar students' faces here and some tutors had turned up, which made sense considering they probably all had contact with Tanya at some point. She'd been a star in drama class of course, but unlike Paulie who studied drama full-time, Tanya had been balancing at least three other subjects. Tutors and students alike swapped all sorts of stories about Tanya – funny things she'd said in class, excellent pieces of work she'd handed in, the way she'd described her dreams of stardom to anybody who would listen. It was hard to believe that one girl could have such an overwhelming ripple effect on so many people whilst Paulie struggled to turn heads at all when she walked into a room.

"She was all set for going to London, wasn't she, Josiah?" Romano Smith was perched at the end of one of the tables, lavishing first cream and then jam onto a particularly large scone. He'd been at the funeral too, although Paulie hadn't noticed him until she'd been sprinting (yes, sprinting) for the bus with Wren. As he wrapped his mouth around the scone, Paulie wondered what secrets he knew about Tanya, and how long he'd been seeing her for counselling.

Swanny sat slap-bang in the middle of all of the students, slightly red-eyed and fidgeting, which was not like him, but also

lapping up sympathies and attention, which was entirely like
him. Paulie felt a sudden surge of conflicting emotions about the
man. She was pretty sure he was the first person in the world
(aside from Aunt Meg) to look her in the eye and give her the
time of day. It had happened at the college open evening over a
year ago, when she'd been brave enough to walk up to his drama
stall and enquire about the very subject that petrified her. He'd
been delighted to speak with her, coaxing her out of herself with
phrases like, "I can see you have what it takes," and "Your potential is dazzling." However, she couldn't ignore how the
outlandish, performative nature of his personality collided
deeply with her own. For a tiny, tubby man with an unremark-
able look about him, Paulie could hardly believe the way flam-
boyance shimmered from his bones.

"Yes, darling. She'd already seen my own agent – that's the
delectable *Augustin* at Champion Talent Agency for those not in
the know. She performed an astounding Shakespearean audition
piece. He snapped her up in an instant. An instant, I tell you!"
Swanny stopped mid-flow and waved his hands at a nearby student
called Rashid who was basically his younger body double. Using a
flamboyant style clearly modelled on Swanny, Rashid stuffed some
Booty Bakes napkins into his tutor's hands. Swanny crushed the
napkins against his face and blew his nose astonishingly loudly.
Rashid took the soiled napkins without a glimmer of disgust which
should have earned him some kind of drama-student-of-the-year
award. "London would have been her first port of call but with
talent like that, she could have taken the world by storm!" Everybody nodded in agreement and Swanny threw himself into another
nose-blowing fit promptly facilitated by the tireless Rashid.

He continued, turning his attention to Sage, who was sitting
on the next table with Debbie Devon hovering around him like a
drunken bee. "I'm sorry, my dear boy. I know you didn't want to

let her go off to fancy London Town. But it was her calling, my dearest. You can't tether that kind of talent."

"Who said I wanted to tether her?" Sage said, through gritted teeth. Paulie noticed his fists clench slightly. "I just wanted to be with her, that's all. Is that such a crime?"

"Nobody said anything about crimes," Romano chimed in. "I think we can all just agree that Tanya is a sore miss for all of us. Now, who wants another scone?" Quite a few of the students followed Romano back to the table of treats and loaded their plates again. Wren shuffled up to sit next to Paulie and nudged her right in the ribs.

"Come on then, get your phone out."

"What? What for?"

"Because you can add it to your notes, Detective Trinket. You caught that, right? Peg Leg was deliberately blunt. Swanny was encouraging Tanya's talents? Sage was dead against it? Look at them. He's furious." Wren was right. Sage was glaring at the floor like he was trying to laser a hole in it.

"Yeah. There's defo something going on. Sage is hiding something. God, Wren, do you think he got so mad about Tanya's plans to desert him that he actually killed her?"

"Dude, you're reaching. But I agree something's off. And look at the socials queen – she's desperate to get Sage's attention. What on earth is she giving him?"

"Looks like a gift," Paulie said, as Debbie Devon presented Sage with a small white box tied up in a yellow ribbon. Sage gave her a mystified look but untied the ribbon and opened the box anyway – all of which was filmed by Debbie on her famous phone. Because of this, every other person in the place suddenly sat up and took notice, straightening their clothes and fixing their hair.

"Dude," Wren whispered. "I reckon she's using that new

feature on BeYu. The live streaming. It only came out this week but she's on it like a bonnet."

"Probs." Paulie felt her phone buzz in her pocket. It would be BeYu notifying her about Debbie's stream. "Why would anyone give a gift at a funeral? And then bloody well film the reaction?"

"Oh wow, Debbie. Thank you." Sage reached into the open box and lifted out a set of three golden, glittering juggling balls. His face was that classic mixture of discomfort and gratitude but Debbie pressed on with her mission from behind her phone screen.

"You're more than welcome, Sagey. I know you have a talent for juggling and we all know that Tanya would want you to hone that talent. Can you hold them up for all of my BeYu fans to see? How about a little demo?" At this very suggestion, everybody close to 'Sagey' murmured in agreement and encouraged him to give his new present a go, including his parents who had watched the whole exchange with triumphant smiles they didn't even bother to hide. Sage looked truly uncomfortable, but what else could he do in this moment, other than obey?

"Dude, he's probably got several thousand people watching him right now," Wren whispered.

"Yeah," Paulie whispered back. "Pressure or what?"

"Pressure," Wren agreed and they both watched as Sage got up from his seat, removed his suit jacket, rolled up his shirt sleeves and planted his feet hip distance apart. Then he started juggling the twinkling balls, using a slow pace at first. Debbie Devon gave a squeal of glee and a small cheer erupted from the people around him. This seemed to spur Sage on to juggle even faster and after a few seconds, he started to move around the café floor whilst showing off his talent, a smile edging over his handsome mouth.

"Here, catch this!" shouted a moustachioed lad from drama

class and chucked a scone towards Sage, who caught it effort-
lessly. He blended the scone into the juggling act, managing to
extract yet more whoops and cheers from the small crowd.
Debbie Devon looked like she was going to do an excited wee on
the floor but kept her phone trained on Sage, chattering away to
her followers as she went.

"This young man is incredible! Here he is, in active
mourning but dedicating this outburst of talent to his late girlfriend, Tanya Withers. Do make sure you all like and comment
as Sage keeps juggling! What's that @nobodysbusiness_123?
You want me to sing Tanya's Tune? Oh, I don't know if it's
appropriate. Is that really what people want right now?"

There was a collective gasp, and Sage took that as a sign to
add more random objects to his act (a milk jug, butter packets
and a mini pot of jam), whilst Debbie cleared her throat and
handed her phone to the nearest person. This was obviously the
most electrifying prospect in the world and cries of, "Please do!"
and "Let's hear it!" eventually gave way to Tanya's crooning
voice . . .

Stray bullet on a pirate ship,
One girl whose sacred life has slipped
Into a void we just don't get.
Tanya, you were so loved by the internet.

"Dude, when did this turn into a David Lynch movie?"

"There is no easy answer to that," Paulie said, shaking her
head and feeling down to her toes that somewhere, in all this
surreal bullshit, there must be some clues. Then it suddenly
occurred to her. "It gives me a way in though."

"What do you mean? I can't take any more weirdness
today."

"Well, Coral said, in the second tip she gave me, that I

needed to *'find a motive . . . get into the minds of the people around Tanya'*. And this is as good a start as any." There was that familiar rise of elation, that overflow of excitement that travelled, with rejoicing anticipation, from her very insides until it shot outwards to the tips of her grasping fingers. "Prime delivery, I'm coming for you." Paulie took her phone out of her pocket, tapped open the Amazon app, and began the familiar ritual of searching, comparing and ordering. It didn't take long at all to find what she was looking for. There are only so many results that can come up from the search term: *'golden glitter juggling balls'.*

"What are you ordering now?" Aunt Meg appeared at her shoulder, bringing with her the scents of cinnamon and earl grey tea. She peered into Paulie's phone with concern, probably knowing that yet another parcel was about to clutter their hallway. "Have Debbie Devon and Sage inspired you with this here performance? Honestly, this was the last thing I expected to see. Good publicity for us though, eh? Debbie's put a link to Booty Bakes in her live and so many people are watching it right now!"

"Three thousand, nine hundred and fifty two to be exact," Wren piped up, checking her own phone.

Meg squealed like a schoolgirl at a boy band concert and she and Wren settled into watching the juggling / singing phenomenon as it continued to build in tempo, volume and ridiculousness. Paulie, meanwhile, hit 'Buy Now' and felt a private euphoria she didn't care to share with anyone. Juggling. Like Sage. That was the way forward.

That was how she'd get into the mind of a killer.

18

Paulie tore open the package the minute the Amazon guy left it on the bakery counter. She left Fickle Fergus to his daily decision-making at the display case and called to let Aunt Meg know she was going upstairs for a few minutes.

These juggling balls were just as bright and glittering as the ones Sage had been showing off with at the wake. They had a good, solid weight to them and they came in a handy little cloth bag, also golden. The instructions inside were printed so tiny, there was no way she'd be able to read them. Luckily, there was also a QR code so she zapped it with her phone and was directed to a You Tube video.

Paulie felt that delicious pinching of attention and just knew she was ready to master the art of juggling. She was prepared to be crap at it at first, but surely the process of learning would help her unlock the way Sage's mind worked and how it might be capable of something as unlikely as murder. She cleared a patch of carpet in the middle of the living room and propped her phone up on the sofa. She stood as she imagined a juggler should stand and waited for instructions.

The video blared out a startling techno jingle and a young

man appeared on the screen, holding juggling balls and standing in a graffitied underground tunnel. It took Paulie maybe a whole ten seconds to realise he wasn't speaking in a language she understood. Her best guess was that it was Mandarin. For a further three seconds, she thought subtitles had saved her, but then quickly realised those symbols flashing along the bottom of the screen were not in English either. Crap.

The obvious answer was to just Google *'learn to juggle'* but a ping from her phone told her that it was time to leave for drama class. Wren was on point with her text reminders these days. Paulie found it annoyingly considerate, but shaking Wren off was something she just didn't have time for right now. It would have to wait.

After downing a pint of water (*'Drink'* sticky note) and grabbing her essentials (*'Keys, money, phone'* sticky note) Paulie bounded downstairs in her comfiest jean shorts and favourite Gorillaz top. She had tied the juggling balls back up in their sparkly bag and slipped the drawstring over her wrist, letting the weight of them swing and sway as she moved. Aunt Meg furnished her with a package of Doubloon Delights not just for her, but for the whole of the drama class ("Your lot probably needs the kindness as much as the sugar") and Paulie made a beeline across the sunny harbour, through the meandering tourists and towards the bus stop. She saw the number twelve waiting at the traffic lights, on its way to pick up its Berryport passengers and felt a dart of happiness trip through her tummy. She was clean, dressed, on time and hydrated. Oh, and she would be an expert juggler in a week, tops.

"For a three ball cascade, you actually need to start with just one." Sage shouted across the drama studio, commenting directly on Paulie's efforts, just as she hoped he would. "Get comfortable with throwing one ball from left hand to right, right hand to left, then add the other two in later. You know, when you're ready."

"Can you show me?" Paulie knew he hardly needed encouragement after his performance at Tanya's wake. "I think we've got time. Swanny's outside on the phone." Sage sauntered over and took the balls from Paulie's hands. All of the other students were watching at first, attuned as they were to admiring Sage's every move, and the attention made Paulie squirm inside, at least momentarily. But when he started to show her the patterns and geometrics involved in juggling, the students quickly tuned out and went back to scoffing Aunt Meg's cookies.

Paulie studied Sage a little closer. He really was quite beautiful, there was no question about that. As he described the techniques with a growing enthusiasm, his cheekbones lifted and his complexion warmed even under his 'tantastic' glow. He had a smile that invited you to mirror one straight back and his stone grey eyes were lavished with lashes that would have made a supermodel question the point of everything. He was the most unlikely killer imaginable. But Paulie had a good imagination and Coral Bombora had, after all, told her to honour her intuition.

"When did you learn to juggle so well, Sage?" Paulie pushed the words out of her mouth with sheer determination, fully aware that just a couple of weeks ago he had no idea who she even was. "You're very good,"

"Not that long ago, actually," Sage replied, with a tilted smile. "It got me out of a difficult time, you could say. Gave me a focus." Paulie's mind flew to Romano's miniature houseplants and her twisting rituals with her necklace. Maybe this was Sage's thing. His coping mechanism. Then he shook his head as if banishing a dark thought. "Anyway, Pauline. I'm sure you'll get it if you keep practicing." And he walked back across the studio, into the eager company of several girls who had probably been waiting for him the whole time.

"Dude, he can't even get your name right. He should be embarrassed." Wren stood up from the floor, where she'd been sitting cross-legged on top of her duffle bag. She'd made it her mission to pick up the juggling balls that Paulie dropped, but that was obviously as far as she was willing to get involved. "Sucking up to Sage Bretton is ridiculous. Do you really think he'd kill the girl he was besotted with?"

"Give me time. I'm just trying to get into his mind. Imagine his motives. Get closer to what makes him tick."

"And you're doing that with a set of spangly balls? It's original, I'll give you that."

"Whatever. Anyway, what's keeping Swanny? It's not like him to start the class late."

"He's still on the phone. It sounds proper important. When I passed him earlier I heard him say, *'The Arching Angel is the perfect location. You couldn't build a more authentic pirate ship. You simply must come and see it!'*" A few heads turned at the uncanny sound of Swanny's voice streaming from Wren's mouth. Her flawless hand gestures weren't far behind. "Dude, he's cooking something up."

"Well, we all know he's got dreams of making a movie. He's hardly kept that a secret."

"I know. He's mentioned it one hundred and fourteen times this term alone. Anyway, the pirate festival distracted him for a bit. Then, you know, everything with Tanya. It basically happened on his watch. Poor bugger."

Then a different voice made both Paulie and Wren jump. "I don't know, for a 'poor bugger' he seems pretty excited to me." The voice wasn't familiar. Like, at all. "Paulie, don't tell me you've forgotten me already?"

The girls turned around and saw Breeze Bombora standing in *their* drama studio. The hem of his black coat was practically kissing the floor, a roguish expression peeked out from behind shards of midnight black and blue hair, and an air of amusement almost broke into a smile. He looked at Paulie as if she owed him something, rather than acknowledging that he was gate-crashing their space and had been rude enough to not only eavesdrop but also invade their conversation. Unbelievable.

"Nope. Haven't forgotten you. Just wondering why you're here? If you're looking for the art block, you took a major wrong turn."

"Already been there. They gave me a message, actually. They want their paint stripper back that Swanny borrowed." He paused and looked around the studio, nodding in approval. "Now I'm here though, I might check things out. Maybe I'll join drama."

Before Paulie could question such a ridiculous notion, Wren stuck out her hand. "Welcome, Bruise. Oops! I mean, Breeze. I'm Wren, Paulie's friend. You'll love drama. It's excellent on all kinds of levels. And Swanny's okay too – when he's not flipping out over mysterious phone calls, that is."

"Yeah, he does seem pretty worked up out there. But like, in a good way. I think?" Breeze dropped a large, transparent plastic folder on the ground, propping it up on a staging block. It was dusted with a film of chalky colour, but you could still see that inside was a collection of papers, all covered in intricate illustrations. There must have been at least a hundred of them, all stashed together, fanning out at a dozen different angles, with no particular order or care. It made Paulie want to pull them all out and organise them right there in the middle of the drama studio floor. But that would be weird. At least, to everyone else.

"Woah, dude. Are those your drawings? They're incredible." Wren crouched down and had a closer look. Breeze crouched down with her and together they pointed out ornate dragons, fiery demons, complex skeletons, fantastical birds and stormy scenes. Paulie sighed audibly and wished Swanny would come back in so they could get started and Breeze would quickly realise this wasn't the place for him and his moody 'art'.

"Thanks. I brought them for an A Level art interview. But really what I want to do is focus on illustration. I want to get into tattooing."

"Oh. Like your auntie? That's what she's doing now, isn't it?"

"Wow. Keep forgetting I'm in a small town now." Breeze glanced up at Paulie and smirked. "Yeah. Like my auntie. My dad sent me down here to Berryport to do work experience with her. You know, once she gets properly opened up. She's a sick tattoo artist, and even where I live in Bristol, there probably isn't anyone else as good. But I won't stay here forever. I want to do an apprenticeship with the Family Iron in Switzerland one day. Filip Leu slays everyone else. Easy." Breeze rolled up his sleeves and reached into his folder to pull out a sheet of tattoo examples to show them. Paulie was sure it was meant to be impressive but, inexplicably, her eyes were glued to his forearms.

"How come you don't have any tattoos, if you're so into them? You look old enough." She felt the need to justify – to herself as much as anyone else – why she was staring at Breeze's arms. But he had obviously answered the questions many times before, judging by the quickness of his answer.

"I am. But I'm still working out what my first one's going to be. If it's a story I'll tell in years to come, it needs to be a good one, right?"

"S'pose." Something inexplicable fluttered down Paulie's spine. "But why bother with drama class?" It was the obvious question. If his drawings were so good and Switzerland was calling, what was he even doing here?

Breeze rose to standing, and for the first time, Paulie noticed his height. Then his proximity. He was standing so close she could smell something like pepper and citrus on his skin. Or maybe it was his hair. Often, this kind of physical closeness would have Paulie lashing out like a wild animal but in this moment, she could deal with it. And anyway, she wanted her question answered. He'd taken in a breath and struck up eye contact that shot arrows to her bones, but his answer was yet to come. It was a simple question, so why hadn't he bloody well answered it?

"Oi. Bombora. What gave you the nerve to turn up here?"

Sage. He yelled across the room as he had done at Paulie earlier, only this time his voice was knotted with anger. Breeze immediately clocked the mood. And rather than shrink back, he turned away from Paulie, strode towards Sage and met him in the middle of the studio floor.

"Just thinking about joining the class after summer. That's all." Breeze tipped his chin and met Sage's glare.

"I saw you at the funeral. You weren't welcome there and you're not welcome here. Just go." Sage's arms shot down by his sides like missiles. He was flexing his fists and it was hard to tell if those were conscious movements or not.

"I'll be staying, actually."

"Haven't you done enough? Tanya wouldn't want you here." Sage's jaw was halfway between grinding and wobbling, as if an outburst of sadness or a fit of fury were equally possible. Either way, he wasn't going to back down.

"Well. She's not here, is she? So we'll never know." Breeze's words rang out like crystal tapped in a silent room and the drama students gasped almost to the point of choking. Wren nudged Paulie hard and they watched as Sage screwed his right fist into a ball and swung it upwards in a motion not unlike the one he'd shown Paulie earlier when they were juggling.

That was when Swanny burst into the room.

"Darlings! No!" He jumped right in the middle of the two boys, who leapt back to avoid his bulk. Sage's swooping fist flew over Swanny's head where otherwise it might have met Breeze's cheekbone and it arced, wastefully, in mid-air. The boys were left staring at each other so that if looks could kill they would have both been floored.

Swanny stretched out his arms and pushed them even further away from each other. "This is an abomination! This is not happening in *my* drama studio. You, Breeze Bamboozle or suchlike? I got a text saying you might be on your way over. Go home. You can join us another day. In fact, class is cancelled today, darlings. I'm not even going to tell you all my good – no not 'good' – my *exceptional* news. It will have to wait. Sage. You stay here. We need a discussion."

A murmur of disapproval pulsed among the students but they knew better than to question Swanny's authority on this one. It wasn't often he cancelled class – especially when it had already started – so they knew he meant business. Everyone started packing up bags, putting on jackets and shuffling towards the doors, leaving Swanny and Sage still standing in the middle of the floor.

As Paulie picked up her juggling balls and stuffed them back in their bag, she saw Sage look down at his feet, whilst Swanny, even though he was much shorter, somehow loomed over him. Paulie caught herself feeling sorry for Sage. *Nope. He could be a killer, remember? He deserves whatever's coming to him.*

"Dude, let's go." Wren tugged at her elbow. "Somebody's waiting for you at the door." Paulie looked up and saw Breeze standing there like some kind of spectre. The intense black of his long coat blended in with the black of the studio doors and Paulie wondered if it would kill him to wear some colour.

"Soz, girls. I didn't mean for my first session to go off so cray."

Wren shrugged and smiled. "At least the *drama* studio is finally living up to its name."

"What's Sage's problem with you, anyway?" Paulie asked.

"Let's do this in the Meadow," Breeze said. "That's if you've got a minute?"

Wren was already way ahead, marching at her usual astonishing pace, headed for the Meadow. Paulie moved past Breeze, breathing in that peppery, lemony scent without even meaning to. She nodded and walked on, deciding he could follow, or not, it didn't really matter. At least, not that much.

19

Breeze, Wren and Paulie followed the gravel path from the drama studio, past the pastoral block and out onto the open aspect of the Meadow. The sun was out at full pelt and the daisies speckling the grass were open wide, making a generous offer of white and gold across the patchy ground. Wren suggested they sit under a large apple tree where there was a luscious splash of grass in between the exposed roots. They sat down and the sun darted playfully through the flickering leaves. Like a very organised mum on a picnic, Wren took three cans of orange Fanta out of her bag and handed one each to Paulie and Breeze. Then she took our her jigsaw tube, unrolled the mat and placed a pot of spare pieces next to it. "Anybody want to help? I finished the Battle of Cape Lopez. Now I'm doing these spilled beans."

Paulie felt her innards cringe into knots. Could Wren be any more embarrassing? "Is now really the time, Wren?"

"Dude, not only do jigsaws improve visual-spatial reasoning, short-term memory and problem-solving skills, but they reduce stress too. So maybe now is *exactly* the right time." Her eyes darted over to Breeze, who was studying the ring pull on his can of Fanta with unnerving attentiveness.

"Flipping heck, there's no arguing with you."

Several moments passed with Wren flicking through jigsaw pieces and Paulie glugging down Fanta, before Breeze spoke. "Tanya and I had a thing."

Wren nearly coughed up her Fanta. "I'm sorry, what?"

"Yeah. And not even that long ago."

"Dude, that's so not enough. More please."

Breeze brushed his hair off his face and closed his eyes for a moment. Then he took a deep breath so that his chest swelled, looking first at the baked bean jigsaw, then at Wren, then at Paulie. "I had a gap year after school and my dad was sick of me knocking round the house. So just before the summer came, he sent me down here to stay with Auntie Coral. That's when I hooked up with Tanya. She used to sit in the Nautical Gardens on her own, all quiet and upset-looking. One day I just started drawing her using an illustration app on my phone and she caught me. That was it. We got tight really quick."

"Woah, dude. That must be why I thought I recognised you. Maybe I saw you with her at some point?"

"Maybe. We hung out a lot even though she wanted to keep us on the down-low so we always met up in quiet places. Like Kingsands beach. That was her favourite."

"That's it!" Wren punched the air. "My kitchen window looks down on Kingsands. I must have seen you there. Damn, I'm good with faces."

"That's how Tanya wanted it. Kingsands worked for her because I guess I didn't exactly fit into her social scene or whatever. But I didn't really care. I just wanted to be around her. It wasn't until she started getting into acting and stuff, that she got a bit up herself if you know what I mean."

"Speak ill of the dead, why don't you." Paulie crushed her

empty Fanta can and shot Breeze a look of disgust. It slid right off him.

"It's just the way it was. She was the sweetest, dopest girl at first. Then, as soon as she went to the college open day, met Swanny and decided to be a performer, the idea of fame just took over."

"Didn't you want her to follow her dreams?"

"Obviously I did. I knew she'd be lit at it and I encouraged her loads at first. But then she started with the fake-tanning and hair extensions. Planning her whole life around nail appointments with her mum and dieting like her life depended on it – totally messed up. But whenever I tried to challenge her on it, she wouldn't listen. She said I was being controlling. And if there's one thing she should have known about me, it's that I will never, ever be controlling."

"So that's why you broke up?" Wren slotted one splodge of baked beans against another splodge of baked beans without taking her gaze off Breeze.

"Kind of. You know, sometimes I have to remind myself of how much I know because of my auntie's police work and how much I know because of Tanya. I don't want to speak about confidential stuff but I have a feeling I can trust you both?"

"You absolutely can," Wren assured him, shooting Paulie a look that said, *we're onto something here, but we have to be careful.* Paulie nodded, already knowing she'd be writing it all in her notes later. What Breeze didn't know wouldn't hurt him.

"Okay, here goes. So she signed up for this acting summer school in London. I was disappointed because it was, like, five weeks long, but I knew she'd love it. That was where she got to know Sage. I'd heard his name knocked about town so once she started mentioning him, I asked my Auntie Coral about him. If you catch her with a few golden rums inside her, sometimes you get what you need." Wren and Paulie exchanged looks. Was he getting to the juicy stuff or what? "Anyway, I found out Sage was involved in low level drugs. Using as well as dealing. It wasn't really risky stuff, but enough for him to be charged with possession and intent to supply."

"Golden Boy Bretton? For real?" Wren was practically squealing. Paulie was gripped too. She just didn't know how to show it.

"For real. My auntie let on that if his parents weren't the local business magnates, it could have got so much worse for him. It's basically one of the reasons she took early retirement. Twisted politics. Anyway, after they got him out of trouble, they threatened him with taking away his entire share in the Bretton empire if he didn't clean his act up. He is your absolute classic example of a privileged white boy hanging around, looking pretty and mopping up generational wealth. Suddenly he had to stay the golden boy or he could lose everything."

"Dude. What happened next?"

"So they were both at this acting school. Sage was there because it was one of his parents' demands, you know, to focus on a hobby and get him away from the gear. He came back with a particular talent for juggling. Oh, and Tanya. He came back with Tanya too."

"So she curved you while she was there? At the summer school?"

"Yeah," he sighed.

"That's brutal, dude."

"Yeah. Maybe. God knows what she told Sage about me because since I got back he's been plaguing me on socials, especially since her death. I don't care if I upset him. Going to the funeral felt important. Really important. Joining drama class might be a bit selfish on my part." There was that look of raw honesty, directed right at Paulie. "But it's a free country. I can join if I want."

"Well, Sage will have to get over it," Wren said. "You saw how disgusted Swanny was with him. He loves Golden Boy Bretton but he loves his precious drama class more. I reckon this time next week you'll be back. Right, Paulie?"

"Oh, er. Probably. Knowing Swanny."

Breeze didn't seem the type to rest his hopes on anybody else's opinions, but after hearing Paulie say that, he seemed to relax somewhat and leaned forwards to gaze at Wren's jigsaw. "Hope so," he said, picking up and fitting in the only missing edge piece.

"Dude, I've been looking for that everywhere."

"You're welcome," he smiled and started scouring the little pot for more pieces. When they started murmuring about the shape, colour and form of baked beans, Paulie tuned out.

Even though he'd figuratively spilled his own beans, given them both an interesting afternoon and smelled undeniably delicious, Paulie wished Breeze would leave now. She wanted to discuss with Wren a delectable new theory that was forming in her mind.

Maybe, just maybe, Breeze was joining drama class as a way to feel closer to his old flame. And maybe, just maybe, that was because he had some sort of guilty conscience. Now, that could be for a number of reasons, all of which seemed equally compelling. Murder, obviously, was number one. But guilt could come from all kinds of places and if there was one thing that Paulie knew about this weirdly fascinating boy, it was that she had to get inside his head.

"I'm off." Paulie jumped up, taking her juggling balls with her. Wren squinted up at her, a question forming on her confused face. Paulie answered it before she could ask. "I've er, got some studying to do. At the library."

"The library? Dude, do you even know where that is? What about getting the bus home?"

"It's fine. All fine." Paulie backed away from their spot under the tree and the ridiculous jigsaw. Breeze had sat up too, possibly freaked out by her sudden exit, and raised his hand to his forehead, blocking out the sun.

"You okay, Paulie?"

Paulie didn't answer. Instead she turned away and focused all her efforts on getting to the library, knowing that about now, Wren would be finding some cringey way to explain to Breeze that Paulie could be like that sometimes. Unpredictable. Emotional. Except Paulie knew she was being neither of those things. If anything, it was the exact opposite. Because she knew that where she was going and what she was going to do when she got there made perfect, diamond-clear sense. She could feel it down to her core. And if those two weirdos sitting under that tree didn't get that? Well that was their problem.

20

The incessant 'kaching' sound of a cash register was getting annoying now.

A while ago, when Aunt Meg had insisted Paulie become more responsible about her finances and set up online banking notifications for her phone, she'd thought it would be funny to choose that particular noise. Now though, it was fraying her nerves good and proper. Which she supposed it should do after her phone 'kachinged' for perhaps the millionth time that day.

Paulie was fully aware that her bank balance was way below zero. That's what interest free overdrafts were for though, right? She hardly needed reminding that she'd spent all her bakery wages and that the required funds were coming from the bank itself. It was just stupid.

Now was not the time to fix it. She was deliciously embroiled in nailing this dragon design. The book she'd got from the library was surprisingly good. 'One Thousand and One Tattoo Designs' had even recommended the types of illustration pens she should buy to practice with. She'd been too impatient to wait five whole days for the fancy drawing paper so was using an old notepad taken from a collection of quite possibly hundreds, from under her bed. The golden dragon she'd sketched was similar to the designs Breeze had been flaunting in his art folder, except this one was wrapping itself through the innards of a crumbling skull. Okay, so the workmanship may not have been so on point, but she would get there.

With every brush stroke, every fine line and every patch of shading, Paulie felt like she was getting closer to Breeze. She reckoned he was nowhere near as mysterious as he made out to be. Like every other male with a pulse, he'd succumbed to Tanya's charms, hadn't he? And he must have been at least a little bit hurt when Tanya dumped his ass for Sage last summer. He'd certainly shown more than a scrap of vulnerability under the tree in the Meadow yesterday. Which, to be honest, made Paulie wonder why on earth he had suddenly started confiding in her and Wren. What was his game?

Paulie picked up a pen again and began to shade the hollow depths of one of the skull's eyes. As she was doing so, she reflected on the effects a hobby like illustration could have on your character. It was a very insular activity. It didn't really require any input from anybody else, at least not when practicing like this. Look at Coral. She may have been a detective all her professional life, dealing with people and their secrets, but her personality must be more suited to sitting still and drawing and not dealing with anybody's crap. *She must be comfortable with silence. And with pain.*

And how did that translate to Breeze? His auntie was obviously his mentor and Paulie was willing to bet it wasn't just about drawing, either. His very presence kept him cut off from those around him. That mask of dark hair. That shroud of a coat. Yet there he was, pushing himself into Paulie and Wren's lives. Dropping them bits of information like you'd give treats to a dog. Paulie was convinced that if she just kept drawing, she'd figure him out.

Just then, she heard the front door of the flat slam closed and several, quick steps banged across the landing carpet. "Dude! You do know it's not Christmas, right?"

Crap. How did Wren get in here?

Paulie dropped her pen, threw a nearby towel over her work and stood up. "Wren? What's going on?"

Wren appeared at the doorway to Paulie's room, her pale complexion glowing far more than usual and her arms trembling under the weight of a pile of parcels all emblazoned with the Amazon logo. "I'll tell you what's going on. Your aunt just made me the delivery guy, messenger and head chef all in one go. All I wanted was a bag of doubloons. Jeez."

"Okay, okay. Just dump them all on there." Paulie gestured towards the clothes mountain / bed and Wren only just had enough time to step an inch forward before all of the boxes tumbled out of her arms. She stood up and fanned her face, then flexed her arms in a stupidly exaggerated way. "Thanks. You can go get your doubloons now if you want. I'm cool here."

"Dude, debatable. I'd ask what's in that lot but first I have to give you a message from Meg . . ."

"Okay."

"Luvver, why didn't you turn up for work? Was it fatigue again? Please can you tell me next time? Just a text, luvver? The summer holidays are almost here and we need to keep this business afloat!" Wren's Aunt Meg impression was sublime, but Paulie wasn't going to actually tell her that.

"Bugger. Was I on shift? Totally forgot. I've been, er, busy." Paulie realised too late that her eyes had flicked over to her desk where the towel lay flung over her dragon sketch. Wren was quicker than a Berryport seagull to a manky chip. She chucked the towel aside and held the drawing up.

"Dude. This is good. I didn't know you were into illustration.

New hobby?" Then Wren clocked 'One Thousand and One Tattoo Designs' also on the desk and flicked through it, finding the college library stamp on the inside cover. "So this is what you went to the library for the other day? Why didn't you just say?" She gazed at Paulie, looking for an answer. Paulie felt her mouth pop like a goldfish but Wren drew completely the wrong conclusion before she could speak. "Aw. Say no more, dude. Say no more. I suppose that Breeze is pretty hot, in his own look-at-me-I'm-brooding kind of way. You're trying to get into his interests? Cute."

"No. Not cute. Absolutely not cute." Paulie felt her cheeks rage and willed them to cool the heck down. "I'm just taking Coral's advice. Getting into the minds of the people around Tanya. Then I might find a motive."

"But he wasn't around Tanya. They split up ages ago."

"We don't know that. We only know what he's told us."

"True. But he seems like an honest type, don't you think?"

"I don't know what I think. That's why I'm trying out the tattoo designs. To get into his mindset."

"Ah, okay. Like the juggling? How goes it with the spangly balls, by the way?" Wren crossed the room and started picking up and shaking the parcels. Paulie could hardly bear it and took each one off her as fast as she could.

"Well, erm, I got the basics. I'll get back to them at some point. Don't you want to go downstairs and get the cookies you came for?"

"I lied. Actually, it wasn't a complete lie because I will always take Doubloon Delights if they're on offer, but I lied about that being the only reason I came. Dude, don't you realise it's supposed to be drama class this afternoon? Judging by your current ensemble, I'm assuming not?"

Paulie looked down at what she was wearing possibly for the first time that day. Okay, so maybe threadbare tracksuit bottoms and a pasta sauce stained vest weren't acceptable attire for college. "These are my comfies. I'm not changing."

"Fine. But did you get any of my texts or voice notes today? I left loads."

Paulie wasn't even sure where her phone was. Probably in the depths of her floordrobe where she'd flung it earlier. "Phone's got no battery. Soz."

"Well, I'm here now. If you don't fancy college today, and you're willing to face the wrath of Peg Leg, I can stay here with you this afternoon? My attendance record is pretty good so it won't matter."

"No thanks."

"I'll take that as a yes." Wren kicked her shoes off and sat on Paulie's bed in a cross-legged position. She eyed the pile of parcels with an appetite for mischief. "Shall we open this one first?" As she picked one off the top, Paulie furtively grabbed the rectangular one closest to her and slid it under the bed. That one needed to be out of Wren's reach. Just in case.

"No, I don't think . . ." But it was too late. Wren had already very precisely torn the perforated pully thing and a neat strip of the cardboard packaging fell away.

"Dude, you're taking up gardening? These are so cool!"

Paulie had to admit, the houseplants had arrived in better condition than she'd expected them to. There were six of them in total, all green and robust, leafy and bright. As she picked them up in their little tray holder, she admired the small ceramic pots and the labels stuck into the soil with care instructions printed on. Wren was grinning from ear to ear and her eyes were sparkling as much as Paulie felt her insides were. For that reason she said, "Wren, open that one next."

Wren picked up the oblong parcel and fiddled around trying to open it the proper way. "Just rip it," Paulie urged, and Wren smiled uncertainly, took a deep breath and burrowed her fingertips into the parcel. Several items fell out, all co-ordinating in a very precise duck-egg blue that Paulie had spent ages looking for. A water spray bottle. A small trowel. A mini rake. Some secateurs. A pair of gardening gloves. "These remind me of what you described in Peg Leg's office. He's obsessed with plants, isn't he?" Wren looked up at Paulie, the innocence of her question dowsing her expression with curiosity. Then – as Paulie returned that curiosity with a steadfast gaze – Wren's expression fell helplessly into complete and total understanding. "Ohhh. I get it. Get into the minds of the people around Tanya. Dude, you suspect Peg Leg?"

"I'm keeping my options open."

Wren gave a shriek of delight which was quite possibly the girliest thing Paulie had ever witnessed her do, and the two of them started ripping into the other parcels. Now that Wren understood Paulie's methods (and the one parcel containing a ridiculously difficult jigsaw was safely tucked away) things were so much easier. And enjoyable too, actually. There Paulie was, in the absolute tip of her room in her scruffiest, most ridiculous clothes, with the last person in the world she'd expect to under-stand her, having the time of her life.

They ripped open a stack of crossword puzzle books.

"Fickle Fergus!" Wren whooped.

Then a 'better-then-the-real-thing' cuddly robot poodle.

"Debbie Devon!" Wren cried.

A state-of-the art manicure set plus nail varnishes.

"Wendy Withers!" They both shouted.

A doughnut baking tray complete with instant doughnut mix.

"Raymond the Police Officer!"

A DVD called 'The Theory of Modern Drama'.

"A DVD? How will you play it? Never mind . . . Swanny!"

A hand-held magnifying glass complete with deerstalker hat.

"Coral Bombora? Dude – you suspect the ex-detective of Berryport?" Wren's smile dropped from her face but the seriousness was lost as soon as she donned the hat and peered through the magnifying glass.

"Like I said, I'm keeping my options open. Plus, short of buying an actual tattoo needle, I didn't know what else to get for her. I think it was about three in the morning when I made that purchase." Paulie flung herself back on the bed, laughing at her own silliness and sighed up at the ceiling. "I'm so pleased with all this stuff!"

"You must have been making some serious bakery dollars to pay for all of this." Before Paulie could worm her way out of that one, her stomach gave out an enormous squawk. "Dude! I totally forgot! Your aunt asked me to get you some food. Remember? She made me delivery man – tick; messenger – tick; and head chef – yet to tick. Let's do it now. What do you want?"

"I don't want anything. I defo don't want a personal chef. I can get my own food, thank you very much." Paulie felt the edges of her merriment dim slightly. She'd been having such a good time and really – like, *really* – wanted to get on with her investigations with all of this new stuff.

"What's that?" Wren asked, cupping her hand against her ear. "A large bowl of spicy beef Super Noodles? A stack of hot, buttery toast? A mug of tea, a can of Fanta *and* a glass of iced water? Well, it just so happens those are all my specialities. Follow me, Watson, erm, I mean, well, I suppose you're Sherlock. Follow me, Sherlock! Time for sustenance." Wren, still wearing the deerstalker and holding the magnifying glass, clambered her way off the bomb-site of a bed and gently took Paulie's arm so that she had to stand too.

Paulie allowed herself to be led away because even she

couldn't deny the hollow clang of her belly. However, she enjoyed a quick glance backwards at the mess in her room. It looked like an Amazon warehouse had been subject to a protest attack and then ransacked by hungry wolves. Her aunt would have a legit fit.

It was kind of ironic that it took a monumental shit-tip in Paulie's room to give her any kind of focus. But as she looked back at the frayed edges of discarded boxes, the translucent billow of empty plastic wrapping and the riot of seemingly random objects piled up against each other, she could feel that focus streaming through her consciousness like an intravenous medicine plumping up poorly, withered veins to healthy perfection. And she wasn't about to argue with something that felt like a medicine now, was she?

21

It never failed to amaze Paulie how Swanny could hold the students' attention like this.

For a seemingly self-assured troupe of individuals, right now – with their mouths hanging open and their bodies leaned forwards into the abyss of Swanny's imminent announcement – they showed the stark truth of their own vulnerabilities. It suddenly occurred to Paulie that in her mission to gain popularity ever since the academic year began, she may have forgotten that these students too had faults, flaws and, probably most of all, dreams.

"Swanny, please. Just tell us. Today's our last session and we don't want to be wondering for the whole of the summer holidays." It was one of Sage's female devotees (Paulie was pretty sure she called herself 'Shazza') currently flanking his right side and using the drama of the moment to clutch his muscular bicep. Sage didn't seem to mind. Or even notice.

Swanny whipped out a travel-size tube of anti-bac and rubbed it gleefully into his hands as he spoke. "Of course, my darling bud of delight, you make an excellent point. And maybe it's unfair of me to reveal this secret right now, before we break up, but you do need to know. You *all* need to know." Swanny was sitting on a drama studio chair at the head of a circle with his stubby legs swinging. Not that a circle could really have a head. The whole point of using circles in class, Swanny said, was to create a sense of equality, to make sure that every single person was seen and heard. But whenever Swanny was in the circle, it had a head. No doubt.

Paulie had been learning all about the sense of equality necessary in dramaturgy. In fact, she'd learned many interesting theories from her new – though admittedly, dated – DVD, 'The Theory of Modern Drama', including that *'a person's identity is not a stable and independent psychological entity, but rather constantly remade as that person interacts with others'*. She wondered what that said about Swanny, with his constant theatrical vibrancy and inability to finish a sentence without the word 'darling' attached to it.

She'd spent so much quality time in the flat lately, she'd lost track of how many drama classes she'd missed. And how many texts she'd ignored from Romano. She was only here today because Wren had sent her about thirty messages reminding her it was the last one before the summer break. Paulie was sure that if Swanny and Romano had known just how deeply she'd got into 'The Theory of Modern Drama' they wouldn't care about the missed sessions. Not to mention all of the other constructive hobbies she'd taken up: the avid growing of miniature houseplants; the self-application of French manicures; the conquering of crosswords in increasingly shorter times; the training of 'better-than-the-real-thing' toy poodles; and experimentation in all kinds of doughnut recipes. She was yet to get round to the rather daunting two thousand piece under-the-sea jigsaw but she had taken to wearing the ridiculous, purchased-at-three-in-the-morning deerstalker hat. She actually quite liked the snug feel of it on her head and it meant that when she forgot to wash her hair, she didn't get the usual lecture from Aunt Meg. Bonus.

Swanny slapped his hands down on his knees so hard, everyone jumped. His bearded cheeks were glowing rosy pink and there was a sheen to his forehead that was nothing to do with the studio lights. He then pressed his hands together and brought his fingertips to his lips, kissing them loudly over and over. His eyes flicked heavenwards like he was in some kind of divine discourse that the students were somehow privy to. And then he let the words stream out, "This is it, my lolloping blossoms of the sea . . . 'For the Love of Pirates' is happening. It's really happening!"

A chorus of *wows, woahs, whats* and *wickeds* flew out across the circle and Rashid skipped around the circle fist-bumping everybody. Breeze, who had been attending drama class for a few weeks now, and ignoring Sage enough to get along, looked at Wren and Paulie with a flicker of a smile. He mouthed at them both, "For the love of pirates?" Paulie stifled a grin but Wren went all out and had to stop laughing to draw breath.

"Dude, don't burst his bubble. It's the script he's been working on for years." Then, behind both hands covering her face so only Paulie and Breeze could see, she somehow twisted her features into a Swanny-like grin and got his clipped, excited tone just right. "'For the Love of Pirates' – a fierce, fantastical, romance of swashbuckling sparkle and swagger. It will put me, er, I mean, Berryport . . . on the map of fame foreverrrrr."

Paulie and Breeze flopped back in their chairs laughing but then immediately worked to mask their mocking convulsions as celebratory shrieks to merge with the rest of the class. Swanny didn't notice anyway and held out his hands like an emperor, quieting the masses, waiting for the perfect moment to deliver the rest of his news.

"So, I've been in talks with movie producers via my agent,

Augustin at the preeminent Champion Talent Agency. My script has been high on their agenda for years now but, well, as you know chickadees, the movie-making market is a complex beast. And until now, the time just hasn't been right . . ."

"And now?" Shazza, the bicep-clutching girl from before asked eagerly, now having moved on to Sage's thigh, along with another equally grabby girl (Cazza?) simpering at his other side. Paulie wondered what Debbie Devon would think about that.

"Now, angels of my lune, you should be tickled pink that you have a theatrical guru in your very midst who has remained so steadfast in his Hollywood dreams."

"Hollywood?" Several people gasped.

"Well, probably Hollywood. Most likely Hollywood. Because it seems that the very tragedy Berryport suffered way back at the pirate festival has inspired the powers that be to visit our town in the imminent future to scope out the movie location ready for shooting next Spring. Tanya, our faithful, beautiful Tanya, has inadvertently got the right people signing on the dotted line. Her death, it seems, has not been in vain." To this, the room fell silent. How else could you cope with the agonising combination of good information and bad, other than with silence?

It was Sage who broke it. "When are they coming? These movie people?"

"A production team will come for a recce sometime before Christmas. They can't be any more specific than that right now but I'm thinking . . . now wait for it, my thrilling little thespians . . . the Berryport Lantern Parade."

Sage slapped his head into his hands so Shazza and Cazza either side of him jumped back in surprise. Everybody else oohed and aahed and generally agreed with what Swanny was now saying about it being the perfect time for a visit. "Just imagine, it will be the Christmas light switch-on after the parade and the town will not only be looking its absolute best but the community will be all together. Let's not forget that we'll be performing our abstract piece on Billowbreak Beach, which I think, this year, should be a moving tribute to our very own angel, Tanya. Don't you, chickadees? This is the perfect plan, my little ducklings of drama, the perfect plan! Sage, what's wrong with you, pudding chops? Don't you like the plan for Berryport to rise to fame and fortune?"

Sage sighed and removed his head from his hands. "It's not that I don't like the plan, Swanny. It's just that my parents are the main sponsors of that event and the minute they hear movie producers are coming, they'll want me in on it all. Getting inside info and 'maximising their investment'. I just don't know if I've got the energy after . . . everything."

"Never fear my golden one, because we are all here for you. Isn't that right my adorable assembly of stars? We're all here for Sage?" Swanny stood up to a circle of nodding heads. "And as for the ever-so benignant Rex and Bex Bretton, you needn't worry about what they may ask of you. As part of my ongoing discourse with sponsorship partners and allies, I have already have dropped a word or two in their ears. This is news to you, my darlings, but not to the two most powerful people in Torbay."

Just then, a bleep came from Swanny's pocket and he fished his phone out. One look at the screen told the students he had bigger fish to fry. "Shiver my titillating timbers, the universe must be listening. I must make haste! Wren! Darling little mouse of magnificence, could you please use the next forty five minutes and your exceptional directing skills to get everyone to brainstorm ideas for Tanya's tribute piece? We'll get into it properly after the holidays." Occasionally, Swanny encouraged Wren to direct the class but only because he'd once heard her extraordinary impression of him and mistook it for a conscientious desire to be his protégé. She nodded anyway because who could say no to Swanny, really? "Yes? Good? Excellent. Term ends today so I guess it's goodbye from me . . . over the next couple of turns of the moon, I wish you all have fair winds and faithful seas." And just like that, Josiah Swan left the room, backing his way out like an aged actor eager for an encore.

Wren stood up straight away and looked directly at the circle of baffled students. "Okay, dudes, who's got some ideas?"

22

Wren's question was met with silence apart from the last couple of people dragging their chairs to the edges of the studio. "Okay, well the performance piece for the lantern parade is supposed to be abstract and it's supposed to be impressive and now, like Swanny said, it's supposed to be in tribute to Tanya." Paulie might have imagined it, but she thought she felt a heated flash of spite in the space between Breeze and Sage. Then, there was yet more silence.

Being in the middle of watching 'The Theory of Modern Drama', Paulie felt brave enough to chuck an idea into the ring. "What about honouring Tanya's last moments? An abstract retelling through expressive movement and physical storytelling?"

It was a bold suggestion and nobody had the guts to answer but Wren. "Last moments? Okay, but we'd need to be careful because the police are still investigating what actually happened."

Cazza, one of Sage's grabby groupies said, "Yeah. Apparently the police are doing another round of interviews over the summer." She waited for a suitable gasp from the circle of students and got it. In abundance. "My next door neighbour, Maxine is the receptionist at the station and she told me that over a chicken bhuna last night. So, just to be safe, maybe we should focus more on the gap she's left behind. You know, like the Debbie Devon song? How her life has *'slipped into a void we just don't get'*." The entire class couldn't help themselves and all sang the next line in unison.

"Tanya, you were so loved by the internet."

From that point on, suggestions rolled in about taking Paulie's idea of physical storytelling to embody the gaping chasm Tanya had left in the heart of Berryport. Somebody linked their phone to the studio's speakers and put 'Tanya's Tune' on repeat, just loud enough to accelerate their ideas as well as dust off recent feelings of grief. There was suddenly talk of giant, heart-shaped lanterns, light-up flags to represent stormy ocean waves and elaborate, fairy-lit costumes. Before you could say, *'Debbie Devon is a dumbass'* there were bodies leaping about the studio in not-so-graceful arcs and swirls. Paulie wasn't sure how any of it related back to Tanya and itched to get back to her original suggestion of examining the poor girl's final moments.

"Dude, I'm dying for the loo," Wren muttered at Paulie's side. "Just keep an eye on this lot till I get back, will you? They're deep in their own egos so I doubt they'll resurface very soon."

This was it. It was now or never.

Whether it was the deerstalker hat on her head that gave her extra confidence, or the fact that both Swanny and Wren were gone from the room, Paulie wasn't sure, but she cleared her throat and found an appetising balance of strength and volume. "Okay, everyone. Let's go from that last bit where you were leaping sideways. That kind of looked like the choreography from the skirmish. Remember?" There were enough nodding heads to keep going. "Great. Now, get into your groups from that day. Feel your way there. Remember the nerves and the expectations and the energy of the festival. Have you got it? It was an emotional time, right? Good. Now let's go with those feelings . . ."

Paulie somehow – for the first time since she used to make all those jokes in secondary school maths lessons – had a group of people in the palm of her hand. She was vaguely aware of Breeze hanging around the sidelines, watching her intently. But he hadn't been part of the group back then, had he? So it was reasonable for him to sit this one out.

Paulie wanted to get to the absolute nucleus of the moment before Tanya was shot and soak up the energies that would run through it. It was risky, yes, and she wasn't sure that even she could stand the intensity of what they were about to do. But if the murderer was in this room then they'd reveal themselves somehow. And if they weren't? Well, there could still be some vital clues. The game was on.

Because they had known their skirmish choreography so well, the students moved as if hypnotised. Paulie grabbed Shazza or Cazza or whoever she was and said, "You. You're Tanya." The girl smiled broadly then the next split second looked like she was about to be hit by a bus. She did what Paulie said anyway. Anything to be Sage's girlfriend, even if it was his dead girlfriend.

Paulie's voice rose high above the hubbub of the skirmish and the ever-present drone of 'Tanya's Tune' as the students played out mock punches, kicks, swipes and slaps. "Now, as you're performing, I'm going to tap each of you on the shoulder, and as I do, I want you to yell out how you were feeling on that day. Not your character, but you. Okay? Right, here we go . . ." Paulie moved deftly among the animated bodies. She could feel Breeze's eyes burning into her, but she didn't care. Her whole body was fizzing with an energy so unbearable it was delicious. She tapped the first person on their shoulder. Rashid.

"Thrilled!" he shouted, proudly.

"Fab," Paulie shouted back. She moved on to the next person, a grungey-type with neon green and black striped hair and insane freckles.

"Nervous!"

"Good!" Paulie encouraged. "Let's keep going!" Her breath shortened and her ambitions boldened as she zipped from person to person, placing her hand on each student's shoulder, sharing their energy for seconds at a time, getting miniscule flares of insight from their chosen words, yes, but also from the micro-movements rippling beneath their skin.

The words came faster and faster as everybody's pace increased – the flow of the scene streaming out like the waters around the Arching Angel itself.

"Excited."

"Happy."

"Focused."

"Skittish."

It was amazing how many contrasting emotions could be had by a group of people performing the exact same thing. Paulie noticed some of them were shuddering with unwelcome memories, but they were all, to their credit, going along with the task. She got swept up with it herself, amazed she'd missed all of this that day whilst frozen in the alleyway of Booty Bakes. She kept moving, placing her hand on each and every shoulder getting ever closer to where Sage and Shazza were at the far end of the studio, which would have equated to the stern of the Arching Angel.

"Proud."

"Alert."

"Concentrating."

"Tense."

"Worried."

"Cagey."

"Edgy."

And now, Sage.

"Arrogant!" As soon as the word shot from his mouth, he started manically juggling imaginary objects. The word and the movements seemed wildly out of place but there was no time to make sense out of them. Instead, Paulie landed her palm on the shoulder of Shazza, who was already crumpled to the ground, as Tanya had actually been choreographed to do. *That's why then,* she thought, *that nobody noticed Tanya had been shot at first.* Shazza didn't disappoint and screamed with a passionate, ear-splitting ferocity, the exact word Tanya probably had felt in that moment, if she'd still been conscious . . .

"Betraaaaayyyyyyyed!"

On her agonising scream, Wren blasted through the studio doors with questions plastered all over her face. Many of the students collapsed dramatically or hung off each other in blistering silence and Breeze, from his vantage point at the edge of the studio, raised his fingertips to his temples mocking up the shape of a gun and said, without any expression whatsoever, "Bang."

23

"I can't believe you dragged me all the way out here. It's so . . . barren." Paulie shifted on her beach towel and squinted at the vast sheet of silvery sands. The sun was beating down in needles into her eyes. She found it hard to admit that sunlight – generally worshipped by the Devon masses – often caused her eyes discomfort bordering on pain. That was yet another weird personality defect that seemed to set her apart from her peers.

"It might be 'all the way out here' for you, but for me it's only down fifty-two steps." Wren took off her sunglasses and threw them into Paulie's hands. "Take them, dude. Or you'll get a headache. Anyway, Kingsands is honestly one of the only places you're going to get a break from the grockles during the holidays. We all need that by now."

Wren was right. Grockles had been *everywhere* this August. Not that it was a surprise. Berryport was one of the most popular holiday destinations in Devon and in a world still reeling from the repercussions of a pandemic, you could almost feel the cumulative glee.

Paulie, however, had spent a lot of time in the flat, doing a deep dive into her new 'hobbies', organising all of her findings on a huge pinboard in her room like a map of obsessions. The pinboard was a physical embodiment of Coral's first three instructions (document everything / find a motive / treat everything as evidence) and Paulie felt proud just looking at it. She'd also had to work a load of shifts in the bakery to make up all the forgotten ones to Aunt Meg, but had kept mostly to the kitchen where it was a lot quieter. "I don't know. Berryport hasn't been stupidly busy this year."

"You're kidding me, right? It's full to bursting. And anyway, you spend so much time holed up in your room 'detecting', how would you know?" Paulie was about to protest, but Wren was on a roll. "Why do you think I suggested meeting here? Dude, you need to get out more. Especially because there's no college. And you can't let what happened in the last drama session bother you. It was just . . . well, drama."

Paulie sighed and thought back to the session in question. Okay, so people might not have understood her methods but she'd felt she was getting somewhere; that the recreation of Tanya's final moments by the people who'd actually *been there*, was a necessary part of her investigations. And she'd managed to cover it up as art so what harm can it have done, really? "No, Wren. It was truth. Some truth was in that session. I could feel it. Out of all the words in the English language, why did Sage choose the word 'arrogant'? There are secrets. So many of them."

"Dude, apparently he stropped about for, like, a week after you directed that session. So did Shazza. All it did was trigger people and it's no wonder when you think that this is all so fresh. It's only coming up to four months since Tanya died. People aren't ready to 'investigate'."

"Well, people are crap." Paulie really meant this statement sometimes. There was so much fuss about accepting and catering for those with neurodivergence in this world, she often wondered whether it should be the other way around. Why did neurotypical people have oh so many layers of secrecy and complexity to their lives? Why have all these unspoken social rules and pointless, unrewarding customs? It would be much easier if people just followed their joy, paid attention to their instincts and made room for each other. Why couldn't the world just shift a little to become more sincere?

Just then, Paulie felt a cold splat against her legs and looked down to see giant pearls of wet sand. There was a young lad, maybe only a few years younger than herself, driving his wellie-booted toes into a puddly patch of sand, causing it to spray out in different directions. His body was set at a determined angle and his entire focus was on kicking. His face was flooded with captivation as the pure energy of his driving foot transformed sluggish sand into forceful, glittering bursts. So much so, that Paulie really didn't care that some of it had landed on her.

A tall, blonde woman – most likely his mum – came up to him and spoke quietly at his side. Whatever she said convinced him to move further down the beach. Another child ran over to the woman and took her hand, dragging her away but not before she purposefully looked up, caught Paulie's eye and, rather than any kind of apology, sent a silent smile of acknowledgement. Something about the conviction of that smile moved Paulie. It was like a fresh cloud wrapping around the unforgiving sun . . . a small gift . . . a relief.

"Oh cool. He's here." Wren jumped up and pointed back towards the precarious steps that led down from the path up near the main track. There was a figure, dressed entirely in black, hopping down the steps and onto the beach. The way he moved – the swish of his long limbs and the confident tip of his head – was unmistakeable.

"Oh god, Wren. Why did you ask him? I thought it was just going to be you here."

"Because he doesn't know anybody else, dude, and he's been trapped in Berryport the entire holidays. Plus we can help him appreciate this 'barren' beach in a whole new way. He used to come here with Tanya, remember?" Fine. Paulie didn't care if Breeze was here. The smile from that woman had put her in a good mood and there was no reason why he should get in the way of that. She'd simply lie back on her towel and listen to him and Wren chat rubbish. There were worse ways to spend an afternoon.

"What do you *mean* 'fond'?" Paulie was kneeling on her towel, her chest to the sky, her hands on her hips and a curiosity coursing through her that singed her very insides. "They've lived in the same town their whole lives and I've never even met your aunt until now. It took an actual person to die for me to meet her. How could your Aunt Coral and my Aunt Meg possibly be 'fond' of each other?"

"I don't know," Breeze sighed. "It's just the word she used. They used to hang about together at school. My auntie gave your auntie a tattoo once. That's it. That's all I know."

"Then why bring it up at all?" Paulie didn't know why but there was a part of her that was fuming. She and her Aunt Meg had always agreed to have no secrets. How dare Breeze rock up here and imply that she wasn't totally clued up when it came to her own aunt?

"Oh that tattoo is cool though," Wren said, magically pulling out drinks and snacks from a nearby cool bag. Thank god. Paulie's belly was about to tear itself out of her skin and go forage for whelks along the shores of Kingsands. They all dived on the treats. Crisps. Scotch eggs. Pasties. Chocolate. Paulie felt soothed in a way she couldn't even begin to describe so kept eating, taking a break from this ridiculous conversation.

"What is the tattoo?" Breeze asked. "My auntie never said. Just that it had been the first one she'd ever done."

"If that's the case, then it's even more impressive," Wren said. "It's a tiny little smoking gun, just on the inside of her wrist. It's a pirate-type pistol. A blunderbuss. A short, muzzle-loading shoulder weapon. Flintlock. Bore flared at about ten centimetres. Forerunner of the shotgun."

"You know all this just from the tattoo?" Breeze asked, mouth slightly agape. Wren looked back at him blankly. He'd get used to her encyclopaedic knowledge. Eventually.

"My favourite bits are the trails of smoke coming from the muzzle. They remind me of a jigsaw I once did of a Klimt painting. Swirly and decorative. But sinister too. So cool."

"Sinister and cool? That's my Auntie Coral for you. That's weird though, because I'm sure she has the exact same tattoo on her left forearm. You'd probably have a job picking it out now, because she's got, like, masses of them but it's definitely in there." At Breeze's description, Paulie cast her mind back to the day she met Coral in the police station, and how hypnotised she'd been by the artwork all over Coral's arms. Had there been a smoking gun in amongst all of those tattoos?

"So, hang on a minute," Wren puzzled. "They've got, like, the exact same tattoo? Coral and Meg?"

"Sounds like it."

"Well, that takes 'fond' to a whole new level. Right?" Wren looked from Breeze to Paulie, Paulie to Breeze. "Dudes, your aunts had a *bond*. Nobody gets matching tattoos without some full-on, soul-tying stuff going down. Have you really never heard either of them talk about the other one?"

Paulie put her third pastie down for a second. "No. Never. But I do remember Coral calling me 'Little Paulie' when I turned up at Odyssey Ink that day. I thought it was weird but, I don't know, got distracted or whatever. Just remembered it now."

"But dude, lots of people call you that. Fickle Fergus does."

"Little Paulie?" Breeze looked at Paulie. "Why would anybody call you that? Patronising much?"

"It's because they remember her arriving in Meg's life." Wren stole a look at Paulie, asking without a word if it was okay to go on. Paulie nodded. What did she care if Breeze knew? He'd be off in Switzerland tattooing skinheads before long. "When Paulie was six years old, her mum died in a mugging on the street."

"What? I'm so sorry." Breeze's arm flinched as if he wanted to reach out to Paulie, but he didn't. She felt the cool absence of his touch across the top of her hand.

"After the funeral, Paulie's dad took her to Meg, said he couldn't look after her anymore. Then he did a runner." Paulie's heart pounded at the memory. Hearing Wren re-tell it was just plain weird. And slightly inaccurate, but it would do. "My parents say it was before Meg took over the bakery, but she was already well known in the community because she used to bake cakes and supply half the town's cafes and restaurants. She was in the bakery at the time, dropping stuff off so the regulars were around. And they just started calling her 'Little Paulie'. That's why you might hear people saying it sometimes. I guess it's their way of showing affection. And sympathy."

Breeze stared out at the lapping waves. They were coming closer. The three of them would have to move soon or they'd be swallowed into the ocean. "So my auntie must know your story. They have matching tattoos. But they haven't spoken in years. This feels odd."

"Maybe." Paulie jumped to her feet. She picked up a nearby rock and threw it repeatedly from palm to palm. Solid and steady. Rhythmical and strong. Without even realising it, she'd started one of the juggling warm-ups she'd learned through her investigations into Sage. She added another rock to the pattern and her nerves thrummed like plucked guitar strings. "Maybe your auntie would be up for a chat, Breeze?"

"Erm, I doubt it to be honest. She's busy inking all the time. And I don't know if you've noticed, but she's hardly the most approachable person."

Paulie added another stone. This was proper juggling now. "But if there are secrets, we need to know about them."

"Why?"

"Yeah, dude. Why?"

Paulie was definitely more than a little curious about her aunt's connections to the local tattooist / detective / ice queen but it could also be important to her investigations. However unlikely it seemed, if Aunt Meg and Coral were close, it could mean access to further expert, murder-solving advice, which she could really do with. But Breeze was here and she didn't particularly want him in on the whole thing. "Because they're our guardians. Our keepers. They should be telling us stuff like that." A fourth stone. Faster. Paulie moved around the beach towels, crossing Wren and Breeze who were still sitting down. She dodged the cool bag and random potholes in the sand and still she was juggling the rocks. She was amazing herself.

"Dude, you're getting a bit close with those."

"It's fine. I'm only just getting into it. So, Breeze, why don't we . . ." Just as she was about to suggest going back to Odyssey Ink, a stone slipped from Paulie's fingertips and fell with a thud to the ground. Except it wasn't the first thud. It was the second. And the first one had caught Breeze square on his upturned face, clashing against his cheekbone and eye socket, eliciting a shocked yell. He thrust his head into the palm of his hands and swore savagely against his skin.

Wren scooted over to Breeze. "Dude. What have you done?"

Paulie dropped all of the stones and stared at him. Suddenly her skin felt too tight for her body and she thought her heart might cave in on itself. "Breeze . . . are you okay?" He took his hand away from his face for an instant and even from this angle, she could see his cheek had blown up like a cannon ball. His eye was disappearing as fast as Paulie's self-worth.

Wren made some mechanical tuts and soothing sounds before looking up at Paulie with that annoyingly familiar judge-mental look in her eye. "Well, you wanted to see Coral Bomb-ora? Dude, you've got it. There's a bus in fourteen minutes. Let's go."

24

Coral Bombora was not happy.

She stood at the back of the renovated Odyssey Ink, up to her elbows in antiseptic and cotton wool, wearing an expression of the calmest, coldest rage. The shameful heat writhing in Paulie's chest, however, more than made up for it.

"With some luck, we won't have to go to A and E." Coral turned her wrist to look at her watch and Paulie noticed Wren crane her neck, looking for the smoking gun tattoo. "That's a wait that could keep us until the early hours of tomorrow which I'm not prepared to do. Already lost three customers this afternoon."

"Soz, Auntie Coral." Breeze, who was lying back on some kind of fancy tattoo chair, tried to smile but the fiery globe on his cheek wouldn't allow it. Paulie couldn't even see if the smile reached his eyes because one of them was packed behind a sterilised bandage. Whatever first aid training Coral had got as part of her role with the police, it had been thorough.

"It's okay, nephew. You're fine. We just need to keep it clean. And stay away from any more . . . falling rocks." Coral threw a look at Paulie that was impossible to read. Humour?

Disgust? Both seemed equally likely, although Coral knew nothing of the juggling episode. Breeze had fabricated some elaborate story about rocks falling on him from the Kingsands cliffs during the hike back up to the main track. Knowing how perilous that track was, it was a plausible story, but the way Coral had looked at Paulie suggested she knew far better. She hadn't been Berryport's only detective for nothing. "You'll have a hell of a bruise for a while, but it'll heal okay."

"Dude, I get to call you 'Bruise' for real now." Wren was beside herself at this, ignorant to the crushing guilt currently stopping Paulie from breathing properly. "I always knew that was the better name for you. From, like, day one."

"Fine. I can take it," Breeze said, wincing as he sat upright in the chair. "Let's just avoid Kingsands for a bit, yeah?" He tried that broken smile thing at Paulie, but looking back at him was hard. Instead she twisted the pendants around her neck until she felt the sharp and familiar nip at her skin. Silently, she cursed them for the pain not being anywhere near what Breeze must be feeling.

"What are you doing?" Coral snapped, jolting Paulie out of her ritual. "You'll hurt yourself. Such lovely pendants. Don't use them to punish yourself."

"Punish myself? I . . . I . . ."

"Whatever you're doing, Paulie, stop it right now. Breeze will be fine. Just fine." The words helped the air to whoosh back into Paulie's lungs but it came with a slash of confusion. Why would Coral use the word 'punish'? And how had she even noticed her twisting the necklace? She'd thought she had this down to a fine, stealthy art. "Come over here and help me clear up." Coral moved over to a bin in the corner of the room and signalled for Paulie to bring over the pile of used cotton wool. "Well?" she asked, once they were practically shoulder-to-shoulder, stood over the bin.

"I'm sorry, I thought Breeze told you. The rocks fell and . . ."

"Great leering limpets, I don't mean the bloody rocks. I mean your murder investigation. I assume you've seen sense by now and given up?"

"Oh, er, that. Right. Well, actually your tips have been really helpful." Paulie thought of her crazy, collaged pinboard at home. The lid of the impossible jigsaw box. Instructions for that weird toy poodle. Homemade swatches of nail polish colours. "I'm getting into the minds of people around Tanya, like you said. Treating everything as evidence."

"Really?" Coral's face brightened for a moment, and then it suddenly smoothed, as if remembering herself. "Well, I think I was a bit too keen giving you those tips. It's the detective in me. I think you should step back. Let the police get on with things."

"Oh. But I think I might be getting somewhere."

"It doesn't matter. The police will be getting further than you. They have resources."

"Resources? Have they even appointed a new detective?" Other than appeal posters on every other lamppost and the occasional officer calming hysterical crowds of grockles around the Arching Angel, Paulie was yet to be convinced.

"There's a whole team on it, Paulie. In the background. Doing more than you know."

"Don't you wish you were in on it?" Paulie couldn't help herself. Standing here, with Coral was just a shining, golden opportunity and she was willing to risk the wrath of the Bombora hard stare.

"It hardly matters what I wish. It hardly matters that I'd be looking at the most rich and powerful people in Berryport. Or that I'd be looking at how they're connected to what happened in those final moments aboard the ship."

"I did that! I got the whole drama class to re-enact it! Shazza thought Tanya felt betrayed and we realised she collapsed as part of her choreography so nobody even knew she'd been shot and Sage, he was whizzing his hands about like a maniac and acting all weird . . ."

"Enough." Coral raised her hand and Paulie felt her lips close automatically. Man, she was good. "Like I said, it hardly matters because the police are on it." She walked over to the now leather studded reception desk and pulled out a full bottle of golden rum from a drawer, as well as a small copper tankard. She leaned heavily on the neck of the bottle and spoke down towards the desk, but loud enough so everybody could hear. "Right girls, thanks for bringing Breeze back here and making sure he was okay. I think we'll shut up shop and turn in now so . . ."

Wren looked up from her inspection of Breeze's injury. "Oh yeah. Cool. We'll go. Come on, Paulie." She strode over to Paulie, grabbed her elbow and swept off to the shop's door. Paulie's mind was a cluster of misbehaving fireworks after that chat with Coral, but even she noticed the door of Odyssey Ink was now festooned in illustrations. Storm-wrecked pirate ships, blackening skies, grotesque sea monsters and devastatingly beautiful merpeople. It was clearly Breeze's handiwork and it was, in a word, amazing.

"Wait." Coral stepped out from behind the desk and brought the bottle of rum with her. "Paulie. Give this to Meggie. I mean, your Aunt Meg." Paulie glanced down at the amber liquid sloshing in the glass next to the embellished skin of Coral's forearm. "I, er, remember that she used to like it. Just say it's from Coz."

"Coz?"

"Yes." Coral's dark green eyes drifted into softness for a time so short it was barely noticeable. And then they were back. Sharp. Centred. "That's it. Bye."

Paulie and Wren walked quickly together down the high

street and towards the harbour, meandering grockles flowing past them like water around a ship's hull. Paulie gripped the bottle with one hand and the other swayed in a motion strong and quick enough to propel her towards the bakery, towards home.

"Did you see it?" Wren whispered.

"I did."

And then they said it together, excitement clenching around every single word, "The smoking gun tattoo."

"So you just hit him? With an actual rock?" After a hearty supper of fish and chips, Aunt Meg was a good way into the bottle of golden rum. She'd accepted it with a twitch of surprise and then an unreadable blankness. Infuriating.

Now though, it was clear that the rum was positively relished and with every second that passed, Meg sank deeper into the old green armchair they'd had forever. Paulie was opposite her, sprawled across the sofa, willing her limbs to sink down as deep as Meg's. But it just wasn't happening. She couldn't keep still. And she couldn't stop thinking of that horrible thud against Breeze's cheek.

"Not on purpose. Obviously. And I feel awful about it."

"Well, luvver, it sounds like he's going to be fine. If Coz – Coral – says he's okay, then he's okay."

"Why do you call her Coz anyway? You two must have been close once."

Aunt Meg downed what was left of the rum and reached to the little round table at her side where the diminishing bottle sat. She poured another glass and held it to her chest, looking at Paulie with that intent stare she had sometimes. A few seconds passed and just before it could turn into tension, Meg swigged the rum right down and said, "You say you were juggling those rocks?"

"What? Oh, er, yeah. You know I was learning juggling, right? Just one of my little ADHD attempts at keeping life varied."

"I'm not stupid, luvver. This is different. I know you took up juggling because of Sage. It was just after his and Debbie's performance at the wake that the Amazon man rocked up with the parcel. So, come on, you sweet on him or what?"

"Ugh! No way. I know half of Berryport is, but not me. Definitely not me."

"Shame. It would do me a favour with the lease and everything if you two were, well . . . it could help. Never mind. Then tell me the score. Why the juggling?"

"It just . . . looked like fun. If Sage Bretton can do it, then I can bloody well do it."

"That's my girl." Meg topped up her glass. Again.

Suddenly Paulie felt a boldness shoot through her whole body. Maybe it was wrong to get Meg talking whilst the rum was running the show, but it seemed a wasted opportunity not to get something out of her. And if she wasn't budging on the whole Coral thing, maybe she'd spill some dirt on Golden Boy. "Speaking of Sage . . . you know the day of the funeral?"

"Yep."

"After you left so quickly for the bakery, Wendy's brother had a right go at Sage and his family. I think Wendy didn't want him in the line-up thingy where everyone gives their condolences. What was that all about?"

"Well, she doesn't like him, does she?" Meg's words were soft around the edges, cushioning each other.

"Oh? Why not?"

"It's obvious, isn't it? Sage, his family, the lot of them . . .

people talk about what they do for this town but nobody talks about the shady stuff."

"Shady?"

"Yep. Shady as hell. Back in the day, anyway, before they rose up the ranks. They gave out loans. High interest ones, to anyone that was stupid enough to take them on. And do you know who was stupid enough?"

"Who?"

"Arthur. Lovely Arthur Withers."

"Tanya's dad?"

"Such a nice fella, but he was troubled, luvver. Spent half his days in the Powder Monkey – that's the pub where our Fickle Fergus works so he'd tell you. Really troubled, Arthur was. Wendy was always in such a state about him. He drank away any money they had and couldn't pay the mortgage or Wendy's business loans. It was a right old mess."

"And he took out a loan with the Brettons?"

"At least one. We'll never really know. When he went missing, the debt disappeared too. Wendy still wonders if they had something to do with it."

"His disappearance?"

"She thinks either they were behind it or that Arthur *made* himself disappear to escape their demands. Who knows? The police were worse than useless."

"Couldn't Coral . . . er, Coz, solve what had happened?" Paulie remembered with a jolt what Coral had said back at Odyssey Ink. '*I'd be looking at the most rich and powerful people in Berryport.*' Is that who she'd meant? The Brettons? And did that include Sage?

"Oh, this was when she was detective somewhere else. London, I think. She probably could have though, if the case had been hers."

"How old was Tanya when all this happened?"

"I think Tanya was only about three when Arthur . . . went. So sad. And now Wendy has to cope without Tanya too. It's just awful. Come over here, maid."

Paulie scooted over to the armchair and sank into the ample spot Meg made for her. Now that her aunt's warm arms were wrapped around her, Paulie felt the fizz of tension start to disperse and wondered if actually, it might be possible to forgive herself for what she'd done to Breeze today. Plus, all this new information about Sage and his family made her feel like she was getting somewhere, even if the whole Meg and Coral thing was still a mystery.

Without even meaning to, she'd found out the reason why Wendy didn't like Sage and could absolutely understand why she wouldn't want her daughter choosing him for a boyfriend. While the rest of Berryport practically swooned over the two most beautiful people in town being a thing, it was poor Wendy's worst nightmare come true. Suddenly it looked like Paulie's mission to solve Tanya's murder was only one cog in the working parts of a much bigger machine. What if figuring out what happened to Arthur was actually the important thing here? What if Paulie had spent the last few months merely scratching the surface of something much bigger and more monstrous than she could have imagined?

Sitting there, cuddled up in Meg's arms and listening to her soft, rum-laced breath get heavy, Paulie felt her pulse beat strong against the fatigue of the day. She knew she could sleep now, in the safety and love of Meg's embrace. But she also knew that when she woke up, a new kind of energy would greet her. A kind of energy that matched perfectly to Coral Bombora's fourth and penultimate tip, which she totally intended to fulfil . . .

Persevere. Never, ever give up.

25

Romano handed the letter to Paulie with a sigh. "I'm sorry, Paulie. I know a formal warning isn't the best way to start the academic year. I did all I could but it comes straight from the top. There were quite a few complaints."

"Quite a few? Or one in particular?" It was obvious she meant Golden Boy Bretton. For all Paulie knew, his parents probably funded the entire bloody drama department.

Romano sat back in his creaky old armchair and took one of his mini plants down from a shelf next to him. He pulled out a few dead leaves and fluffed up the rest. Paulie wondered who had looked after them over the six weeks' holidays, or if Romano himself had come back every few days, armed with his pruners and some secretive growth serum. Her own miniature house-plant collection back at the flat was surprisingly not dead yet. She'd quite enjoyed tending to their simple, quiet needs for the entire summer and now wondered how much longer she could make them last.

Suddenly, his cool, blue eyes were on her. "What were you trying to do anyway, using a drama session to make everybody go through the moments before Tanya's death? You must have known it would have been traumatic for them."

"I don't know . . . I was just trying to figure things out."

"Why do you need to figure things out?"

"Well, because the people who loved Tanya deserve answers, don't they? And the police aren't giving them. In fact, I'm not sure what the police are doing."

"And what is it you think the police *should* be doing?" Romano put his plant down and stared at Paulie, propping his ginger-bearded chin up on his steepled hands.

"I don't know. Sweeping about town in trench coats with upturned collars. Making ambiguous comments in places they can be overheard. Consulting psychics and serial killers."

"Paulie, come on now."

"Okay! But they should be giving us some answers. I know I'm hardly qualified or anything but at least I took some initiative during that drama session, looking the event in the eyes, working with the people who were actually there. That's got to count for something?"

Romano held her gaze for a few moments, indulging in that annoying habit of his where, rather than answering her questions, he just left them hanging in the quiet air between them. "Paulie, have you heard of the acronym, INCUP? It stands for the five motivating factors for somebody with ADHD."

"Motivating factors?"

"The qualities an activity or task needs to make it, let's say 'worthwhile'. Shall I go through them with you?"

Paulie sighed. A surrender. She knew what Romano was like once he got started on the ADHD thing.

"Okay. So INCUP stands for: interest, novelty, challenge, urgency and passion. Do you think those are things you need in a task?"

"Wouldn't anybody?"

"Not necessarily. A lot of people can get a job done with just one of these factors but quite often, ADHDers need all five things to be present. So, it makes me wonder . . . when you were leading the whole drama class – without Josiah – through the events leading up to Tanya's death, did the task tick all these boxes? Were you truly interested? Did it feel novel? Did it challenge you in some way? Was there a sense of urgency and did you feel passionately invested? In fact, do you feel all five of these things when you think about working out how Tanya died?"

"You mean, working out how she was *murdered*?"

"Listen, Paulie, it's my job to advocate for you. I don't want to see you kicked out of college. But it's also my job to challenge you inside these four walls so you can get to know yourself better and navigate college life properly. I wanted to tell you about INCUP so you could perhaps open yourself up to the possibility that 'solving' Tanya's case, is just a way to keep your ADHD, I don't know, happy."

"Keep it happy? You talk about ADHD like it's something separate to me. Like a pet I have to keep. Romano, I didn't even know I had it until a few months ago and I've always just . . . got through." Paulie stopped, took a breath and remembered that spark her mum had told her about: *'It's like a spark of truth deep inside you. A bright, powerful spark that leads to wonderful things.'* That's what was driving her. "I don't think me wanting answers for Tanya has anything to do with being an 'ADHDer'. I think it has to do with being an actual human with actual compassion and INCUP or not, I feel it in my bones that Tanya deserves the truth to come out. Is that so hard to understand?"

"No, Paulie, it's not. Especially after what you went through as a child. Don't you think it's likely that you feel some sort of responsibility towards Tanya because of what you saw happen to your mum?"

Paulie wasn't a huge fan of silence but right now she welcomed it. It was way better than responding to that ridiculous notion. Tears pooled in the corners of her eyes and a lump of something hard and spiky formed in her throat. She twisted her necklace, hoping it would retreat back to the depths of her windpipe, perhaps disappear into her chest. No such luck. It stuck hard and fast and stabbed at her resolve. Romano offered her the tissue box but she ignored him.

"Look, Paulie. These last few months have been a challenge for everyone and not least, you. I'm on your side and I'm here for whatever you want to talk about. Just please know that management have said if you try to 'investigate' Tanya's death in any of your lessons again, there will be consequences. They need to mitigate risk. So, if I were you, I'd use this new term to turn everything around. Turn up to your lessons on time. All of them. I'll set up timetable reminders for you if you like. Hand in your assignments. Let Josiah decide on the content of this 'tribute' performance for the lantern parade. Just get on with student life and you'll be fine. How does that sound?"

Paulie raised her head and found the courage to look him right in the eye. She had an important question for him. A question she couldn't leave this room without being answered. "Why were you seeing Tanya?"

"What?" Romano tuned white as sea foam.

"I know Tanya was having sessions with you. I saw a pile of her papers on your cabinet. Why was she coming to you before she died?"

"Oh god, I thought I'd . . . never mind. Paulie, you know I can't discuss other students with you. Confidentiality, remember?"

"Did she have something on you? Did she say or do something you didn't like? Why did she need to see you on the day of the skirmish? Come on, if you can't tell me in 'these four walls' then where can you?"

"That's enough." Romano's cheery demeanour transformed into a rock-hard flatness. He was suddenly so deadpan, not even anger showed behind his eyes. "I'm going to pretend you didn't ask me this. I won't put it in my notes. Now, please do as I say about college. For your own good. This session is over." He stood up, strode over to the office door and opened it with a sharpness to rival the swooping of a sword.

Paulie gathered up her things and shuffled through the gap, past Romano's stiff and silent body and out into the creamy-coloured corridor of the pastoral block. It was empty but there were anonymous voices not far away, murmuring conversations, chatter rolling like waves. She chanced a look behind her, to try and get some sort of clue, some sort of answer to her question. But the door had been softly closed and Romano was gone.

26

Paulie pulled her puffer jacket collar up around her ears and brought the edges of the (surprisingly warm) deerstalker hat down to close the gap. The air wasn't icy, as such, but the wind sweeping in from the English Channel had got a whole lot colder during November. It was a wonder she was surprised. It happened every year. The balmy temperatures Devon boasted for so many months were always shoved aside by the bitter bite of winter around now.

It had been much earlier in the season when Paulie's mum used to wrap her up against the elements in the Midlands. Gloved hands, booted feet, always a fluffy pom-pom hat. Paulie had loved the way her mum tugged and pulled at her body, making sure everything was secure before they went outside. Squeaky, scratchy hugs. Hand-holding that felt tighter for the extra layer of wool between their fingers. All this came back to her now, as Paulie was trudging along the harbour path, heading away from town and towards Billowbreak Beach.

She wasn't exactly part of the lantern parade. At least, since the crowds had left the marketplace, she was trying her best not to be. It was tricky not to get caught up in the slow-moving shuffle of all of those families carrying glowing, home-made constructions of sea creatures. She kept her body at the edge of the glimmering herd yet firmly behind her fellow students who strode on, wearing a dazzling collection of neon, fairy-lit garments. They had spent practically all week in the drama studio, putting the final touches to what had fast become known as 'Once Upon a Tanya' and was billed in the Lantern Parade programme as *'a bright, blazing routine in tribute to Berryport's tragic angel, Tanya Withers'*. Paulie was currently battling with her fury over the gaudiness of the whole concept and a bone-deep desire to slip on one of those shimmering costumes herself.

"Come on, dude. Keep up!" Wren boomed over her luminous shoulder. "We're nearly there!"

"Okay, okay. I'm coming." Paulie hitched the canvas bag of spare battery packs across her body and kept walking. Swanny had shown a kindness giving her this job when she had refused any invitations to perform. He could well have kicked her off the project – or even the course – considering the complaints he'd had about *that* session. However, she suspected he quite liked having people around to do the jobs nobody else wanted to do. Especially when he was busy impressing the movie producers who were apparently somewhere in the crowd.

Paulie hadn't actually seen Romano at all since their last session at the beginning of term. Well, she had *seen* him – she'd actually seen him earlier tonight, buying his kid some whirling hand-held torch thingie at one of the market stalls – but she hadn't been to any of their regular appointments. It would be too weird to face him. She felt a pounding sense of guilt at questioning him so blatantly about Tanya, but was also kind of mad that he hadn't been straight with her. Why were there so many bloody hoops to jump through in the world of adulting? It was stupid.

The lively samba beats coming from the band up ahead

started to slow, so Paulie knew they must be approaching Billowbreak. The college students would be performing 'Once Upon a Tanya' on a temporary stage on the beach, accompanied by Debbie Devon who would sing a brand new mash-up of Tanya's Tune. If Paulie was lucky, she'd be able to retreat to a corner somewhere to watch the madness unfold.

When they got to the beach, she spotted a large, smooth rock just a few yards away from the corner of the stage and sat on it before anybody else could. It was sufficiently tucked into darkness so that she could see everything but nobody would really notice her. She unzipped her jacket so she could actually breathe and placed her bag at her side, ready to reach into should anybody need to re-illuminate their head-dress or cloak or whatever. She heard Swanny trill at everyone to point out where she was, but they were so busy clambering on stage and taking their places, they didn't even glance over.

The moon was huge and bulging in the sky, and together with the jagged outline of Billowbreak rockface, provided a staggering backdrop. It hung low, with streaks of silver raging across its pearly surface, throwing just enough light to provide the bodies now positioned on the stage with eerie edges of translucence. Paulie could see now, that the jet-black, fine-line illustrations Breeze had added to the neon costumes at the last minute, lifted them out of their potential tackiness. They had suddenly, under the moon's gaze, become truly beautiful. Elegant even. She felt Breeze's eyes land on her like a warm raindrop. He smiled from his place on-stage, his eye and cheek now fully healed, leaving a star-shaped scar across the top of his cheekbone. Without even meaning to, she smiled right back.

Then there was a loud tapping noise followed by an earsplitting squeal of audio feedback. "Berryport! Can I get an 'Oh yeah'?" Debbie Devon. Obviously.

"Oh yeah!" Sang back the crowd, whilst lanterns bobbed

and pebbles crunched beneath hundreds of pairs of feet. Debbie stood centre-stage, her coppery locks reaching almost to the backs of her knees, feet astride in purple, sequinned platform boots with tiny but powerful fairy lights spiralling up her calves. Her short shift dress was bright white and plain but she wore a pair of ridiculously fluffy angel wings that spread so generously outwards from her shoulders, they practically took up the whole stage. It was lucky the ocean winds weren't even a tiny bit stronger otherwise she might well have taken off. *Now that would be a BeYu moment.* A fluorescent halo hovered above Debbie's hair-sprayed head and she gripped a microphone whose wire was wrapped in shining white flowers. "Amazing! Now, before we start the performance, I have something to say."

A hush fell all around, all except for a few whispers or bleeping phones. Paulie could have sworn she heard the words, "Insufferable braggart," murmured under somebody's breath so she looked around to see who was on the same wavelength as her. There was Coral Bombora dressed from head to toe in black winter gear, stamping against the cold, lacking anything that would pass for a lantern. She clocked Paulie's eyes on her straight away, strode over and without even asking, sat down on the rock next to her. "Where's your lantern, Little Paulie?"

"I'm dazzling enough as it is."

"Same." Coral offered her a ghost of a smile before focusing her eyes back on the stage and the 'insufferable braggart'.

Debbie continued with the microphone pressed up against her lips, her voice suddenly breathy. "It's more than six months since our precious angel, Tanya, was wrenched away from us. I know that since then, we have all been in utter torment over what could have gone wrong that day." Debbie tipped her head to the starlit sky and let out a small moan. It was timed perfectly. "I know the police are doing all they can to get us some answers, to get Tanya's *family* some answers." An expertly posed pout

gave the whole crowd just enough time to look over at Wendy
Withers, who was standing stiff and straight on a podium up
front, next to some ancient bloke draped in medallions. With
the whole of Berryport's eyes suddenly on her, she practically
disappeared into the folds of her chunky-knit scarf.

"Oh dear god. Poor Wendy." Coral clapped her gloved
hands over her mouth and probably – no, *definitely* – muffled a
stream of vicious swear words. Paulie agreed with the sentiment
she supposed Coral was expressing: this was exploitation.

Still, Debbie pressed on. "It's important that we all come
together as a community, and nobody feels that more than our
very own business magnates, Rex and Bex Bretton!" A cheer
whooshed throughout the crowd, giving Paulie's tummy a brief
and sickening spasm. Coral sneered behind her scarf.

"Paulie, are you still . . . 'investigating'?"

"Erm. Well, yeah. Sorry. I know you said not to."

"Well if you are . . . watch those two. In fact, watch their son
too. They're all corrupt as hell and that lad of theirs . . . there's
something not quite right."

Before Paulie could respond, the Brettons appeared on
stage, standing either side of Debbie in winter coats so expensive
they were probably worth more than Paulie's annual Amazon
bill. Their golden boy was just metres away, beaming like an
idiot in his luminous get-up. Debbie cocooned Rex and Bex with
her outrageous wings and droned on yet more. "Not only have
the Brettons commissioned a selection of exquisite new illuminations throughout the town – which you'll be able to see in just
a few short moments – but they have also made it possible for
me to co-produce Tanya's Tune to a whole new, kick ass level!
That's right people, tonight you will witness the performative
prowess of the Bay Community College Drama Department in
their moving tribute, Once Upon a Tanya, accompanied by me
and my upgraded version of Tanya's Tune. So, before this year's

illuminations are officially switched on, can we have three cheers for the amazing Rex and Bex Bretton?"

While Coral picked up some pebbles and literally crushed them in her bare palms, the requested cheers rose in swells across the crowd. Rex and Bex beamed with shockingly white teeth, taking little bows and batting off the attention. Debbie Devon wiped some non-existent tears from her cheeks and next thing Paulie knew the whole beach was bathed in an artificial glow of gold. She and Coral looked over at the podium where Wendy was and saw her hand had been placed over a selection of switches by the medallion-adorned geriatric.

"Oh god," Coral spat. "They actually got her to switch on the lights."

"Lights? Coral, they're monstrosities." How in the actual world the Town Council had agreed to over a hundred cherub / buxom wench hybrid light fixtures dotting the path along the harbour towards town, was perhaps the biggest mystery yet.

"Paulie, I'm going to rescue Wendy. Remember. Watch them." She dropped the crushed up pebble dust onto the ground and pointed at the Brettons. She slinked off before Paulie could get anything else out of her which was, quite frankly, infuriating.

Just then, the infamous introductory notes of Tanya's Tune started up. Rex and Bex helped Debbie Devon move her panoramic, feathery mass to the side of the stage so the performance Paulie was so familiar with could begin.

After just one verse, it became apparent that much of the swooping, looping choreography had to be repositioned and the students, who were otherwise ridiculously well-rehearsed, actually appeared quite cumbersome. The new mash-up of the song included audio snippets of Tanya reciting lines from Shakespeare, which, as well as seeming wildly irrelevant, was also pretty spooky. And although the words were to do with lovers' tongues and boundless bounties, as soon as Paulie heard Tanya's voice, all she could ever remember her saying was: *'It's like you've got a death wish or something'*.

Towards the end of the tribute, just as the students were coming up to the most intricate part of their performance which involved body-rolling into a human pyramid with a succession of spinning neon flags and banners, Paulie's phone pinged in her pocket. It was the BeYu alarm. She shrugged. It would be something to do. She yanked off her gloves and held the phone up so that it framed the whole stage, as well as positioning her face for the obligatory selfie.

As she looked through the screen of her phone though, Paulie could hardly believe what she was seeing. Sage had inexplicably deserted his allocated spot in the human pyramid, causing every one of the students to tumble, slip or plummet, grabbed Debbie Devon by the hand and pulled her centre-stage, right in front of the action. Out of the corner of her eye, Paulie spotted Bex Bretton clutching a remote control and beaming up at her son with an offering of vigorous nods. Sage took a stony-faced breath and, just as Paulie tapped the button on BeYu, he planted his lips firmly onto Debbie Devon's mouth, whilst Bex brought a finger down on the remote control and Debbie's feathered wings exploded into a million starbursts of rainbow-coloured light. The crowd went wild and local history was instantly made.

Paulie lowered her phone and wondered if anybody else had noticed what she had.

Sage's fingers crossed behind his back.

"Paulie, your BeYu pic! It's total vibes! At least one person came through for us tonight." Paulie couldn't quite believe what she was hearing. And from Shazza too.

"What do you mean? I just caught the kiss like probably a hundred other people tonight." The drama students were gathered around Paulie, zipped up into coats and jackets now that the performance was over, ruddy cheeked with anger as well as the cold. Sage, Debbie and the Brettons had been whisked away by the Town Council and were probably enjoying a slap-up meal at Billowbreak Hotel by now. Swanny, who flapped after them like a highly strung seagull, had most likely wangled himself in too.

"Yeah, but nobody else got that little detail, right? Why was he crossing his fingers like that? He's a total put-about, that's why."

"Yeah," Cazza growled. "And he's never, in all the time we've been rehearsing, told us he was planning to do that. He ruined the entire finale!"

"This is truly devastating to our theatrical cause. Eternal damnations to that intolerable show-off!" Rashid threw his hands in the air and looked like he might cry.

"Well, Paulie seems to think it might have been more than that. Right, Paulie?" Cazza held her phone out for everyone to see.

"Do I?" Flustered wasn't the word. Paulie's veins whooshed with a gratifying adrenaline. The new cherub / buxom wench lights throbbed overhead and the sound of the waves gushing nearby matched the rapids in her tummy. She was flattered by the attention but words left her high and dry. She looked over at Wren, who was shrugging on her coat by the stage. Breeze stood next to her, his head bowed solemnly over his phone. She'd been making her way over to them when she got intercepted.

"Yeah, I mean, look at your caption: '*Other than the best part of the show, what else is this kiss hiding?'* Tell us, Paulie. What do you think Sage is hiding? Why on earth would he jeopardise our chances with the movie producers?"

"Erm, what? Well, I just . . . I just thought . . ." All of their faces were angled up at Paulie, waiting with bated breath. She'd never had people hang on her words like this. It was all at once wonderful and terrifying. She looked again for Wren and Breeze, hoping they might come and back her up or something. But they stayed away, seemingly waiting for her to join them. "I just thought it was a bit odd. You know, the crossed fingers. I wouldn't trust him as far as I could throw him."

"I agree. He's totes shifty. I want to break his neck for what he's just done to us. Paulie, you know more, don't you?" Shazza whispered. "Come on, you can tell us. We're your *friends*."

Friends. That sounded nice.

"I have lots of thoughts on Sage and why he's not trustworthy. In fact, I've been thinking about it for months." The words fell out of Paulie's mouth before she could apply any kind of filter. "He's tormented by something and I think that means . . ."

"What? What does it mean?"

"Yeah, Paulie, tell us!"

"Well, I think that means he had something to do with Tanya's death." There she said it. Out loud. In front of people. And now that she'd started, she just couldn't stop. "And I tell you something, I will use all of my energies to find out what that was." Paulie noticed movement at the corner of her eye and looked up to see Wren and Breeze with Coral and they were showing her something on their phones. Maybe the BeYu photo? Next thing she knew, Wren and Breeze had turned away, walking across the beach, but Coral stayed an extra few seconds. She gazed at Paulie, mouthed the words, *'Told you,'* and then delivered a sharp nod. It was a nod of agreement. A nod of alignment. And, in a strange way, it seemed to be a nod of permission.

Paulie turned back to her classmates and told them something she meant from the bottom of her heart, "I am going to prove that Sage Bretton was instrumental in Tanya's death."

Shazza's eyes widened and the whole lot of them gasped dramatically. "Oh, can we help, Paulie? Can we *all* help? Anything to nail Bretton, that show-stealing creep."

"You can. And this won't take forever, either, not now that we can work together. I reckon we could solve this case by . . . by . . ."

Cazza yelped, "When? When will we solve it by, Paulie?"

A warmth flooded Paulie's entire nervous system and the response came so swiftly, so naturally that she knew it was right. "We will solve it . . . by the next Berryport Pirate Festival."

27

Meg set the plate of Doubloon Delights down on the table and beamed. "There you go, my luvvers. That'll keep you all going for a good while. What are you working on, anyway? Anything exciting?" Meg peered down at Paulie's blank notebook, her smile broadening so far across her face, the edges of it disappeared behind her curls.

"Erm, nothing really," Paulie said. "Just college stuff." Cazza and Shazza grabbed the two biggest doubloons on the top of the pile and sank back into the booth to devour them. The other students followed their example and there were numerous, crumbly thank yous mumbled at Meg.

"Okay, luvvers. You just let me know if you need anything else, won't you? It's a quiet day, what with the weather being so bad." Meg practically skipped back to her spot behind the bakery counter and began boxing up cupcakes like it was the most joyous task on earth. *Jeez,* Paulie thought. *It's only a few college friends.* Truthfully though, her innards trembled with gladness that so many people had come to Booty Bakes. If only she'd known all along how much support she'd have had if she'd just spoken to somebody other than Wren.

"So, where do we start then, Paulie?" Rashid looked at her expectantly. "Did anybody see that article online? The one that leaked the stuff about the pistol that shot Tanya?"

Everybody whipped out their phones and followed a link Rashid quickly pinged to them all. Paulie had already seen it. In fact, Wren had WhatsApped it to her that morning, along with a voice note spoken in dull tones: "Dude, you'll probably want to see this. Let me know if you want to chat about it or whatever. Over and out." Paulie had been far too busy prepping herself for the students turning up at the bakery to get back to Wren. She'd do it later.

The article, in its capacity as a non-official theory, had every chance of being taken off the internet really soon. Luckily though, Rashid had screenshot – and potentially memorised – the entire thing. "So, remember how Torquay Museum gave us enough pistol replicas for the skirmish?" A succession of wide-eyed nods. "And remember how half of them didn't do a thing, but half of them were loaded with blanks?"

"Of course," Shazza sighed. "Those of us on the losing side of the skirmish had the duds and those of us on the conquering side had the firing ones. The safety talks were boring vibes all over, right?" Various voices agreed and sighed along with Shazza, remembering the visits from the theatrical firearms experts and the many, many demonstrations.

Rashid continued. "Yep. But as Swanny said, it was utterly important."

"And still, one of us got shot." This came from the freckle-faced girl with the neon green and black fringe, named Beau.

"Anyway, the pistols that were loaded with blanks, as you know, didn't actually have bullets inside them, just the explosive combination needed to make an ear-splitting bang and release a flare. Plus – and this is the important bit – the barrel of each pistol was fitted with a small, circular gauze, better known as a 'gate', fixed just ahead of the explosive bits and bobs." Rashid stopped, took a swig of his bubble tea and carried on. "That gate is meant to make the explosion safer and make the flare that comes out of the muzzle even more dazzling. Remember? Swanny said we needed that so that people on the harbour could see, as well as hear, when we fired the pistols."

"Well, considering we were meant to fire the pistols at the same time as the first cannon shot, it was uber important for the shots to be seen, right?" Cazza pondered this as she dusted crumbs off her lap. She'd been on the conquering side, if Paulie remembered rightly, so she'd have known all the pistol timings.

"Exactly," Rashid replied. "And it was all part of the skirmish story."

"For the conquering side to shoot their pistols in the air as a sign of intimidation to the others. That we were going to steal their loot." Cazza filled in.

"Exactly again. We were supposed to fire into the air to get all of the drama but none of the risk."

"Famous last words," Paulie offered. She figured she should say something.

"Indeed. So, according to this article, the gate in one of the pistols was faulty – basically not attached properly – so that when it was fired, it shot out and hit Tanya."

"What? That little gauzey thing could kill someone?" Shazza wailed.

"Of course," Beau answered. "It says here that it would have typically been travelling at two thousand, seven hundred feet per second." At this there was a small hush in the group and a distinct tightening of shoulders. "How would you like something like that – anything, actually – bolting through your heart at that speed?"

"Hang on, her heart? We were supposed to be pointing our pistols in the air. How could it possibly have gone through her heart?" Cazza had gone a bit white. As had Shazza. It was suddenly much harder to tell them apart. Paulie knew this was her moment.

"Seems a bit too precise, doesn't it? I knew something wasn't right. And who was standing closest to her on the day? Sage. Who had a loaded pistol in his hands? Sage. Who messed up the entire tribute performance last night? Sage. I'm telling you, he's got something to hide and we need to find out what it is."

"Now might be your moment," Rashid whispered and then nodded towards the door of the bakery.

"What?" Paulie spun around to see the bakery doors slam shut, a downpour suddenly darkening the harbour streets behind the glass. A surge of bitter air hit the back wall and, caught in its slipstream, a stony-faced, heavy-footed figure strode towards her.

"Trinket. Would you like to tell me what the hell you mean by this?" Sage thrust his phone in Paulie's face, which displayed the photo she took on BeYu and the caption underneath it. He'd obviously screenshot it. Or somebody else had and sent it to him. She couldn't imagine that he was a follower of hers. She looked from the phone to his face and saw that it was turning really quite red. His bottom lip tremored slightly and the corners of his beautiful grey eyes turned downwards with the sagging weight of imminent tears. It didn't matter. She mustn't sympathise with him. Larger things were at stake.

"I'm just telling it like I saw it, Sage. First you sabotaged the performance, betraying everybody on that stage . . ." Paulie glanced around her and the students that weren't petrified by Sage's very presence nodded at least a little. ". . . and then you acted well dodgy when you kissed Debbie Devon. What's the deal with all of that?"

"It's none of your bloody business, that's what. Who I kiss and when I kiss them is entirely up to me."

"Pfft. Debbie Devon though?" Shazza spat the words out like they were dirty.

"Oh leave off it, Shazza," Sage bellowed. "You've had it in for me since I turned you down at the wake."

Paulie sensed an exquisite moment to show Shazza – and the others – that she was on their side. "Well, we just wonder what Tanya would think about you and Debbie Devon. Did you ever stop to think about that?"

Sage's chiselled chin wobbled precariously but then quickly set into the shape of a brick before he extended his whole body and towered over Paulie like she was a baby seagull caught in a gutter. "I'm warning you, Trinket. Leave well alone, understood? The last thing I need is you making things even more . . . complicated."

Paulie didn't know what came over her. Maybe it was the audience, the energies, or the sugar from the Doubloon Delights. Whatever it was, the words streamed from her mouth as quickly as Sage had brought in the cold, "Or what?"

Sage laughed a breathy, disbelieving laugh, his eyebrows rising to new heights. "Or what? Okay. I'll show you." And with that, he walked over to the bakery counter, drummed his fingers on top and squared up to Meg.

"What can I get for you, luvver?" Meg asked.

"Nothing, Ms Trinket. I've been sent here by my parents, your landlords. As you know, the commercial lease on this establishment is almost up for renewal?"

"Oh, er, I do, yes. But I thought that . . ."

"I am now your Landlord Liaison Manager and I'll be considering the best commercial strategy for this building."

"Commercial strategy?"

"Yes. For such a prime spot, there's a lot of interest. However, I can take into account the commercial impact of the business to inform the tentative renewal of the lease."

Meg touched the back of her hand to her forehead. "Tentative?"

"Not certain or fixed." He returned Meg's panicked stare with a resolute one. "Here's my business card. Please email me and I will list the documents I need you to provide. Goodbye." He didn't even need to look back at Paulie to punctuate the point. His sharp exit was quite enough.

Not really getting the gravity of the situation, the drama students had already started scoffing another round of doubloons whilst conferring even more about the article. But Paulie was struck into stillness, only her eyes able to move around the room in fearful, sweeping arcs. It wasn't until the heat of her Aunt's gaze became unbearable that she looked up and their eyes locked. Paulie realised that all of that heart-driven fear or rage or whatever Sage felt over her BeYu post, was now fully and completely channelled into an entirely different person. Her lovely Aunt Meg.

28

Paulie didn't think she'd ever seen Swanny in such an exuberant state. And that was saying something.

So far, he'd quoted Shakespeare seven times, performed over-zealous impressions of Captain Hook, Jack Sparrow and (weirdly) Taylor Swift, grabbed a large, golden vase from the props box to mime accepting an Oscar and now he was draping himself in swathes of striped fabric bound by his very own skull and cutlass belt buckle, asking if he would pass for a buxom wench. All of this with the entire drama class's camera phones trained right on him with a special request to, "Immediately spread the fantastical news on your social thingamabobs."

With an immense stroke of luck, the daily BeYu notification came in around the time Swanny gave this instruction so there was an almost melodic burst of chimes, pops and whooshes. Paulie could hardly blame him for being excited. He'd told them repeatedly of his years of dedication to writing 'For the Love of Pirates', how he'd had countless meetings in London and how it had come so close so many times. "But it's never come this close my little thespian fledglings. It's so painfully close now I can actually smell it. Can't you? Come on, breathe deep my darlings. Fill those lungs. Success is in the air!"

Everybody did as they were told, or at least pretended to. And because Swanny awaited their reaction with the expression of a three year old waiting for a lollipop, they all agreed they could, indeed, smell the scent of success. *This is madness*, Paulie thought, and nudged Wren for a reaction. She got it. Well, she got a small smile, at least.

"So, Swanny," Rashid asked, "how come our disaster of a performance didn't put the movie producers off?" Everybody's eyes flicked towards Sage who, after a miniscule twitch of his mouth, kept his head held high. "After the human pyramid fell apart, we thought it was game over."

A shriek of laughter escaped Swanny's smacking mouth. "Because, my dearest boy, it takes more than a little tumble to put powerful people like this off. They know a profitable cinematic opportunity when they see it. And see it they did! They saw it in the streets of Berryport. They saw it in the glistening waves of the sea, the panoramic skies across Torbay, the charming cobbles of the harbour. They saw it in each and every one of you and they see it in my script. Finally!"

"What happens next, Swanny?" Shazza was teetering on the edge of her seat like she was ready to run a marathon. Only Cazza matched her in quietly tethered eagerness.

"Well, no doubt I will be needed in London over the coming weeks to secure the deal. But I can tell you whispers of something that I heard, if you promise that you will keep it between these four, heavily curtained walls?" Everybody instantly agreed and leaned further forwards on their chairs, if that was even possible. "Now that sufficient time has passed since our terrible tragedy, the producers are keen to film some crowd scenes during Berryport Pirate Festival. And what that means, my bountiful little buttercups, is that we need to make next year's skirmish bigger and better than ever!" He flung his arms in the air and spoke the last few words in a not-very-secretive fashion at all, causing the whole class to cheer.

This unified glee poured into the remainder of the session as Swanny handed out 'top secret pages' from his script and invited the students to come up with various interpretations in small groups. To Paulie's surprise, Rashid immediately made a beeline for her to be in his group, but Wren and Breeze stepped in front of her. "Paulie's with us," Wren said, giving Rashid a glare that would have made Coral Bombora twitch.

"He could have joined us if he wanted to."

"Not right now. Breeze and I want to talk to you."

"Okay, but let's at least make it look like we're working. I can't bear to be pulled up in Romano's office again." The three of them sat cross-legged on the floor in a quiet corner of the studio, putting the scripts down in the middle and huddling over the papers as if deep in creative discussion. Wren took a deep breath, but it was Breeze who kicked off the conversation.

"Paulie, are you okay after the whole BeYu thing? And that article that got leaked?"

"Why wouldn't I be?" Paulie glanced at Wren. How much had she shared with Breeze about her investigations?

"Well, we know Sage is on the warpath. We know the article was quite an eye-opener. And we know you've got half the drama class hounding you to be Berryport's answer to Sherlock Holmes."

"Dude, the hat doesn't help." Wren reached up to snatch the deerstalker off Paulie's head, but her own reflexes were way too quick. She would decide when the hat came off. Not Wren.

"Look, Wren's told me how certain you are that there's more to Tanya's death than the police even know. And that's why you were hanging around at my auntie's shop the day we met. She said you even suspected me at one point." He chuckled, the scar on his cheekbone creasing.

"I've suspected everybody at one point," Paulie said, not sure if her tone indicated that meant Breeze was nothing special or if she was making some kind of apology.

"Fair enough. It's just that, if the article is right and that faulty gate thing in the pistol means it was just a horrible accident, then Wren and I were wondering . . . don't you think that's enough now?"

Paulie didn't know why but his words smarted. "No. I don't. There are still so many questions. Why didn't the safety checks pick up on the loose gate? Whose fingerprints were on the faulty pistol? Why was Tanya shot in the heart when those pistols were supposed to be shot into the air? Why is Sage acting so shady? I don't think the police have looked into any of that properly. And anyway, I reckon your Auntie Coral thinks the same."

"What makes you say that?"

"Just something she did on the night of the lantern parade. It was, well, the way she looked at me."

"The way she *looked* at you?" Wren interjected. "Look, I know she's got a death stare to rival the dude from The Shining but that doesn't mean you should give your whole life up for this. Tanya's gone. Things are changing. We all need to get on with college life."

"You sound like Romano," Paulie sighed.

"That's because he, along with me and Breeze, just wants what's best for you. You're really flipping clever, dude. You could slay college if you wanted to. And what's with the new band of groupies?" Wren gestured over to the other students who were diligently flinging themselves into a dramatic enactments whilst also throwing occasional smiles over to Paulie. This was the first time Paulie had ever felt remotely popular and Wren couldn't possibly understand that.

"They're not groupies. They're just . . . friends." Wren made a 'pfft' sound and Breeze grimaced. She ignored them. "They also think Sage is hiding something. So we're working together to figure out what that is."

"And how's Golden Boy taking that?" They all looked over at Sage, who was, for once, working with a group of quieter students. Paulie shuddered as she remembered him staring down her aunt at the bakery counter. Poor Meg had been glued to a laptop ever since, trying to make the accounts look more profitable than they actually were and writing an entirely new business plan for the next five years. She was stressed beyond words.

"He'll get over it," Paulie mumbled.

"I wouldn't count on that," Breeze said. "He can be a nasty piece of work."

"Exactly," Paulie threw her hands up in the air, then waved them in an appropriate captured-by-pirates kind of way as Swanny swept past them. Then she lowered her voice. "You can see why I need to work out what happened. Properly. Ever since that moment in the alleyway, I've known something's off."

"Dude, she was just arguing with Sage. The police have probably interrogated him to within an inch of his life about that. You know the two of them blew hot and cold all the time. It had nothing to do with her death and as much as I'd love to see Golden Boy get his reputation hauled through the dirt, I'm worried that you're going to come out of this far worse than him."

"Ditto," Breeze added.

Ripples of fatigue pulsed at Paulie's skin, trying to work their way inside. She knew it was a matter of moments before she'd feel like death itself. Right now, words were just too tiring and totally useless anyway. The only ones she could manage were spoken slowly and deliberately, her energy reserves funnelling carefully into each syllable. She needed to keep a tiny bit of that energy to stand up and leave. "Fine. I can do it myself. Don't worry about me."

Once she got to the bus stop, however, Paulie felt the energy drain from her body. She stared hard at the bus timetable but the numbers, letters and lines swam in a blurry clump, making her eyes water. She squeezed them shut, flung her back against the bus stop wall, slid slowly down the Perspex surface, sat on the stone cold ground, and waited.

A bus would come. Eventually.

29

The month of December was totally exhausting. Meg was overwrought with worry about the future of the bakery and spent countless evenings perfecting the last twelve months of accounts as well as shaping a new business plan. If her frenzied, wide-eyed look and incessant coffee consumption were anything to go by, then her strengths in figures and forecasts were nowhere near as adept as the ones she had in baking.

She'd finally submitted the paperwork to Sage and had so far been met with a resounding silence. Paulie wondered if he was just flexing his landlord muscle to get back at her about the BeYu post rather than actually planning to revoke the lease. Either way, it threatened Aunt Meg's wellbeing and that just boiled Paulie's blood. She was sick of the Brettons swanning about this town like they owned it, especially when it was likely that they were involved in actual murder.

Sadly, she was no closer to proving that. Of course, she now had 'help' from the drama students who had started showing up at the bakery around closing time. Paulie had no idea how this arrangement had come about but wasn't going to challenge it now that she finally had some friends in her life. The problem with them showing up so late was that Aunt Meg had a habit of ushering everyone upstairs into the flat so she and Rita could get on with cleaning chores. That meant Paulie had to have people in her room. And people in her room was not something she was used to. At all.

"Ugh. Why's it such a mess?" Shazza had asked, on first entering. "My Mum would go mental if my room was like this."

"How do you ever find anything?" Rashid had wondered, his eyes wide and disbelieving.

Paulie didn't really have answers for them so had just cleared a space on the bed for them to sit. It went fine the first few times. That was, if she ignored the way they kicked their shoes through piles of stuff on the floor; the way they casually sifted through books, lip balms, t-shirts and phone chargers then put them down somewhere completely different. Watching all of this happen was like having tiny but constant electrical shocks ripple through her body. It was almost impossible to concentrate on what the students were there for in the first place. Hence why Sage was yet to be nailed for anything.

When Wren turned up one day, uninvited, it was really confusing. She only ever sat on the floor by the door, quietly working on whatever jigsaw she was on with, meaning people had to step awkwardly over her if they needed to go to the loo or something. Paulie wondered what on earth she was there for, especially since the intervention from her and Breeze in drama class. However, there was something about the way Wren methodically looked up from her jigsaw, watching the students in Paulie's room, that made her feel reassured. Protected.

This was especially true the evening Cazza started re-organising Paulie's pinboard.

"Paulie, I've always wondered about this random stuff up

here. Why are you displaying all this? Weird plant care leaflets. Not-even-completed crossword puzzles. Samples of really disgusting nail varnish colours."

"Yeah! And what are these?" Shazza chimed in. "Instructions for a robot dog. An ancient DVD case. A stupidly boring chart of juggling patterns. Crappy drawings of dragons. What the actual?" Both girls started giggling and most others in the room followed suit.

"That's enough." When Wren rose from her spot on the floor, Paulie quickly scanned the board to check for the lid of the jigsaw because Wren would only take it the wrong way. Then she remembered it was all safely tucked away under the coffee table in the living room where she'd been working on it just last night. Ice filled her tummy as Shazza and Cazza prodded at the other items one by one. She twisted her necklace hard against her neck, hoping some warmth would rush back into her gut.

"Paulie, we could be using this as a murder investigation board or something. Let's just take all of this rubbish down and start fresh." Shazza looked at Cazza and an obnoxious nod passed between them, then a millisecond of silence before they started ripping everything off the board in a fit of discordant giggles so that the items soared to the ground along with a pelting shower of multi-coloured push-pins.

Paulie jumped back and fell against her bed, clashing against the warm bodies of Rashid and Beau. She was almost blinded by the number of things going on: tearing, laughing, ripping, shouting, meddling, destroying. Overwhelm flushed through her system and there was that distant sense of acceptance that she was in the thick of it now, so much so that stillness and silence were the only concrete things to rely on.

And Wren. She could rely on Wren.

Because the next time Paulie opened her screwed-up eyes,

the students were filtering out of the room, carefully stepping over Wren's jigsaw with a sense of urgency at their heels. Paulie couldn't understand what Wren had done because there were no traces of conflict lacing the energies of the room. She would have felt it if there had been.

The sound of the front door clicking shut reached Paulie's ears and she shifted on her bed to stretch the muscles that had been wound up so tight. Wren walked back in and handed Paulie a can of Fanta. "Dude, drink this." Paulie took the can and watched Wren move over to the pinboard, hands on hips, a small sigh escaping her lips as she surveyed the empty space.

"Wren. Why did you . . . how did you do that?"

"Dude, it's amazing how quickly people will move for free booze." She showed Paulie her phone which displayed Debbie Devon shooting a live video at Berryport's local supermarket, giving away samples of locally-made, organic ale. "No need for me to body slam Shazza or Cazza. Yet."

"Oh. Okay," Paulie whispered.

Wren didn't say anything else. Not even her usual roguish smile accompanied her while she worked. She just gathered up everything that had been torn from the pinboard and started to put it all back together again. It was amazing that she could even remember the arrangement of everything because, to be quite honest, it probably wouldn't have made sense to anybody but Paulie. However, it seemed Wren's jigsaw-solving skills were being given a chance to shine.

Paulie stayed rooted to the bed, her limbs feeling lumpish and weighty. In fact, as she watched Wren work, her eyelids began to feel that way too. It wasn't long before she dropped into a deep sleep and when she woke up, close to midnight, she found that her favourite blanket had been thrown over her, her pinboard was once again complete and there was a plate of sandwiches on her bedside table. Her phone, which had been plugged in to charge and was lying next to the film-wrapped food, blinked brightly in the darkness with a new text message.

Dude, wake up. Your real friends are here for you.

30

There was no other time of the year when Paulie felt more grateful for her Aunt Meg, than in the weeks leading up to Christmas. They'd lived together long enough now to know all of each other's triggers and although Meg clearly thrived on the holiday spirit, that didn't stop her from putting Paulie's needs first.

The bakery became Meg's channel for expressing her festive cheer. It didn't matter how many times Paulie pointed out that it was unlikely pirates ever festooned their ships with tinsel, Meg still draped it across all of the shop's nautical fixtures. She also played on repeat a playlist of 'Yuletide Sea Shanties' complete with sound effects of jingling bells, crackling fires and Santa-style 'ho-ho-hos' punctuating every other verse. As far as Paulie was concerned, it was a musical travesty.

Custom was at an all-time high too. This wasn't just because people were tempted by Meg's cinnamon-dusted mince pies – it was because the prices were always slashed in December. "People have a hard enough time affording Christmas as it is, without me hiking my prices." Paulie was surprised she'd kept up that tradition this year, when she was trying so hard to prove to the Brettons that Booty Bakes was a profitable venture. But some values run so deep no amount of fear will make you compromise them.

Upstairs in the flat though, Meg held back. Paulie loved the *idea* of getting cosy around a Christmas tree, exchanging cards and gifts, but the reality felt vastly different to the fantasy. The pressure was unbelievable. How were you supposed to know which were the right cards for the right people? How were you supposed to remember everyone's names or choose the right words or send them at the right time? Gifts were even more stressful. How much should you spend? What should the gift be? How would you remember what you'd given different people? What should you wrap them in? Who qualified for a gift and who didn't? It was a minefield.

Instead, the Trinkets' flat was devoid of Christmas cheer unless you counted the pockets of space where Paulie had occasional bouts of festive energy. This year, for example, there was a cluster of fairy lights around the tv, a stretch of tinsel along the window sill and jewelled stars hanging from the living room ceiling. All of these things graced their living space in the understanding that they could be snatched away at any moment, if Paulie suddenly experienced a flare of Christmas-induced stress. Which was entirely likely.

The Yuletide Sea Chanties were banished to downstairs and Paulie could play whatever music she liked up in the flat. This was obviously going to be Gorillaz. With the outside world screaming at her to 'be jolly' and 'shop til you drop', their humorous fusion of musical styles gave Paulie an intuitive sense of peace. And the louder, the better.

In fact, she'd been playing Gorillaz at quite some volume when her aunt finished work on Christmas Eve. The repetitive cracks, ominous whistles and sparse vocals of their one and only Christmas song, encouraged her to sway right there at the kitchen sink where she was supposed to be washing dishes. That's why it was so embarrassing when Aunt Meg knocked gingerly on the kitchen door to find her dripping soapy water on the linoleum and tick-tocking her hips in time with the music. "Luvver, erm . . . we've got a guest."

Paulie spun around to be greeted by the apologetic face of Wendy Withers. She stood in the doorway with Aunt Meg, holding a small leather holdall and tapping her stiletto-booted foot nervously. "Maybe this isn't a good idea, Meg," she almost whispered. "Maybe I should spend Christmas at home after all."

"Nonsense," Meg answered, ushering her in to sit at the kitchen table. "There's no way you're going back to that empty house. Paulie, please make Wendy a cup of tea. And stick a slug of rum in it. One for me too."

Paulie snapped off her gloves and made her way to the kettle. She filled it up and flicked it on whilst an army of butter-flies had a dance-off in her belly. It was very strange of Aunt Meg to bring someone else into their space at Christmas, but she supposed she could understand it. Wendy was all alone now, after all.

"Now, Wendy, as I explained, Paulie and I don't have the typical Christmas. We take things very easy because all those bells and whistles? Well, they're a bit much for our Paulie. To be honest, it's nice for me to have a break from the kitchen so we don't have a turkey dinner or elaborate puds. But we do have each other and loads of snacks and plenty of peace and quiet and that usually suits us quite well. What do you think, Wendy. Does that sound doable?"

There was an audible tremble in Wendy's voice, but she was just about holding it together. "Oh yes, Meggie. It sounds just lovely. If you're sure I'm not a hassle."

"Anything but. It will be a joy to have you. Now, Paulie? Where's that tea?"

Paulie realised she'd been meticulously stacking herbal tea boxes into the colours of the rainbow. "Oh yeah. It's coming." She set the fragrant tea down on the table in chunky, mismatched mugs and suddenly wondered, if she focused really hard on the task, how many secrets she might be able to get out of Wendy over the next twenty four hours. She nipped back to the kitchen counter, picked up the bottle of rum and returned to the table with a forced smile. "More rum, anybody?"

> Merry Christmas, dude! How goes it in the Trinket household? Did you like the hoodie I got you?

Wren's text woke Paulie late on Christmas morning and served as a reminder that there was a parcel still sitting at the bottom of her college bag.

> Spoiler much? Haven't opened it yet.

She yawned and grabbed her bag, which was inexplicably hanging out of her underwear drawer, and rooted through it. She tore open the silver wrapping and a soft, grey hoodie fell onto her lap, emblazoned with the Gorillaz logo and their trademark band of illustrated faces. She actually loved it.

> Thanks. Really bloody like it. Sorry I didn't get you anything.

> Aw, it's cool. I know Crimbo freaks you out. Have a good one though!

It was a relief that Wren wouldn't expect any more of an

exchange than that. Anyway, she was probably busy with her parents who were actually back home for a short spell before jetting off to their next failing hotel. Paulie wondered briefly what Breeze might be doing and then remembered him saying something about going back to Bristol to spend Christmas with his dad. She had no idea what the other students were up to and wondered if there would be any festive greetings in her BeYu inbox to sift through later.

Paulie padded through to the living room and found Meg and Wendy up and dressed, albeit in comfy, slouchy clothes, with their feet up on the cluttered coffee table. They were watching some kind of Christmas dross on the telly. "Good morning, beautiful niece! Happy Christmas. Is this okay with you?" Meg gestured to the telly situation as well as the numerous bowls of chocolates, crisps and mince pies.

"I'll allow it," Paulie smiled as she crouched to kiss Meg on the cheek and give Wendy a nod. "So, is this, like, breakfast?"

"If you want it to be," Meg laughed. "Or there are some left over pasties in the fridge."

"Maybe later." Paulie dropped into her favourite armchair and eyed the bottle of golden rum sitting between her Aunt Meg and Wendy. She hadn't managed to ply them with much of it last night, but today would be different.

And how right she was. Because a few hours later, after a brisk harbour walk and a whole lot of vegging on the sofa, Wendy seemed taken over by a sudden sense of gratitude. "You know, I can't thank you two enough for inviting me here, into your home, at a time that's really hard for me." Meg tried to bat off her thanks but Wendy kept going. "The only comfort I have, really, is that Arthur and Tanya might be together. Maybe they're pulling crackers or eating turkey or something. Tanya always liked her turkey dinners." Wendy's beautiful, almond-shaped eyes reddened slightly and she sniffed daintily. "Anyway, I'd like to do something for you, if that's okay?"

"Wendy, there's really no need. Is there, Paulie?"

Paulie opened her mouth to dutifully agree with her aunt but Wendy was already pulling something out of her bag. "I couldn't buy you gifts because, well, the nail salon has been closed for so much of the year so my income is miniscule. But, there are two things I can give you: my time and my expertise." Wendy unfolded a spotless black, leather pouch to reveal a collection of manicure equipment. "It's just my travelling kit, but it'll do the job. Now, who's first?"

Meg practically leapt at the chance of getting her nails done. It wasn't the kind of thing she'd ever usually spend her money on, not only because she wouldn't have made the time for it, but also because she usually had her hands so deep in dough, it just didn't seem practical. "I doubt you can do much with these stubby little horrors, Wendy, but you're welcome to give it a go!"

Paulie watched as the two women spent the next hour or so laughing and chatting during the treatment. Wendy came alive once she had Meg's hands in hers and the slickness of her move-ments was matched by the smiles appearing more often across her face. Paulie busied herself by fetching towels and bowls of warm water but really she was entirely occupied by listening to their chat about 'the old days'.

She'd had no idea that Meg and Wendy were old school friends; that they used to smoke together at the Nautical Gardens after school; or that they would meet up at Billowbreak on weekends to see which boys were around. Apparently, Wendy only ever had eyes for Arthur though, who had also gone to Berryport High. There was no mention of who Aunt Meg had eyes for.

Once it was Paulie's turn for a manicure, the rum was really flowing. "Now don't you worry, Little Paulie," Wendy slurred slightly. "I can hold my drink and I could do a manicure blind-folded. I promise your nails will be beautiful." Truth be known, Paulie was starting to get a headache from the stink of acetone but she had a feeling now was not the time to back out. There was a current of something exciting in the air. As sure as the Christmas day fireworks now bursting in the night sky across Torquay, Paulie could feel it.

She sat cross-legged on the floor, on the other side of the coffee table from Wendy. She lay her hands out on the folded towel and Wendy gently placed them in a fresh bowl of warm water. This felt like such a kind gesture that Paulie thought for a moment she might cry . . . until she saw something dark and definite on the skin of Wendy's slender wrist. It was only just visible beneath a stack of glittering bracelets, but Paulie was sure her eyes didn't deceive her. So, she took a deep breath and just asked the question outright, "Wendy, is that a tattoo?"

31

Wendy's eyes flicked down and she seemed to take a second to decide what to say. She then reached across to rearrange the bangles on her wrist so that the full design of the smoking pistol could be seen. "Why yes, it is a tattoo. My only one."

Paulie gasped. "It's a blunderbuss, right? Flintlock or something. My Aunt Meg has the exact same one." Meg, who'd been lounging on the sofa admiring her nails, tensed up when she heard mention of the tattoo. Paulie jumped on it. "Haven't you, Aunt Meg? They're identical."

"You always were a clever one, Little Paulie," Wendy sighed.

"It's okay, Wendy. You don't have to talk about it," Meg eased the words carefully from her mouth, as if it was a creaky old letterbox. "Paulie, you shouldn't ask personal questions."

"What's the big secret? You were at school together, you were great friends. You got a tattoo. Why can't I ask about it?"

"It's not really up to me." Meg ran her fingers through her hair then immediately ripped them out again when Wendy yelped to remind her of the fresh manicure. She sighed in some kind of defeat. "Wendy, it's up to you, luvver."

Wendy completely drained her glass of rum before taking Paulie's hands out of the bowl and patting them dry with a towel. "We can talk about it. Dammit, we *should* talk about it. Especially to girls Paulie's age."

"What?" Paulie looked from Wendy to Meg. Meg to Wendy. "What about girls my age?"

"Okay, it was just something that happened when we were at school. Well, something that happened to *me* at school. And your aunt was very supportive. So we got a tattoo."

"Sorry, you're going to have to give me more than that. And . . ." Paulie practically glowed with determination. ". . . I know Coral Bombora has the same tattoo."

There was a beat of confused silence and then Wendy looked her right in the eye. "Okay. Here we go." She picked up some kind of filing tool and went at Paulie's nails like there was no tomorrow. "I was attacked. By a man. A boy. And Coral found us. I mean, she found him, trying to, well, you know."

"I do," Paulie whispered, feeling suddenly sick to the stomach.

"It happened at school. I was running an errand for a teacher and was passing the back of the school hall. Do you remember it, Paulie? That weird little corridor where they store all of the lost property?" Paulie had tried to wipe her memory of Berryport High but she knew exactly the spot Wendy was describing. It was cold and dark. Rarely populated. "This lad just went for me. The weird thing was, that he was masked. I think he'd stolen a balaclava thingie from the lost property cupboard because I remember it stank of damp. Anyway, he got as far as ripping my clothes before Coral came across us and wrenched him off me. She always did have the strength of an ox, even as a young girl."

"What happened?" Paulie stole a glance at Aunt Meg,

wondering when she came into all this, but her expression was uncharacteristically unreadable.

"He got away. Coral clocked him one good and proper but he got away and she stayed with me rather than run after him."

"Did you report it to the school?" Paulie thought that was the obvious course of action.

Aunt Meg sat up from her horizontal position and looked Paulie square in the eyes. "It's hard for you to understand, luvver, but times were different then. More than half of the school staff were male and Wendy didn't feel comfortable going into a room with a man to report this."

"Coral could have gone with her. Backed her up."

"True. And you did consider that, didn't you Wendy?" Wendy nodded, still grinding away at Paulie's nails. "But there was more. I mean, look at Wendy. She's a real bombshell, right? And she was back then too. She had so much male attention, completely unwanted, but attention like that, in those days, clung hard. And your reputation was decided for you."

Wendy grimaced. "I only ever had eyes for Arthur. We fell in love from a young age. But that didn't make a bit of difference to all the other boys. They thought they could do anything. Say anything. Grab anything. I was known as the school tart yet I'd never even kissed a boy."

"So, you felt that nobody would believe you? Because of your reputation?"

"Exactly. And they wouldn't have. Plus I was okay really, aside from a few bruises and hurt feelings."

"Hurt feelings?" Paulie gasped. "Wendy, that was trauma in action."

"Maybe. But that's how I dealt with it at the time. And then there was the tattoo. That helped me deal with it, no doubt." Wendy looked up at Paulie's face and there must have been questions plastered all over it. She shot a glance at Meg, who gave a tiny shrug, so she carried on. "Shortly after Coral picked me up and dusted me down, your lovely Aunt Meg arrived. She was horrified, bless her and they both virtually carried me back to Coral's place. First and only time I ever bunked off school."

"Me too," smiled Meg.

"We knew Coral had been teaching herself how to tattoo because she never stopped going on about it. And when we got back to hers she was so fired up, so angry at the men in the world, as well as herself for not catching my attacker, that she proposed something. She proposed a tattoo."

Meg joined in now. "We wanted to do something to remind ourselves that we would never be victims. That we would look after each other and if another unwelcome man ever came near any of us ever again, we would . . ."

"Shoot the bastard!" Wendy and Meg said in unison, notes of determination edging at their voices.

Meg carried on, "Coz, I mean Coral, has pirate ancestry – or so she tells everybody – so she suggested a pirate-style pistol."

"Then I had the idea for the smoke trailing out of it. You know, as if we'd already shot it. Like a warning." Wendy added. "Coral sketched this beautiful design, got out her kit and we went for it."

"Didn't it hurt? How old were you?" Paulie asked.

Meg shrugged. "Yes it bloody well hurt. And we were sixteen."

"Didn't your parents freak out? Aunt Meg, you'd go mad if I got a tattoo even now."

"That I would," she agreed. "But we basically wore jumpers for a hell of a long time and then, in the summer when we had our arms on show we just told our parents we'd drawn it on. By the time they realised we'd been tattooed, we were at college, off doing our own things and we really didn't care. Your grandparents, may their souls rest, weren't the most observant people in the world, Paulie."

Paulie slumped slightly whilst she took in all of this new knowledge. It was going to take some processing. She had no idea if this story could be in any way linked to what happened to Arthur, or even what happened to Tanya, but she now had a far deeper insight into the psyches of three women who, until now, she hadn't even known had a connection.

"Hang on, did you ever figure out who attacked you, Wendy? That must have been scary, not knowing."

"It was." She shuddered from her spot on the living room carpet. "But no, I never fully figured out who it was." She clearly didn't want to speak further on this so Paulie didn't push it.

Glancing down at her hands, Paulie saw that Wendy was applying a coat of silvery-grey glitter to her now perfectly shaped nails. It crossed her mind that the colour matched the new hoodie from Wren, like pieces of a puzzle slotting together by some force of good luck. "I'm so sorry that happened to you, Wendy. This being female is rough sometimes."

"True," Wendy agreed. "But I honestly wouldn't trade my femininity for the world. People round here, they look at me and they see lipstick, lashes, nails, legs. These days they see tragedy too. And all of those things are there, for sure. But please, little Paulie, don't ever feel hard done by as a woman. We are not the weaker sex. If anything, we have strength that permeates not just our muscles and our bones . . . it drips in abundance from our very spirit. My Tanya had it. You have it. We all have it. And without Coral and Meggie, I might not have known I even possess it. Or it possesses me. I'm never quite sure!" Wendy half-sighed, half-laughed, leaving the power of her words floating on the air. Suddenly Paulie could see where Tanya got her talents. It was obvious now.

"Wendy, can I ask you one more thing?"

"Of course."

"How did you feel about that article that got leaked out about the faulty pistol? It implies what happened to Tanya was an accident but do you ever wonder . . . do you ever *worry* . . . that it might actually have been murder?"

"Now Paulie, I think that's enough," Meg quickly stood up, placing her hands on her hips.

"No, it's okay, Meggie. I can talk about this now. Why don't you go make us one of your famous hot chocolates? It's not Christmas without hot chocolate." Meg hesitated, giving Paulie a quick warning look, before leaving the room and muttering something under her breath. Wendy turned back to Paulie and blew gently across her fingertips. "Paulie, I know your background, with your mum, and that what happened to Tanya has probably affected you more than some of her other friends." Paulie flinched inwardly at the assumption of friendship, but now was not the time for corrections. "I did worry at first, that somebody was out to get Tanya. Of course I did. Because I never got any answers about my Arthur."

"What about the Brettons? Didn't Arthur owe them money?"

Wendy blinked in surprise but then shrugged sadly. "I suppose most people know about that, even if it was years ago. Yes, he owed them money. He was an addict, you see. Gambling. Alcohol. I did my best to help him. I did everything . . . but until he disappeared, I had no idea about the volume of debt he got into. I suspected for ages that the Brettons had seen him off or that he'd, you know, *left* on purpose just to save Tanya and I from the financial mess."

"There was no note? No sign he would be leaving?"

"Not a thing." Wendy's voice was becoming smaller,

shakier. She began to pack up her manicure kit with tremoring hands.

Nevertheless, Paulie pressed on. "And now?"

"Now I suppose I'm used to not knowing. There was never any evidence the Brettons had anything to do with it. The police did all they could. He really did just . . . disappear."

"That's so hard." Paulie really wanted to launch into her next question but left what she hoped was an appropriate beat of silence before speaking again. "And what about Tanya? What do you believe happened to her?"

As soon as Tanya's name was mentioned, Wendy dropped her kit and everything fell to the floor. She left it there, staring at the glinting metal items as she spoke. "I just, well, to be honest, we constantly fell out over Sage. I never liked him. I never wanted her to be with him. I thought it was the worst thing that could happen, her being with a Bretton, until . . . well, you know."

"Yeah. I know. But Wendy, what do you think *really* happened to her?"

Wendy rubbed at her chest, leaving red marks across her skin, not unlike the ones Paulie inflicted on herself with the frequent twisting of her necklace. Her face became vacant as she lifted her gaze from the manicure items on the floor to the blackness of the window. Fireworks from Torquay were still bursting across the sky, creating flashes of colour that aggravated a headache Paulie had been trying to ignore. It was an effort to listen to Wendy's small voice, but she was determined not to miss a word.

"I did suspect Sage, at first. I wondered if he could hurt my girl . . . but then I saw how cut up he was and realised he had no motive. He was obsessed with her, with Tanya. Who could blame him? He didn't even want her to go to London. He couldn't bear the thought of life without her." Tears suddenly began to stream down Wendy's face, her head tipped back towards the star-strung ceiling and the next words rushed from her throat with a deep, mournful cry, "I just don't know."

"I don't know either," Paulie echoed, completely taken aback by the surge of Wendy's grief.

It was then that Aunt Meg came back into the room, carrying a tray laden with steaming mugs of spiced hot chocolate. As soon as she saw the state of Wendy, the tray was clattered onto the table and Meg crashed to the ground, wrapping her arms around her friend's small, quivering body. Paulie was amazed at how quickly the claws of grief could sink into a person and all at once felt overwhelmed by the multiple streams of action flowing around her.

Hot chocolate spilling. Nail files glinting. Manicure drying. Fireworks bursting. Headache pounding. Wendy sobbing. Aunt Meg glaring. And her heart, suddenly shamed and dark, throbbing so hard, she thought she might be sick.

32

"I don't know why you brought me here. I don't deserve this."

"Too bloody right you don't. But maybe I need it more than you do." Meg shouted over the music and handed Paulie an extortionately priced bottle of water. "Absolutely no alcohol for either of us tonight. Nightclubs are not about drinking."

"Duly noted. What are they about then?"

"Dancing, of course!" And with that, Meg started popping her body to the beat of the electro-trance tunes pounding from all corners of the dark, cavernous space. Paulie looked up to see a torrent of angular sculptures hanging from the ceiling, twitching and flashing under the soaring lighting rig. They were faces – made from brightly coloured foil, plastics and wire – twisted into all manner of weird and wonderful grimaces. Rather than being creeped out, Paulie immediately loved them because they reminded her of the ghoulish faces of her beloved Gorillaz. Which was kind of why they were here in the first place.

Since upsetting Wendy with her questioning on Christmas Day, Paulie had struggled to get out of a self-induced pit of shame. Okay, so Wendy was a grieving mother and the smallest thing could probably set her off, but things had been going well with the whole manicure thing until Paulie had dared to breathe the word, '*murder*'.

After Wendy went home, Aunt Meg had started Paulie on the silent treatment. That had gone on for at least two days. Then there had been an exhausting rush of questions: "*How could you . . ?*", "*Why did you think . . ?*", and "*Couldn't you just . . ?*". Frantic Google searches were made around ADHD and social infelicity. Eyes were rolled heavenwards. Hands were wrung out. Doors were slammed and swear words were whispered. Through all of this, all Paulie could offer was silence.

When Meg presented her with the tickets for tonight, it came as something of a shock. Nightclubs had never been her thing, what with the crowds and the sweat and the presumably awful music. However, Aunt Meg had decided they should do something different for New Year's Eve and when she'd seen a Gorillaz tribute DJ was playing at Hanwi, her favourite nightclub in Bristol, it hadn't taken much for her to reach for her credit card. The cheap hotel and the train fares seemed like pennies after that.

Being here, inside Hanwi, was a classic paradox for Paulie. She was thrilled by the very thought of being somewhere so cool and diverse. She really wanted to hear the Gorillaz DJ, but there was that thing about being in crowds that made her feel anonymous, worthless even. And she'd felt quite enough of that all week.

Paulie swallowed back her fears, tethered down her jitters and decided to do what she often did in times of doubt – follow her Aunt Meg.

She might have been imagining it, but Paulie thought she felt his presence before she heard his voice. It was like a cool sheet of silk settling over her clammy skin. "I should have known you'd be here. Gorillaz at New Year is perfect for you, right?"

"Breeze! I knew you were in Bristol but how crazy is it that you're here?"

"Same. I thought you'd be living it up in Berryport. But here you are. Partying with mad vibes." He grinned, his blue-back hair shimmering under the flashing lights and the tiny star-shaped scar at his cheek rising with the effort. Paulie felt bizarrely comforted by him turning up out of nowhere. She'd managed to lose herself in dancing over the last hour or so but now she was ready for some human interaction that didn't involve having drinks spilled on her or her toes trodden on.

"Who are you here with? Surely not your dad?"

"Yup. And Auntie Coral too. This is her favourite club. Apparently she used to come here in her youth. I think it had a different name back then, the Moon Club or something?" Breeze pointed up to the next floor where there was a split-level balcony holding a bar and another dance floor. There was Coral Bombora, her normally ruler-straight hair frizzed up to rocker heights, moshing wildly with a man who looked very much like her.

"Wow. She looks amazing. Actually, Aunt Meg just went up that way to get a drink. Maybe she'll bump into . . ." Paulie's voice trailed off as the two of them looked up towards the balcony where the energy had blatantly shifted. Coral had frozen solid, and was staring across the head of her moshing brother, towards a spot in the crowd. They followed her gaze and found that it landed, unquestionably, on Meg.

The two women surveyed each other, first practically boring into each other's eyes and second scanning up and down their bodies with a slow, steady intention, almost unbearable to watch. And although Paulie never would have guessed it, it was Coral who softened first, her tight lips blossoming into a hint of a smile that Paulie had never seen before. It was kind of beautiful. A mutual smile hovered distantly somewhere behind Aunt Meg's eyes. Even from this distance, Paulie knew it was there. Coral must have known it too because in the next moment, the next flash of lights, the next clash of music, they were deep in each other's arms.

Breeze gave a low whistle. "What was that all about?"

"Not a clue. Except, we know they're old friends. The tattoos, remember?" Paulie would tell him about Wendy's attack later. Maybe.

"Oh yeah. Listen, shall we go somewhere quieter? I've got intel." He leaned closer in and brushed her hair away from her ears. "About Sage."

Minutes later they were sitting on a large, squishy sofa, bumped up against a diverse range of people with varying degrees of audacity, energy and body hair. Paulie wriggled next to a giant man in a fairy costume and tried not to lean on Breeze too much. "Hey, it's okay," he said. "I'm not gonna bite. You sure you don't mind leaving the dance floor? You looked well into it."

"I was. Erm, I mean. I don't mind. The Gorillaz guy isn't back on until the countdown. We've got time. So come on. Sage. Spill."

Just like the day she'd met him outside Odyssey Ink, Breeze somehow, with his body and his words and his attitude, built a private space around them where he could tell her everything he knew. Apparently, he'd overheard Coral speaking with an old police associate about Tanya's case. "I was meant to be doing a stocktake but she was having this conversation in the back yard with the window open and Paulie, I know what I heard."

"What? What did you hear?"

"She was trying to get to the bottom of whether or not that

article had any truth in it and also, I think, how close they are to cracking the case. She acts like she's not bothered about Tanya's death but I know she totally is." *Too right she is,* Paulie thought. *She can't bloody help herself.* "Anyway, long story short is that when the pistols were forensically examined, quite a few of the firing ones were covered in one person's fingerprints."

"Sage."

"Dead on. Including the pistol that fired the fatal shot at Tanya."

"But that doesn't make any sense. He'd be in prison right now if the police knew that. And why would his prints be on more than one gun?"

"I guess that's what we figure out next."

"We? So you're in on this now?"

"Paulie, don't underestimate how much we want to be there for you. Me and Wren."

His words created a tension she wasn't at all interested in. "Somebody would have seen him shoot her. He's not clever enough to mask it. He's good but not that good. Damn, I wish now that I'd been on the Arching Angel that day . . ."

"Arseing Angel," Breeze said, deadpan.

She couldn't help but laugh. "Yes, the Arseing Angel. Then I might have seen something."

"Listen, I overheard Auntie Coral checking that the investigation team had been through everything. Social media photos, videos, CCTV, people's phones, witness accounts. They've done the lot. And there's no evidence to show he shot her. She just . . . collapsed."

Paulie swallowed down this new information like a lead bullet. "I guess I can share it with the others. They might know something. There's got to be an explanation."

Breeze shifted on the sofa, creating a micro-thin gap of cool air between them. "Listen, I get that you have some new friends.

I get that you want their help with your . . . investigations. Just be careful who you trust, okay?"

"Breeze, I don't even know if I can trust *you*. I've only just met you, really."

He laughed, but it settled gently over her because it was infused with such kindness. "Come on. Give yourself more credit than that. You've got to be one of the most intuitive people I've ever met."

"Apart from when I hit you with an actual rock."

"Yeah, well, the actual rock did hurt. A bit." His fingertips brushed his hair back to reveal his scar. "But I kind of like this. Gives me Scarface vibes. Plus I think it's shaped like a kind of star, or maybe . . . a spark."

"A spark?" Paulie's mind leapt straight into the memory of her mum describing how she would recognise her intuition. *"It's like a spark of truth deep inside you. A bright, powerful spark that leads to wonderful things."*

"Yeah. You know what a spark is, don't you Paulie?" He left a few beats of silence, presumably to demonstrate said spark. And the worst thing was, Paulie couldn't deny it was there. "Of course you do. And I just find you so . . . oh god, what's the word? Sorry, but sometimes when you look at me like that I can't, I mean, I forget my words. Paulie, I wish you could see. You're just so . . . well you're so unbelievably likeable."

That word, *likeable*. Another memory, an entirely different one, crashed into her consciousness.

She was being dragged out of a strawberry-smelling taxi. Her little hand pulled so forcefully her arm was on fire. Legs barely able to keep up. The heavy stomping of her dad's booted feet. The tight feeling of a scratchy, black dress that had been waiting for her on her bed that morning. The glossy tracks of tears still burning down her cheeks.

"Paulie, are you okay?"

The door of the bakery was different back then. Scruffy. Peeling paint. Splats of seagull poo all over the ground. Just-baked scents floating on the air, clashing with the salty brine of the sea slapping against the harbour walls just metres away. A pirate ship. A big one. At any other time she would have begged to climb aboard but the way her dad yanked her body, she didn't dare.

"Paulie, seriously. I need to know you're alright."

Aunt Meg had rushed out, surprise plastering her face. Whatever the adults were talking about, it was bad. She ached for her mum profoundly and twisted the pendants on her necklace deep into the soft skin of her neck. It felt . . . not good, exactly, but gave her pain a place to go. To burrow. Then her body catapulted forwards with a force she'd been unaware her dad possessed. Meg took her hand and gently placed her behind her legs, as if that would create some kind of sound barrier for the words he was about to say.

"You take her. I can't look after her anymore. She's not an easy child to like."

"I'm not easy to like," Paulie murmured.

"What? Are you kidding?" Breeze went to grab her hand but then thought better of it. "Listen. Can I hold your hand for a minute?" She was gradually coming back to the night, to the club, to him. So she nodded. "Good. I don't know where you get this idea from, that you're not likeable but I can tell you, from personal experience, it's the opposite of true."

"You have to say that," Paulie whispered.

"No, I don't. Paulie. I like you." He took a deep breath that brought colour to his cheeks, then lifted her hand and pressed her knuckles to his mouth. It wasn't exactly a kiss, but it was intimate. Tender. "I've liked you from the first moment I saw you."

"The first moment?"

"The first moment."

There was a sudden roar that screeched off the walls of the entire nightclub. "Ten, nine, eight, seven . . ."

"Oh my god, it's midnight already," Paulie yelped.

"Six, five, four . . ."

"Well, what are we waiting for? Your DJ's back on now, right?" Breeze took her hand with an intoxicating combination of grace and excitement and whilst the surrounding cries of, "Three, two, one!" exploded around them, they dashed back to the dance floor, finding a spot just big enough for the both of them.

Paulie closed her eyes, imagined what it would be like to be someone who didn't care what people thought of her and used Breeze's presence to lull her into a state of immense wellbeing. The addictive bass line of 'Feel Good Inc' immediately flooded her with the most delicious sense of familiarity and her body moved with a confidence she'd always hoped had been hiding in there somewhere.

Maybe it didn't have to be so hidden anymore.

33

Wren slammed the paper and pens down on the table and said, "There. Use these."

"What's the point of this again?" Cazza asked, her lip-glossed mouth framed by the froth of a mocha-chocca-latté.

"The point of this, is to stop you lot from shouting over each other. It's just not helping." As Wren spoke, Paulie shrank her stiffened body into the corner of the booth, trying not to seem like the reason for this sudden change in strategy. "Look, I know you're all in a bit of a state after what Paulie said about Sage and the fingerprints. And yes, maybe we are getting closer to the truth. But seriously, dudes, what's with all the shouting? We're in a public place, remember?" Wren swept her arm out to gesture towards the bakery, which was full to the brim with customers. Meg's January offers were enough to get anybody in off the streets.

"I don't understand why we can't go up to Paulie's room anymore," Rashid wailed. "It was kind of comfy and nobody could overhear us."

"Just because, okay?" Wren stared him down. Paulie was grateful she didn't mention the dismantled pinboard. The last thing she wanted was to scare her new friends away with seeming too precious about her stuff. But she had to admit she was happier with this new arrangement. It did run the risk of being overheard though, especially when it was becoming increasingly obvious that the drama students *really* liked the sound of their own voices.

Paulie took a deep breath and tried to find her own voice, which had diminished rapidly when the shouting started. "Wren's right. This is a much better idea. Okay, so we're all clear on what we're doing? You take a piece of paper and write on it anything – and I mean anything – that you noticed was even slightly out of place on the day of the skirmish. Then fold it up and put it in . . ." She looked around for some kind of container and Wren handed her an empty cake box from one of Meg's displays. "Here. You put it in here."

"Then what happens?" Shazza whinged.

"Then, when I've got time, I'll look at them all individually and see if there's anything that helps us understand the finger-print thing."

"I don't understand why we can't be in on that. It's our project too."

"Investigation," Paulie corrected. "And you can be in on it. Next time we meet, okay?"

"Fine," was the resounding response and everybody grabbed a pen and paper. The cake box filled up gradually during a welcome quiet that gave Paulie's nerves a chance to settle. Over the heads of the concentrating students, she glanced around the bakery and watched as her Aunt Meg moved swiftly from table to table, offering smiles and endearments as generously as she did pots of coffee and sweet bakes. Meg had been in a strangely good mood since New Year's Eve and Paulie wasn't about to challenge it, especially if it helped her get through the torturous wait for Sage's verdict on the lease.

Today Meg had enlisted the help of Rita the cleaning lady who was currently stood behind the counter, waiting for Fickle Fergus – who was rocking a velvety tricorne along with this tracksuit – to make up his mind from the day's specials. She held up various plates of delicious things, clearly trying to sell the virtues of each, but Fergus maintained his constant chin-stroking. Poor Rita. She'd learn soon enough to get on with something else until he reached the winning decision.

"Right. Is that it? Because I'll never forgive myself if I miss the script reading." Rashid sprang to his feet and brushed some doughnut crumbs off his belly in an extremely Swanny-like fashion. "Who's coming?" The rest of the students nodded eagerly and started draping themselves in scarves and big winter coats.

"Yeah, fine. Just go. I can't because, erm, I've got to work. Tell Swanny for me." The students were so used to Paulie skipping class by now that they didn't think anything of her ducking out of the session. Wren, however, gave her a shrewd look that could have bored more holes in her than one of Meg's crumpets.

"Dude, is that the best way to start the year?"

"Wren, I'm just tired. I can't face it."

"Breeze will be there."

"And?" The thought of seeing Breeze again made her stomach flip at the same time as warming her right through. But it wasn't enough. The fatigue was winning this one. "It's since the clubbing at New Year. And meeting up today. I just need . . ."

"Your blanket and a bowl of Super Noodles," Wren finished for her. "I get it. I do. But you'll have to convince Swanny. And probably Romano too. Here. Take the box with you and we'll look at it together later, yeah? Bye." Before dashing out of the bakery, Wren handed the box to Paulie and, with the now tantalising thought of her blanket and noodles, she spun out of the booth smacking hard and fast into another person. A cloud of expensive perfume erupted on the impact.

"Wendy!" Paulie exclaimed.

"Oh! Paulie. I'm sorry about that. I was just going to the loo while waiting for my coffee. Look at the mess we've made!" They looked down at the floor where the entire contents of the box had spilled out, as well as the innards of Wendy's handbag. The last thing Paulie wanted was for her to see anything the students had written, so she quickly knelt down to sweep up the papers. "Oh look, your nails are still so nice. Good for you for keeping them like that. I doubt your aunt has managed the same."

"Oh, yeah. Thanks. You did a great job." Wendy scooped up the contents of her handbag, including a multitude of lipsticks, mini perfume bottles, tissues, chewing gum, quite a few crumpled white envelopes and some photos. There was one of Tanya and one of a very handsome man with striking, smiley eyes, who she presumed was Arthur. "Wow, Wendy. Arthur was fit. I mean, erm, handsome."

"Oh yes. He really was. Best looking lad in Berryport. Until the drink took him, anyway."

"Buccaneer Bounty. Wasn't it, Wendy?" Fickle Fergus was now settled inside the booth Paulie had just vacated. After all that, he'd decided on a cherry flapjack and a chai latté. "His favourite ale?"

"Oh, er, yes, Fergus. He loved a bottle of Buccaneer. Anyway. Best get on." Wendy zipped up her bag and gave Paulie a quick squeeze on her shoulder, eyes glistening ever so slightly. "You look after yourself, Little Paulie. And Happy New Year." And with that, she dashed into the ladies' without a backward glance.

"Nice one, Fergus." Even Paulie knew that reminding

Wendy of the very reason she'd lost her husband was a conversation no-go.

"What?" Fergus asked, straightening his tricorne. "It was his favourite ale. We used to get it in, just for him at the Powder Monkey."

"Fine. Whatever. I can't believe it's me saying this, but just think before you speak next time, okay?"

"Okay, Little Paulie. You run along now. You look shattered."

When Paulie slumped on the sofa in the flat, wrapped in the very blanket Wren had referred to earlier, it was the box of papers she reached for before Super Noodles. She unfolded the first few bits of paper.

Shazza's lip gloss was basic.

Cazza was wearing my earrings.

Swanny's hands were dirty.

Useless. When Paulie next dipped her hand into the box, rather than a piece of paper, she pulled out a white envelope. She immediately recognised it as one of the envelopes that spilled out of Wendy's bag and realised she must have put it in the box by mistake. No worries. She would leave it behind the bakery counter and somebody would give it to her next time she was in. Paulie was far too tightly wrapped in her blanket to do it right now.

She turned the envelope over in her hands and noticed the seal had already been ripped open. It was crumpled too. She might have been reading too much into this, but it seemed like the crumples were deliberate rather than a result of being bashed around in a handbag. They had a concentric quality to them, as if they'd been crunched inside a fist. Should she open it? It went against everything she'd ever been taught to invade a person's privacy in that way, but the inquisitive sensors seemingly embedded up and down her spine were on deliciously high alert.

Before Paulie knew it, she was removing a note from the envelope and smoothing it out. She read carefully, trying not to let her eyes race ahead of her brain.

My darling Wendy,

My love for you grows stronger every day, even when I think it must be impossible. I know you're alone and I never meant it to be that way. Hold out a little longer and we can finally be together. After all these years.

Always yours,

R

xxxxx

The words on their own were enough to throw Paulie's brain into somersaults, but there was something else, something more physical and immediate that made her nerves erupt into a million, potent starbursts. She *totally* recognised the hand-writing.

Paulie grappled for her phone that was hidden in the folds of her blanket, and bypassed some stern texts from Romano about attendance. She opened the 'Project Skirmish' WhatsApp group Rashid had set up weeks ago and started to tap her thoughts into a message. They'd go mental over this, definitely. However, because her senses were firing on all cylinders, she immediately felt this wasn't right. It was like her instincts were acting on her behalf so she copied the text, deleted it and pasted it into a message to Wren.

Can you turn around and come back? I've just found something. Something big.

34

The wind was chopping over the waves like a knife but it wasn't quite severe enough for the Town Council to have closed the pier. Paulie had hoped the rubbish weather would deter Romano from his idea of a 'walking appointment', but sadly not. The man was wrapped from head to toe in co-ordinating winter gear whilst Paulie was dressed in a mish-mash of the warmest clothing hastily snatched from her floordrobe. She had on her trusty deerstalker, obviously, with a pair of furry, rainbow earmuffs over the top. She pulled them more snugly over her earlobes and burrowed her nose into a soft, woollen scarf.

Romano was an insanely fast walker for somebody with a missing leg. "Are we in some kind of rush?" Paulie asked.

"Not at all. Sorry, Paulie. I'm just stoked that the college has agreed to this idea of mine. Isn't it good to get out of the counselling room?" He slowed his pace and gestured at the silvery sea crashing against the breaks surrounding the length of the pier. "And it must be easier for you too, considering we could do this so close to your home."

"I guess."

"I want to make things easier for you, Paulie. I know you're keen to stay on track at college but the only way I can help you is if you actually turn up to our appointments. So, I thought you could help me trial the whole outdoor counselling thing. Is that okay with you?"

"Yup. This, I can do." To be fair, it was a far sight easier than getting on a bus and if Romano was willing to come to Berry-port, then there wasn't much she could do to duck out of it. Plus it helped to bridge that awkward gap since she'd confronted him about Tanya in her last appointment. Not that she didn't still want to know why the hell Tanya had needed to see him so badly on the day of the skirmish.

As they strode along the pier, Romano banged on about the winter wildlife of the Torbay coast as if she'd actually asked him about it. Maybe she had. She often doled out mindless plati-tudes if it meant keeping up the appearances of being socially adept. For all she knew, she might have hit him with a "Wow. Tell me more" and that would have been enough to propel him into this current monologue about the winter habitation of seals.

While Romano droned on, Paulie reflected on the recent discovery of Wendy's love letter. Wren had, predictably, rushed back to the bakery and examined it with Paulie. Both of them were sure they recognised the handwriting but couldn't quite place it so the question of who 'R' was had flung them into a bout of fruitless list-making. Neither of them could work out how old the note might be, although Wren agreed that the paper wasn't ragged enough to have been knocking about in Wendy's handbag for long. She'd even taken a photo of it so she could go away and examine it some more. Paulie had put it under the bakery counter, meaning to return it to Wendy when she got a chance.

The obvious assumption was that Arthur was somehow alive and well, operating under an alias and planning to come back for Wendy. Those words, "*I know you're alone and I never meant it to be that way,*" were more than a little haunting. But if the letter was from Arthur then why was it crumpled? And why were all the other letters that had spilled out of Wendy's bag also scrunched up? Surely Wendy would have taken care of any communication that came from her beloved Arthur?

Paulie had kept the story of Wendy's school attack mostly to herself. She knew with a visceral shudder that it wasn't something to tell to just anyone but she had shared it with Wren and Breeze. They'd been pleased to get an explanation for the tattoos but none of them had any idea what relevance this had to Tanya. Nevertheless, Paulie couldn't shake off the third tip Coral had given her back in the early summer: *Treat everything as evidence.*

Once Romano reached the lighthouse at the end of the pier, he spread out his arms and for one horrible second, Paulie thought he might beat his chest like Tarzan. Instead though, he turned back to face her and grinned in a way that was almost infectious. "Doesn't it make you feel glad to be alive? Makes your worries seem smaller, doesn't it?"

"So, do you have a lot of worries?" Paulie couldn't help herself. Romano dropped his hands and his playful grin transformed into something softer, imbued with a patience that seemed tailored just for her.

"Okay, Paulie. I get it. It's not fair for me to always be asking you stuff. So go on, shoot."

"What?"

"I mean it. With the time it takes us to walk the length of the pier back to Billowbreak, you can ask me whatever you like. But remember I can't speak about others, okay? Confidentiality is something I'm very strict about."

"Fair." The two of them headed past the lighthouse and tracked their steps back to the beach. Mercifully, the wind was behind them now, so it was like walking along a calm, quiet tunnel but with all the same scenery. Without the wind and the shivering and the spray of the waves, Paulie could actually hear her own thoughts. "So, do you have a lot of worries then?"

Romano chuckled. "Define 'a lot'."

"Erm, enough to keep you up at night."

"Sure. Sometimes. Don't we all?"

"I don't know. As a college counsellor, I thought you'd have your worries lined up in a row and, like, shelved or something." She could just imagine his shelf of worries. It would be neat and tidy and there would be succulent, green houseplants at either end.

"I'm not a fan of shelving, Paulie. It's hard to explain but, over the years, I've learned that the hard feelings have to be felt too. Perhaps even more so than the pleasant ones."

"That sounds suspiciously like hippy shit to me."

"Maybe so. But what other option do we have?"

"Smash them. Squash them. Crumple them up in your fist." Wendy's letter sprang to mind.

Romano rubbed the back of his neck, seemingly inviting the sea air into the space between his scarf and his skin. "Obviously, those are human instincts. It's the fight or flight mechanism. But our brains have advanced remarkably over thousands of years and we're now capable of reasoning, feeling and experiencing without fear. Or actually, maybe alongside it."

"Alongside fear? So you've been feeling fearful recently?"

He shot her an amused glance. "Wow. That escalated. Okay. Fear. Have I been feeling it recently? In all honesty? Yes."

Hoping that it was nothing to do with where the Berryport seals were going to stay over the winter, she ventured, "What are you fearful of?"

"Wow. You're getting good with your open questions. I'm hoping you've got a compassionate ear too?"

"Absolutely. I have my special ear muffs of compassion on."

Paulie twanged the insanely colourful earmuffs against her ears and immediately tried not to show on her face how much that had just hurt.

"Well, without divulging anything that would mean telling somebody else's story, I'll say that my fears have mostly been centred around my tendency to hesitate. I sometimes worry that I've let people down by not acting more quickly for them."

"Let's unpick that, shall we?" Paulie giggled, knowing she was directly quoting Romano on at least a squillion occasions. And the joke wasn't lost on him. Damn, it felt good when she got these things right.

"So we're unpicking now? Okay. Sometimes, being a trained counsellor means finding the correct balance between intuition and all of the rationale from the training I've undergone. It's a tricky line to walk. Compassion and rigour."

"Are you talking about hesitations you've made in your work? With students?" Paulie knew she was digging but this was too much of an opportunity not to. Plus, in all its moody, silver-stoned glory, Billowbreak was almost upon them.

Romano brought his fingers to the rim of his thermal beanie hat and adjusted the way it sat on his head. Were those beads of sweat Paulie spotted? Surely not in these temperatures.

"Not necessarily. I sometimes think I'm too hesitant in many areas of my life. At home. With my kid. With friends and family. Contrary to popular belief, us college staff do have lives outside of the building." Something had changed in his voice. It was subtle but it was there. A tone higher? A beat quicker? She wasn't sure but the embedded conviction of his earlier statement about feeling fearful was gone. "Anyway, I hope that convinces you that I'm human like you? Now, we've got a bit of time left before my next walking session. Shall we get a hot drink to warm up?"

They arrived at Billowbreak and the wooden picnic tables

that lined the periphery of the beach were mostly vacant. Romano was intent on switching the dynamic back around so Paulie said yes to the hot drink, knowing that it was her turn to be under the microscope. He left her at one of the tables after dumping his jacket and phone on top of it. Yes, the winter sun was streaming down on them but she didn't think it was warm enough to even consider removing a coat. Maybe he was sweating about something after all.

Just then, Romano's phone buzzed. For some unfathomable reason, it made Paulie's nerves jangle so she scooped it up with shaky hands and pushed it under the folds of the coat. A tinny voice streamed out from beneath the fabric. "Mable, is that you?"

Crap. She must have hit answer by mistake. Now what? She pulled the phone back out and wondered if she could get away with just hitting the end call button. "Mable, it's Dev. Can you get a message to Romano? I know he usually leaves his phone with you when he's with a student." Mable was the counsellors' secretary. She'd set up Paulie's initial appointments with Romano shortly after her diagnosis. Dev, she wasn't so sure about.

It was no good. The people-pleasing part of Paulie struck hard. "Yeah. Sure."

"Great. Because in his voice message, he gave the impression it was important. Tell him that formal complaints do have to go through HR procedures which can be found in the staff handbook. It wasn't clear if he was talking about a complaint from him or a student. Or even if the complaint might be *against* him. Do you happen to know?"

To be fair, Paulie did answer truthfully. "No."

"Fine. Well, the process is slightly different but either way it's in the handbook. And he hinted that it might be a historical complaint, which makes things a bit trickier but all the more reason for him not to be hesitant, you know?"

Hesitant. Romano had been fearful of hesitation. Could this be at all connected to what he'd said on the pier? Paulie said a quiet goodbye to Dev and had to decide quickly what to do next. Give Romano the message or keep it to herself?

She knew down to her core that she shouldn't have taken the call, but at the same time, felt elated that she had. What with secret love letters to Wendy Withers and historical, mystery complaints concerning Romano Smith, Paulie's day had just got a whole lot more interesting.

And that's what made her hit delete.

Romano returned from the bistro with two cups of something hot in his mittened hands. The smile he wore was unsuspecting. Paulie felt a credible tremor of guilt before squashing it, shelving it, keeping up the pretence of obedient college student. The nutty aroma of milky coffee found its way into her nostrils and made her stomach lurch. How on earth was she supposed to consume something in this state of agitation? She made a decision to herself then and there that she wouldn't drink it at all. Twenty minutes of pretending to sip whilst babbling about herself should do the trick. She could do that.

Then she'd be out of there.

35

The damp, dingy WWII look-out shelter smelled vaguely disgusting but it was the only place in the Nautical Gardens where the students could meet away from the wind that whipped the cliffside. Meeting in the bakery wasn't a great idea because going through the papers in the box required some privacy. You never knew what prying ears might be around in Booty Bakes and even the Doubloon Delights weren't enough motivation to risk being overheard.

Shazza sighed and dusted some WWII brick dust off her ankle-length golden gilet. Apparently nobody told her she wasn't going on a red carpet today. "Can we just get on with it please? Paulie, do these papers that we wrote the other day actually have anything interesting on them or could I be spending valuable time with my eyebrows?"

"I don't know. I only had a chance to look at a few of them. Here you go." Paulie handed Shazza the box and the students practically tore off the lid to get inside.

"What was wrong with my lip gloss?" Shazza demanded, holding up one of the notes. The question was addressed at nobody in particular, but Paulie didn't miss the scarlet flush across Cazza's cheeks.

"And those were *my* earrings, actually," Cazza stated to nobody in particular again. "I've had them, like, forever."

"Let's just pull out the notes that might have something to do with Sage and the fingerprints. Or that look interesting," Paulie suggested. "I know we have to be diligent, but there will be loads in here that's useless."

"I don't know. Lip gloss is important." Wren muttered it from where she stood at the entry to the shelter, a smile edging at her mouth. As usual, she was stood on the periphery of the group, only getting involved when things got a bit messy. It made Paulie wonder if Wren actually wanted to solve this thing or just be in on the action. Whatever. She had enough mysteries to deal with without musing over Wren's motivations.

Rashid held out his satchel, the lid peeled back. "Stick all the useless ones in here," he said. "We can keep the promising ones separate." After filtering out statements about the weather, random costume details and Swanny's new and varied terms of endearment for the group that day, they were left with just four notes.

"Right. Let's go through them one by one. Who wrote this one?" Paulie held up a slip of paper that read:

Tanya and Sage did a massive snog.

Beau raised her hand. "Okay, Beau. What was so weird about the kiss between Tanya and Sage?"

Beau attempted to blow her heavy fringe out of her eyes with an instantaneous lack of success. "There was just something about the urgency of it. She came sprinting onto the ship, just before everything was about to start and basically threw herself at him. Then she snogged his face off. Like, properly. I remember thinking it was strange because they'd been huffy with each other at Booty Bakes. But this kiss, guys. It was as if it was the last time she was ever going to kiss him."

"Bleurgh," Shazza retched.

"Poetic," Rashid crooned.

"Maybe they were just having a mammoth make up sesh after the fight Paulie saw them have in the alleyway?" Cazza was potentially better at joining the dots than any of the other students, but Paulie couldn't help thinking that Tanya throwing herself at Sage was unlikely after what she'd witnessed. How could they be on smooching terms after such a short amount of time? The facts hopped about in Paulie's brain like perky little elements of an algebra equation wanting desperately to be solved. And the very idea of algebra was enough to make her feel unsteady on her feet.

"Okay. Let's move on. Now what's this about an extra pistol?" Paulie held up a note that read:

Where was the extra pistol?

"That's mine." Wren joined the group now, bringing the cold snap of the wind into the shelter as she moved away from the entrance. "It suddenly occurred to me that there may have been a floating gun."

"Explain please." Paulie couldn't believe she was only hearing about this now.

"Well, I was thinking about the list of students that the safety company had. Paulie, your name would have been on that list because you were originally supposed to be in the skirmish. And you were cast in the conquering troop of pirates, right?"

"Right."

"So, you would have had a loaded pistol. Right again?"

"Right again. I even had the safety training." Paulie remembered all too well trying to play along with the assumption she'd be in the performance with everybody else.

"So, that means there was one too many loaded pistols and nobody would have even noticed. Except, perhaps, for the person who was wielding it. Like, with intent."

"Damn, Wren. Wouldn't the police have picked up on that?" Beau was as wide-eyed as the rest of them.

"You'd think so. But not if they had the original cast list and Paulie's name was on it. I don't know. I guess I'm reaching a bit. Just thought it was worth noting."

"Totally," Beau agreed. "So, somebody could have been messing about with two pistols, maybe? Or they could have intentionally replaced an empty gun with the faulty one? Woah. That opens things up a bit."

"Yeah, that means we could be looking at somebody from the losing side of the cast." Cazza shuddered.

"This is ridiculous," Shazza whined. "We're not supposed to be implicating other people now. We all know Sage's fingerprints were on the faulty pistol. Can we get on with proving that please?" It wasn't often Paulie felt on the same page as Shazza, but these were strange times.

"Okay, okay. Let's do these last two. Now, who wrote this one?"

Peg Leg waved at Tanya.

A tall lad with an impressive moustache raised his hand. He was potentially the love child of Snoop Dogg and Luigi from Super Mario Bros and although Paulie was getting better at names, she couldn't quite grasp the certainty of his. Adam? Axel? It was probably best not to even try. "Can you elaborate?"

"Yeah. Like, it's probs nothing. But, like, he waved at her just before she took her position. From the harbour. Like, in a way that, like, looked as if he was going to be waiting for her afterwards. Like, after the skirmish." Swanny's absolute favourite phrase ran through Paulie's mind whilst she listened to Adam / Axel speak. *"It's not* <u>*like*</u> *anything, darling. It either is or it isn't."* Unfortunately, she didn't credit herself with quite enough charisma to pull it off.

"Can you describe the wave? Friendly? Aggressive?"

"Neither. It was, like, reassuring. Like, an agreement."

"And nothing was said?"

"Nothing was said."

Paulie figured there was no way forward if she didn't share at least some of the stuff she knew with the students. So, she told them not only that Tanya had been looking for Romano that day, but also about the call she'd received on Romano's phone about the historic college complaint. Remembering her rainbow 'earmuffs of compassion', she didn't feel right disclosing exactly what Romano had said about being fearful of hesitancy, so she left that out. Her brain didn't seem to know where her moral boundaries were these days but at least her body was good enough to give her warning signs.

After her disclosures, everybody started talking at once.

"So there's a chance the complaint was something to do with Tanya?"

"Maybe Peg Leg had something on her."

"Or she had something on him."

"We all know he saw her for counselling."

"Maybe Tanya was complaining about Peg Leg . . ."

". . . and he wanted to talk her out of it?"

"Yep. Yep. Loads of possibilities," Wren stepped in, stopping the overlapping voices in their tracks. "Shall we do the last one? It's getting dark and I don't fancy sticking around to see if there are any WWII ghosts that guard this thing at night."

Paulie held up the last slip of paper for everyone to see.

What she hadn't realised, was that during the seconds before, when everybody had been talking over each other, the daily BeYu notification had come in and phones were instantly released from the confines of pockets and bags. The timing of it was perfect in the eyes of Shazza, Cazza, Rashid, Beau and probably the rest of the drama crew. But to Paulie, who now had an excessive number of phones pointed right at her, it couldn't have been worse.

Because the note she was holding up, right next to her stupidly smiling face . . . the note she was holding as phone cameras snapped, totally inappropriate captions were added and photos were irrevocably posted . . . was possibly the note they'd been looking for all along:

Sage juggled the pistols and then Tanya was dead.

When Paulie arrived home, her Aunt was sat motionless at the kitchen table, staring at her open laptop. There was no 'Hello, luvver,' or the usual mug of tea shoved into her hands, so she knew immediately that something was up. She didn't even drop her bag or shrug off her coat. Instead, she moved straight over to stand behind her aunt so she could see what was on the screen.

It was an email from Sage.

Sent ten minutes ago.

After reading the words, Paulie felt a kind of numbness take over. All she could think about was the fact that the laptop might short circuit if any more of her aunt's tears fell onto it. She waited for a crackle, a flare. She almost willed it. At least it would snap them both out of this unbearable moment.

Meg's tears were silent. Paulie tried to focus on the words again. It was an arrogant display of harsh, black letters and she actively wished she could transport those words back through time and into one of the school books she used to purposefully drop in muddy puddles. Damn the advancements in technology that meant communication like this couldn't be ignored, hidden or destroyed. Because even if Meg's tears did short circuit the laptop, the email would still exist.

Finally, Meg spoke. "Who's this prospective tenant? Why would he even think about offering my tenancy to somebody else? And that increase in rent? It's ludicrous. Paulie, we'll never afford it."

Paulie opened her mouth to speak, to offer her beloved aunt some appropriate words of reassurance. *Everything will be fine. We'll find the money. There will be a way.* But the words, although clinging to the fringes of her voice, couldn't be said out loud. Not when the whole reason that email existed was – to all intents and purposes – her fault.

36

"I don't know, dudes. I honestly expected tea and biscuits rather than . . . this." Wren took a swig from a toddler-sized bottle of blackcurrant squash, it being the only non-alcoholic drink on offer. Her whole face squirmed a bit and she set it down on a nearby shelf. "I might go looking for teabags and a kettle."

"If we'd known, you could have brought flasks from the bakery, Paulie." Breeze was sat on the carpet at the girls' feet and the mention of the bakery nearly made her kick him. But he wasn't to know about Sage's email. As far as anyone else knew, Booty Bakes was there for the long run, and she'd keep it like that for now.

Paulie worked hard to pull her focus out of that dark place and force it back into Swanny's so called 'office'. Because the drama studio was in constant demand by other departments, Swanny had wangled the most swanky space on campus. It came complete with floor-to-ceiling windows, squishy sofas and glass cabinets he'd packed with trophies that archived his entire history of thespian accolades. The room, Swanny always insisted, was infused with a theatrical magic perfect for audition prep, note runs and solving any and every drama-based crisis.

That's why, Paulie was guessing, he'd offered it up for tonight's pirate festival committee meeting. That and the fact that the usual venue, the Arching Angel, was out of the question because of the winter storms currently wreaking havoc on the harbour.

Luckily, Sage hadn't turned up, which was a blessing because she just wasn't ready for Golden Boy rage. Apparently he was 'busy with Bretton business', which Swanny had been less than impressed with judging by the clipped tone in which he delivered the message to the rest of the students. Paulie didn't even want to think about what the Brettons were up to other than finding ways to turf her and Aunt Meg out of house and home.

Swanny's office was quite large really, but the ambition of squeezing in the entire drama class and the committee was pretty bold. People were perched wherever they could find a space and were dressed from head to toe in pirate gear, aside from the students, who clearly hadn't got the memo. The only refreshments available were laid out in two huge pallets at the door – bottles of the Devonian ale, Buccaneer Bounty and tiny, packed-lunch sized bottles of purple squash. Paulie quickly figured they must be left over from last year's festival because every time a bottle of ale was snapped open, somebody some-where muttered the words, "Waste-not-want-not".

"When does the meeting actually start?" Paulie whinged. "And can we duck out after we've talked about the skirmish?" She suddenly realised she hadn't eaten all day (again) as dizzi-ness washed over her. "This is all a bit 'peopley' for me."

"I wouldn't fancy being the one to tell Swanny he has to get things moving, would you?" Wren gestured over to where Swanny appeared to be doing a little dance of triumph next to an animated group of ageing pirates. The group included Romano Smith (who had resurrected Captain Corvus and the gross-out crow skull hat) and Raymond the doughnut-loving police officer, who was waving a copy of the Torbay Gazette in Swanny's face. Paulie knew all too well what the paper said on its front page, as people had been talking about it all day at the bakery.

'LOCAL DRAMA TEACHER BRINGS HOLLY-WOOD KNOCKING.'

The article described how, thanks to *'local theatrical aficionado, Josiah Swan'*, the movie-making company, Picaroon Productions, had made the necessary planning applications to Torbay Council for permission to shoot some of the scenes from 'For The Love of Pirates' at the next pirate festival. The story continued from the front page through to a double-page spread and an open-armed image of Swanny in full pirate get-up standing in front of the Arching Angel. It must have been taken at last year's festival, before everything went so horribly wrong.

"It's my character, don't you know," Swanny boomed loudly so that the whole room came to a stand-still. "The character I *always* bring out for the Pirate Festival is the very same one at the centre of my epic, swashbuckling tale." He gestured at the length of his body which was adorned in the same costume he wore in the photograph, right down to the same grubby old palm gloves and over-sized, glinting belt buckle. "Of course, an ageing old luvvie like me couldn't *possibly* play Captain Roger Salt-beard in the actual movie version." There were immediate cries of *'Of course you could!'* and *'Why on earth not?'* but Swanny batted them away with two very limp wrists. "Darlings, don't be absurd. I shall be leaving all of that to the youngsters. Who knows who they'll cast as Saltbeard? It could be an A-lister!"

Somewhere in the proceedings of the entire room fawning over Swanny, some stuff about the skirmish was actually discussed. An email had been sent by Picaroon Productions, outlining the kinds of shots they needed, and they were mostly made up of crowd and aerial shots, which Breeze quietly observed would be, "CGI'd to death."

"That's all fine. But what about using explosives?" Romano ventured. "Here at Bay Community College, we want to make sure that some sensitivity is exercised. The town has been through enough, don't you think? And obviously we need to consider Tanya's poor mum, Wendy." At the mention of Wendy's name, nearly every middle-aged man in the room went gooey-eyed, weak-kneed or both. With the exceptions, of course, of Romano who stood resolute, waiting for an answer and Swanny, who rubbed his palm into his heart as if it had broken in two in that very moment. Damn, he was good.

The committee, in all its collective wisdom, agreed that there should be no explosives involved this year and the emphasis instead, should be on sweeping fight choreography involving flags, rigging and ropes that would look impressive from above. "We've got to give those drones something to fly for!" Swanny bleated, as everyone joyfully clashed bottles of Buccaneer Bounty together. Quite a lot of it sloshed on the carpet and Rashid jumped up, looking for a cloth. "Oh, it's quite alright," Swanny said. "Lovely Rita will sort it in the morning."

"Better give your mum a heads-up when you get home, Shazza." Cazza elbowed her friend in the ribs and Paulie could sense the scowl from the other end of the sofa. "Tell her she'll need to bring her best carpet cleaner to work tomorrow."

"Shut up, Cazza."

"Hang on a minute." Despite Paulie's brain feeling outstandingly sluggish, some of the synapses must have been working. "Shazza, is Rita your mum? Our cleaner at Booty Bakes? You never said."

"So what if she is?" Shazza used her narrowed eyes to throw daggers first at Cazza and then at Paulie. "Why does the world need to know what she does for a living anyway?"

"There's nothing wrong with cleaning," Paulie frowned. "She's probably my Aunt Meg's most valued worker. I don't understand. You never say two words to her when you're at the bakery."

Shazza rolled her eyes and stood up from the sofa. "Whatever. I need more squash." She flounced off and Paulie felt the cold and instant stab of having been the cause of somebody's discomfort. It made her realise that even though she'd been meeting up with the drama crew for the last few months, she didn't know any of them all that well. She'd have to fix that. On another day, when she had more energy and was less threatened by imminent homelessness, she'd totally fix it.

The talk about skirmish choreography continued as committee members suggested their individual ideas to Swanny. To be fair to him, he did a pretty good job of appearing to consider every single one of them – eager as they all were to have their suggestions included in an actual movie. But in reality, Paulie knew he would have already decided. He must have been waiting for this moment for over a decade and now that it was here, he'd be putting his stamp on it, for sure.

"I did used to live on the Arching Angel itself, you know, darlings. So I understand with meticulous complexity the technical composition and structure of the ship."

Rashid's mouth hung open, but the adults in the room didn't bat an eyelid. "Hang on, Swanny. You *lived* on the Arching Angel?"

"That I did my bright-eyed boy. It was back when I first returned from the thrills and spills of London town, way before I began as Head of Drama. I did it as a favour to Torbay Council." Swanny grinned at his captive audience and continued. "They snapped me up as soon as I stepped foot back in Berryport, and I was commissioned to devise a pirate persona with which to beguile the tourists – it's how Roger Saltbeard was born, no less! And I knew that to truly get into the character I must employ the Stanislavskian 'method' approach. The Arching Angel had just been renovated and was waiting for licenses with which to invite the general public aboard, so I suggested we make use of that gap in time by planting me – the original Captain Saltbeard – into the ship. It really was the only way to go. By spending several months on that dark, creaking vessel, I gained a familiarity that has been wildly beneficial to my final script. And planning the town's annual skirmishes of course!"

"Yo-ho-ho!" The cry came from the ageing pirates. The ale was really sloshing now. Rita would have her work cut out for her in the morning.

"Indeed!" Squealed Swanny, camper than he perhaps intended. "I even won awards for my contributions to tourism. Among other things. Like my long ago appearance as Vladimir in Godot at the National. That one's obvious. My trophy cabinets aren't something I usually point people towards but, as you asked, Rashid . . ." Swanny fanned his hands towards the tall, glass cabinets on the opposite side of the room that were filled with gleaming cups, medals and figurines. The students looked from Swanny to the cabinets. The cabinets to Swanny. Then there was a unified realisation that he expected everybody to get off their arses and go admire his multitude of honours.

A steady roll of 'ooohs' and 'aaahs' erupted from the students' mouths as they meticulously viewed the awards Swanny had achieved over the years. Paulie was vaguely aware of Breeze and Wren giggling at her side, perhaps over the fact that Swanny had included small plastic trophies from his school days for things like 'Most Enthusiastic Performer' and 'Biggest Drama Queen'. Paulie could understand why he'd kept them though. She would have loved to have such positive reminders of secondary school.

As the students scrabbled around her, Paulie tried really hard to focus on the items behind the glass. She wanted to show willing but was feeling woozier by the second. At that precise moment, she would have done anything for a bit of Gorillaz music, just to crisp up her concentration levels. Was it her frazzled brain, or was that an empty bottle of Buccaneer Bounty on the top shelf of the tallest cabinet? It was positioned as if it was the star accolade, with rolled up papers stuffed inside it. Maybe somebody had stuck it in there tonight as some kind of joke? To give poor Rita even more of a clean-up in the morning? Whatever. Paulie tried examining the rest of the polished, brassy items but they clouded like puffs of glitter as her eyes became glossy and her vision distorted.

"I need to go home," she whispered, in the hope that one of her classmates would hear her. Her legs felt like they were about to give way and her tummy twisted with a nausea whose likely source was hunger. When *had* she last eaten? She honestly had no idea.

"It's okay, Paulie, I've got you." Rashid most definitely did not have her, but was fussing in a manner he had probably seen in the movies. Nevertheless, Paulie allowed her weight to drop, because somebody – she thought maybe Cazza and Shazza – had linked her arms and were helping her stand. So much for Wren and Breeze being there when she needed them.

"Come on," Cazza crooned. "Let's get you home. Our part of the meeting is over now anyway."

Once out on the Meadow, the furious wind made itself known with stubborn lashings across their faces. "Oh god, I forgot there was a storm," wailed Cazza. "Paulie. You look a better colour. Will you be okay from here?" It was true that Paulie felt instantly more awake out here. Her stomach still howled for attention but she could feel her feet on the ground and the cold had snapped her vision back to normality.

"Erm . . ."

"Look at her, she's fine. Let's go." Shazza's expression was one of pure terror and Paulie could guess why by the way she was trying to hold down her perfectly curled hair with one hand and shield her Russian lashes with the other. Before Paulie could even bring herself to either ask for more help or approve their request to go, they were, indeed, gone.

She wrapped her coat tightly around her body. Because the bakery closed ages ago, she knew her Aunt would come get her with just one carefully worded text. After tapping it out on her phone, she turned in the direction of the car park, as well as into the unforgiving blast of the wind and managed, tiny step by tiny step, to warm herself with thoughts of the place she called home.

37

The late morning sun whooshed through the bakery window and slashed across the tray of Polly Pirate Pasties. From her spot behind the counter, Paulie watched it in a trance of sorts. It flashed sporadically as people outside moved around. With a heavy sigh and an even heavier heart, Paulie had to admit that the onset of a bright and beaming March meant that blanket season was over.

She continued to gaze at the humongous pile of pasties. How could there be so many of them left when there were hordes of people outside? Like, literal hordes. Why couldn't at least some of those people come inside and bloody well buy something? It wasn't like Paulie actually *wanted* to serve hordes of people, but Booty Bakes needed the sales now more than ever.

She twisted the rope necklace hard into the sinews of her neck. It pinched, like she knew it would, but it did nothing to realign her senses. The sun kept whooshing in, the bakery remained empty, and that feeling that she was somehow letting the world down skulked at the boundaries of her heart.

Since the email from Sage, it was becoming painfully clear

that Booty Bakes was in no position to withstand the ridiculous rent increase. Aunt Meg had summoned a small amount of fighting spirit in the first few weeks and had done anything she could to bring in extra cash. She'd changed suppliers, tried out new recipes, come up with special offers and invested in a social media marketing campaign. She'd even messaged Debbie Devon for a bit of help. Paulie had tried to explain that what with snogging Sage in front of the whole town and being Rex and Bex Bretton's new best friend, there was no way Devon's most influential digital creator was going to help them out. And she'd been right.

Suddenly, the phone in Paulie's apron pocket pinged. It would most likely be Wren. Texts from the 'Project Skirmish' WhatsApp group had dried up recently, mainly due to the fact that she was yet to come good on her promise to nail Sage, or anyone for that matter. Plus there was the fact that her personality was clearly not sparkling enough to hold their attention. Instead, Swanny's promise of fame and fortune had become the current obsession. A new WhatsApp group had been set up called 'Hollywood Here We Come'. Paulie didn't even know if she was in it.

She checked her phone and yeah, it was Wren.

> Dude, am assuming college is not on your agenda today? Swanny is asking after you. Again. Golden Boy is also AWOL so, obvs, he's having a meltdown. Anyway, did you know Debbie Devon is doing weird crap outside Booty Bakes? She's live-streaming. Here's the link . . .

Paulie blinked and looked out of the window. She'd had no idea that Debbie Devon was the cause of the hordes. But now that Wren mentioned it, she could definitely identify that grating voice shunting through the bakery windows, the exaggerated rolling of the Devonian 'R' that thrilled her followers so much. "Okay everybody. This is a trrruly spontaneous sneak peek at some rrrrreally exciting news I have to announce in the next few weeks. And I wanted you to be the firrrst to know that this building, that I'm standing in frrront of rrright now, holds the key to something utterrrrly grrrroundbreaking. And no, I'm not talking about pasties forrrr once!"

"What the heck is she up to?" Aunt Meg stormed out of the kitchen, icing sugar up to her elbows, and flung the bakery door open. Fickle Fergus, the only customer in the place, followed her out, a tatty but flamboyant scarf trailing out in dramatic ribbons behind him. Paulie knew, deep in her actual bones, that she couldn't face going outside right now. The sunshine was getting distinctly more crisp and bright, and she just wasn't up for it.

Instead, she slid down to sit on the floor behind the counter. She tapped on the link Wren had sent and watched what was happening on her very doorstep from the perspective Debbie Devon intended her to.

"That's right, people. Whilst I can't give any promises yet, I can say that this prime spot in the heart of Berryport Harbour, is most likely where I'm going to be hanging out in the months to come." The camera angle suddenly swooped down to Debbie's glitter-booted ankles where her army of snow-white poodles were hankering for her attention, "Isn't that right, Trixie, Dixie, Lixie and Nixie? We're going to have so much fun here, aren't we little ones?" The camera whizzed back up to reveal rather too much of Debbie Devon's nostrils if Paulie was honest. "So, to keep my lovely followers guessing *and* to reward you for your eternal commitment to me and my passion for local brand awareness, I'm going to treat you *all* right here, right now." A cheer burst from the crowd which Paulie received in strange and startling stereo from the real-time event going on outside first and the phone's tinny speakers second. "Now, can we have a round of applause for my *favourite* man at the moment, the gorgeous Mr Sage Bretton!"

Sage slid up next to Debbie, a fixed smile on his handsome face. The smile didn't reach his eyes one little bit and Paulie felt somehow pleased to notice this. He had a tray of lavishly iced muffins in his hands and a stupid paper hat on that gave the impression he'd come fresh from some country kitchen or other. There was no way, surely, that they were going to give out muffins right outside Booty Bakes? Could they stoop any lower?

Apparently they could. Because not only were they giving out free cakes, but Debbie was also screeching on about some discount link she was putting in the comments so that all of her followers could get a taster box delivered to their doors. She droned on about some local brand or other and how "simply incredible" it was before feeding a muffin straight into the unsuspecting mouth of Sage. Through gaudy yellow icing, his smile remained fixed but his eyes flared with something Paulie could have sworn was fury.

After stuffing Sage's face, Debbie swung the camera over to his parents, who stood nearby, grinning from ear to ear. "And here are our local business pioneers, Rex and Bex Bretton, my mutual masterminds behind this latest venture. Rex, Bex, I know we can't reveal all just yet, but what can you tell my followers about the way we are going to transform this particular unit on Berryport Harbour?"

"Well," Rex began, "rest assured the innovation we are bringing to the town is the first of its kind in the country and will put Berryport well and truly on the map."

"And local creators will be thrilled," Bex added, flicking her hair in a sad attempt to mimic Debbie, "it really is an opportunity to showcase talent as well as maximise turnover. And can I just say, Debbie, between you, me and your lovely followers . . ." Bex leaned forwards and Debbie did too, angling the camera to capture the both of them, almost forehead to forehead and whispering, ". . . I'm delighted to see you and my son on such cosy terms." The two women shrieked with laughter and sprang backwards from each other to reveal a yellow-mouthed, bewildered looking Sage holding an empty cupcake tray and appearing, to all intents and purposes, like he'd just been ravaged by vultures. Simultaneously, an ocean of hearts washed across the phone screen, meaning Debbie Devon's BeYu followers were just as euphoric as the cackling onlookers.

Seemingly forced inside by the torrent of laughter, Aunt Meg appeared at the door, followed by Fickle Fergus. Both of them wore defeat like a heavy cloak, their slumped shoulders leading the way. Fergus pressed the door closed behind them and gently nudged Aunt Meg forwards. "Come on, Meg, love. It's not all bad. Come and help me with my crossword, eh?"

Meg's voice trickled out of her like water from a broken tap. "No thanks, Ferg. I think I might go upstairs and start, um, packing."

"Packing?" The word was enough to get Paulie off the floor and rush from behind the counter to face her aunt. "Isn't that a bit hasty? I mean, we don't really know what's happening, do we? Aren't you, well, jumping the gun?"

Maybe it was the word, 'gun' that did it, but the look that Aunt Meg gave Paulie just then could have sunk a thousand pirate ships. "Luvver, let me past."

"But, but . . ." Suddenly there were a million routes for Paulie to choose from. Take Aunt Meg's hand. Rub her shoulder. Engulf her in a huge hug. Make a brew. Force feed her a pastie. Submit to Fergus's crossword idea. Open a bottle of golden rum. Say nothing. Scream, cry, kill Debbie Devon. All of the options were equally mad and equally logical. And by the time she'd filtered through them all in her head, Meg was already upstairs, banging cupboard doors and shifting furniture.

"Oh god, Fergus. Is this really happening?" Paulie slumped into a chair and found her necklace with grappling fingertips. No amount of twisting was going to fix this.

"Oh, it's okay, Little Paulie," Fergus smiled, joining her at the table. "We've got to be a bit nine across about all this."

"Huh?"

"Nineteen ninety-two rock hit with driving bass and hopeful message. Three words. Four – three – five. First word begins with K. Middle word, 'the'. Last word begins with F." Fergus swooped his biro down to fill in the answer at the same time that Paulie wondered if she had the energy to even contemplate the possibility of what the crossword clue was suggesting. If she was going to keep anything in all of this, it was going to be her relationship with Aunt Meg. Because when all was said and done, that's where her home really was.

38

Meg had spent all month packing boxes. Since Debbie Devon's livestream outside Booty Bakes there hadn't been confirmation that she'd be taking over the building, but there were plenty of rumours flying around to keep even the most gossip-hungry satiated. Paulie wasn't sure whether she preferred the rumour about the strip club or the shamanic colonic irrigation centre, but she was pretty sure about one thing: she and Meg were getting turfed out.

Paulie was fully aware she wasn't a grand master at making (or implementing) plans but she had a feeling that stuffing, emptying and re-stuffing boxes would only get them so far. She looked at the empty boxes stacked up in the corner of her room and promised herself for the bazillionth time that she would get round to filling them. Meg had even bought her the multi-coloured markers, sticky labels and stripey parcel tape she'd insisted she'd needed before she could start. And there they were, several weeks later, gathering dust.

Dust. That made her think of Tanya. She remembered that BeYu photograph of her dust-covered collection of origami shapes on her windowsill, the one that Tanya had compared with her own sun-catcher art. It was the perfect metaphor because back then, Paulie was dust and Tanya was sparkling sunshine. Since Tanya's death, there had been the chance to switch it. But sparkling sunshine, to Paulie, seemed as out of reach as the bank balance needed to save Booty Bakes.

"Luvver," Aunt Meg popped her head around the door. "Rita's coming over to help me pack up the kitchen. Is that alright with . . . Oh, Paulie. Come on. You still haven't started with the boxes?" Notches of energy in Meg's voice faded with every word she spoke until the end of the sentence was practically at one with the carpet.

"Oh yeah, er, soz. Will get round to it later. Promise."

"Later? Why can't you start now?"

"Erm, well, I've got counselling."

Aunt Meg brightened. "Oh, that *is* good. Is it another one of those walking thingies? Along the pier?"

"I think Romano said to meet at the Nautical Gardens this time."

"Nice."

"S'pose." At the thought of going outside, Paulie felt her muscles droop. That would mean washing her face, brushing her hair, finding a jacket, putting on shoes. Where was she going to get the energy for all of that?

"Here." In quick succession, Aunt Meg chucked a series of objects at Paulie. A flannel, a comb, her denim jacket and a pair of Converse. Damn, she was good. "Don't leave the man waiting."

"On it." Paulie heaved her body off her bed with such an effort that it almost brought tears to her eyes. Aunt Meg planted a weary kiss on her forehead and sloped off to get on with reducing their whole lives to boxes. The jarring clang of kitchen items forced Paulie to hit play on her favourite Gorillaz album and stuff her earbuds in so far, they might never come out. *This is it*, thought Paulie. *This is what defeat feels like.*

In a shock happening, Paulie arrived at the gardens early. Once the fresh air hit her lungs, her body had found some ease and the walk along the coastal path had been quick.

The day wasn't the crisp, bright kind that Devon usually boasted in early April. Instead, there was a silvery edge to the light, a damp cotton hint to the sky. A refreshing vapour tumbled through patches of air, probably meaning it could rain at any minute. Paulie dug her hands deep into her denim jacket pockets, wishing she'd picked up something even remotely waterproof. That's when she found her deerstalker hat which she decided she may as well wear. It would keep off any rain as well as hide her greasy roots.

Just as she was walking the winding path along to the spot where she was meeting Romano, she saw Breeze sitting on a bench overlooking the cliff. He sat with his shoulders pressed right against the back of the bench and his knees drawn up, heels grabbing the edge of the seat. He had an iPad balanced against his lap, a stylus in his hand and his face was bent towards whatever he was drawing so that his hair cascaded over his face in streaks of blue and black. Despite his face being covered, Paulie knew for sure it was him. Who else could pull off the brooding on a cliff thing quite like that?

"Hey." She sat next to him and took a breath. Maybe the walk over here had been a little too quick.

"Hey you. Nice day for it, right?"

"Nice day for what?"

"Oh, you know. Skipping college. Cliffs. Stormy skies. Dramatic, Devonshire seascapes."

Paulie glanced at his iPad screen and tried to get a look at what he was working on. "But that's not what you're drawing."

"Well deduced, Sherlock." He flicked the peak of her hat with his stylus and smirked. "No, I just couldn't get into it so I started on something else." He turned the iPad towards her and with a brush of his fingers, zoomed out so she could see the whole illustration. She gasped.

"Oh wow, Breeze. That's . . . it's totally beautiful." Paulie's hand shot to her necklace and, in particular, the compass charm because Breeze's drawing was of a compass, glowing with gold and embellished with jewels. She might have been wrong, but the basic structure of the drawing was uncannily like the tiny pendant she now held between her fingertips.

"You don't miss a trick, do you?" Breeze said. "It would make a mean tattoo, right?"

"It so would." Paulie held her arms and legs out straight as if deciding where she'd place a tattoo like that, then flopped them down again just as quickly. "I'd never have the guts, but it would be cool."

"Never say never." Breeze shuffled on the seat and nudged Paulie playfully. She felt a lightness infiltrate her bones that had eluded her for weeks. How did he *do* that? "So what are you doing out here? Meeting your murder posse or something?" Before Paulie could answer Breeze's question, they were distracted by footsteps coming their way and a couple of voices rising in volume. One of the voices was clearly distressed, judging by the ragged edges to the words. Paulie had never heard Sage speak in that way before, so it took her a few seconds to realise it was him.

"Romano, it had to have been me. There's no other explanation. I can't believe I did this to my own girlfriend."

"No, Sage. The police obviously think otherwise. You need to let this go."

They were standing on the main path leading out of the small woods at the boundaries of the Nautical Gardens. There was a huge old tree in between the bench Breeze and Paulie were sitting on and the spot where Romano stood with Sage. There was just enough space between the leaves and branches to see what was going on, but there was every chance that from the other side, the view wasn't so clear. "Can they see us?" Breeze whispered to Paulie.

"I don't think so." Paulie's heart pummelled the insides of her chest. Could this be it? Could this be the moment she'd been waiting for all this time? Breeze gave her a searching look which was freakish in how accurately it said, *I know you want to nail him with every fibre of your being, but is this the right way to do it?*

"I can't see how to make this right," Sage continued, tears dowsing his voice. "Maybe, now that my parents are in on it, and you are too . . . maybe I should just tell the world, you know? Swanny's been great. You've been great. But all this secrecy, it's exhausting."

"But what is there to tell, Sage? Your parents filed a subject access request with the police and the report said there was insufficient evidence you shot Tanya. The fingerprints alone weren't enough. It looks like she collapsed before you even picked those guns up to juggle them. And the police must have other lines of enquiry otherwise you would have been charged. Come on, you must know that."

Sage's voice, which had been so heavy with tears just seconds before, suddenly turned hot and sharp. "No, Romano. It was me. I picked the guns up. I juggled them when I'd been told a million times not to. Only my fingerprints are on the faulty pistol. It was me. I killed my girlfriend." At this, there was a

crunching twist of gravel underfoot and Sage shot out from
behind the tree. He can't have managed two or three steps
before he clocked Paulie and Breeze on the bench, followed by
Romano who almost ran into the back of him. Rather than look
like he wanted to strangle Paulie on the spot, his expression
slackened to one of pure relief. The deep exhalation that catapulted from his body pierced Paulie with tiny stabs of shock
because the energy of the moment felt all wrong.

"Sage. I . . . I . . ."

"It's fine, Paulie. I'm glad you're here." Sage turned to
Romano who gaped at the scene, his mouth popping open and
closed as if the words he needed could be swallowed from the
air around him. "Did you arrange this?"

"No. Definitely not. In fact, I highly advise that we stop
right now . . ."

"Stop? You're kidding, aren't you? This is an absolute gift.
Paulie, you can finally tell everyone on BeYu or whatever, it was
me. I'm the one who killed Tanya. It was an accident. But I did
it." Sage slumped down on the bench beside her.

"What? I don't understand."

Sage muttered to himself for a moment. "Tanya. I owe this
to Tanya." He lifted his chiselled chin, flicked a toxic gaze at
Breeze for a millisecond, then looked Paulie straight in the eyes.
"What do you want to know?"

"Really? We're doing this?" Paulie could hardly breathe.

Sage nodded.

"Really? We're doing this?" Romano repeated, looking from
Sage to Paulie to Breeze in a lost puppy kind of way.

Sage nodded again.

Over the next half an hour, as Romano played mediator and
Sage poured out his guilt-ridden story, Paulie felt her contempt
for him scatter like a flock of frightened birds. She was vaguely
aware of Breeze by her side, tutting at points in the story that

must have been hard for him to hear, but primarily she was focused on Sage. No. Who was she kidding? She was *absorbed* in him.

Right from the day of the pirate festival, Sage thought he might have killed Tanya. After the initial blasts from the cannons, he'd spotted some discarded pistols on the deck of the Arching Angel and couldn't help but pick them up and juggle them. "I was showing off, pure and simple. And I wanted to cheer Tanya up because we'd been rowing that day about Debbie bloody Devon." Not long after that, Sage looked over at Tanya and saw blood. Then somebody else screamed and everything changed. In a panic, Sage thought he must have triggered one of the pistols whilst juggling. He confided in Swanny in those first few moments when they were herded off the ship by the police, who advised him to wait until investigations were done. "He told me there was no way I could have done it. That all the loaded pistols had already been fired. I suppose I believed it for a while. I wanted to believe it."

During intense questioning in those first few weeks, video footage of Sage juggling was uncovered. Sage broke down and confessed to the police, but there was something about the time-lines that wasn't right. "They let me go home and I couldn't quite believe it. My parents were over the moon though, like they'd won the lottery or something. Not that they'd ever need a lottery win." Sage explained how his parents were furious at first. The last thing they wanted was for his previous record of drug offences to surface and what with a murder charge to top things off, that would really dent their business egos. "I was told in no uncertain terms that should I get in trouble with the law again, I'd have my inheritance taken away. All of it." Sage's complexion paled as he explained, "I mean, what have I got to offer the world apart from some half-decent looks and a pretty unexceptional acting talent? So I told my parents to let me prove it to them that I was trustworthy. I begged them to give me one of their contracts to work on. And they did. They gave me yours."

Paulie swallowed down something hard and horrible. It must have been around that time that she posted the BeYu photo of Sage snogging Debbie Devon with his fingers crossed. Just as she was wondering how Debbie Devon fit into any of this, Sage volunteered, "I don't like her. I never have. But, like everything else in the world, my mum and dad see her as a business opportunity. Tanya sensed it even before I did." Sage rubbed his face with the heels of his hands and sat back on the bench, blinking at the silvery stare of the sky. "I don't know. I've been so weak in all of this. I've let them pull me along in their current of greed. And that's just it. Because I've been greedy too."

"Okay, I think that might be enough." Romano placed a hand on Sage's shoulder. He'd been sat on a nearby tree stump the whole time. "I hope you both know that I need to write this up in your files. And Paulie, I've got something to give you before you go."

"Hang on, just a bit," Sage said. "If I'm doing this properly, Paulie needs to know about the fingerprints."

"I do know about them." Breeze tensed up beside her, but it was too late now. She'd said it. "I know your fingerprints were on the faulty pistol."

"Well, that's the end of the story then. My parents sucked that information out of the police by doing what they usually do – stretching red tape as far as it will bloody well go."

"Well, the subject access report is a legitimate thing, Sage," Romano added.

"Whatever. They did it. We found out about the fingerprints. And now, I don't care what anyone says. I killed Tanya. With my stupid, swaggering juggling moves. When I saw your most recent BeYu photo, Paulie, it just confirmed everything. *Sage juggled the pistols and then Tanya was dead.* I was so unbelievably angry that I sent Meg that email about the rent increase. It's not like Debbie Devon isn't standing by to leech her way in with some stupid idea for a social media hub. It was easy."

"A social media hub? Honestly? And where are we supposed to go, Sage?"

"I don't know. And I'm sorry. Really. I shouldn't have taken my rage out on you and your aunt. But, then, what else can you expect from an actual murderer?" As soon as Sage said those words, no matter how full of angst and shame they might have been, Breeze jumped up and lunged towards him. That's when Romano's role as college counsellor kicked into turbo charge and Sage's now quivering, folded body was scooped up and carted off.

Romano shouted over his shoulder as he and Sage darted along the path, "Paulie, we'll reschedule properly. Keep an eye on your WhatsApp."

"I thought you had something to give me?" Paulie yelled, not knowing quite how her brain had managed to pick out that tiny, insignificant bit of information after those mammoth disclosures.

"It'll have to wait," he called back. "But it'll be soon."

Breeze and Paulie were left standing alone on their cliffside, the wind picking up and spots of rain pinching the skin on their faces. Paulie was scarcely able to bring her eyes to meet his, but she did it. Somehow.

"How . . . how are you feeling?" he asked. There was no answer. None at all. But the sense of triumph she'd expected was weirdly missing. "Hey, looks like this is for you." Breeze bent down and picked up a formal-looking envelope off the ground, exactly next to the tree stump where Romano had been sitting. Paulie took it off him and turned it over to see who it was addressed to. It took a few seconds to make sense of the words, but once she focused really hard, and stopped looking for the victory she so wanted from Sage's revelations, the words jumped up and grabbed her by the throat:

For the parent / guardian of Miss Paulie Trinket.

39

Technically, the envelope was addressed to Aunt Meg but Paulie ripped it open anyway. It was from Bay Community College. No surprises there. Aunt Meg had received these things before and apart from sometimes having to attend a meeting or two, she mostly just needed reassurance from Paulie that things were in hand. Not that they ever were. Paulie just got good at convincing herself, as much as Aunt Meg, that she would get her act together.

Reading it out to Breeze who was still at her side, she skimmed the first part about interventions, support and guidance and finally got to what the letter was really about.

. . . therefore, we have implemented a suspension until further notice . . .

"Oh, Paulie. I'm so sorry. That sucks."

"What? What sucks?" Paulie's head was like a washing machine on full speed.

"You know. Being suspended from college. Can I do anything?" Breeze stepped forward and attempted to rub her arm but she snapped it back as if he'd given her a shock. Which, in a way, he had.

"I can't . . . You can't . . ."

"Hey. I just want to help. There's so much going on. Shall we talk about it? What do you want to do about everything Sage said? I might kill him, but you can have first dibs if you want. And all this about a suspension? Paulie, what are you going to do?"

Paulie's hands flew to her head and she grabbed the fabric of her hat, bunching the fabric and catching the hairs beneath so that jolts of pain streaked across her scalp. She wanted to say, *please don't fire all those questions at me at once.* She wanted to say, *the wind is cold, Sage is guilty, my hat keeps blowing off, maybe Romano knew all along, Sage is guilty, your compass design is awesome, the rain's getting worse, Sage is guilty, I need to get home, I'm suspended, I love how you smell, Sage is guilty . . . .* But none of those words made it anywhere near her lips. Instead, she flung her hat at Breeze's feet and screamed at the top of her lungs, "Get out of my face!" She had just enough time to register his wide, imploring eyes before she spun on her heels and ran like her life depended on it.

When Paulie got home, she was surprised to see Meg had shut up shop for the day. The episode with Sage must have lasted longer than she thought. She let herself through the bakery door and stood for a moment in the quiet, her back pressed up against the 'Closed' sign, catching her breath.

Without really thinking about it, she focused her attention on the tips of her toes and began to scan it slowly up through her body. This was something Romano had once taught her during a mindfulness session. Granted, he'd said mindfulness wasn't goal driven, but she needed clues from her body. Was she sad about the college letter? Angry with herself for screaming at Breeze?

Triumphant that she'd finally caught a killer? Maybe her chest would be tight or her tummy squirmy or her shoulders unknotted. But there was none of that. It felt more like her body was reaching for something invisible. As if it would gladly cling to the nearest rock like a limpet.

When Paulie got upstairs, she shrugged off her totally ineffectual denim jacket and knew she'd be heading straight for her bed and her favourite blanket. That was, until she heard voices coming from the kitchen. A glance through the partially open door told her that the contents of the cupboards were now in labelled boxes stacked all along the counters and Meg was at the kitchen table having a cuppa with Rita. She knew she should go inside and face this college suspension thing head-on, show the letter to her aunt and find ways to soften the blow. But that would be embarrassing for Rita, right? And besides, since she'd left Breeze on the cliffside, she wasn't sure she yet had the power of speech.

Paulie was just about to go to her room when she heard her name. But it wasn't from Meg, it was from Rita. "So, hang on, the college is *suspending* Paulie now?"

"Looks like it," Meg sighed. "I don't know. Maybe we've come to the end of the line with this whole college thing." Crap. Perhaps the college had emailed Aunt Meg? Sometimes they did that as well as send a letter.

"Meggie, you sound knackered, mate. And this packing isn't doing you any good, is it?" Rita reached out and took Meg's hand.

"It's not. But I have to get on with it. Lord knows where we'll actually go, but at least we'll be ready when the time comes."

"You're right. But I can see how much this is taking out of you. You haven't been right in the bakery for months now. Paulie should know how hard things are for you. Can't she just apply herself a bit more? I'm always telling my Shazza to do that. Just get your head down and focus on your college work. Paulie should be doing it for you as much as herself."

"There aren't really any 'shoulds' with our Paulie, Rita." Meg took her hand away and used it to rub her neck. Paulie could see how exhausted she was from the red rims around her eyes and the flighty way her fingers brushed over her skin.

"God, you did a grand thing taking her in all those years ago. And the amount you gave up for her. Do you think she knows?"

"No." Meg sat up straight. "I've never told her. It doesn't matter anymore."

"But you and Coral were so in love. Ready to take on the world, you were. Didn't you have plans for travelling? I remember you saying you were going to marry in LA, then travel all over the world. You'd learn new baking skills and Coral would train with the best tattooists. You had it all figured out."

"We did."

"It would have been amazing."

"Agreed." A glimmer of a smile brushed Meg's mouth, but it was followed by a drooping arc which Paulie involuntarily mirrored from her spot in the darkness of the landing. Coral? In love? Marrying in LA? What the actual? "But what else could I do, Rita? My brother rocks up, hands over his daughter then disappears into thin air. Doesn't bother to tell me she has, well, issues. He must have known even from that age, goddammit." That word, 'issues', struck Paulie like a boulder. "And if we're really being honest here, of course I regret it sometimes. Of course I regret leaving Coral and suddenly becoming a guardian and compromising all of those adventures. How could I not? She can be such a difficult kid and there isn't one minute I don't wonder what life would have been like if I'd stuck with Coral. Regret is an ugly thing and Rita, it's gnawing away at me. It really is. I just wish things had been . . . different."

That other word, 'regret', hit Paulie in the heart just as hard as the first one and she knew she had to get out. For the second time that day, but this time with tears flooding her throat and heartbreak threatening to crack her whole body open, she pounded down the stairs and ran as fast as she could.

40

The rain was really coming down now. The sodden denim jacket scenario had reached the point of no return and so too, it seemed, had Paulie.

How could she go back to the flat? Meg and Rita had probably cracked the golden rum open by now and would be having a good old laugh about Paulie's 'issues'. Maybe they would toast a future where Meg could run off with Coral and desert everything else. Too late. She already felt deserted. At least, that's what the pain ripping through her chest was telling her.

She stood on the shore of Billowbreak Beach and watched the rain slice into the surface of the choppy sea. Slabs of wet hair stuck to her ears as if they were trying to close off at least one of her senses. It wasn't working. Her system was engulfed in the roar of rain, the thrash of twilight, the sting of wet skin, the colossal stench of soaked seaweed. She wished she could crawl under one of Billowbreak's rocks. Just shut it all out.

She clambered over to the steep steps carved into the rockface and began to climb. There was something about becoming breathless that felt better. With each step she took, the constriction of her lungs pushed against the walls of her chest and gave her heart less of a chance to throb. *That's what I'll do,* she thought. *I'll push the pain out.*

Once at the top of the steps, she didn't stop. In fact, she broke into a run. This was the third time today that she'd run to escape something horrendous and she didn't know how it would end. The more fire screeched through her lungs, the less chance she had to think. She ran along the top road where hotels, pubs and holiday flats sloped perilously towards the sea. She pounded down the curved path towards the saltwater lido where dozens of greedy rockpools shared the ocean's spill. She sprinted up and over the ragged cliffs, nearing Daisy Dark Point, the knife-like precipice on the outskirts of Berryport. She ran and ran and ran until, despite the rain, it seemed fire would fly from her limbs and her chest might explode more violently than the pirate festival cannons ever could.

Paulie couldn't quite believe it when she realised where she'd stopped. Looking up and through the driving rain, she recognised the salmon-pink tint on the walls of the house in front of her. She'd seen it a million times in BeYu photos. Selfies showing off new earrings, a different hairstyle, the latest fashion trend or, sometimes, if her followers were lucky, a monologue from some cool and current Hollywood movie. This was Tanya's house.

"Paulie, luvver. You're like a drowned rat! Come inside." It was Wendy. She must have spotted Paulie from the window and hadn't hesitated to dash outside and scoop her up into a fluffy towel. "Let's get you warm."

Once inside, Wendy busied herself around Paulie, rubbing her down, pulling her jacket off and even removing her soggy shoes. Standing there in the neat and tidy hallway, Paulie just let her do it all. The moment that Breeze had tried to comfort her on the cliffside earlier that day flashed through her mind. Then, she hadn't been able to bear the weight of his hand on her arm and had reacted as if he was out to get her. Yet here she was now, being pummelled with a towel and tossed about like a baby.

"Alright. You're a bit drier now but those clothes aren't helping. Come upstairs and we'll find you something cosy." Before Paulie knew what was happening, she was being led by the hand up a set of richly carpeted stairs and into a bedroom. A bright pink, sparkly bedroom.

"Oh no," Paulie moaned. "I can't. Not Tanya's stuff."

"I know. It's weird. But Tanya would want to know she could help you. She'd be glad to offer you her stuff." Paulie highly doubted that, but found a small smile to offer Wendy. "Right, you have a look through the wardrobe and pick something out. I'll nip downstairs and call your aunt. Does she know you're out in this weather?"

"Oh erm, it's okay. I'll call her myself." The last thing she wanted right now was Aunt Meg rocking up. She wasn't sure she could bear to even look her in the face after what she'd heard.

"Alright then, if you're sure. I'll be downstairs. And I'll put some cocoa on to heat. How does that sound?"

"Great. It sounds great." Wendy closed the door behind her and left Paulie alone in the room. It wasn't until she was rifling through endless pairs of hotpants and crop tops in the (very) tidy wardrobe, that she remembered she had information that could change Wendy's world. For that woman downstairs right now, probably stirring milk on the stove and putting out a plate of biscuits, a few words from Paulie could break her. Just when Paulie thought the day couldn't get any heavier, it smacked her again with a force that hurt like hell.

She collapsed on the bed with a sigh, clutching a pair of bright pink jogger bottoms and a black, mohair jumper with silver strands all over it. They were about a tenth of the size

Paulie would usually wear, but hopefully there was enough give in them that they'd do. She peeled off her sodden clothes and they fell to the floor with a splat. Tanya's clothes just about fit, although Paulie was sure she would turn in her ashen grave if she saw how stretched and strained the fabric was.

She suddenly felt stuck. Stuck in Tanya's room. Stuck on her bed. The thought of going downstairs to face Wendy with the kind of information she had in her head was unthinkable, let alone share a cup of cocoa. However, the thought of being here, amongst all of Tanya's things seemed equally impossible. What the hell should her next move be?

Her phone interrupted her thoughts. She wrangled it out of her jeans pocket and wiped off the film of water across the screen. Wren.

> Dude, Breeze told me you were upset. You screamed at him or something? What's up? He said I should just ask you but I don't know when you're next going to be in drama class. Tell me! I'm dying here.

Typical Wren. Thinking all of this could be communicated in an actual text. Where was the compassion? The sympathy? The concern? And what did Breeze think he was doing, bad-mouthing her like that? Especially before she'd even had the chance to process any of this herself. The thought of them gossiping behind her back was just too much and she flung herself back into the soft and frilly folds of Tanya's bed to stare at the ceiling. The glittery, chandelier-adorned ceiling.

There was no point in lavishing details upon Wren. Instead of that, Paulie would text the Project Skirmish group and make some kind of announcement. All this murder investigation stuff? It was over. And this would be the perfect full stop. So much for Coral's top tips. So much for everybody helping her get to the bottom of things. And so much for proving to everybody that she was worth something.

Now that she'd overheard Aunt Meg's deepest thoughts, Paulie knew the truth of things. She was, and always had been, utterly unlikeable.

41

With a satisfying click, Paulie slotted in the last corner piece. The jigsaw she'd found on Tanya's shelves might not have been as taxing as one of Wren's but it at least gave her mind something to do. Out of the five hundred pieces that made up the iconic Hollywood sign, she'd probably only managed to put together about eighty. Who knew if she'd get it anywhere near finished? She could add it to the never-ending list of incomplete projects.

Wendy had been kind to let her stay overnight. It had become obvious, after a few hours of Paulie not budging from the room, that something was up. Instead of allowing her to wallow without interruption, there had been a series of knocks on the door including the delivery of towels, trays of food, stacks of magazines and manicure paraphernalia. "Would you like me to come in and do your cuticles, Paulie? It really is no trouble. You can take your favourite colours home if you like?"

Home. Funny word, that. Did Paulie even have a home now? For all she knew, Meg could have boxed her room up and chucked it out on the street. She'd had about a dozen missed calls from her aunt and it wasn't until she heard Wendy's phone ringing and some kind of not-very-whispered conversation going on that the calls stopped. Of course, there had been texts too.

> I know about the suspension.

> Can we talk about this?

> That's enough now. Time to come back.

It was amazing that Meg thought Paulie would disappear just because of the college thing. She'd had to hold herself back from responding with, *'Nope. Not coming back to a woman who regrets ever knowing me.'*

Paulie abandoned the jigsaw laid out on Tanya's dresser but kept a few pieces to rattle in her palm for comfort. She walked over to the bed and rescued her phone from under the frilly pillow. Did anybody from the Project Skirmish group have any reaction whatsoever to the text she'd sent yesterday about Sage's disclosure? For people who, only a few months ago, had wanted to out him as a killer, there was a disturbing lack of feedback.

Finally. Some replies.

> Yeah, saw sumthing about that on BeYu.

> He says one thing, the police say another.

> Yawn. Old news.

Old news. Old bloody news? How could it be old news when it was still – along with many other things – causing fire-works in Paulie's mind and body? It was enough to make her want to dive in among the frills of Tanya's duvet and never come out.

So much for that though, because just then, Wendy knocked softly at the door and said there was a visitor downstairs. Would she please come down and see to them because she needed to come in and air the bedroom anyway. Fine. Whatever. She supposed she should move her arse at some point. As long as the visitor wasn't Aunt Meg.

"Dude. You look like Barbie went a bit Noel Fielding." Wren stood in the hallway and took in the ensemble Paulie was still wearing from Tanya's wardrobe. She had her rucksack on her back, her sturdiest walking boots on and her rose-coloured sunglasses propped up on her forehead. The sun must have come out then.

"What do you want?"

"Okay. Always a pleasure . . ." Wren eyed up the sofas in the living room adjacent to where they were standing but Paulie was having none of it. "Fine. I'm here because Meg told me you were here. She says you didn't come home last night. That you've been suspended from college. And obviously there's the stuff about Sage, which is all over social media."

"It is?"

"Right. I forgot you live in the dark ages. He put a statement across his socials last night. Told everyone he was responsible for killing Tanya with the whole juggling thing. Then the police jumped in with their own statement and now there are press conferences happening left, right and centre. It's back in the national news. But the police are adamant it wasn't Sage."

"Anything else?"

"What, that's it? You don't have any other reaction to what Sage told you and how it's exploded into everyone's lives? The boy you've been trying to nail for Tanya's death for almost a year comes forward and you don't even move a muscle on your face? Did you even see how upset Wendy was?"

"Wendy knows?"

"Of course she bloody knows. She was just telling me that the police came early this morning to inform her. I suppose you slept through that. She's in pieces. And here you are, taking advantage of her hospitality when you could be at home with your aunt who loves you."

"Pfft. I wouldn't be so sure about that. I overheard something." Paulie's throat closed up. Should she explain it all to Wren? How could she ever understand?

"Well, whatever you overheard, you can go back and speak to Meg about it. And if things were really that bad, why didn't you come to mine? You know I'm in the house by myself. There's always a bed for you. To be honest, dude, I don't know why you didn't tell me about the Sage stuff. You posted on the WhatsApp group before even thinking about trusting me with it first? What was that about?"

"I, well, I don't need to explain myself to you."

"Exactly. That's the point. You don't need to explain yourself to me which is why – at least from my perspective and the fact that we've been best friends for a while now – you would have been safe at my house. Safe and comfortable and trusted. And no explaining needed. Dude, that's what real friends are about."

When Wren put it like that, Paulie had to admit it did suddenly seem like the obvious choice should have been going to Wren's. But really, 'best friends'? That was stretching it a bit. "It was just, well, you know how I am with the buses."

"Crap. Total crap. I know you. It had nothing to do with buses."

"Okay, Wren. Did you come out here just to yell at me or is there something else?" Paulie folded her arms across her chest and stood her ground. There was a jigsaw upstairs with her name on it and she wasn't going to let Wren keep her from it much longer.

Wren took a long, hard look at Paulie's face, as if she was waiting for it to change into something completely different.

Which it didn't. Then, she wriggled the rucksack off her back, dumped it on the floor and unzipped it. "Actually, I've brought you some stuff for your birthday tomorrow. This is from me. And this is from Breeze. Oh, and the whole drama class did this for you. They thought I'd be the first to see you on your birthday. Can't think why." She handed Paulie a couple of parcels and a large card in a black and white stripey envelope that looked a bit like a movie-making clapperboard.

"The whole drama class?" Paulie couldn't believe anybody had even known about her birthday, let alone given her anything for it.

"Yup. They're stupidly busy with preparing the skirmish, but they didn't forget. Turns out you *are* popular. Just like you always wanted. Dude, what's that in your hand?" Wren noticed that Paulie was struggling to hold everything because she still had the pile of jigsaw pieces in her palm.

"Erm. Nothing. Just a jigsaw I'm doing."

"You're doing a jigsaw? You?"

"Yeah. I found it in Tanya's room and . . ."

A cold wash of realisation rippled over Wren's face. "And you thought you'd try to find a motive for somebody other than Sage? You thought you'd get into the mind of a different suspect?"

"No, Wren, I didn't. Honestly, it's just a distraction."

"Yeah, right. Dude, you're unbelievable. I can't believe you're turning this on me now." With that, Wren flipped her sunglasses over her eyes, threw her rucksack over her shoulder and stormed out of the open front door into the harsh, streaming sunlight.

42

Paulie stood at the window and watched Aunt Meg traipse towards the cliff path that would lead her back into town. The plastic bag she'd been carrying on the way in was now empty, ballooning in the wind as she walked. She'd probably dropped off some birthday presents or something. The very thought caused a flutter of something pleasant in Paulie's tummy which was instantly crushed by the damning reminder of those two overheard words: 'issues' and 'regret'.

It felt ridiculously childish to refuse to come out of Tanya's room. Especially on her birthday. She didn't want to come across as a spoiled kid in a strop. But what other choice was there? She couldn't face Meg just yet.

She went to sit back on the bed and twisted her necklace deep into the side of her neck. The things Wren had given her yesterday were dumped in the folds of the duvet, a sickening reminder of the way things were between them now. The jigsaw meant nothing. Paulie knew that. In fact, the pieces were now strewn across the bedroom floor and the Hollywood sign would probably never materialise. Just like it never would for Tanya.

Paulie picked up the parcels and turned them over in her

hands. She got a flashback of ripping open Amazon parcels with Wren all those months ago. The joy she'd felt that day had now morphed into the cold, hard truth that it had all been in vain.

She opened the card. The front was full of black and gold letters spelling out the words, 'Lights, Camera, Action' and inside the message read, 'Have a Hollywood-style Birthday!' It was signed by pretty much everyone she knew at college, including Swanny, who had lavished his name with swirls and flourishes, and Romano who simply wrote, 'Keep being you'. *Thanks, Romano,* she thought, *but I so wish I didn't have to.* Nevertheless, Paulie took a quick selfie with the card so she could pop it on the WhatsApp group later to say thanks. That seemed to be the correct birthday etiquette.

She moved on to the parcel from Breeze. She gasped when she saw what was inside. It was a framed print of the compass design he'd been working on. How on earth had he found the time since then to finish it, print it and frame it? He'd even signed it in the bottom right corner like a proper pro. On second thoughts, maybe he had a whole stack of these things sitting at home, ready to dish out as and when they were needed. Nothing said, *hey, I might act like I give a crap about you but I really don't,* like a bit of card grabbed from a stack of hundreds.

Wren's present was the last one sitting there. It had a small note attached. *Something to save your neck.* What the hell was that supposed to mean? Her neck was perfectly fine and to prove it she pulled the pendants up to her lips and gave them a quick kiss. Then she ripped open the parcel and found a little wooden box. Inside was a silver ring with several layers of tiny beads and flexible wires. It was very pretty and as Paulie slipped it onto her finger, she found that the beads slid backwards and forwards across the edges of the ring and the wires rippled in response. She peered inside the box and there were two words stamped across the inside of the lid: *Anxiety Ring.*

Anxiety? It felt like a slap. She pulled the ring off and chucked it across the room so that it disappeared with a clatter behind Tanya's dresser. How dare Wren suggest she was some kind of psycho? Or that her necklace needed replacing? If she knew Paulie *at all*, she'd know that this was the most insensitive gift she could have chosen. Damn Wren.

A text chirped from Paulie's phone and saved her from screaming out loud. Rashid.

> Happy birthday, Paulie! Now you're old enough, maybe you could join us at the Crow's Nest tonight? We're all going. Wanna come?

Paulie did not, under any circumstances want to come. However, sitting there on the bed and realising that the birthday card signed by everyone was actually the only thing that made her feel remotely wanted, she wondered if she should.

The Crow's Nest was Berryport's only nightclub and was likely packed with all of the elements she hated. Rubbish music. Sweaty people. Crowds. Still, if Rashid could be bothered to ask her, maybe she could be bothered to go. Before her mind could dive into the scenario where she stayed here and festered further in Tanya's overstretched clothes, she quickly typed out a reply.

> Rashid, I'm in.

Paulie had been right about the sweaty people and the rubbish music. The Crow's Nest had both things in abundance.

Inside a booth right next to the dance floor, she shifted in her seat and peeled the skin of her thighs away from the pleather covering. It would have been great if she'd been able to find something other than hotpants in Tanya's wardrobe, but these were the only things in there with a stretchy waistband. The crop top with the word 'Juicy' emblazoned across it didn't do much to complete the ensemble but again, it was pretty much the only thing Paulie could wriggle into. At least they were both the same shade of magenta pink. Because looking like a Kardashian *and* wearing clashing colours would have been a total embarrassment.

She watched her friends shaking their stuff on the dance floor. They were really living it up due to the fact that the next few days would be fraught with the hard work of staging a successful skirmish. Shazza and Cazza were giving Rashid some kind of boppy Tikok dance tutorial that looked more like he was suffering from a series of electric shocks. Beau was swirling alone on the sidelines, proper Kate Bush style, her black and green hair billowing under the glow of the disco lights. Adam / Axel was involving some of the other students in a semi-circle of enthusiastic head-banging. It was quite the thing to watch.

They'd been so kind when she'd first arrived, with whoops and cheers and a rendition of 'Happy Birthday'. A nearby gang of lads had insisted on buying her a drink called 'Caribbean Curse' which was every bit as gaudy and over-decorated as they were. One of them had flung a feather boa around her neck. Another one had pressed a rainbow bowler hat on her head and squealed that it was the ultimate in millinery chic. Far from finding the attention enjoyable, Paulie's fractured system could only take so much. That's why she'd found this booth where she could babysit everybody's drinks as well as smile occasionally as if she actually meant to be there.

"So, what's wrong with the birthday girl then?" It was the lad who'd given her the bowler hat earlier, accompanied by his boyfriend who had quite possibly the most outstanding eyeliner she'd ever seen. They crashed into the booth with her, bringing a festive kind of vibe with them. "Don't feel like dancing?"

"Erm, well, nope. Not really my thing. At least, not right now."

"You conserving your energy, babe?" said Eyeliner Guy. "You're one of the drama lot, right? So you'll be in that pirate movie thingy? Oooh, I bet you even know that Bretton boy who reckons he shot his girlfriend last year. I read about it online."

"I do. I was." Paulie puffed out her cheeks and let the air escape from her mouth. The umbrella in the drink she hadn't touched twirled around in its own mini-carnival moment. "I mean . . . I'm kind of between drama opportunities right now."

"Story of my life!" Bowler Hat Guy shrieked with laughter and made the whole table wobble with the force of the slap he brought down upon it. "Seriously though, babe, like, what ails you? You're the birthday girl! You're supposed to be up there with that lot, dancing for your life. Eighteen is an important birthday."

"So they say," Paulie shrugged, knowing full well there was no way she was getting up on that dance floor. "I'm just . . . having a moment."

"Fair enough. So, you're not at college anymore? What was it, the teachers doing your head in?"

"Oh, they're okay. They're not really the problem." Paulie thought that if she kept her answers brief, the lads might go away. It's not that they weren't perfectly lovely, she just couldn't possibly explain to them all the many reasons why college was failing her. Or she was failing it. Plus there was a lot going on. Glittering drinks. Swirling lights. Pounding music. Spilled cocktails. Sticky thighs. That internal dragging feeling that she was somehow disappointing the world by not behaving in an appropriate birthday / nightclub fashion. For all of those reasons, a decent conversation was never going to happen.

"Oh, come on. I used to go there myself. Who have you got?"

"Swanny for drama. Romano Smith for counselling."

Bowler Hat and Eyeliner Guys exchanged a look Paulie couldn't quite determine. "Oh yeah, Romano. He's a good guy. Helped me through a few tough times myself."

"Is he the ginger dish with the prosthetic leg? Hmm. Tasty, I say."

Paulie feigned a laugh as the two lads slapped each other in a mock fall-out. "He's alright I suppose. Swanny's a laugh. He makes drama fun."

"Yeah. Everyone seems to think so." Bowler Hat Guy's face suddenly darkened, as if a shadow had passed over it. "Good old Swanny."

"But you don't mean that." The words were out of Paulie's mouth before she could filter them. It was obvious though. Bowler Hat Guy was not Swanny's number one fan.

"He knows his stuff about drama and acting and all those shenanigans, that's true. But, well, Paulie, is it?" She nodded and edged forward in her seat, eager to hear more. "Paulie. Listen. I've never really said this out loud to anyone apart from well, you know, my *community*, but . . . I just don't buy it."

"What? What don't you buy?"

"The way he presents himself. The exuberance. The mincing about. The campness. He's like a pantomime dame."

"Oh no he isn't!" roared Eyeliner Guy. Bowler Hat Guy flat-out ignored him, and continued with an expression that betrayed his jolly, rainbow-striped jumpsuit.

"I can't say I've got any real evidence but something isn't quite right. Paulie, I'm letting you in on a Berryport secret here but the word on the street is . . ." he leaned forwards across the table and beckoned her with his finger. She didn't want to miss a word so she edged as close as she possibly could, barely teetering on the edge of her seat, elbows pressing on the table with the full weight of her body. ". . . Nobody that gay is that gay."

"Wah?" That's when Paulie felt her whole world – or at least the table with about fifty billion glasses of Caribbean Curse on it – suddenly topple and crash to the ground, taking her with it and quite possibly chinning both Bowler Hat and Eyeliner Guys on its journey. It wasn't until she found herself slammed to the floor, her scraped elbows burning and her bum cheeks screaming with the impact, that she realised what had happened.

And of course, because her life was never as easy as picking herself up and dusting herself off, the entire drama class abandoned their dancing efforts and sprinted over, their phones open, their camera flashes at the ready. There wasn't even a second to shake the drinks out of her hair, pull her limbs into order or assemble her face into anything resembling good humour before the clicks and taps were dutifully performed.

BeYu had struck again. And this time, it was Paulie who was on the mortifying end of it.

43

"More waffles?" Wendy piled three more onto Paulie's plate without waiting for an answer. "Can't have you wasting away now, can we?"

On her birthday night, when Paulie had come back to Wendy's house covered in dregs of Caribbean Curse and bruises from her fall, Wendy had slapped her hands to her face and exclaimed, "It's because you're not eating, isn't it?" That's when Paulie realised that the distinct lack of contact from Aunt Meg probably meant she'd provided Wendy with some kind of 'How-To Guide'. It was insulting. Okay, so sometimes she forgot to eat and sometimes she ate like her life depended on it – both versions taking their toll on her body – but that didn't mean she needed spoon-feeding like a toddler.

Wendy sat down at the table with her, hugging a mug of green tea with her perfectly manicured fingers. "So, are you going to make it into town today?" It was the day of the pirate festival and Paulie suspected that Wendy would want to stay home just as much as she did. It might have felt lately like the walls of Wendy's house were closing in on her, but anything was preferable to being at that skirmish.

"Doubt it."

"Hmm. I understand. But wouldn't you be happier amongst your friends?" *Friends*. Is that what they were? The bunch of cretins who'd posted a BeYu picture of her splayed across the floor of the Crow's Nest? The boy who gossiped about her behind her back? The girl who wanted her to wear jewellery that advertised to the world she was a screw-up? As if. Paulie muttered something non-committal and mopped up a pool of maple syrup with the last corner of her waffle. Wendy sighed heavily and started clearing plates away.

"Are *you* okay, Wendy?" Paulie suddenly realised she should ask this question. Wendy had been good enough to let her stay in her home and surely that meant Paulie should be showing some charity back. Today couldn't be an easy day for her.

"Honestly? I'm okay as long as I'm distracted. But I have you. I'll concentrate on you." The smile on Wendy's face was bright but it plastered over a very deep pain. Paulie could feel it in her chest, along with everything else.

"Actually, if you want a distraction, I do have a question for you."

"Anything."

Paulie took a deep breath and willed the words to stream from her mouth. "Did my Aunt Meg and Coral have like, you know, a thing."

"Oh, Paulie. I'm not sure it's my place to say."

"It's okay. Go on."

"They did. Yes, they did. A big thing."

"What do you mean, big?"

"Big, like epic. They were in love from a young age. Anybody with eyes could see it. If me and Arthur were the golden couple then they, without doubt, were the platinum one."

"So what happened?"

"Life."

"Come on, Wendy. One word isn't going to cut it."

"Paulie, I'm really not sure I should."

Paulie needed to change tack. Like, now. "Okay. Let me tell you what I know." It wasn't an easy tale to tell, but Paulie described to Wendy what she'd overheard in the flat between Rita and Meg. It ran the risk of Aunt Meg finding out, but that didn't even really matter anymore. Paulie just wanted the truth.

And she got it. Like a stab to the heart, she got it. Meg and Coral had been on the verge of getting on a plane to Vegas when Paulie's dad had turned up with her in tow. In fact, that was why Meg hadn't made it to her mum's funeral, because she was preparing to jet off with the love of her life. It was all very movie-worthy.

When Paulie's dad seemingly disappeared off the face of the earth, Meg told Coral this was it, she was now a parent. Everything had changed. Her outlook, her ambitions, her responsibilities. Coral had been furious, especially when Meg explained she needed to funnel all of her energies into caring for Paulie and earning a living. The bakery came up for rent and Meg threw her travel savings at it. Coral – high on heartbreak and betrayal – threw hers at training with the police force. In London.

"Why the police though? I thought Coral wanted to be a tattooist?"

"Well, yes she did. But she comes from a family of detectives. It's in her blood. And the whole idea of tattooing just reminded her of Meg. It was a sad time for her. Listen, Paulie, whatever's keeping you from going back to your aunt, don't let it spoil what you two have got. This stuff is ancient history and what matters is the here and now. Meggie bloody loves you, and what you overheard will have been part of a much bigger conversation, I'm sure of it. Maybe you didn't hang around long enough to hear the bit about how much you've changed her life? How she wouldn't change a thing?" Paulie couldn't bring herself to meet Wendy's eyes now. Instead, she stared at some waffle crumbs on the table, languishing in tiny puddles of sticky, brown syrup. "I hope you don't mind, luvver, but I'm going for a lie down. This day . . . well, it's giving me a headache. If you want any more food, please help yourself."

Paulie didn't even get a chance to whisper any thanks before Wendy left the room. She was left alone, with nothing but a jangling energy tugging at her limbs. The kitchen table juddered as her leg twitched and she had flashbacks of the table tipping in the nightclub. It wouldn't do to repeat that episode so she got up and started pacing around the kitchen.

Every surface in this place bloody well gleamed. As much as Paulie loved the idea of order, when she was confronted with it, it often felt like an immersion. A drowning. She paced even quicker and squeezed her eyes open and closed repeatedly, in a perilous game where she could easily lose her footing or walk into a piece of furniture. But opening her eyes on something new in the room every few seconds was kind of thrilling. She was basically making her own fun, like she used to when she was little.

There was the fancy Smeg fridge. There was the fruit bowl. There was the light switch, a blender, a chopping board, a metallic splashback. With every squeeze of her eyelids, the items she was seeing took longer to come into focus, to sharpen. She enjoyed the way there was a fuzzy edge to her vision and experimented with how long it took to clear every time she zoomed in on something different. Door handle. Tap. Cactus. Rug. Photo.

Photo.

Paulie wanted to see what was in the photo so she strode over to it. It hung in a silver frame on the wall above the cutlery drawer and for a few seconds, was so blurry it could have been an abstract painting. Eventually though, three faces emerged and the starry borders faded back to reveal features belonging to a much younger Wendy and Arthur with a golden-haired, toddler-aged Tanya nestled between them.

The photo must have been taken on pirate festival day because they were all in costume. Arthur looked really quite handsome in a brown leather tricorne and eye patch ensemble. Wendy had her hair gathered up in a fabric wrap and wore huge, hooped earrings and a striped top. Tanya, as adorable as could be, wore a bandana printed with a skull and crossbones and was waving a plastic cutlass about.

In the background there was the blurred outline of the Arching Angel as well as a handful of people milling about the harbour. Some of them had stopped to appreciate the beauty of the Withers family and looked on with what? Admiration? Wonder? It was hard to tell. There was one young pirate in particular, who had an entirely different expression on his face though. His presence was miniscule, and he may have been looking beyond the Withers family and at something else entirely, but his twisted features were very out of place. If Paulie didn't know better, she'd say they showed rage. Real rage.

And the only real reason she knew this was that she felt rage too. So much of it. It gushed from her heart to every extremity of her body so that her fingertips, toes and scalp blazed like hell. It didn't feel right to be feeling such things here, in the Withers household, where joy had once been so prevalent and sorrow now saturated the walls. She needed to take this rage some-where else. Somewhere pain would be allowed, welcomed, perhaps even intensified.

She knew exactly where that place was.

Odyssey Ink.

44

Running through Berryport was no easy task. Far from the wild sprint she'd done across the cliffs days ago, dashing through town on Pirate Festival day was doomed from the start. It didn't help that every single pirate in town knew that there were movie cameras about.

People moved in packs. Dense and deliberate packs. Their costumes were even more on point than usual; friends preened and adjusted each other; there were whispers of excitement and desperate, flitting eyes searching every corner of the town for signs of Hollywood. Ordinarily, Paulie would need to work hard at not being consumed by such potent energies but right now she had one task and one task only: get to Odyssey Ink.

She needed to hear everything Wendy had told her from Coral's mouth now. Why hadn't she stood by Aunt Meg when Paulie arrived on the scene twelve years ago? If they were supposedly so in love, how come Paulie never even had an inkling of it? She felt stupidly, ashamedly in the dark and she needed light on this matter immediately.

As she moved along the harbour, Paulie shimmied past a rather sparkly group of middle-aged mermen, ducked under a giant skull and crossbones flag and narrowly missed a wheel-chair that had been transformed into an open clam shell, the person inside it dressed as some kind of sea nymph. Before she could become too transfixed by the brilliance and variety of costumes, an audible gasp swept across the harbour. Every single person looked up to see a drone arcing gracefully across the sky. Nearby, a rather portly Smee whispered to an octopus, "I've heard they're doing practice sweeps ready for the skirmish later." Paulie shook her head vigorously, driving out distraction, and pressed on towards the tattoo shop.

"I want to know what happened between you and Aunt Meg." Paulie let the words tumble out of her as soon as she burst through the shop door. The only way to deal with somebody like Coral Bombora was to just come out with it. Otherwise, she might lose her nerve.

"Erm . . . she once gave me a doughnut with extra filling?" Breeze emerged from the shadows at the back of the shop which was otherwise empty, his sleeves rolled up and holding a broom. Damn. Why hadn't she bloody well used her eyes before storming in, all guns blazing?

"Oh, it's you. Where's your auntie?"

Breeze blinked and some of his fringe caught in his eyelashes. He pushed it away with the back of his hand and treated Paulie to one of those smiles that wasn't quite a smile. "Wow. I'm fine, thanks. How are you?"

"I mean it, Breeze. Where is she? It's important."

"She's at the festival. With your auntie, I believe."

"Really? Why aren't you there? Don't tell me. You've been suspended from college too?"

"No. That's only for special people. My contribution was painting the flags for the skirmish. You know, for the aerial shots for the movie. I'd be there to watch the others but I told Auntie Coral to go instead. She's been working like mad since she opened this place and, well, I have a feeling she really – like, *really* – wants to see your Meg."

"Yeah, twelve years too late," stormed Paulie. This was not good news. Now what was she supposed to do with herself? Berryport on Pirate Festival day was the last place she wanted to be. "How come she's left you to run the shop on such a busy day? Are you, like, allowed to do tattoos by yourself now? I thought you were still training."

"Well, it's busy out there but we probably won't get any bookings on a day like this. I'm just holding fort. And to answer your question, yes, I am allowed to do tattoos myself now. I'm most likely better at it than you think I am."

"Are you now?" An idea was forming in Paulie's mind. An idea that would help her channel her pain, assert her independence *and* give her time to think. "So tattoo me then."

"Tattoo *you*?" If he hadn't been leaning on the broom he might have fallen over in surprise. "You want *me* to tattoo *you*?"

"I do."

"Have you thought this through, Paulie? Is it something you actually want? Or is it another one of your spontaneous interests?"

"That's not really any of your business, is it? I can pay you. And I'm eighteen now. Let me see your designs and I'll choose one. We'll do it now." Paulie strode over to the wall that was completely covered in tattoo designs and looked it over. She didn't want to admit it to Breeze, but she was so unbelievably consumed by this new idea that her eyes wouldn't allow her to focus on any of the pictures in front of her, let alone make a decision. She could hear Breeze behind her, spraying down the tattoo chair and gathering his tools. Her heart pumped with the possibility of marking her body in this way. Why hadn't she thought of this before?

She spun around to face Breeze. "I know what I want."

"Okay."

"I want that compass design you did. The one you gave me for my birthday."

"Oh. Right. It's quite intricate."

"You're not up to it?"

"Course I am. It's just, for your first tattoo it's a commitment. I mean, for you."

"I don't care. I want it. And I want it here." Paulie pulled up her sleeve and stuck out the soft underside of her forearm.

"That'll hurt."

"Duh," Paulie scoffed. "Just do it, Breeze."

"Well, seeing as you asked so nicely." Breeze gestured towards the empty chair, and bowed as if he was her butler or something. Once she was sat down he walked over to the shop door and turned a sign over so that to the outside world it read three very important words: 'Tattoo in progress'.

Breeze was right. It did hurt. As the needle worked its way over her skin, and her arm began to burn with the pressure, Paulie realised she'd never felt a pain like it. Breeze kept stopping to ask if she was alright. She wished he wouldn't.

Looking down at the black outline appearing across her skin was a thrill. Despite the pain. Or maybe even because of it. Yes, the soreness was intense and it increased by the second but what was interesting, was that it was almost as if it was *giving* her brain something. With every second that passed, her mind came alive, feeling more alert, attuned and, well, happy. How could it be that pain could do that to her?

She suddenly remembered Romano's tentative introduction of the INCUP theory all those months ago. He'd explained people with ADHD often needed activities to tick five specific boxes. What was the first one? 'Interest'. Yep. She definitely had an interest in the way Breeze was carving out forever-lines on her skin. She was pretty sure the second one was 'Novelty', and you couldn't get more novel than having your first tattoo. The third was 'Challenge'. She knew that one for sure. Sitting here, in this chair and getting through the whole thing was going to be tough, but she was sure as hell going to do it. 'Urgency'. That had been the next one. The spontaneous idea for this had filled her with an immediate sense of haste. Like this tattoo was going to solve everything and the quicker she got started, the better. When Breeze had flipped that sign on the door and sat her down on the chair, she'd have thanked her lucky stars if she actually had any.

The last word in the INCUP theory was 'Passion', and that's where the compass design came in. The compass pendant she'd worn around her neck for the last twelve years was, according to her beautiful mum, for guidance and protection. Paulie had practically worshipped both of her pendants for so long but wasn't sure she'd always felt guided or protected. That's why this tattoo was important. If she had guidance and protection gouged into her actual skin, surely she'd reap some of the metaphorical benefits her mum always meant her to have?

"Breeze. Can we put some music on?"

"Sure. You got something you want to play?" Paulie already had her phone out and was scrolling to her favourite Gorillaz playlist. She found the shop's smart speaker on Bluetooth and hit play. The tinny beats of 'Dare' bounced into the empty shop, turning quickly into a tormenting base and solid dance rhythm which, when combined with the sensations of the tattoo, felt unbearably good. She willed her muscles to hold still as Breeze pressed harder, sending shots of pain up her arm and into her brain. Would it be wrong to tell him how much she was enjoying this?

Paulie let her eyes roam around in a bid to still her body. They landed on a stack of newspapers within arm's reach. She reached out and took one, realising straight away that it was the edition of the Torbay Gazette with Swanny on the front cover. As the music swelled in her body and the pain rippled across her soul, Paulie opened up to the double page spread where the photo had the caption, *'Local hero, Josiah Swan, seconds before boarding the Arching Angel as Captain Roger Saltbeard'.*

That photo, of Swanny with his arms spread wide and a grin plastered across his chubby face, was quite stirring. It was a year to the day since it was taken and at that point, nobody knew what was about to happen to Tanya. Not even Sage, her actual killer.

Paulie looked closer at the scene unfolding behind Swanny. The Arching Angel looked magnificent in the golden rush of afternoon sunlight that Devon was so famous for. Turquoise waves curved with sparkling elegance across the hull and seagulls swooped in the sky. The ship was loaded with figures. That would be the students, getting ready to perform their skirmish, totally oblivious of the hell that was about to be unleashed.

In fact, if she skewed her eyes a bit, Paulie could make out figures she actually recognised. That must have been Wren with the crazy beard and the upright stance. And there was Rashid, looking out at Swanny as if frustrated that he hadn't joined them yet. Then there was a couple, snogging like their life depended on it. Sage and Tanya, obviously. So Beau's account of the kiss was true then. Sage had Tanya locked in an embrace to put any romance movie to shame and Tanya looked like she'd found everything all at once in Sage's arms. As the tattoo needle went over a particularly sensitive patch near her wrist and the Gorillaz track came to a satisfying crescendo, Paulie intuited that the total collapse of Tanya's body against Sage's meant that fear had been coursing through it only seconds before.

Seconds before . . . what must have happened only seconds before this photo was taken? The argument in the alleyway? Surely, this was about the time Paulie herself had frozen against the wheelie bins? On her sprint out of the alleyway, Tanya had bumped into Raymond the police officer, told him she'd had an argument with her boyfriend and he'd seen her onto the Arching Angel to be with none other than . . . her boyfriend. Sage might be a golden boy, but even a Bretton couldn't be in two places at once.

And at that time, when the skirmish was about to start, everyone should have been present and correct on the ship. Especially the drama tutor who had organised the whole damn thing . . .

Paulie looked again at Swanny. She couldn't see much that was unusual about his image other than he should have been *on* the ship, not in front of it. His giant belt buckle of a demonic skull and crossed cutlasses gleamed from his portly midriff, and Paulie noticed that his hands were filthy. Although what that meant she didn't know. It could have just been the camera angle or something . . .

There was a sudden and violent smash against the shop window. Both Breeze and Paulie looked up to see a troop of drunken sailors staggering past but no actual broken glass in the window. Not even a crack. "What did they do?" Paulie asked, her heart pounding fast.

"Looks like they kicked a bottle and it smashed off our window. Idiots. I'll clean it up later. You okay? Shall I keep going?" On closer inspection, there was a broken bottle of Buccaneer Bounty now scattered on the ground outside. Amazing that such a small thing could make such a startling sound.

"Yes. Please don't stop." Breeze folded back over Paulie's arm so that she could feel his breath meandering through the pain as it picked back up. It added another dimension she couldn't say was unpleasant. And the tattoo was coming along great so she slid back into whatever kind of focus she'd been in before.

Except this time, something was tugging her brain away from the photo in the newspaper. For some stupid reason, the smashed bottle outside wanted her attention. Other than it being Arthur Withers' favourite ale, she couldn't think why else it was significant. Maybe after this tattoo she'd go out and buy a bottle. She could toast her bravery.

Then the joyous cries of, "Waste-not-want-not" echoed through her mind as she remembered everybody in Swanny's office glugging down masses of the stuff. It was shameful the way they'd sloshed it over the carpet for Rita to clean the next day. There had even been a bottle of it stuffed inside Swanny's trophy cabinet.

Like the correct answer pinging on a game show, Paulie knew she'd hit some kind of jackpot with that last thought. The empty bottle of beer hadn't been placed there by some thought-less guest at all. It had been placed there deliberately, like an actual trophy, and it had rolled up bits of paper inside that had to mean *something*. A seemingly random catalogue of thoughts suddenly flew into order inside her head. No, not inside her head. Inside her whole body. She felt them stack and sort and systemize themselves into an electrifying collection of very real and very thorough evidence. How had she never seen it before?

Swanny used to live aboard the Arching Angel.

The Arching Angel was directly opposite the Powder Monkey Pub.

The Powder Monkey pub had been Arthur's local.

Arthur's local was the last place he was seen.

Using a miraculous part of her brain raucously unleashed by the pain now searing into her arm and the music speaking to her heart, Paulie realised she was sure of one more thing. The man in the background of the Withers family photo that hung on Wendy's kitchen wall, the man looking right at them, the raging, furious man, was the one man who had been clever enough to get the whole town to worship him. Flipping genius.

"Breeze. We're going."

"Huh?" He looked up, his fringe dropping across deep green eyes of concentration. "What do you mean?"

"I mean stop that. We're going."

"Where?" The tattoo gun stopped buzzing. Breeze sat upright on his stool.

"Out. Now. Close up shop. I need you."

"What about your tattoo?"

Paulie looked down at her arm where the black outline of the compass design already looked stunning. "You can finish it later."

"Later? Paulie, what can be more important than the eternal art you're currently branding yourself with?"

"You'll understand if you come with me. Come on, do you trust me?"

Breeze looked hard at her and only left it a couple of beats before saying, "Actually, with my life." Then he switched off the tattoo gun at the wall, knocked off the lights, grabbed a set of keys and gave Paulie his hand to help her out of the chair. "Come on then. Take me on an adventure."

"Oh, I will," Paulie promised. And they left the shop, crunching the shards of broken beer bottle beneath their feet as they went.

45

"This is all good. We're headed in the right direction. But I need to do something first." Paulie stopped sharp on the corner of the back street that led to the harbour. Yes, it qualified as an alleyway but they would have to take that route to avoid the hordes of people now heading to the Arching Angel. She would just have to get over it.

If the frenzied mob was anything to go by, the skirmish would start in the next few minutes and that meant Picaroon Productions would be watching. The thought of that many cameras caused Paulie's stomach to flip into a thousand consecutive somersaults. "Breeze, I need you to call Wren."

"She'll be about to go into performance mode."

"I know, but you have to."

"Well, I *could*, but I really don't think it's me she wants to hear from."

Paulie sighed and just wished he would do as he was told. "She's not speaking to me. I can't do it."

"Paulie, that's precisely why you *should* do it." Breeze folded his arms across his chest and gave Paulie one of his classic Bombora stares.

"Okay, whatever, I need to call Shazza first anyway. Or maybe I'll text her. She's better with texts." Paulie found Shazza in her contacts and tapped out the message:

> Shazza, I know this will sound weird but I just need you to answer. Is your mum cleaning at the college today?

Shazza, glued to her phone as she always was, got straight back:

> Erm, interruption much? We r about 2 b discovered by Hollywood. Yeah, she had to work today. Why?

> Get her to go into Swanny's office. She needs to look in the tallest trophy cabinet. There should be an empty bottle of Buccaneer Bounty. There are rolled up papers inside. Ask her to unroll them and send a photo of whatever's on them. Then send it to me. ASAP.

> Weird. But 'K.

"What the heck was that all about?" Breeze asked, scratching his head in an extremely cartoon like fashion.

"I thought you trusted me with your life?"

"Oh, I do. But it wouldn't hurt to know at least a little of what's going on in that brilliant brain of yours."

"It is the little grey cells, mon ami, on which one must rely."

"Alright, Poirot. But some insight? Please?" Paulie looked up and down the street to make sure nobody was about. It was a miracle on a day like today but they were definitely alone. Unless you counted scavenging seagulls, of course.

She spoke in fast and rattled words, describing every place her head had gone whilst getting her tattoo. There was the alleyway argument and the timing of Tanya getting back to the ship and the fact that Sage had already been onboard so it couldn't have been him she was arguing with after all. There was Arthur's disappearance and Swanny's habitation of the Arching Angel and Arthur's love of Buccaneer Bounty. Then there was the missing pistol and the lack of fingerprints and Swanny's discoloured hands and the love letter to Wendy and the raging man in the background of the Withers family photo . . .

"Woah, woah. I get it. You know stuff I don't know." Breeze smoothed the fabric of her top down over her shoulders. Until that point, she'd forgotten she was wearing Tanya's sparkly t-shirt. "Paulie, are you totally sure about all of this? I can hear your passion and I'm guessing that's because there's a lot of truth in what you're trying to say."

"Indisputable truth. Breeze, I can feel it here." Paulie drew his hands down from her shoulders and placed them on her belly where they lay for a few seconds, rising and falling with the dogged determination of her breath. They looked so far into each other's eyes the rest of the world may as well have put itself on pause but, of course, it didn't. Because that's when Paulie's phone bleeped. "It's Shazza."

Opening the message, Paulie gasped. She'd expected the photo to reveal something, but this? It was a gift. A strange and terrible gift. Held between Rita's fingers, the rest of Swanny's lit up trophy cabinet hovering in the background, was an unrolled note where the paper was shabby enough that it could have been a decade old. In fancy flourishes and swirls, the note read:

The whole town knows your debt to the Brettons is insurmountable. Bring this bottle to the Arching Angel tonight for a way out.

"Let me see?" Breeze asked, moving behind her so he could peer over her shoulder. "Jeez, Paulie. Is that from Swanny's cabinet?"

"It is," she whispered, "and look." She flicked through her photo library until she found the selfie with her birthday card from the drama class. She zoomed in on Swanny's signature, which was undeniably written in the same hand as the note in the bottle.

"So . . . Swanny's been sus this whole time?"

"I'd say yes." A resolve surged through Paulie's gut where Breeze's hands had been placed just seconds ago. "Right, because I haven't got time to go home, and I don't even know if I have a home to be honest, now we need to speak to Wren."

"*You* need to speak to Wren."

"Whatever," Paulie huffed and hit the call button on her phone. The thought of speaking to Wren excited her heart as much as it terrified it. What if she hadn't got past the jigsaw thing? What if Paulie had really blown it? Regardless, it was an all-or-nothing kind of day and she knew she just had to go for it.

"What?" Wren's tone was clipped. Even with that one word, Paulie knew she had her work cut out for her.

"Wren? It's Paulie."

"You don't say."

"Listen, I know you're about to go into the skirmish. And I know you probably haven't got much time . . ."

"And . . ." Wren invited.

"And I know I was crap to you the other day."

"Dude. Don't break your back over it or anything."

"Okay, how's this? I'm really sorry. I never show enough appreciation for you. I never really suspected you could do anything to hurt Tanya - I just got carried away with my investigations. I've been stupid and I know it and although it hurts my actual body to admit, I want you to hear this. It's taken me too long to realise this but you, Wren Taylor, are the best friend I could possibly ask for, the best friend anybody could ask for and the best friend I could even dream up in my admittedly different, but obviously incredible, neurodiverse brain. You're just, well, you're the best."

There was a scuffling sound on the line and Paulie thought she detected a sigh that was bordering on happy. "It'll do. For now."

Paulie felt a tempting flood of tears in the bottom of her throat but when Breeze placed a reassuring hand on her arm, she got back on track. "Good. I mean, we'll talk properly later but for now, please know that *because* you are my best friend, I really need you. Like, right now."

"And you're saying that out loud." Okay, now there was definitely at least a hint of a smile to Wren's voice.

"I'm saying that out loud. Look, before the skirmish starts, can you please send me that photo you took of Wendy's love letter? It's back at Booty Bakes - still under the counter for all I know. I haven't got time to go and get it and I don't even know if Aunt Meg's been kicked out yet . . ."

"Whatever, dude. Done. Check your photos. Soz and all that but I've got to go now. The skirmish is afoot, as Swanny says."

"Okay, okay. But Wren? One more thing."

"Yep."

"When I get there, just go along with whatever I say, right? And tell the others I'm about to come good on that promise I made the night of the lantern parade, just in a different way than I thought. Breeze trusts me." Breeze smiled properly and broadly in a way that almost lifted her off the ground. "And I need you to do the same, okay?"

"Dude, as if you need to ask." The line went dead, but

Paulie already knew Wren was on her side. She always had been.

"Check your photos then." Breeze was getting into this now. Paulie flicked through to Wren's message and there it was, plain as day, the love letter written to Wendy in a hand that was so individual, Paulie was stunned she hadn't made the connection before now, however implausible it seemed.

My darling Wendy,

My love for you grows stronger every day, even when I think it must be impossible. I know you're alone and I never meant it to be that way. Hold out a little longer and we can finally be together. After all these years.

Always yours,

R

xxxxx

"R though?" Breeze asked. "I don't get the R."

Paulie mentally flicked through all the Rs she'd considered up until now. Raymond. Rita. Romano. Rex. Rashid. All of those seemed so ridiculous now. "Really? I thought you would have figured it out."

"Nope. My grey cells are no match for yours."

"What about if I asked you to think of the most popular pirate in town? The one that's going to put Berryport on the map? The one with more dramatic gravitas than you could shake a cutlass at? The one that's taking us all the way to Hollywood?"

Breeze's eyes widened and a rosy glow spread across his cheeks. Whether it was embarrassment or excitement, the result was the same. "Ohhh . . . Captain *Roger* Saltbeard."

Then they shrieked together, in perfect unison and hands joyfully interlocking, "For the love of pirates!"

"Come on, we've got to go. Now!" Paulie kept hold of Breeze's hands and tried dragging him towards the harbour. He didn't budge.

"Wait, I think you're forgetting something." He reached inside the pocket of his skinny jeans and pulled out Paulie's deerstalker hat. It looked like it had been through a decent wash cycle and when he handed it to her, it smelled like him. Pepper and citrus.

"How did you . . ? Oh right. Yeah. I think I may have thrown this at you in a fit of rage."

"I think you may have done. Never mind. You've got it back now. Now come on, let's go do some detecting." Paulie pulled the hat down firmly on her head and felt the snug fit of it propel her further into her mission.

This was it. This was really and truly it.

46

Paulie and Breeze had pushed through the hordes and were taking a breathless moment at the roped off viewing area.

"Woah. The Arseing Angel never looked so good." Breeze gave a low whistle and even Paulie had to admit that he'd done an amazing job of painting the sails and flags. Somehow, with a mesmerising swirl of colours and illustrations, he'd paid homage to the pirating heritage of Berryport as well as the modern day beauty of the place.

The Chair of Berryport Town Council was just finishing his speech to the masses and was now handing the mic over to Rex Bretton, who was standing on a platform next to the ship with a grinning Bex. For once, they weren't dressed in stiff power suits but as ghost pirates covered in gnarly barnacles. The costumes were astoundingly good and Paulie wondered how many other poor tenants' rent they'd put up in order to pay for such Hollywood standards. Sage stood behind them, wearing a rather infantile parrot costume, with huge, googly eyes, a beak and a fluffy, rainbow mohawk attached to a red hoodie. If he'd opened his arms out wide, there would have been an impressive display of feathers in blue, red, green and orange, but he kept them crossed over his chest, in a stubborn, silent stillness.

"I think Bretton should keep the mohawk," Breeze whispered into her ear. "It suits the whole eighties sullen thing."

"Really? *You're* pulling *him* up on sullen?" He threw her a look that combined pride and shock in equal measure. "Anyway, shut up. Once Rex has done his spiel, that's my moment."

"Me hearties of Berryport! I'm sure you can understand why we are not employing the signature cannon blasts this year. We are exercising quiet respect and courtesy at this year's festival." Rex hung his head at exactly the same time as Bex and Sage, an obviously choreographed piece that the whole of the town had no problem following. It astounded Paulie that everybody had pretty much forgotten Sage's revelations about his supposed guilt in Tanya's killing, but at times like this, money talked.

Rex lifted his crustacean covered face and continued, "Instead you will hear – streaming through the speakers set up on every street corner – the most exquisite piece of bespoke music which has been composed specifically for the forthcoming Hollywood hit, For the Love of Pirates!" There was an instant roar from the crowd and it felt like Berryport itself might levitate off the ground, leaving the sloshing sea below. "Yes, yes, our friends at Picaroon Productions have excelled themselves. And if you'll allow me, I'd now like to introduce to you our annual skirmish performed by the Bretton Inc sponsored, Bay Community College!" He turned around to address the students, who were each frozen in dramatic images of impending conflict, as focused and impressive as any troupe of professionals. Swanny was right in the centre, like a spider in the middle of its own web. "Avast ye! All hands on deck! Dead men tell no tales so skirmish thee to the bitter end!"

As the deep, resonant thud of timpani drums infiltrated

every nook of the harbour, Paulie wondered if she really could interrupt this epic scene. The students were beginning to move. There were cameras literally everywhere, including Debbie Devon practically hanging off the edge of the harbour wall – dressed (or not so dressed) in a sparkling blue mermaid costume. She had her phone stretched out on an intricate-looking telescopic stick covered in mock seaweed and was chatting away to her BeYu followers. Trust her to livestream a scene that one year ago today had ended in devastation.

Wren had already spotted Paulie and was throwing her questioning looks as she tumbled into fight choreography. Out of the corner of her eye, Paulie was aware of the fancy drone buzzing high up in the sky. It would be capturing every single detail of what was happening on the ship and – for an earth shattering moment – she pondered on how helpful it would have been if it was around last year to catch what really happened to Tanya.

Tanya. Her face flashed into Paulie's mind. Those amazing, cat-like eyes, that incredible, golden hair, that smile that lit up rooms. She felt with a burning intensity not just the fresh pain where her half-done tattoo was, but the ghostly call-back of the bruised shoulder that Tanya had rammed into on her hurried exit from the alleyway. Paulie had known from the start that alleyway moment had meant *something*. She grabbed her pendants and rubbed the glittery eye between her fingertips. Intuition. The spark deep inside her. That's what she had to listen to now.

Casting one last look at Breeze, Paulie slipped under the rope, dashed up the wooden walkway and hopped onto the bow of the ship. She heard one or two people gasp but she kept going. She slipped under the jib sail and swung under the bowsprit, standing mere yards from the confused looking Brettons on their podium. Now what?

"Paulie, here!" It was Wren. She was forward-rolling out of an intricate cutlass fight with Rashid and on springing to her feet, had reached out and grabbed the microphone from under Rex Bretton's nose. She threw it to Paulie and winked. "You've got this, dude!"

Standing there, with the microphone in her hand, Paulie knew that all she had to do was speak into it. The whole festival would come to a stop. But did she have the words? Did she ever have the words? One affirmative glance towards Wren told her that, yes, she would bloody well *find* the words.

"Berryport! I have something very important to say." Her voice boomed over the music and Paulie remembered the sound was being cast across the whole of town. She'd better make this good. "I have to tell you what really happened to Tanya at last year's festival." The music stopped. The action stopped. This was it.

"Get off!" Somebody yelled, from the back, near the ice cream shop.

"Let the police get on with it!" A voice rippled into a thousand agreements.

"You're ruining our movie!" This instigated a jeer that Paulie would have to work hard to get around.

"What if I told you that Josiah Swan is not what he seems?" She flung her arm back to gesture towards Swanny, who stood in the midst of the students, one booted leg propped up on a barrel and his arms raised high with a telescope in hand. He lowered them slowly and watched Paulie with a perfectly crafted expression of anguish on his face.

"Paulie, angel of my loon. You're spoiling the skirmish."

"I don't care what I'm spoiling," she ranted. "You spoiled Tanya's life. I think you also ended it."

Swanny's hands flew to his heart. "Desolate darling, how can you say such a thing?" He stepped forwards, threw his telescope aside so that it smacked a nearby Rashid in the face so hard that his dad jumped onto the ship to see if he was okay. In this mere second of distraction, Swanny snatched the mic away from Paulie and began imploring to the crowds. "The girl is maddened with grief! Even a year on, this poor young woman is steeped in the terrors of sorrow. I beseech you, kind souls of Berryport, to have mercy on her. She doesn't mean to trigger your own trauma or toss around such wild accusations."

"Yes I do!" Paulie cried, trying to wrangle the mic back off him. But it was no good. This little man was freakishly strong.

"Alright then, my heckling hen of innocence, why don't you tell us why you've brought these great proceedings to a halt?" He turned to the crowd, commanding them to sweep their attention his way with his mere physicality. Paulie had to get that mic back. "This, honoured guests, is an ex-drama-student from my very own class. She's usually such a sweet little thing. Would you like to know why she's hell-bent on thwarting the filming of the opening scene of my – I mean, *our* – feature movie debut?"

The crowd answered in a rousing cry of "Yes!" peppered with the odd, "Get 'er off, Swanny!" and "Let's get on with it!" For the first time, Paulie also noticed a group of people in solid black clothing, with definite ninja vibes, standing near Rex and Bex on the podium. They either wore headsets with mics, iPads around their necks or both, and their expressions were of stony steel. One of them, with a burgundy cravat, a buzz cut and horn-rimmed glasses flapped his hands at Swanny, urging him to wrap up whatever the hell this was and get back to filming. Swanny, in that moment – which would hardly have been decipherable to anybody else – nodded resolutely and turned to Paulie with a flashy smile.

"So you think I'm not what I seem?" He flipped the mic in Paulie's direction but retained a firm grasp on it. There was no way she could get it off him without biting him or something, and that would hardly make the crowds take her seriously now, would it?

"I believe you are hiding a lot of dark secrets," she said into the mic, surprised at how raspy her voice sounded. *Come on, get a grip.*

"Hilarious!" Swanny doubled over in merriment for a second, and Paulie briefly wondered if the ridiculously jagged belt buckle he was so precious about might actually puncture his gut. Then he snapped back up and glared hard at her. "To be fair, my meddlesome madam, I am a *drama* teacher, so it's my very occupation to employ trickery of the emotions. It's a ritual obsession of mine. But anyway, I digress. So, before we get this skirmish underway again, can you give us all an example? Of something you think I might be hiding?"

Paulie could hardly believe the bare-faced cheek of the man. No wonder he'd got this far in his blazing trail of deceit. He had total confidence that the town was on his side. Right. She'd show him. And them. "I think you're in love with Wendy, Tanya's mum. And that you're behind Arthur Withers' disappearance all those years ago. What have you got to say about that?"

For probably a billionth of a second, Paulie clocked a tell-tale twitch of Swanny's cheek, a fleeting sheet of white across his face. And she knew, with the same certainty that she knew her own name, that she was right about this. But he was quick. Quicker than her. He was a pro, after all. "What have I got to say about that?" Swanny turned to the crowds again, sweeping his very limp-wristed arm out before him and making flourishes across his body. "I'm sorry if it comes as a tragic surprise but I am *not* that way inclined."

"Well I don't believe you!" Paulie yelled it from behind him, not needing the mic to project her outrage.

"You don't believe me? She doesn't believe me, folks!" The crowd burst into laughter and Swanny's chest swelled to proportions that rivalled the ship's giant sails billowing above them. "Well, it's not often I perform on demand, but if you insist . . ." His little beady eyes swung around wildly until they landed on the closest male victim – Rashid. As corrupt as the man was, he must have known that using a student to demonstrate his romantic preferences would not be the best move. Instead, his attention turned to Rashid's dad, who was standing mere feet away, still tending to his son's battered face.

Swanny looked out at the crowd once more. "Berryport? I shall show you exactly what I am *not* hiding!" Then he held out his arm, did a mic drop that would have had Eminem quaking in his boots, strode over to Rashid's dad, grabbed him by the ruffle-necked pirate shirt and planted a slobbering, smacking kiss right on his lips.

Paulie's cries of, "But that proves nothing!" were immediately drowned out by the cheers, whoops and whistles now exploding across the harbour. One of the iPad clad movie-ninjas scooped away the mic, another one of them grabbed Paulie by the elbow and escorted her off the ship, and a third one pulled Swanny off Rashid's dad, gesticulating about time, money and overhead drones. The cheers, whoops and whistles morphed into one single, rhythmical chant that – with every sickening repetition – pulled on Paulie's guts and twisted them into a trap she had no chance of escaping from.

"Swanny, Swanny, Swanny!"

Now what was she supposed to do?

47

"Swanny, Swanny, Swanny!"

While Swanny performed a series of extravagant bows, Paulie was escorted to the podium where Rex, Bex, Sage and the posse of movie-ninjas had previously stood. The Brettons were now in the crowd, chanting along with the rest of the town, and she was stuck between two of the ninjas who wouldn't let her out of their sight. The one with the buzz cut and crazy glasses had now flounced off somewhere but not before instructing his co-ninjas to, "Keep an eye on that one."

The same music she'd interrupted with her dramatic accusations against Swanny streamed through the harbour for a second time. The skirmish started up again and Breeze's beautiful flags were being used to their best advantage for the drone camera hovering above. They rippled with astonishing effect. Ghostly illustrations flashing like mirages of palm trees, ocean waves, broad skies and birds in flight. Even sickened by what had just gone down, Paulie felt unbelievably proud of Breeze. His artwork was as amazing as him.

Breeze. Where the heck was he? She scanned the crowd for his signature shock of blue hair but couldn't find it. And that was because he'd somehow already made his way through the mobs and was practically hanging off the edge of the podium just below her. "Paulie!" His face appeared through the gaps in the railings. "Are you okay? You were so brave up there!"

"Brave didn't work though, did it?" She knelt down to speak to him, her ninja security guards still flanking her sides. "Breeze, what now? The crowd thinks Swanny is an actual god. It's going to be nearly impossible to convince them otherwise."

"Yeah, maybe. But since when do you let that put you off? Miss *I'm-going-to-learn-the-hobbies-of-every-single-suspect-in-this-case-and-just-you-try-and-stop-me*. If there's one thing you can do well, Paulie – and I'd argue there are many – it's going ahead and doing what the hell you want."

"Fair," Paulie shrugged, although she didn't see how she could claw this one back. She'd already given everything she had to that get up in front of all those people in the first place and now there was a literal buzzing inside her gut that resounded at her extremities with a sickening thrum.

"Look. Aunties o'clock." Breeze pointed in the direction of the bakery where Coral and Meg stood, a direct line of vision to the Arching Angel. Even from here, Paulie could see that the bakery was dark, unoccupied and all closed up – absolutely unheard of on the day of the Pirate Festival. Her aunt looked upset, naturally, though Paulie felt her bewildered demeanour may have had more to do with the spectacle she'd just been subject to rather than her precious bakery.

Precious. That was the word she should try to focus on. If her aunt's slack-jawed, teary-eyed expression was anything to go by, it was telling her that she – Paulie – was even more precious to her than her bakery. She could see it in the comforting arm Coral had slung around her shoulder; in the way her body was tilted, unconsciously, in Paulie's direction; in her wide, blinking eyes, her knitted brows, her mouth paused open as if words of love and concern were about to tumble out. *It's okay*, Paulie mouthed at her, unsure if the distance between them was too much for her to be understood. *I'm okay.*

Holding the gaze of Aunt Meg was all a bit much and what felt like millions of possible future conversations with her bolted through her brain. If there was anything that needed to be clear right now, it was her brain, so she tore her eyes away and scanned the crowd.

It seemed she was already old news as everyone was focused on the ship, oohing and aahing at every twist and turn the students made. So much for explosives being the one thing that drew in the crowds – Swanny's choreography and the students' performance was on another level this year.

Of course it is, she mused. *He needs this Hollywood thing to be pulled off, because he thinks that's what's going to win Wendy over. That's what he's always thought.* Man, she needed to make everyone else see the pieces she'd put together in her mind.

Just as she had this thought, Paulie's brain somehow conspired with her eyes and filtered out a collection of faces amongst the thousands, that were not trained on the Arching Angel. They were trained on her. Suddenly, these faces appeared like the rosiest apples in a bad lot, suddenly so strong and important that there was no way she could ignore them. She gave herself a few seconds to absorb them, really *feel* what they were trying to tell her. Because, right now, what other option did she have?

Fickle Fergus was easy to spot because he was waving manically. He was dressed from head-to-foot in pirate gear, finally bringing together his ensemble of pieces from throughout the year into one, singular, spectacular look. It was his face that really stood out though – a visible flush to his cheeks, a smile pouring out of him making his one eye that wasn't behind a patch all glossy and bright. He was rooting for her. Even if

Paulie didn't know why, it was bloody obvious he was rooting for her.

Then there was Romano Smith. He stood slap bang in the centre of the crowd and had his little boy sitting high up on his shoulders. He held tightly onto his son's ankles and jiggled slightly in time with the music, but he was looking right at Paulie, offering her not only the concern and validation he always had done, but a sense of strong-willed encouragement. She was sure of it.

Even Raymond the doughnut-loving police officer was looking her way. She didn't know him so well, apart from his preference for a sugar-pearled frosting, but she would swear his slowly nodding head was confirming something. Something he'd either known all along or had just seen the light about.

Not far from Raymond, hanging off either side of a tall lamp post, was the couple she'd met in the Crow's Nest on the night of her birthday. Although Bowler Hat Guy had swapped his rainbow hat for a bandana complete with a Jack Sparrow wig, she was absolutely sure it was him. His eyelinered, merman of a boyfriend was fixed on the skirmish but he watched Paulie as if she was about to make some bold and terrifying move. It was almost like he willed it.

It was Coral Bombora's face that really roused her though. It was a steely display of astonishment that barrelled across the crowd, straight into Paulie's gut. With one arm still protectively curved around Meg and the other balled into a fist in the air, Coral projected the support from where she stood. The ferocious, unfaltering, rock-hard support.

I've got Coral Bombora on my side.

"Dude, quick, what are you going to do?" It was Wren. She was pressed up against the structure of the podium, her chest heaving with the physical effort of the skirmish. "Tell me how I can help because I've got to go back on and pelt doubloons at Cazza any second now."

"Wren, I – I just don't know. People love him too much."

"Do they though? Come on, dude. Do you absolutely, categorically, believe all the stuff you're saying about him?"

"I do."

"Then find another way to say it!" And she was off, hurling doubloons at poor Cazza, who dipped and swerved in an intricate piece of choreography timed precisely to the music which was now building in drama, pace and volume. Breeze reached out and squeezed Paulie's hand through the railings.

"She's right," he said. "Find another way."

"Paulie! Look, whatever's gone between us I need you to know that I think you're onto something." Sage had somehow escaped the clutches of his parents and was now breathlessly hanging onto the edges of the podium, the hood of his parrot costume now dropped back and his face wide and shining. "I think you're right about Swanny."

"What? Last time I saw you, you were adamant you'd killed Tanya yourself. You put it all over the internet."

"Yeah, I know. But I think a lot of that is down to him. Now that I look back on it, every single conversation I've had with him since Tanya died, he has allowed me to think I did it. Sure, he placed just enough doubt in my mind to *appear* to be supportive but he needed to keep me on side because my parents are match-funding his whole movie. I was easy pickings for him. It all makes sense now. Paulie, if you know more about Swanny that can expose him, then just do it. I'm behind you. Breeze, you're behind her too, right?"

"Always." Breeze didn't even square up to Sage to prove his statement. Which was an achievement in itself.

"See? You can do this, Paulie."

"Yeah, but I'm getting stuck on the 'how' part." Paulie

rubbed her arm where her freshly scorched tattoo felt like recent sunburn.

"Be careful," Breeze said. "Try not to rub it." He took her arm through the railings and blew cool air across her skin. The emerging shape of the compass reminded her of the guidance and protection her mum always meant her to have. With her free hand she went to twist her necklace into her skin but it didn't strike the part of her soul she needed it to. The burn across her arm was speaking instead.

At that precise moment, Debbie Devon sauntered past below, her selfie stick held high as she continued to livestream the skirmish. She 'accidentally' brushed Sage with her scaly hips and made some fuss to her followers about bumping into him 'by mistake'. It was while she was lavishly ruffling his parrot feathers and engaging him in some stupid, soulless prattle that Paulie saw her chance. The phone and its stick were so temptingly close, it would have been crazy not to.

She grabbed the stick, ignored Debbie's shrieks and positioned herself into the frame. The skirmish continued to rollick and roll behind her as she channelled the buzzing energy in her tummy straight into her voice box so she could find the appropriate words . . . "Hi everyone. I'm Paulie, and I'm going to tell you a story."

48

When Paulie grabbed the phone, Breeze and Sage saw their chance.

With Debbie Devon sandwiched between them, the choice couldn't have been clearer. This would distract the movie-ninjas from Paulie's side, give her a chance to commandeer the livestream *and* it was totally believable. After all, it wasn't like the weird emo kid from Bristol and the Golden Boy of Berryport hadn't fought over a girl before, right?

The fight choreography they'd learned in drama class came into its own. With swooping fists and a string of soap opera insults, they did an amazing job at making people believe they were fighting over Debbie. The movie-ninjas jumped down from the podium and tried to break things up, but Sage and Breeze kept things going as long as they could so that Paulie could tell her story. Debbie screeched in an *oh-my-actual-god-how-terrible-these-boys-are-fighting-over-little-old-me* kind of a way and the loss of her precious phone became a secondary concern. Paulie knew it wouldn't last forever so she got on with things as quickly as she could.

"I've already tried appealing to the crowds here at the skirmish," she continued, breathlessly, "but Josiah Swan's choreography is, as ever, designed to bedazzle and distract from what he's really got going on. People of Berryport, and people all over the world, I need to tell you what I know about this man, the death of his student, Tanya Withers, last year and the disappearance of her father, Arthur Withers, more than a decade ago." Paulie glanced at the number of people watching the stream right now and her heart nearly flipped out of her chest. She glanced back at Wren, who was body rolling her way out of a cutlass attack from Axel / Adam. She would be well impressed with these figures, and would be using that feeling to show everyone how the pieces of this jigsaw had finally come together. *Right, Paulie. Make like Wren and get this bloody well done.*

So she did. She rattled through all of the facts she'd uncovered, as well as the gut-feeling-vibes that threaded everything together. Because those vibes, she now knew, were just as important as cold, hard evidence. It was like Coral Bombora had said in her fifth and final tip for solving a murder: *don't underestimate the power of your intuition.*

Or, as Paulie had come to know it, a spark.

She started with the place it had all kicked off a year ago. Tanya was arguing with somebody in the alleyway only moments before her death. That person had to have been Swanny because of the timings suggested in the newspaper photo. She popped a link to the Gazette article in the comments so people could see for themselves.

Wendy had been attacked years ago by a masked boy and Paulie would bet money that the perpetrator was Swanny. The likelihood was that Wendy knew it too, but once he 'adopted' his camp persona, if she'd said anything to anyone she would have been laughed out of town.

Paulie was certain that Tanya had somehow found out

about the attack on her mother and was going to report Swanny to the college authorities. Romano would have been supporting her with this. Regardless of the outrage Tanya probably felt, it must have been conflicting for her because Swanny had organised her entire acting career to start in London. Now, with hindsight, it was crushingly clear that all Swanny wanted was to get Tanya out of the way so he could have Wendy to himself. When Tanya stuck a big old spanner in the works with threats to report him to the college authorities, perhaps he elevated the plan of packing her off to London to a plan to pack her off for good. Like, from life.

"I don't know exactly how he fixed the pistol so that it was faulty but I'm one hundred percent sure he tampered with it." Paulie paused to catch her breath and really think through what she was saying. Out loud. To thousands of people. "We think there was an extra gun onboard the Arching Angel that day and chances are Swanny had it stowed away somewhere ready for the attack. Maybe somebody could check the Gazette photo I've just shared and get back to me? Also, I wouldn't be surprised if he somehow encouraged Sage to juggle those pistols after the deed was done. I mean, having somebody else to so readily take the fall was pretty convenient, right?"

Out of the corner of her eye, Paulie noticed some comments starting to pop up on Debbie's screen. If she filtered out the lines that read, *'Who does she think she is?'* and, *'Where's Debbie gone?'*, there were actually some people starting to invest . . .

Sounds plausible.

Stranger things have happened.

Tell us more, Paulie!

Then there was one that made her heart stop:

```
Checked the gazette photo. He has a gun in his
waistband and another one in the pocket of his
frock coat. See for yourself.
```

@Devon_Beats, whoever they were, had attached an image to their comment that showed a zoom-in of Swanny's midriff. Sure enough, there was a pistol – probably the non-firing one – tucked into his bright red sash. Then a lump, an unmistakably pistol-shaped lump, inside the chest pocket of his long, waxed frock coat.

"Oh my god, @Devon_Beats, you've a keener eye than me. Thank you so much for sharing that. While we're sharing damning photos, let me show you what I've found too." Slamming all assumptions about ADHD and multi-tasking out of the park, Paulie used one hand to keep the livestream going and the other to fish out her own phone and send pictures to Debbie's live post of the love letter to Wendy, the notes from the bottle and, for good measure, the signature from her birthday card.

Once those images were out in the world, she looked over her shoulder at what was going on with the skirmish, to see Swanny hanging from the standing rigging of the Arching Angel, performing some elaborate twirling that would have ordinarily had the crowds roaring for more. Looking at the audience though, something was beginning to shift. Not everybody was focused on the ship. In fact, a good deal of people had their noses in their phones and yet more were looking right at her.

"Dude!" Wren shouted, from her spot on the ship. "Whatever you're doing, it's working! They're losing interest." Paulie nodded and swung her focus back around to the phone. She had to ride on the waves of whatever this was.

"I hope you can all see how I've managed to piece this together. I don't know how it's taken me an entire year to see it, but this man is dangerous. He's obsessed, he's a phony and he's already taken Tanya's life – possibly her father's too – who knows what else he could do?" Paulie was struggling to keep track of the comments now, but could see they were overwhelmingly in her favour.

@Rainbow_BowlerHat_Guy:
I told you, Paulie darling. Nobody that gay is that gay!

"You were right, lovely Bowler Hat Guy. You were so right!" Paulie directed this to the phone but then cranked her head over the top of it to see that Bowler Hat Guy was still hanging off the lamp post but now blowing a stream of kisses in her direction. What a gem.

@ChampionTalentAugustin:
I'm just going to come out and say it. Josiah Swan has been threatening me for years that if I didn't get his pirate movie off the ground, he would ruin me forever!

Wow. Even Swanny's agent was willing to out him. "Oh my god, Augustin! That's awful! I know it must be hard to admit that. He's a manipulative swine."

@ChampionTalentAugustin:
He also insisted I lock Tanya into contracts that would have taken her out of the country. I knew he had it in for her for some reason. Wish I'd been stronger. Thank you, Paulie for showing his true colours to the world!

"I'm all about true colours, Augustin. I can't believe he would have done that to Tanya!"

@BrettonBigBoy:
He's been manipulating me all year. Making me think I killed my own girlfriend. You're right Paulie, he's dangerous.

"Sage, I'm so sorry you went through this. What a weight you must have carried for the last twelve months." The comments were coming in thick and fast now and Paulie's neurons were firing faster than she could even speak. "Sorry, guys. I just want to read everything you're saying because you're adding more than I could have even hoped for!"

@ShazzaRulez:
Sorry we didn't figure this out with you, Paulie. But this all fits!

@RealLifeRashid:
I hate to say it, but I think you might have something here. #paulieisalegend

@CazzaRulezMore:
We're with you, #paulieisalegend

@Actually_Axel:
You're doing it . . . you're really outing a murderer!

@BeauJustBeau:

Wren was right that you'd figure it out in the end. And that's clearly because #paulieisalegend

@WrenT:
Look up, bezzie.

Paulie looked up. The music was still blaring through the speakers but the Arching Angel was like a ghost ship. A very weird ghost ship where flags had been laid down, weapons were scattered on the floor, and every single pirate was standing still, holding a phone in their hands, a solid combination of devastation and satisfaction on their faces. Every single pirate, that is, except one.

Captain Roger Saltbeard.

"What? Why has everyone stopped *again*? Darlings, put your blessed phones away. Can't you stay off BeYu for more than a millisecond? This isn't a rehearsal! I don't think you understand the gravity of the situation. That drone will wait for no man!" As Swanny cranked his head to the sky to check out what the drone was doing, he clocked that all was not well even beyond the Arching Angel. He cast his gaze across the stunned, motionless crowd, over the inert group of students, towards the movie-ninjas (who were now also glued to their phones) and, last of all, at Paulie who still held the selfie stick up high and didn't need to do or say anything else for her audience. Swanny was doing it all.

He yelped like an injured puppy and sprang over to Rashid, grabbing his phone and pushing him forcefully into a stack of barrels. He tried scrolling on the screen but something about the fingerless gauntlets he was wearing wouldn't allow it. He yelped again – louder this time – and yanked them off with his teeth. When they flopped to the ship's deck, they appeared to take his fingers with them. There wasn't much time to register this obscure happening, but one word flashed through Paulie's mind: latex.

She focused back on Swanny and saw that he was now scrolling through all of the comments on the livestream. His face literally flickered to white, like somebody had passed a strip light across it. Then there was something about his body that changed too. It was as if he was removing a costume, a heavy, uncomfortable costume. The familiar hold of his muscles was released; the limpness of his limbs was discarded; his shoulders squared outwards; he grew to a height that seemed impossible and the broadness of his torso filled with a solidness that obliterated the soft and playful persona of 'Swanny'.

"What the . . ?" Paulie's whisper towards her invisible audience was greeted by thousands of shocked face emojis rupturing across the screen and when they finally cleared, there was a brand new comment waiting to be read. Paulie read it slowly and carefully because as soon as she saw who it was from, she knew that accuracy was everything.

@WendyInfinityNails:
I can confirm that it was Josiah Swan who
attacked me when I was sixteen years old. And
yes, he has been sending me 'love' letters
ever since. I despise the man, but I never
imagined he could hurt my Tanya. Or my Arthur.
Paulie, take him down.

Before Paulie could even swing her attention back around to Swanny, she heard an almighty, "I will KILL you!" and after a freakishly rapid succession of heavy booted steps he was on her. Heavy, kicking, screaming and raging, he was on her.

How he'd managed to leap as high as the podium she had no

idea but somehow he had done it. He was attached to her back like a wild animal and lashed out at anybody who came near to try and prize him off. Breeze, Sage, Wren, the movie-ninjas. None of them could get past Swanny's crazed limbs thrashing and whipping with an energy fuelled by decades of passion, rejection and secrecy.

Paulie's brain wasn't capable of much in that moment, other than the fact that he was a murderer scorching her consciousness like lightning. What if he killed her right here, right now, in front of the whole town? Was her aunt still watching? How would she ever get over witnessing something like that? How could she stop it?

Debbie's phone and selfie stick clattered to the ground and all Paulie could see was her own face cowering into the livestream, a swearing and screaming Swanny, wild-eyed right behind her. At first she couldn't figure out why her lips were turning blue, why her face had tinges of purple. But then she realised that breath was completely eluding her and a tightness around her neck was the cause of it all. She focused really hard on touching the area where her necklace should have been dangling freely, but of course it wasn't. Swanny must have had it gripped with a death-like clutch because it was twisted with a toxic, vengeful force into her windpipe. Suddenly, Tanya's voice echoed through her mind with a meaning so potent, Paulie thought everybody in the vicinity must surely have heard it, *"It's like you've got a death wish or something."*

With her last scrap of energy, Paulie dug her fingers deep into the skin of her neck and managed to curl her fingertips around the edge of the rope that held her pendants together. Her vision was blackening and her awareness fading so she used all the strength she had to yank her fingers forwards and away from the beast on her back. There was a violent twang, the sense of objects flying freely and two bodies, hers and Swanny's, catapulting backwards against the steel podium.

The last things she experienced were the vibrant determination of blue sky spinning across her vision, a scorching pain tearing into her ribs and the dull, metallic crack of a skull.

And then . . . black.

49

When her eyelids finally fluttered open, it was her aunt's face she saw first.

"Luvver, it's okay. I'm here. We're here."

Paulie tried to shift her body in crinkly sheets but her head was ridiculously heavy and her side hurt. Like, a lot. She looked to her right where Meg's glance had shot and saw Coral. The two of them were stooped over her, a human-shaped frame to a very weird picture. A bed with barriers and buttons. A thin, dimpled blanket thrown over her body. An ache on the back of her hand where a cannula sat. Blue walls. An eerie kind of bleeping. A tiny sink. The light was syrupy and thick. Not natural at all.

"How - how long have I been asleep?"

"Maybe don't try to move right now, maid. You've been through so much."

A short woman dressed in pale blue suddenly drifted into her field of vision. She was busy tapping on an iPad but then looked up and gave Paulie a smile so warm she knew she could trust it. "Hi Paulie. I'm Roberta. Your aunt's right. Maybe don't move around too much right now. Do you know where you are?"

"Erm, I'd hazard a guess I'm in hospital."

"That's right. You're actually in intensive care, just so we can keep an eye on you after your small laparotomy. All that means is that we gave you a minor operation on your abdomen to prevent any further bleeding."

"My abdomen? Further bleeding?" Paulie felt a flash of panic and moved her hands to her tummy. That's when she realised there were tubes in all kinds of places, which did nothing to ease the panic.

Aunt Meg seethed, "When you fell backwards, that monstrous man's belt buckle cut right into your side. I mean, who wears a belt buckle made out of actual cutlasses?"

"A homicidal screwball?" Coral suddenly spoke up.

"It's okay though." Roberta's calming tone somehow funnelled the contemptuous atmosphere into something more nurturing. "The op went really well. It's all going to heal just fine, but you might be in here a few days yet. Also, you might feel a bit sick or groggy until the anaesthetic wears off. Is the IV comfortable? How's your pain on a scale of one to ten?"

"Erm, somewhere around a seven?" Paulie was certain she'd feel better if she could just elevate herself a little. "Can I sit up please?"

"Yep, of course. But see that button there? Let's give it a press to increase your pain meds. This might be sore." Roberta, Meg and Coral worked as a team to plump up pillows, grab her elbows and facilitate a half-decent sitting position. "How's that?"

"Thanks. That's better. I think."

Roberta checked a softly bleeping screen, threw Paulie yet another cheery smile then went through a few details about sign-offs from surgeons, visits from consultants and how she was off to check on other patients now. "See that button at the side of your bed? Press that if you need me but I'll keep popping my head in anyway."

When Roberta left the room, a few silent moments passed when Coral and Meg dropped into chairs either side of the bed and their gaze joined, soft smiles drifting towards each other.

Paulie couldn't help herself. "So, you two then?"

Aunt Meg beamed. "Yeah. Us two. Well, we'll see at least, won't we Coz?"

"I'm hoping so," Coral's smile slipped behind her long, straight hair and Paulie thought that was perhaps the first time in her entire life she had appeared remotely cute.

"I'm glad. Really. I saw you together at the festival and I . . ." The festival. The crowds. The Arching Angel. Swanny. Paulie squeezed her eyes shut and saw an instant flash of her own face turning blue, Swanny's savage eyes bulging behind her. She opened her own eyes and saw the whole drama etched onto the faces of Meg and Coral. Her hands dashed to her neck, searching for the familiar click-clack of her pendants but, of course, there was nothing there.

"Sorry luvver, you whipped your necklace off good and proper. You had to or that awful man might have . . . but then that made you both catapult back and that's when you got injured." Meg paused and took a deep breath, wiping back tears that followed the silvery tracks of ones that had clearly gone before. "Anyway, the sea must have pulled your necklace out. It was low tide tonight and Breeze and Wren, bless them, scoured the entire harbour floor. Wren texted me a few hours ago to say they didn't find it."

"Oh."

"But Breeze says he's got a plan," Coral said. "He made me promise to tell you that when you woke up." Coral gently pulled the blanket away from Paulie's arm and the incomplete compass tattoo shone upwards with stinging determination. "And if I know my nephew, I'd say it's something to do with this."

"Crap. Aunt Meg. I should have . . ."

"It's okay, luvver. I'm cool with it. You're an adult now. I mean, if the last few hours hasn't shown that then I don't know what has."

"Was I right though? About Swanny?" She already knew she was. She'd known it from that moment in the chair at Odyssey Ink. But her mind was still gloopy like jam and she needed to hear it from the most important person in her life.

However, it was Coral who spoke first. "You were. The police have got him now. He won't be going anywhere for a very long time."

"Have you, like, heard anything? Anything that matches my theories."

"All of it matches."

"All of it?"

"All of it. As soon as the team got a camera on Josiah, he was away. Raymond said it was like he was giving the performance of his life. Which I suppose, in a way, he was."

"What did he say?"

Coral looked over at Meg as if asking for permission. Meg shrugged and leaned back in her chair. "Like I said, she's an adult."

"Are you sure you're ready to hear it all? And it will have to just be between us for now, before it goes public, okay?"

"Totally." Paulie attempted to straighten her spine against the stack of soft pillows behind her. The pain in her tummy was pulsing intensely, but it matched the avidity of her heart so she looked squarely at Coral and focused hard.

"He says Wendy is the love of his life. Contrary to how he presents himself to the world. He says he's loved her since he was a boy and knew that one day they'd be together. He admitted that he has demonstrated his love on many occasions, including numerous love letters and what he described as the 'private encounter' at school. Man, it kills me that he was the one that attacked Wendy that day. Not least because I could have taken him down given even a fraction of an opportunity. I wish Wendy would have told me. All of this could have been . . . avoided."

"You did the right thing that day, Coz. You looked after Wendy." Exhaustion laced Meg's voice, as if she'd been telling herself that very thing for decades.

Coral sighed, nodded and continued. "Josiah saw Tanya as a barrier to Wendy. He'd seen how tightly the family had formed as soon as she was born. When she showed an interest in drama, he jumped on it and vowed he'd get rid of her by shipping her off to London with his agent. The agent, I forget his name . . ."

"Augustin." Paulie dragged it from the depths of her brain. "He commented on my live. Said Swanny had been trying to get Tanya out of the country."

"Exactly."

"But I don't understand. How did he go from wanting her far away to wanting her dead?"

"It's not even that much of a leap. As you guessed, Tanya found out that Josiah had attacked her mum all those years ago and confronted him. She threatened to report him to the college authorities but was biding her time. Romano Smith corroborates that. She went to him with it, but didn't name Josiah, so he couldn't do much about it."

The phone call at Billowbreak Beach, Paulie thought. *That's what it must have been about.* That's why Romano said he was worried he'd been 'hesitant'. That's why Tanya had been looking for him the day of the festival, and why he'd waved at her from the harbour, as if to reassure her they'd meet. "But, hang on, how did Tanya suddenly find out about Swanny and her mum?"

"Here. Look at this." Meg scrolled through her phone then passed it over. It was one particular text embedded in a lengthy discussion with her aunt.

> In the end, Tanya demanded to know why I was warning her off Josiah. I had to tell her about the attack. How could I let her trust him with her whole future? I'm sorry I didn't tell you and Coz. I put my head in the sand for so many years. And now I've lost my only daughter.

"Oh." What else was there to say? Wendy's secret had ended up being the one thing that ruined her life. "So, *was* it Swanny that Tanya was arguing with in the alleyway the day of the festival?"

"Of course. Tanya was threatening to out him on that very day, after the skirmish, even though she'd sat on the info for weeks."

"Weeks? Why didn't she tell someone sooner?"

"Raymond says Josiah really relished this bit. Tried to paint Tanya as some kind of blackmailing demon. But from what I can make out, she was scared to report him because he had her future in his hands. She was an ambitious young woman, we all know that."

"And some."

"And during those weeks, little did Tanya know, Josiah was plotting it all out."

"Oh god. I don't even know if I can go through this again." Meg stood up, her chair scraping back. "It turns my stomach. Luvver, you okay here with Coral while I go find a coffee machine?" Meg leaned over and kissed Paulie's cheek, leaving a sweet and scented patch of lip balm.

"Yep. You go. I need to hear this." Meg left and Paulie turned back to Coral, who was now up and pacing the room, making a rhythmical shush-shush with her footsteps. She doled the facts out one by one, like a sail being hoisted up to the sky notch by notch.

"Tanya confronts him with the truth. Threatens to report *him* for historical assault. Josiah freaks out. Threatens to end *her* acting career before it's even begun."

"So they were at a stalemate."

"So it seemed. But Josiah, never one to rest on his laurels, started planning how he could take her down. Literally."

"Well, we know the gauze thing in the pistol was faulty, but I can't even imagine how he engineered that."

"Paint stripper."

"I'm sorry, what?"

"He took paint stripper from the art department at college, knowing that it contained a substance called Methylene Chloride. God knows how he found this out, but Methylene Chloride has the correct chemical make-up to dissolve epoxy resin. Are you sticking with me?"

"Was that a pun? Sticking?"

"So you are." Coral stopped, grinned then resumed her pacing at the foot of Paulie's bed. "This resin stuff is what stuck the gate to the inside of the brass barrel of the pistol. Because Josiah drip-fed paint stripper into the barrel over a period of weeks, it was enough to slowly but surely dissolve the bond, without harming the pistol itself. It would have passed safety inspections. It was just a matter of pocketing the right pistol on the day."

"And Sage? How on earth did he get caught up in all of this?

I was convinced it was him for so long." Paulie felt the clang of something heavy in her heart, but was immediately reassured by Coral.

"You and me both. At least, I think we both knew something wasn't right about him. And that was true. He had a terrible guilty conscience because he really did believe he'd shot Tanya accidentally."

"First there was the juggling . . . I don't understand how Swanny got him to do that."

Coral sneered and looked suddenly like the same woman Paulie had met in the police station a whole year ago. "Don't underestimate this conniving piece of dirt, Paulie."

"Tell me."

"Apparently he was particularly proud of this bit. Said he was practising some kind of mentalism with Sage. From what I deduce, all he did was rely on the fact that Sage is a spoiled, rebellious young man by presenting him with the correct tools and actively discouraging him from doing the exact thing he wanted him to do."

"Juggle." Paulie's mind suddenly started working like a pinball machine, zapping her with memories of Swanny warning Sage not to juggle the pistols in rehearsals. Like, for weeks before the skirmish. She could hear him clear as day: *'Sage, enough with juggling the pistols – I've told you umpteen times we'll never get that past health and safety.'* "Wow. He bloody well *knew* Sage would rebel against that."

"Agreed. So Josiah shot Tanya on that cannon blast, just as she was choreographed to collapse anyway. He knew exactly where to stand and how to do it so that he was in a blind spot on the ship – he used to live there apparently, so he'd scoped it out. After that, all he had to do was drop both of his pistols to the floor, knowing full well Sage would pick them up and plaster them all over with his . . ."

"Fingerprints." Paulie relished in the few moments of silence that Coral allowed, taking some deep, steady breaths to help still the pinball machine that was her brain. "And once the police investigated, they must have found that the timings didn't work? That Sage's juggling happened too late?"

"Yep. I imagine it would have been immensely frustrating for them. They couldn't charge Sage because there was video evidence from bystanders to show he juggled moments *after* she collapsed. I would also bet that his fingerprint wasn't actually on the trigger. But I don't suppose Josiah considered that."

Suddenly something else pinged with a startling resonance across Paulie's mind. "Gloves. Swanny pulled off some kind of gross, latex gloves before he attacked me. Were they significant somehow?"

"Nice, Paulie. No stone unturned. Yes, they were supposedly an ageing bit of costume from his days of playing in Waiting for Godot. Raymond struggled to get him to shut up about it. Torbay Gazette photo shows he was wearing them on the day of the murder so he admitted they were used to mask his fingerprints."

"I knew he wouldn't allow his hands to get dirty like that. He's forever anti-baccing them."

"Paulie, you do realise you've been an exceptional detective in all of this, don't you?" Coral stopped pacing and stood at the end of the bed, her tattooed forearms leaning on the bed frame. The expression of worry she'd worn earlier, as Paulie awoke, was switching up to something a whole lot more animated. "The police were already onto some of it, but by no means all of it. Now, I'd have suggestions to refine your methods, and I'm not sure you followed my tips the way I intended but . . . whether it was your determination, your creativity or your incredible intuition, you showed a lot of promise, Little Paulie. A lot."

"Thank you," Paulie whispered. Her tummy was sore and

her eyes were heavy with fatigue but her heart filled with something gorgeous. "What about Arthur? How does his disappearance fit into all of this?"

"Oh, now that's slightly more cryptic, but your message in the Buccaneer Bounty bottle was a really big clue. Are you sure you've got the energy?"

"Defo." At that moment, the door to the room swung open and Roberta swept back in, Aunt Meg right behind her. She looked at Paulie with a quizzical frown and then seemed to make a decision on the spot.

"You're looking a bit pale, Paulie. I think that's enough now. No more 'big talk' today." She directed this last statement at Coral, probably knowing full well what they'd been up to while she was gone. "I'll see to it you're both allowed in to visit her first thing in the morning, ladies."

"Are you sure she'll be okay?" Aunt Meg trilled, stealing a kiss from Paulie before Roberta practically booted her out.

"Yes, yes, she's fine. I'll be around if she needs anything. Don't worry. But she's exhausted now."

Paulie couldn't argue with that. It turned out that lying in bed whilst receiving news about the murder you'd been trying to solve for a whole year was downright knackering. But Coral hadn't finished yet, and she doubted she could sleep before she knew more about Arthur.

Just as she had that thought, Coral strode right past Roberta and went to hug Paulie. Well, not hug, exactly, it was more like she leaned in and dropped something in her lap. An A4 brown envelope. She lingered long enough to whisper into Paulie's ear, "I called Breeze to drop this over earlier. It'll answer everything you need to know about Arthur. At least, that's what Josiah told the team. Night, Paulie."

"Night," Paulie answered, her voice trailing after the three of them as they left the room. The door hadn't even closed all the way before Paulie tore open the envelope, emptied the paper contents onto her lap and read, not for the first time, the words on the title page . . .

For the Love of Pirates
By Josiah C Swan.

50

As she turned the final page, Paulie leaned back in her creaky old desk chair and sighed.

So it was in the script all along.

The script of For the Love of Pirates had been leaked on a massive scale and was all over BeYu like a rash. People were recording live reaction videos as they read key scenes aloud. The hashtag, #FTLOPscandal, was trending almost as quickly as (much to her horror) #paulieisalegend, and the daily notification pictures were a flood of stupefied faces and highlighted passages.

For this reason, Paulie knew how damning the story would be before she even finished it. Hospital had been draining, but once back home she'd managed to get through it bit by bit, with the help of snacks bestowed upon her by a still-concerned Aunt Meg and the familiar warmth of her own bedroom. It was good she was venturing out into the world today though. It was time.

It was difficult to believe the script hadn't condemned Swanny sooner. It was so obvious that Captain Roger Saltbeard was him. That the young woman he lived for, named Trudy, was actually Wendy. Trudy even had a husband and a daughter and in all Captain Saltbeard's swashbuckling escapades, his main motivation was to find enough treasure to return to shore and convince Trudy to leave family life to be with him. It wasn't even a clever metaphor.

In amongst the ship wreckages, pillaging and storm-swept seas, was the answer to Arthur's demise. In one particularly harrowing scene set at midnight, Trudy's drunk husband stumbled across an empty bottle of his favourite ale as he was leaving his usual drinking establishment. When he picked it up, he realised it had a handwritten note inside, luring him to board Saltbeard's ship with promises of treasure. There ensued a sporadic brawl in which Saltbeard knocked him out with the base of a telescope, sending him plummeting into the sea below. Just as Saltbeard contemplated if the husband was alive or dead, a passing fishing boat unwittingly caught the flaps of his coat in the cod end of its net and dragged his body out to sea. That was it. Davy Jones's locker had claimed him.

Poor Arthur.

Obviously, the police had some work to do to prove the theories outlined in For the Love of Pirates, but Coral would keep her updated on that. In fact, she had a feeling she'd be seeing a lot more of Coral Bombora from now on.

Paulie stood up carefully and scanned her floordrobe. Comfort would be key today, for what she had planned. Just as she was pulling the hoodie Wren had given her for Christmas over her head, Aunt Meg knocked sharply then strode in.

"Luvver! You're up. Good. Fickle Fergus has been asking about you all blinking morning and Wendy wants to give you a hug. She's fragile, but she's okay. You coming down? How's the tummy?"

"Yeah I'm coming down. I'm going out, remember? And the tummy is okay. Loads better, in fact."

"Great. Oh! Before you go, you must see the plans Wendy's

brought with her. It's ridiculously exciting. Oh, maid, I can't believe you're back after everything you've been through. I thought I'd lost you for good." Meg threw her arms around Paulie in a hug as solid as an anchor on the ocean floor. Then her fingertips found Paulie's neck, tracing the rosy welt marks with caution, yet more physical signs of her tussle with Swanny. "Maybe I can find a cream for that. It looks nasty."

"Later," Paulie smiled. "It'll be okay. I'll be down in a minute. Just got to do my hair . . ."

"You mean find your hat."

"Yes, I mean find my hat. Then I'll be down."

"Perfect." On her way out of the room, Aunt Meg tripped on one of the empty boxes still stacked in the corner. "Really, Paulie, I do wish you'd . . ."

"Yeah, but aren't you glad I didn't pack them after all? Sometimes you've just got to . . . oh, now what was that cross-word clue Fergus was trying to get me to solve? Oh yeah. Keep. The. Faith."

"Okay, almighty one. I bow down to your vast and omnipotent knowledge. Now get your arse downstairs. People are waiting."

It only took Paulie a few minutes to find her deerstalker under her pillow, spritz herself with some perfume and smile at her image in the full length mirror hanging on her door. It had taken a hell of a lot, but that girl looked happy. She really did.

The inimitable scent of freshly baked cookies greeted her at the top of the stairs and her quickly healing tummy roared out for attention. And that was okay. Because Paulie was ready to give it the attention it deserved.

"Oi! Luvver! Leave some for the grockles, won't you?"

It was going to be tricky to close the lid on the box anyway, so Paulie stepped away from the display cabinet. "Soz, Aunt Meg, but us youngsters, we've got to keep our strength up, right?"

"I'm only kidding. Take as many as you like. Here, let me tie that up for you." Meg took the box and balanced it on the counter, where Fickle Fergus was tapping a cluster of gem-encrusted knuckle-duster rings and deciding what to have for lunch. She pushed the Doubloon Delights inside and secured the edges with tape. Then she added her signature black ribbon printed with tiny skulls and crossbones. While she was busy with that, Paulie turned to Fergus.

"Can I get you anything, Fergus? Have you decided?"

"Oh, Little Paulie, I can't think straight with you standing there like that!"

"Standing here like what?"

"You know, all 'legend' like." He pointed at the chalkboard behind her where Paulie was horrified to see the words '#paulieisalegend' scrawled across it. Then he waved a copy of the Torbay Gazette in her face which was, for once, not turned to the crossword page but to the front page, whose headline read, *'Berryport Teen Condemns Drama Teacher as Double-Murderer'*. As well as ample screenshots of her BeYu livestream, were photos of Raymond the police officer prising Swanny's curled and clinging figure from the Angel's rigging. "I can't believe you did what you did, Little Paulie. You really are a legend. A Berryport legend."

"Stop. Just stop. Change of subject please."

"I'll change the subject, if I may? What do you think about this?" Wendy Withers approached the counter with an iPad and placed it on top of Fergus's paper. Paulie noticed she looked completely worn out. Red rings hovered beneath her eyes, her complexion was pale and she wore a hoodie and leggings which was a first in the Berryport history books. Paulie felt a sharp pang dig into her chest and wondered if the way she'd exposed Swanny could have been better thought-out to protect her. After all, she was the real victim in this whole sorry mess.

Before Paulie could even finish that thought, however, a particularly handsome man in a suit walked up behind Wendy and helped her find what she was looking for on the iPad. It was miniscule, but a sudden, sunny energy flashed across Wendy's entire being. "So these are the plans for the hybrid venue. Give it a few weeks and Booty Bakes and Infinity Nails will be joining forces! Akito here drew them up with me and Meg. What do you think?"

"I think Debbie Devon will be quaking in her boots."

"What? Nah," Aunt Meg replied, pouring over the impressive designs too. "She had that huge surge in followers after you commandeered her live, so she's been far too busy with new sponsorship deals to even think about this social media hub nonsense. And anyway, with Wendy onboard we can make the rent so there's no need for the Brettons to chuck us out. I don't know why we didn't think of it sooner."

"Yeah, manicures and pastries. That classic combo." Paulie couldn't even imagine the sensory onslaught. She would need to dig out that pack of face masks left over from the pandemic.

"It will be. Just you wait and see. Oh, Fergus! Your rings just reminded me. I found this in our Tanya's room after you left, Paulie. Is it yours?" Wendy delved into her handbag and produced something small and silver, placing it on the counter next to the iPad. It was the anxiety ring that Wren had given her for her birthday. She'd totally forgotten that she'd flung it across the room in a fit of something . . . rage? Desperation? Actual anxiety?

"Oh yeah, that is mine. Thanks." Paulie slipped it onto her finger where it fit perfectly. Fergus, Meg, Wendy and the random architect guy, Akito, all leaned closer to get a better look. The ring glinted and the tiny little wires and beads clinked as Paulie moved her fingers. It was funny, but after the events of the last few days, Paulie couldn't feel prouder to wear this ring gifted by her best friend. How had she ever seen a problem with it in the first place?

"Dude. Sorry. Am I late?" As if by magic, Wren appeared at the bakery door, heaving for breath like she'd just run a marathon.

"Erm, did you get me a ring with magical powers? Are you about to produce a dwarf, an elf and an enigmatic wizard?"

"Wah? No, but dude, I'm pretty sure that lot followed me – even though I tried my best to outrun them." Wren's skin glimmered with sweat and it looked like her legs might give way at any second.

"Who?" Everybody asked at the same time.

"Them!" Wren shoved her thumb behind her towards the harbour. Paulie heard them before she saw them but the chaotic buzz of the students was unmistakeable. Yelps of *'Is she really there?'*, *'I want to talk to her first'* and *'I knew all along that she'd crack it!'* careened through the door and the stampeding colours and shapes of at least fifty determined young people swung into view, crashing past the statue of Prince William of Orange, bowling through the tables and chairs outside the Powder Monkey and blasting past the slowly rocking bulk of the Arching Angel.

"Blimey, Wren, how are there so many of them?"

Wren shrugged and her chest kept heaving. "Dude, How would I know? Friends? Family? Random admirers you acquired during your livestream? Are you going to speak to the masses, or what?"

"Hell no!" She wanted to see her friends. Of course she did, but not like this.

At that moment, Meg's phone beeped and she checked it with a glowing smile. "Well, it looks like now's the time to leave anyway. Quick! Grab the cookies and follow me!"

Wren staggered inside the shop and smashed into Paulie with a hug. "Are you ready for this, dude?"

"Ready as I'll ever be. And you?"

"Course. If you're there to hold my hand."

"I've got you."

"Girls. This way!" Meg held the kitchen door open and they shot through it. The galloping students were hitting the bakery doors like flies against a windscreen and, as Paulie glanced over her shoulder, she could see that Wendy, Akita and Fergus were fending them off with doughnuts and false promises. Meg raced to the other end of the kitchen and pushed the back door open. "Go through here. If you're quick at the other end of the alley-way, you should make it. And Paulie?" Meg grabbed Paulie's elbow just before she exited Booty Bakes and said, "Tell Coz I said hi."

"Done." Paulie was astounded by how much warmth those words infused her bones and she used that to propel her through the alleyway, across the harbour and through the doors of Odyssey Ink.

"About time. You do realise we've booked the shop out for the whole afternoon for you two?" Coral was busy scouring her hands at the sink at the back of the shop. Her tone was as clipped as ever but there was a smile behind her eyes.

"We three." Breeze looked up from the tattoo station where he was lining up tiny pots of colour. "I think you mean we three."

"What? You're going to get your first tattoo? Like, with us?"

He shrugged and a smidge of his famous surliness completely fell away. "Yeah. It feels right. I'll finish your tattoo,

Auntie Coral will do Wren's and then when she's finished, she'll do mine. That sound like a plan?"

"Erm, well, I think . . ." Paulie wasn't sure how she could make herself heard over her hammering heart right now. Breeze Bombora was going to get his first tattoo. With her.

"What she means is, yes, of course it sounds like a plan. And look. We brought sustenance." Wren held up Paulie's arm like she was manipulating a puppet and the box of Doubloons bobbed in the air.

"Sound. Do you want to see the designs?" Breeze led them over to the counter where three illustrations were laid out in front of them. "This one is Paulie's, obviously." He pointed to the original compass design, but right in the centre, where before there had been patterns and flourishes, was a sparkling, turquoise eye, just like the one she'd always worn around her neck, next to the compass.

She gasped, "Oh, Breeze. I love it."

"Hoped you would. This means you can still wear both charms even though your necklace is no more." He held her gaze for a few glorious seconds before Wren had to clear her throat to break up . . . well . . . to break up whatever it was. "Er, sorry. Right. Wren, what about this for you?" He pointed at the exact same compass design but this time it had a jigsaw piece in the middle of it. "I think it's pretty self explanatory. What do you think?"

"I don't think anything, Breeze. I *know* it's perfect. Thanks, dude. What about you? What are you having?"

There was a third compass illustration that had a kind of burst of electricity running through the centre of it. It looked a bit like a star, a mini explosion or something. Wren looked from the drawing to Breeze's face. From Breeze's face to the drawing. "Dude, you do know what you've done, don't you? You've basically drawn the scar that Paulie gave you the day she dropped that rock? Erm, intentional much?" Breeze didn't reply. He just smiled and tossed his fringe away from his eyes.

"Come on, let's get started."

And it wasn't until the tattoos were well underway, the pain was mainlining euphoria to her brain, Gorillaz was blaring on the smart speaker, Doubloon Delights were settling in her tummy, Wren had a death grip on her hand and Breeze's breath was skimming the tender surface of her skin, that Paulie realised what was at the centre of his compass.

And it was her mum's voice, clear and true as the bell of the Arching Angel, that told her . . .

It's a spark.

THE END

MORE BY ABIGAIL YARDIMCI

ACKNOWLEDGMENTS

Because Murder at the Pirate Festival is my first venture into the genre of murder mystery, I have a lot of people to thank. It seems a writer cannot get by on ideas alone . . .

I'll start with my youngest son, Azad. Thank you for being there when I dragged you through the streets of Brixham during the pirate festival in 2023. Thank you for nodding sagely when I suggested it might be possible to get away with murder during the astoundingly loud firing of the cannons. Thank you for sticking with me for an entire year whilst I scribbled, wrote, stressed, dreamt, panicked, chattered and toiled. You have outdone yourself and all I can say is . . . I hope you're ready for the next one.

Thank you to my team of ADHDers. You helped me with my initial research by being so open and generous with your own experience. I wanted Paulie's character to be full, flawed and neurodiversely authentic and you helped make her the loveable young woman that she is: Susan Appleby, Rachel Brown, Eliza Kelly, Sasha Lavinski, Ailsa Ronsdale and Nix Ward.

The committee of Brixham Pirate Festival and Brixham's crew of swashbuckling pirates have been incredibly supportive. You showed interest in my idea from day one and didn't once laugh out loud that I may be some kind of mad wench who should be walked off the nearest plank. That didn't go unnoticed.

My next door neighbour, Mark Fellows helped me see that

not everybody at the pirate festival wants to be a Johnny Depp replica. Your 'Captain Corvus' costume gave Romano his special moment in chapter six.

I'll keep it local and express my thanks to the Brixham community in general. You are a very special kind of people and I love the grace and wit with which the book has been received. Berryport is pretty idyllic but it's not a patch on our gorgeous town.

I've had all kinds of intel on all kinds of topics including the mechanisms of flintlock pistols, police murder investigation procedures, college discipline processes, chemistry, commercial property law, Bristolian nightlife, abdominal trauma, fishing boat anatomy and even tattoo culture. So, huge props to the following people who dealt with my inane questions: Neil Caughey, Rob Claydon, Jacqui Bowley, Natasha Farmer, Phil Hoffmann, Ruth Jackson, Leslie Leggett, Alan Scales (courtesy of Bridget Ward), Ian Stapleton and Nix Ward.

Louize Cattermole - you are always first to insist on an advance copy and I take that as nothing but a compliment. You know how much your literary opinion means to me as well as your general lushness. I mean, how lush are we?

Sarah Hislam and Natalie Nuttall - you let me take over more work Zoom meetings with my bookish talk than was probably allowed. You always showed such unswerving belief, even when I was ready to pack it all in. Maybe especially then. We can take it off the weekly agenda now. At least, until I start writing the next one.

My fellow authors have been ever-wonderful. Margaret Amatt (your cover advice flowed like a fine wine), Chris d'Lacey (I still can't believe how much you helped me improve Paulie's story), Chrissie Parker (my own personal angel on my shoulder) and the rest of the writing community who are continuously generous in offering, support, understanding and motivation.

Team Yardimci - you rocked your ARC team duties once again. Thank you so much. Book bloggers and reviewers - never underestimate how important you are to us authors, especially us in the indie camp. Keep doing what you're doing.

Manuel Diaz did an amazing job of the artwork for the front cover from all the way on the other side of the world. Thank you for being patient whilst I attempted to describe my vision.

READERS . . . You are my rock and my comfort blanket all at once. I love building connections with you through my books as well as my socials and it is YOU who gets me at my writing desk / bed / sofa every day. A million thank yous for buying my books as well as reading, reviewing and sharing them the world over. It's down to you that I was brave enough to venture into the world of cosy mystery.

Finally, because my head has been down and in author mode for most of the past year, I want to make sure my family knows how much I appreciate them. Azad had a special mention because of just how invested he's been in all this murdery nonsense, but the rest of you have been just fab too. Thank you for giving me the space and flexibility I needed to get this book done. Fair warning that it shall be starting all over again very soon. Sorry not sorry.

ABOUT THE AUTHOR

ABIGAIL YARDIMCI is a neurodiverse author, painter, mindfulness practitioner and Humanist celebrant.

She is a Geordie girl living by the sea in South Devon with her Turkish husband and two terrifying kids. She loves to blog and gets her kicks through mindful parenting styles, creative living and chocolate.

Abigail's writing inspiration comes from scratching the surface of everyday life to find the underlying magic that connects us all. The fire beneath the frustration, the creativity beneath the boredom, the stillness beneath the chaos.

All of Abigail's books are published by Soft Rebel Publishing and there are more books on the way.

Abigail LOVES connecting with her readers so check her out on social media and sign up to her mailing list now to get a FREE digital copy of her first novel, Life Is Yours.

www.abigailyardimci.com

Printed in Great Britain
by Amazon